THE HUNTED

KRISTY BERRIDGE

Shadow Ink Press

P.O Box 352n, Cairns North, Queensland 4870 Australia

Email: shadowinkpress@hotmail.com

First published in Australia 2011

This edition published 2015

Copyright © Kristy Berridge 2015

Cover design, typesetting: Chameleon Print Design

Berridge, Kristy

The Hunted

ISBN: 9780987524775

pp580

B orn in Perth, Western Australia in 1982, Kristy Berridge was ushered into the world in a decade of bad hair, parachute pants, and blue eye shadow. Fortunately, she managed to  avoid all three by immersing herself in the business of growing up, and hitched a ride with her fun-loving, and adventure-filled parents to the sunny state of Queensland. Here she completed most of her education.

Besides learning that boys *don't* have cooties, and that algebra *wouldn't* kill her, she pointedly set the path of her high school career towards success in Art and English-based subjects, and won numerous awards for her efforts.

After high school she went on to study Graphic Design and Illustration at James Cook University, furthered her studies at the local TAFE college with an Interior Design course, and then undertook a three-year Design course at Rhodec International in London.

Clearly the girl just can't sit still. Kristy now pens fanciful fiction novels in her spare time finding creative new ways to scare herself and others in the dead of night, promote girl-power with gritty action sequences and, of course, highlight teenage idiosyncrasies with hard-hitting hormonal moments of lust.

She currently resides in Cairns, procrastinates constantly, now studies nutrition and tries desperately to avoid the delicious temptation that is the peanut butter aisle at the supermarket.

To my mother Stephanie—for her constant enthusiasm about my work, and her inability to put the story down even though it's way past bedtime. You make my ego soar and keep me grounded, all at the same time.

To my brother Peter—for your ability to make me sound a lot cooler than I really am, and also for re-educating me on the twisted inner workings of the rebellious teenage mind.

And to the rest of my family, my brother Glen and my father Peter—although you quietly work in the background, I cannot survive without your love and support. Thank you for always believing in me.

PREFACE

espite the fresh sea air, William could smell the scent of sweaty bodies, overpowering aftershave and cheap perfume, all mingled with the enticing scent of fresh blood. The very idea of his tasting its tantalising warmth sent shivers of anticipation across William's skin. He'd spent centuries trying to ignore the enticing aroma of human blood and its sweetness that promised fulfilment and frenzied excitement. But he was still somewhat vulnerable to its call, despite that he was almost five hundred years old.

He tilted his head back and tried to locate the other underlying scent that had led him to this beach in the first place. It was faint now, almost a whisper across the air.

Strange.

If the Vânător was going to be anywhere, then he imagined that it would have stopped here at this human party, drawing him in with its assortment of sensory distractions.

He could smell hundreds of different scents in the wind, plenty of blood and nourishment for a beast that showed no mercy. So why had it not stopped here?

Shaking his head in frustration, William took off at a run. He started circling the entire area, giving it a wide birth of at least five kilometres so that he could catch wind of any scent that may be lingering in the air or a new path that may have been forged.

He took to the trees on the mountain's edge, traversing the cliff face that overhung the sea before running back down along the highway again. This led back to the beachfront.

Where has he gone?

The scent had well and truly dissipated now. Perhaps the Vânător had jumped into the sea? But why? Did he know we were hunting him?

He shook his head again in growing irritation.

'No luck?' Thomas said to William, as he came up behind him. Marianne was only a second behind him.

'No. I just did a perimeter check, but the scent is gone. I think he must have jumped.'

'Damn!'

'My thoughts exactly.'

'Can we go home now?' Marianne whined. 'I don't want to be out hunting anymore.

William inclined his head. 'Do whatever you want, but I'm going to check out that party just in case he passed by and tried to cover up his scent with that of those humans.'

'Do we have to come?' Marianne pouted.

William ignored her and made his way further down the beachfront and towards the group of languid dancers. Most were inebriated and stumbling over one another, embarrassing themselves. He'd never understood the impulsive teenage notion to addle your own brain to a point where you lose yourself completely in the stupidity and irrationality of alcohol consumption. Although, if he was completely honest with himself, he'd realise how hypocritical those thoughts were, particularly since he had his own small substance abuse problem. Drugs and alcohol were a passing trend to these teens, but for him blood was an eternal form of intoxication that no Alcoholics Anonymous programme could ever quite cure.

Marianne caught up to him and wound an arm around his waist and cuddled up close to him. He tried not to cringe at her touch. It wasn't that he didn't like her, exactly; he just didn't reflect the same feelings that she had for him, and her constant attempts at seducing him had become tiring.

'I do love to dance, William,' she said, fluttering her eyelids at him. 'Will you take me for a spin across the sand?'

He looked down at her sapphire blue eyes and her pouty, pink lips. She was stunningly beautiful, but he'd never really been attracted to blondes, and particularly not this one. He liked a girl with spirit, self assurance, and individuality. This was probably why he was still single after four hundred and forty-odd years of existence. Women possessing his giant list of expectations probably did not exist. Either way, he was picky, and the picture of who and what he wanted was clearly etched in his mind—and Marianne wasn't it. He untangled himself from Marianne's embrace and patted her shoulder endearingly. 'Not tonight, Marianne. Perhaps Thomas will oblige you with a dance.'

Thomas shot William a filthy look. William turned away quickly, hiding his growing smile.

How those two had ever shared a womb for an extended period of time was beyond him. They fought like cats and dogs. Serving in the Roman Guard had been a piece of cake compared to keeping the peace between these constantly warring siblings. In truth, though, the Roman Guard that he had served in was a little different to what the humans would probably consider to be the actual 'Roman Guard' of today, if in fact it still even existed. The human version protected the interests of the Italian nation, whereas his had been formed to preserve the way of life for blood drinkers, something his original coven had institutionalised and enforced.

He sighed as he reluctantly thought back to his time with Lucius, the Master Vampire.

Things had been different then. William had been young and impressionable, and Lucius's plans to create an army protecting the interests of vampires had appealed to William's sense of self preservation. It had also fed his desire to belong, creating enough of a distraction to block out the painful memories of his human past.

The distraction had worked for a while. One hundred years to be precise.

Lucius Valerius was the first and most powerful vampire in existence, and kowtowing to his needs was not just a question of choice or a desire to please, but a fulfilment of duty that William had been happy to perform.

Though he had disagreed with many of his former coven's choices when it came to feeding habits, he understood their needs as if they were his own. After all, they were all vampires, and blood was simply a necessity of their existence.

What soured his opinion of his peers, the reason he had left the comfort of his home with Lucius and the command of the Roman Guard, was the coven's decision to kill innocent people beyond mere satiation of thirst. Killing the guilty was one thing, but to kill for the sake of killing was a travesty that William did not wish to be a party to.

For over three hundred years now he had led a life that was varied, but essentially the same as his old one in so many ways. Instead of hunting rogue vampires and serving Lucius's version of justice, he now had made his own path by trying to kill off the very biggest mistake in history.

The Vânătors.

These creatures were born from the blood of vampires, a tainted mix of malevolence, a creature not far removed from the fur-backed, fanged imaginings of our darkest night-mares. They were werewolves with a potent mix of vampire. They had no mercy and fed on the blood of all, including his own kin. Hunting them was the only true justice he could see, incontestable in his life.

And, while out hunting vânători, he had met Thomas.

He glanced backwards and saw that Marianne was tugging on her twin brother's arm, begging him to dance with her. Thomas was less than pleased by the proposition as he was a terrible dancer.

William smiled in spite of himself. He knew that there was a good chance that Thomas would pay him back for this. It was likely he'd endure a few filthy looks. He also suspected a sucker-punch to the arm was the on the cards, but William figured Thomas's displeasure was a small price to pay for avoiding the unrealistic expectations of a blonde who held no interest for him.

While Thomas and Marianne made their exit towards the makeshift dance pit in the sand, William slipped down through the covering of trees and scouted the perimeter of the party, assessing each way and every scent one by one until—

What was that?

He sniffed again, drawing in a scent so deliciously pure and unusual that he actually staggered back a few steps. On later reflection, William thought it had been his first clumsy movement in over two hundred and twenty years.

Righting himself, he sidestepped cautiously, looking out over the crowd, trying to pinpoint the source of his intoxication.

And then he saw her...

The wall of scent slammed into him, sending him staggering back again and hitting a palm tree at his back. He watched soundlessly and with unabated awe as the perfect embodiment of everything physical that he had ever been searching for in a woman caught his gaze, widening his eyes.

She had long, chocolate brown hair and creamy white skin. Her limbs were slender and perfectly proportioned. She had soft pink lips and a face so exquisite that his highly-developed senses found no imperfections. If he hadn't have known better he would have assumed her Vampire, as it was typical for a born vampire to be exceptionally featured. Yet her scent still proclaimed her as human.

Her cheeks were slightly flushed from dancing and her veins throbbed under her skin like tiny strands of molten honey just begging for him to brush his teeth against the flesh of her neck and taste. She was the first person to evoke that insatiable hunger in him in over four hundred years and he wasn't sure whether to be excited by the prospect or innately nervous.

He sniffed and tried to dismiss the thought. And yet despite his best efforts to push her from his mind, there was something about her that kept reeling him back in. It wasn't just her blood or that she was sublime to look at, but more to do with the fact that she was oddly familiar.

A pity she's only human.

He crossed his arms in front of his chest, immediately dismissing all thoughts of the hunt. He leaned back against the palm's trunk, crossing his left ankle over his right, and watching her intently as she laughed and danced with the people around her.

It became immediately obvious that he was not her only admirer.

The men closest to her were closing in like hungry vultures circling their prey, waiting for the right moment in order to strike. That should have been his intentions towards the Vânător, but he couldn't seem to find enough focus to pull away from her.

Her hips swayed seductively in time with the music, and her hair ruffled in the breeze, wafting strawberry scented shampoo in his direction. Watching the way that her lips curved into a smile as she closed her eyes and wiggled her toes in the sand made him forget why he was on the beach in the first place. She was downright distracting.

The blonde girl, assumedly a friend, had an enthusiasm for liquor and gritty dancing, judging by the bottle in her hand and her overly-sensuous moves. Her friend was caught in a world all of her own, oblivious. The blonde tried drawing her attention from across the crowd by waving and shouting, but William observed that once the girl's eyes were closed, she was lost to the music and its beat. It was as if she danced only for her own pleasure, revelling in the serenity of such a simple activity, unaffected by the audience around her.

A growl sounded in the back of his throat as he watched one man rest his large, sweaty hands on her slim hips and gyrate suggestively against her rear.

William almost tore through the crowd right then to snap the guy's fingers off, but he stopped himself, roughly pressing his back against the trunk of the palm tree, concluding that irrationality would get him nowhere. Besides, she'd halted the man's advances, breaking contact by zigzagging through the crowd to talk to the boisterous blonde.

No need for dramatics.

He took a breath and calmed himself.

What am I thinking? Since when do I get possessive over a girl I don't even know? And for that matter—a human!

He shook his head from side to side.

No need for dramatics, alright. I have enough of that hunting.

His eyes snapped back to her as she threw her head back and laughed as her friend whispered something rather impish in her ear.

William couldn't help but smile at the crass comment. His sensitive ears heard the smallest of sounds—it sounded as if the blonde had meant the whispered comment especially for him, but he knew better. Instead, he focused his ability on ignoring the sounds of those around the girl, and listened to the heartiness of her laughter: slightly throaty, and sexy, just like the rest of her.

On an impulse that surprised even him, he flooded her with his scent, using his innate abilities to entice her toward him, to make her look up so he could see into her eyes.

What am I doing?

He almost cursed out loud. This wasn't like him. He didn't go around luring unknowing humans just to satisfy his own curiosities. Actually, for the most part, he tended to avoid humans at any time possible. Being around them made sticking to his oath very difficult to uphold. William had not indulged a drop of human blood since the night after his turning. The constant torment of dark memories from that night still battered his soul and fed his guilt, hence why he'd avoided all temptation…until now. But there was just something about her that was worth the momentary discomfort he felt in his throat, as hunger seared his skin and begged for reprieve—to taste her blood.

Besides the draw of her obvious beauty, the sense of familiarity he felt looking into her eyes was astounding, though he had no idea why. She was like a distant echo from his past, a calling to his spirit and a reminder of a life he had once had.

Strangely, through the oppressive fog of his growing

thirst, he began to conjure alien images in his mind that showed her as a part of his life.

He thought about caressing her skin and tasting those soft pink lips with his, but the visual imagery of such acts was distorted by a greater urgency to devour blood. It was a burning reminder why he *should* ignore the feelings of desire he felt for the human stranger.

He was a vampire and he was dangerous. The night still held promise for the capture and kill of an Alpha Vânător who seemed determined to populate the area with a new pack. At least that was a realistic prospect that he could really sink his teeth into. Killing was second nature to him.

Time to leave. But still ...

A whisper in his mind told him not to walk away from her, told him that she was important, told him that she needed to be protected and taken to the ones with whom she belonged. He wasn't crazy, but it was an odd sensation, an act of compulsion even stronger than his own abilities, an outside force turning the whisper into a pressure on his conscience. And the whispers filled him with the recognition that had previously evaded him. She wore an uncanny resemblance to someone he'd spent the last few centuries avoiding. She looked just like ...

No. *It couldn't be true.*

Yet it was hard to deny. The whisperer in his mind had guided him to this point in time, following the Vânător from London to Australian shores where he now stood on the beach directly across from the daughter of, from the daughter of ...

He still couldn't admit it. Not even in his head.

She turned in his direction, her body swaying seductively in time with the music while the wind that tousled her hair blew a fresh surge of pure blood scent in his direction. It was maddening, yet at the same time, enticing to the point where his earlier notions of disbanding interest in her and continuing with the hunt were once again put on hold.

He looked at the crowd of people who had once again begun pressing themselves in around her, distorting his view. Without thought or hesitation, he touched their minds gently, asking them to step aside so that he could see her and she could see him.

It worked.

The sea of people parted, and he immediately exuded another wave of his scent to bring her to him. Compulsion or 'glamouring' was not difficult for his kind. It was one of the many gifts of the born Vampire that helped implant suggestions in the humans around them. It was handy for acquiring things that required money, and good for covering tracks if humans had seen more than their frail minds should allow. Blending in was easy when you could make everyone around you turn a blind eye to your presence.

Surprisingly, she kept dancing. It appeared that she was immune to his compulsion, or at the very least, tolerant of its effects—an enigma in itself; no human had ever been immune to him. But undeniably he had indeed caught her attention, because then she looked right at him, staring with eyes that he had seen before—eyes that mirrored those of someone he now despised.

His breath caught in his throat and his muscles tightened in response, his jaw hardening as his teeth clenched together.

Though he could clearly see a definite resemblance, the longer he looked, the more he realised that her eyes *were* slightly different. They were a strange combination of green and brown that seemed to swirl haphazardly like a kaleidoscope, captivating anyone who looked into their depths. Or perhaps just him.

William swallowed, a lump rising in his throat, and hurtled another torrent of his essence in her direction.

She watched him with growing interest, but continued to weave her hands through the air and roll her hips in time with the music without moving any further towards him.

He smiled at her, keeping his lips pressed shut and hiding his canines which had begun to slowly extend thanks to her most appetising aroma. He just prayed that his eyes were still green instead of black. He didn't want to scare her off by revealing his true form.

When the change begins, the extension of teeth comes first. They are easier to hide than the other changes—his eyes a prime example. They are usually emerald green, but once tainted by vampirism, they cloud over like a stormy sky, swirling the iris's together until they are as black as pitch. It increases his vision and helps him to see at night, but the result for humans is terrifying, reminding them of demonic creatures that haunt their nightmares.

This is just the beginning.

Once the teeth extend and the eyes turn into empty pits of darkness, the talons grow. Fingernails morph into long black talons as tough as steel and sharp enough to slice through flesh like butter, but again, that is not all.

The final stage is the skin.

Though generally pale and milky, it almost becomes transparent, revealing the corded muscles underneath and the spidery veins of blood that pulse just beneath the surface. At this stage, vampires are at their fastest, strongest and deadliest.

William didn't often reveal that side of himself. It meant

that he had been pushed beyond his boundaries, and he hated the idea of losing control.

Tiny rivulets of pain teased at the edges of his mind before he felt the cord he had plugged into the minds of those around him finally snap. The crowds surged back in and around her, blocking her momentarily from his view.

Damn.

'Hey, you found anything?' Thomas asked, coming up beside him and looking out over the crowd.

'I might have, but it's not a vânător,' William answered throwing his friend a smile.

Thomas cocked an eyebrow in interest. 'Where is she then?'

William was amused. His friend's mind was always on finding the next pretty skirt.

Thomas was nothing if not predictable in his efforts to bed every decent looking vampire that he laid his eyes upon. He reminded William of his own brother in that regard.

As William pointed through the crowd, Thomas looked back at him indignantly, his nose turning up at what William was proposing. 'Trust you to be attracted to the one thing you spend your entire life avoiding. You do realise that delectable morsel is a human?'

William gave him a wry look and ignored him. He watched her making her way out of the pit and heading over to a bunch teens profiteering from a lack of decent alcohol. Thomas tugged on his arm. 'Are you ready to go?' he asked urgently. 'We need to keep hunting.'

William shook his head. 'Not yet, I want to talk to her.'

'Do you think that's a good idea?'

'Probably not,' William agreed, 'but I feel compelled to do it anyway. There's something different about her, something intriguing me.'

Thomas grimaced and touched a concerned hand to his friend's shoulder. 'I hate to tell you this, Brother, but as much as their outer packaging varies in colour, height and size, they all still have the same, delicious, creamy red centres that *you* seem to want to avoid.'

'She's different. I can feel it.'

Thomas scoffed. 'She's human, William.'

William stood idle for a moment as he watched her, thinking about the uncanny resemblance. 'Perhaps.'

Thomas frowned, looking more than confused as he glanced back and forth between William and the girl. 'What's that supposed to mean?'

'I'll tell you when I know for sure,' William answered abruptly as he pushed himself off the tree, leaving his friend behind to ponder over his comment.

Thomas reached out to hold his friend back as he began to cross the sand, but something stopped him.

After all, she was the first woman in three hundred plus years that had actually piqued William's curiosity, and Thomas was more than a little keen to see how this all played out. He just hoped that she wasn't afraid of the dark or the creatures that preyed upon those that dared to stray into the shadows, because if she was, she was in for one hell of a shock.

CHAPTER ONE: HUNTING

The shadows of the night stalked across the ground and wrapped themselves around the shipping containers on either side of me, providing the cover that I needed in order to avoid exposure.

It was dark tonight. A full moon was only just rising, but it was nowhere near at peak luminosity. Still, I wasn't about to stray from the protection of the shadows. My fingers slid against the side of the rusted metal carcass of the container, feeling the coolness of its surface and the uneven texture, as both dirt and eroded metal clung to my fingertips. It felt safer somehow, using the container to hide from the night and the creatures that stalked within it, yet I was still keenly aware that that wasn't exactly the case.

Whether I was in the relative safety of my house, or standing in the middle of a shipping yard sixteen hundred kilometres from home, there were always going to be things that went bump in the night, things that hunted me in return. Given the very nature of what I was, it seemed naive to think that I was invulnerable to persecution from any given race, particularly the clan that harboured me. But I didn't have time to consider that now.

I was hunting.

I glanced quickly behind me, scanning the shadows with narrowed eyes just as I had been trained to do, checking if anyone was approaching from the rear. It appeared that I was still on my own.

I had left the family about ten minutes ago to follow the inklings of my nose rather than the common sense in my head. Probably not the wisest decision I had ever made. But since when did I ever do anything sensible?

Simple answer … never.

The biting, cold night air swirled around me and I looked up, just to make sure that the creatures had not taken to the tops of the containers. Surely I would have heard them if they had? Their nails alone on the metal surface would have given away their position.

The coast was clear above, or so it would seem. Unless of course they were in human form? But then wouldn't I catch scent of them in some way shape or form?

Crap! Why did I wander off on my own again?

Because I'm a total tool.

I shuffled forward a few more steps, ignoring the cold wind that danced through the tendrils of my hair and blew them across my face. Walking between the rows of containers was oddly like being trapped in a wind tunnel. The breeze itself may have been icy cold and biting into my skin, but it did little to calm my nerves or ease the perspiration that was running in beads down my spine.

I treaded quietly across the roughened concrete, taking care not to trip over any of the uneven surface, pulling my coat tighter around me to abate the chill. I continued forward, attempting to track the scent of blood that wafted across the top of the frigid night air. The smell was unmistakable.

It was all encompassing and thick with the stench of both life and death.

Although I was still yet to turn, and my very nature meant it should be appetising and somewhat enticing, I still wrinkled my nose in mental revolt at the smell. I knew it was only a reaction from my stubborn human nature that repelled me. If I was completely honest with myself, I was actually not offended by the smell at all.

I kind of liked it.

I was more offended by what the scent represented for my future, not how it affected me physically.

In the back of my mind I felt deeply disturbed that both the taste and the scent of warm, rich blood was not something that my body or my senses willingly rejected. In fact, my body seemed to rejoice internally at the thought of its taste across my tongue.

But I had never gone there.

I had never tasted blood.

At least not that I remember.

I had no intention of taking that next step until it was absolutely necessary, or on the off chance that my stupid curiosity got the better of my more prudent nature.

Unfortunately, to anyone that knew me well that meant there was an extremely good chance that my somewhat rational intentions were going to blow away with the next wind. Who was I kidding, anyway? I'd probably be chugging down pints of the red stuff before I even turned seventeen.

For now, I would only allow myself to scent blood.

That was enough.

I didn't need to taste it to know that it was strangely sweet even yet laced with lashings of salt and corroded iron. The idea of those combinations in the one liquid was a total paradox. Still, that's what it smelt like to me and I was attracted to its scent. As tempting as it was given my intended nature, for the sake of not scaring little children and small dogs, I'd try to avoid crossing that line. It shouldn't be too difficult given that I only had a normal set of human chompers and the idea of piercing flesh with my teeth slightly sickened me.

Some vampire I was going to turn out to be.

It was probably just a product of my upbringing. My family hated vampires. Teenage girls, too, or maybe that was just me when I was acting out. Honestly, they pretty much hated any being from the undead realm, which of course left me feeling less than inclined to really relax around any of them. After all, I was going to be joining those ranks in just a few short years, and I certainly did not want to be on the receiving end of bad juju.

I looked ahead again, focusing on the unknowns. I was satisfied that I did not have someone tailing me. Besides, the scent of blood was coming from somewhere further on, not from the path that I had just tread. Although the wind blew strongly down these passages, and smells could often be lost during harsh wind gusts, I could not mistake *that* scent even if I had wanted to.

A frenetic tension was building in the air. I could feel it in my bones—feel it under my skin. I knew I was heading in the right direction. It was the same kind of excitement that was coursing through my bloodstream each and every second that I caught wind of the blood trail.

I tilted my head upwards, drawing in a long deep breath, inhaling the different scents on the night air. They must have been feeding, hence the feeling of growing satisfaction I could taste on the wind. The blood odour that danced just inside my nostrils hinted at warmth and freshness.

At least they were distracted.

If I got too close with the ferocity of this wind then they might have been able to scent me as well. But I figured that with their snouts all covered in blood it would prevent them from detecting my presence for a little while yet.

I smoothed my hair back behind my ears and took a few

more steps forward, cursing myself silently for not tying it back. Not to mention the fact that, despite the cold, I was sweating and my hair and perspiration didn't exactly see eye to eye. I was almost surprised that my ringlets had not taken over and devoured my face entirely or turned me into something resembling Medusa.

I looked around again. It was time to get on with the job and stop procrastinating. Where was the rest of my family anyway? Surely they should have found me by now, if for no other reason than for George to scream at me for running off—probably giving him increased blood pressure and a greater risk of heart attack in the future.

I closed my eyes briefly, summoning a new wave of courage to wash over every nerve that was racing out of control in my body. I started to count to ten, hoping that it would be enough to calm my rapidly beating heart. I shouldn't be scared. I had been training with the Institute of Magical Intervention, or IMI, since I was twelve years old. While regular kids went off to regular high schools, I learnt I would eventually become a member of the undead and was destined to spend the next six years studying how to destroy various members of the supernatural realm. So given that I had been trained to deal with these kinds of situations, there was no reason to be sweating bullets now, not when I knew how to defend myself in an attack.

It wasn't like I could actually get hurt anyway. Well, not unless someone decided to chop my head off, then I was really going to be upset. But I was seriously hoping that that was not going to be on anyone's agenda for this evening. That would certainly put a dampener on my Saturday night plans, not to mention seriously piss me off.

Perhaps I was just terrified and letting my nerves get the better of me because this was the first time that I had branched off on my own. The last time that we went hunting there had been backup all the way. But tonight I had no idea where everyone else was.

Well, that wasn't exactly true. I had a 'vague' idea where everyone else was wandering around, but they were going in entirely the wrong direction. That much I was sure of, hence why I'd ditched them all in the first place.

I did try to tell them.

Undoubtedly by now, Susan and George would have realised that I was 'missing' and already started stewing over just exactly *how* they were going to punish my obstinacy this time. I had to say that they weren't very creative.

I smiled, despite my current state of affairs. I'd probably be grounded again which was somewhat inconvenient for my social life, but never the less, only a slight obstacle in perverting my nightly activities. I wasn't about to let a little thing like not being able to use the front door stop me from fulfilling my desire to have social interaction with people other than The Protectors. Besides, there was a rave happening this Saturday that I was determined to attend.

Grounded or not.

I suppose that meant I had to get out of this alive first.

That would be super.

I slapped my head mentally.

Focus Elena.

I wiped the sweat that was building on my upper lip and across my forehead, then grabbed my hair and quickly threaded it into a plait, and then tucked it down into my jacket so that it would at least stay off my face. I couldn't afford to have it swinging about my eyes and blinding me from an impending attack.

I skedaddled quickly down to the corner of the container and peered around the corner before flicking my head back around again, almost giving myself whiplash in the process.

Geez, calm down.

No one was there. My nose still told me that they were further ahead yet, but not by too much.

I looked around the corner again, just to make sure that there was no danger.

Taking a deep breath, I quickly dashed across the open path that exposed me to soft bathing of moonlight, and then ducked back against the next container, folding the shadows around me while I steadied my breathing. My heart beat seemed to quicken in my chest at the prospect of only being a couple of metres away from the targets.

I mentally ordered my heart rate to calm down, but it appeared to be just as stubborn as the rest of me. Although I didn't really want to admit it, not even to myself, I was shit scared right now, despite the years of training. If there was one sure thing that could possibly alert the creatures to my presence, it would be my heart beat. It would be difficult for them to ignore and resist the sound of fresh blood pounding through my veins, particularly blood that was laced heavily with vampiric scent.

Why did I separate from everyone else again?

Oh yeah, that's right, I forgot … I'm a frigging tool.

After a few deep breaths and a notable fall in heart rate, I crept along close to the new container, my fingers still grazing against the metal as I walked, my other hand shaking slightly as it hovered protectively over the knife that was lashed to my leg. I wished now that I had had the good sense to stay behind Lucas instead of wandering off on my own. Why I felt the need to always disobey everyone around me was beyond me. But I guess being sixteen years old made me susceptible to bouts of irrational behaviour and the occasional notion that I was in fact smarter than everyone else, regardless of whether or not that was true.

If I was smart now, I would simply walk back the way I had come instead of proceeding forward into the face of danger. Obviously there was a part of me that had considered facing the two vânătors alone and had decided that was a good idea. Perhaps it was PMS? What other logical reason could there be for continuing on a path this ridiculously dangerous and stupid? Unless of course the only plausible explanation left was that I was in fact a total moron, with a capital M?

I thought about that for a second.

Nope, I just can't see it.

I pulled back in closer to the side of the container, withdrawing my dirty fingers from the metal and brushing them lightly across the front of my jeans to wipe away the orange rusted tinge. I could feel a slight tremble across the surface of my skin, and it had very little to do with the cold weather. I was scared, despite how many times I had told Susan and George on the way here that I was more than capable of participating in tonight's hunt without being chaperoned like a nun at a Manpower concert.

Again, not exactly true.

This was only the second hunt that I had been actively allowed to partake in. The first hunt was more of a 'watch and learn' experience. I 'watched' all right, and Susan and George 'learned' to lock the car. But one thing was certain, I was not about to let some grievances regarding my personal welfare interfere with tonight's intended outcome. We had a job to do and I didn't want to be the one to screw it up because I was too scared to follow through. We couldn't afford to let them get away. I was going to have to swallow my fear and accept that sometimes if fate dealt you a less than desirable hand, then the only option left was to suck it up and play the very best damn game that you could, or bluff like hell until you won a round.

I was intending to bluff, which of course was ridiculous because I was a crappy poker player. But given my current situation, which I had absolutely no one to blame but myself, I had to do the best that I could with the hand that had been dealt to me—a pair of wolves perched just down the end of this container …

I touched the hilt of the silver blade that was lashed tightly to the side of my leg and stroked its length in a reassuring gesture. This blade had been my constant companion since training had started and I was accustomed to how it felt in my hand and the comfort it brought me by having it near. The weight of the hilt in my palm and the way my fingers wrapped tightly around it as I sashayed it through the air in arcing motions felt as natural as breathing. This blade had only plundered blood once and it had been brief, but it had sliced through flesh as easily as a bread knife through butter.

All I needed tonight was a couple of well placed slices and the beasts would be dead. They didn't heal the way that a vampire could, or even the way that I could for that matter. Werewolf flesh was as vulnerable as a human's, and any blow could be fatal. But tonight's outcome depended entirely of course on whether or not they decided to tag team me.

That could mean one of three things.

Drain me dry of all my blood.

Impregnate me with wolf spawn.

Or tear my head right off my shoulders.

Not exactly a pleasant thought. But it didn't change the fact that if I wasn't careful or controlled in my movements, it could easily happen.

Crap why am I doing this again?

I couldn't even claim the last kill as my own because Lucas had incapacitated the beast first with his magic. I may have delivered the fatal blow that killed the last wolves that strayed into our territory, but it was only after they had been frozen to the spot with the Hevannatara spell. It's not much of a challenge if the target in question doesn't defend itself because it's nothing more than a doggie popsicle. Was I even ready for this now given that once they sensed my presence there would be no magic to slow them down?

You have to be.

I blew out another chilled breath and decided to change my tactics. I could do this. I hadn't spent the last four years getting knocked on my ass in training just to stand back and watch. After all, how was I ever supposed to learn the true thrill of a hunt or gain insight from the challenge of a worthy opponent if the opportunity was always muted?

I could do this. Nay ... I needed to do this.

I needed to prove that the IMI had not been wasting their time on me and that I was in fact capable of defending human rights just as well as my family, despite the fact that sometime in the near future I would be a natural enemy of the clan. After all, I may have been human now, but that was not going to be the case forever and when that time came ...

All bets were off.

I fingered the blade again and instantly felt better knowing that I was at least armed against these creatures should their senses stir and become aware that we were hunting them.

Correction. I was hunting them.

I certainly did not have the same magical abilities that the rest of my adoptive family had when it came to fighting these beasts, so I had to be circumspect.

These beasts ... What a joke.

I shook my head in dry amusement.

In so many instances I was just like the creatures that we were hunting this evening. I may not have had the blood lust just yet, but when my turning finally occurred on my eighteenth birthday, I was going to be just as blood driven and deadly.

A beast to the core.

That was certainly something that The Protectors were trying to change by conditioning me to fight against my own kin. I knew that it probably served their ends more than it did mine. I wasn't stupid. But I also didn't know any better either, having never grown up around anyone other than a Protector.

The IMI had long since been training The Protectors in magical defence against the darker realms of the supernatural. Namely the Vampires and the Werewolves, but I had been the exception. Despite the fact that I was going to turn into a vampire on my eighteenth birthday, the IMI saw me as an opportunity to mould a weapon that might one day be of benefit to their side in the fight against the Vampires.

I wasn't exactly sure how I felt about that just yet. After all, I had never actually met a vampire before, so I could only trust in the judgement of my family and the other Protectors when they said that they were a race worthy of annihilation just like their creation ...

The Vânǎtors.

But if that was true, what did that say about me? Was I only worthy of life because they had raised me to fight for their causes? Or would I be just as expendable as the werewolves that we hunted this evening?

I shook my head. I needed to keep my wits about me. I couldn't let my mind wander into the unknowns when there was something lurking in the darkness ahead that was far more dangerous than the thought of meeting a vampire or betraying the IMI.

I ducked down low to the ground when I heard the snapping of snouts and low feral snarls erupting from behind the next container. If nothing else tonight, I wanted to prove to myself that I could defend and protect just as well as the others, despite my lack of magical skills.

I sucked in a breath, the scent of blood now heavy and thick in my nostrils. I could almost taste the saltiness in the air and the sharp after taste of metal as each breath danced across my tongue. I could feel my veins constricting in response, the desire to feed was building in a pit deep down inside of me, which was ridiculous considering I still loved to eat regular food. Perhaps that was the problem with being a born Vampire and not a turned one—you always wanted blood even though you didn't technically need it in order to survive. Despite all born vampires being human for the first eighteen years of life, there was always the underlying desire to taste blood, even if the actual turning did not occur until the stroke of midnight on their eighteenth birthday. It was a total Cinderella cliché, but nevertheless entirely true.

I shook it off and glanced at the containers of rusting metal that loomed impressively above me, closing the darkness in over my head and hiding my figure in the shadows.

Unfortunately, I was close enough to them now that they would be able to catch my scent and quite probably hear my racing heartbeat. So there was definitely no going back.

I wrapped my hand around the hilt of the knife and pulled it slowly from the enclosure on the side of my leg.

My fingers found their usual position on the handle as I

lifted the blade in front of me, moonlight bouncing off the silver surface and dissipating into the darkness beyond.

I held the blade in front of me and edged my way quietly to the corner of the container.

Rather than duck my head around the corner and risk being seen, I tilted the blade on an angle that allowed me to use it like a mirror so that I could see around the other side. In the reflection I could easily see the two vânǎtors that we were hunting tonight. 'Vânǎtor' was the Romanian word for 'hunter', a name adopted by the early descendents of The Protectors over three hundred years ago when the Vânǎtors were first created by the Vampires.

It was a big mistake in hindsight.

The Vampires had never expected that their guard dogs would eventually turn on them. The main problem with the Vânǎtors was that not only did they enjoy the taste of human flesh and blood, they also enjoyed that of the Vampire, and they replicated faster than a warren of horny rabbits. Not to mention the fact that they were remorseless and took on the human figures of anyone they had ever tasted.

The Vânǎtor's creation had been one of the first stories that George had ever told me when they had finally decided to explain the parts about me that could no longer be explained away. It was hard for a twelve year old not to question her surroundings when she never seemed to get sick or injured and her older, adoptive brother could somehow shoot fireballs from his hands. The story of how the Vânǎtors were created was what led to the formation of The Protectors and the creation of the IMI, and also to the story that unfolded my true origins.

I was born a vampire.

Interestingly enough, vampires apparently dated back longer than anyone can remember but, as I had never met one myself, it wasn't like I could ask one to flip out his ID and prove he was older than Father Time. On the other hand, The Institute of Magical Intervention was only created in 1923, consolidating every member of The Protector clans around the world. At last count, these amounted to around five thousand inductees.

None of it would have been necessary if it weren't for one coven of vampires back in 1713 that persisted on plaguing a small village in central Romania.

Too many people went missing, too many people wound up dead.

Needless to say, the villagers were not about to take the assault lying down. They sought out information via the old texts, from campfire stories, and by travelling to other villages that were rife with the superstitions surrounding the practice of witchcraft.

The dark arts banishment was sweeping across Europe at the time, encouraging the burning of innocents at the stake for any suspected acts of witchcraft. But for each of those people that were trialled and found guilty of legitimately practicing different forms of witchcraft ways were found by the villagers to smuggle them to safety.

In exchange for their freedom, the villagers asked to be trained in all manner of magical defence and attack. It came easily to some, but not to others; the villagers' descendants later learned that magic was inherent, unlocked only if it was predisposed of by the blood.

As the power of the villagers' magic grew, so did the Vampires' fear, and what resulted from that fear—the Vânătors. The details of their creation were a little sketchy. The Protectors had never really been too forthcoming with the information they'd given me. Somewhere in the backs of their minds some probably thought I was always going to be the enemy and too much information would be dangerous.

My adoptive parents and my adoptive brother were the closest thing to a loving family I had ever had and I owed them everything for taking me in. I didn't really want to put them in an awkward position by asking too many questions because, if it weren't for them, then I might have been destroyed at birth.

Again, that was another area of my life that was a little sketchy.

Each member of the IMI was more than a little reluctant to discuss my origins, and unrelenting questions had constantly burned at the back of my mind. I was hoping that the older and more resourceful I got, the more they would realise that putting off those vital answers would be more tiresome then just telling me the truth. I only wanted to know the reason that I existed in the first place, and just exactly who my real parents were.

I shook my head and willed myself to concentrate harder. No time for reminiscing or game playing. There were some big bad wolves just around the corner of this container and no hunky woodsman with an axe to chop them all up.

I stared at the metallic surface. The Vânătors were still engrossed in their kill. I could quite easily see the both of them in the reflection of the knife.

I peered closer, my eyes narrowing slightly as I tried to make out just exactly what it was that their bodies were slumped so possessively over.

I clutched a hand to my mouth to prevent any sound from escaping and took another cursory glance at the image reflected in the blade. There was so much blood and torn flesh that it was almost impossible to decipher just exactly what the remains belonged to. I probably wouldn't have recognised it as human at all if it hadn't have been for the torn uniform, flash-light, and hat that was strewn across the ground to the left of the body. It was probably the night patrolman.

My instincts kicked in and I weighed up all of my options, assessing the situation from every angle and trying to work out the best approach.

From what I could tell by the way both of the wolves draped themselves across the carcass, one of them was higher up in the pack hierarchy than the other. The one on the left seemed to pick at the extremities as he fed, glancing back at the other one before he took another portion of flesh. The one on the right, however, draped his body across the carcass, claiming the bigger portion. The low growling in the back of his throat indicated that he didn't appreciate the other wolf sharing his bounty. I wondered if that was going to work to my advantage.

I had learnt that the characteristics of vânǎtors were not that much different to the rest of the animal kingdom: there was always someone a little higher up in the pack order than the other, although neither of these beasts looked like an Alpha or pack leader. An Alpha was larger than a standard vânǎtor, and a whole lot meaner. I hadn't exactly met an alpha before. My field experience was truly limited in that regard, but I was a solid reader, and the texts at the IMI pointed out a few discernable differences between an Alpha and the two wolves I was looking at.

For one, Alphas were rare. No one ever really saw them, but The Protectors that had, recorded that they were at least twice the size of a standard Vânǎtor.

Two, they were supposedly slightly darker in colour— closer to black than grey.

And three, they were really freaking hard to kill, hence

why no one had done it yet. The two vânători that were with me now were definitely nothing special, but I still was shaking in my boots at the prospect of having to face them.

I doubted that the leader of the two would leave his kill until he had taken his fill. If they sensed danger, then I hoped he would send the other one to investigate. Separating them seemed to be the only chance I would have at avoiding the razor sharp teeth and long pointed claws.

I looked around my feet, searching for anything useful, like a rock or piece of broken concrete. There was nothing. *Damn.*

Then I realised that I had my cell phone on me. I smiled lightly. This would do the trick just nicely.

I dug into my coat and fished around in the pockets until I found my phone. I kept the blade in my hand, just in case, and then quickly edged my way back around the container, in the direction that I had just come.

When I got to the end of the row, I used the blade's reflection once again to check if the coast was clear and then darted across the opening, while sticking to the shadows and trying not to make too much noise. After all, their hearing was exceptionally good.

When I got to the very end of the row I turned left and dashed as quickly as I could down to the next passage. I stopped at the corner of another container and took a quick second to peer around the edge.

About seven shipping containers away I could just see the two vânători, and thankfully, it appeared that they were too engrossed to notice me, so I made a run for it while the going was good.

Once I'd cleared the opening, I leant back up against the rear of the next container and listened for any sounds of movement. There was nothing, just the same scent of blood in the air and the distant sound of snapping snouts and tearing flesh. I swallowed down another lump of rising bile.

Gross.

I took off at a run again, putting as much distance between me and the Vânǎtors as I could.

When I got to the far end of one container, I grabbed my cell phone again and turned off the silent option, making sure that when it did ring that the tone would be very loud.

I sent a quick text message to Lucas.

— *Lucas, found the targets. In 5 minutes I need you to ring me, don't hang up until the phone goes to message-bank. Don't bother trying to text me back either, just do as I say, okay?* —

I sent the message. It seemed to take forever with my shaky fingers, but I managed to get it done, and then place the phone on the ground. I had roughly five minutes before that thing was going to go off like a siren, possibly less if Lucas decided to be an ass, ignored my instructions, and called me back straight away.

I took off in a run again, this time keeping to the rear of the containers so I could put a bit of speed into my step without drawing any attention.

Stopping at the corner of the passage that led directly to the Vânǎtors again, I quickly peered around the corner. They were still quite clearly engrossed in their meal.

I darted across the opening while their snouts were buried into the flesh and then stopped short behind another container to try and steady my heartbeat again. The wind had died down a little bit; this was a good sign for me. Windy weather made hiding from creatures such as these difficult, as scent travelled easily on the air.

I took in another deep breath, shuddering slightly as the

scent of warm blood danced across the night air, making my mouth water and my tummy rumble.

Shaking my head to dispel the sensation, I pushed off from the side of the container and headed back up the same path as earlier.

It didn't take me long to get back to my earlier positioning. I clutched the blade in my hand more tightly, feeling the leather of the hilt becoming warm and soft in my palm.

I waited patiently, hoping that Lucas would just do as I asked instead of running in, spells blazing. Then again, if my plan didn't work, it would be a godsend to have a little bit of magical backup. But of course that also meant I had to deal with the fallout from Susan and George once we'd finished kicking vânător butt. It was funny that the thought of taking on two bloodthirsty werewolves seemed to be less of a scary prospect than receiving a tongue lashing from the parentals.

Five minutes soon turned into what felt like an eternity. Small droplets of sweat were already forming across my top lip and forehead as I waited. I was quietly shuffling from foot to foot, doing an imitation of the 'pee dance' because my nerves would not keep me still and my skin was crawling with anticipation. I was ready for action, but at the same time I was *so* ready to throw up.

I checked the mirrored image again. Good. They were still engrossed and completely unaware of my presence. I couldn't ask for more than that.

I briefly closed my eyes, but when I heard my cell phone start ringing, quickly opened them again when I heard the snarls erupting from around the side of the container. There were also a couple of short barks and then a brief snapping sound before a following whimper.

I peered back into the silver of the blade. The subordinate

was getting up to investigate the noise, the other one was still slumped greedily over his kill.

In the distance, the cell phone kept ringing and the Vânător took off in a slow trot towards its sound, disappearing behind one of the containers a few metres away and parallel to the one I was hiding behind. With each step, I could hear its nails clinking against the concrete surface. I decided to give it at least twenty seconds to make sure there was a good distance between us and it.

Twenty seconds passed. I could no longer hear the retreating claws against the ground. I tightened my grip on the blade and edged my way around the corner.

The vânător looked up immediately from its kill. I had never seen such ferocity in a beast's eyes before. They were as black as night itself, framed by grey fur that narrowed in the corners which suggested I was being weighed and measured. The flesh then wrinkled across his brow, narrowing the eyes even further as my scared reflection stared back at me from the pits of obsidian darkness.

I moved my gaze from his eyes and focused on the part that could kill me—his teeth. The greyed fur was thinner in this section, pulled tight across the snout revealing a vicious sneer that showed off every single one of the Vânător's sharp, pointed fangs.

I debated for just under a second whether or not I should just put my head between my legs and kiss my ass goodbye. The last vânător I had killed had been frozen with magic first and there had been nothing but shock on its face.

This was different.

This was primal.

I could see that this beast desired nothing more than to tear me to pieces.

As I stepped forward, the muzzle on the beast pulled back, revealing even more deadly fangs at his disposal.

He snarled at me, the deep, throaty sound tearing through the silence of the night and stripping me of my self confidence. I felt a tremor quake right through me and my heart sped up. He would smell my fear. I had no doubt about that. Hell, if he kept looking at me with those blood thirsty eyes, I was going to smell my fear too … in my pants.

The Vânător straightened up from his slouched position, his limbs stretching, hackles rising.

Wow, they're a lot bigger than I remember.

He slinked towards me, his thick talons clinking against the ground with each step that he took.

I clutched the blade even tighter, the skin of my knuckles stretched taught and white against the bone. I mirrored his steps until we were standing only a few metres apart. I didn't have much time. The phone had stopped ringing and the other wolf would soon be back.

The Vânător leaned back slightly, his weight shifting to his rear legs. It was ready to pounce and I watched for the slightest sign of movement.

The wolf displayed his fangs with a menacing snarl, snapping his snout together with a thunderous clap that echoed through the night. It startled me and I jumped. I guess I'd thought that once he saw the knife in my hand that he would back down.

No such luck—a bucket load of ludicrous wishful thinking on my part.

The next few seconds happened as if in slow motion. His claws left the ground in an instant. He was sailing towards me quicker than I could blink.

Then I was ducking down, raising the blade and, in my mind, running over the skills I had been taught. As he sailed over me, I nicked the underside of his belly, drawing blood, but not enough to wound, just enough to seriously piss him off.

I dropped and rolled, but was not fast enough. His back claws caught the side of my shoulder, tearing through the material of my coat and piercing the flesh beneath. I cried out in pain. Nausea swept over me in an instant as blood poured quickly out of the wound, the sweet, salty scent tantalising to my nostrils, yet churning my stomach in response.

I clutched at the wound with my other hand, waiting for my self-healing abilities to kick in. But the Vânător did not wait. He was circling me and flying through the air again before I could defend myself. He knocked me completely to the ground, his front paws landing heavily across my chest. I felt the air whoosh out my lungs as I gasped for breath.

It felt like he'd cracked one of my ribs.

But, even worse, the bastard had ruined my new coat.

A thick globule of drool landed on my chest and rolled off to one side. The smell of its breath was fetid. Beyond bad; it was all I could do not to bring up what I had for dinner.

In a flash, I drew the blade up and stabbed the wolf's left flank. Blood spurted from the gash and the Vânător, howled out in pain, immediately pulling away from me.

I scrambled back to my feet, fighting for breath, crouching down low and ready for the next attack.

The wolf came fast and was on me in moments.

This time I was ready.

I ducked to the side, avoided a swipe of his claws, and dug the blade of my knife swiftly into its other flank. It dragged briefly through furry flesh as I hung onto the hilt tightly. The skin parted in gory detail, spilling intestines, torrents of blood and other body parts that I was not overly familiar with. They slumped onto the concrete with a sickening *slap*, forming a mound of bloodied organs by my feet.

Sick.

He slumped to the ground, another howl erupting from his muzzle, laboured and tainted with pain.

I turned in time to see the second vânător stalk up behind me from another container. Sensing the two of us were no longer alone reminded me of periphery checks, and it was just as well. He looked down at his badly injured pack mate and then zeroed in on me with his obsidian coloured eyes, howling so loudly that I had to reach up and cover my ears.

Oh yeah, this one was pissed.

I took a few steps back, my heel touching something soft and gooey.

I cringed. I didn't need to look around to realise that I'd stepped in what was left of the patrolman.

I side stepped the body, my eyes quickly flickering to the injured vânător. He was still slumped on the ground, blood pouring from his wounds. He was incapacitated for the moment.

My gaze immediately darted back to the other one, watching every one of his movements as he started to pace backwards and forwards in front of me, never letting his eyes stray from the blade in my hand.

I felt my confidence grow. My heart was still racing, but not from nerves. Now it was purely from the rush of excitement.

One down, one to go.

I tossed the blade from hand-to-hand, back and forth, showing the beast I was no longer afraid. I even smiled a little, growing cocky.

I swirled the hilt in my palm and—

Dropped it. As the blade clattered loudly on the concrete, I cringed.

Total amateur.

Wasting no time, the beast leapt directly at me.

I dropped to the ground, rolled to the side and scooped the blade back up into my hands.

The Vânător landed on the ground not more than a couple of metres away and immediately whirled around to charge again. But instead of jumping, he bared his teeth and ran straight for me.

I wildly swept the blade in front of me, backwards and forwards, hoping to at least pierce some flesh so I didn't have to come up against those sharp teeth.

Faster than death, his muzzle caught my blade-wielding arm in a vice-like grip.

I screamed. The pain of his putrid teeth piercing through my flesh was excruciating.

I screamed again, swallowing back tears as I pounded my fist against his snout, to no avail.

My tortured gasps of pain echoed through the stillness of the night. I was hoping that my screams would alert the others to my whereabouts. If they weren't too far away now then at least they could finish what I had started. At the very least clean up what was left of my remains if the vânător happened to win this tug of war.

The vânător's teeth dug deeper into the flesh of my arm. I could feel their pointed lengths grazing against the bone. I could also hear his talons scrambling for purchase on the concrete surface, scratching his way towards more leverage.

I moved with him, not conceding, but moving to abate the pain in my arm and avoid a severed limb. Despite how well I could heal myself, I didn't know if I could actually grow missing parts back again, and I'd be buggered if I was going to test that theory out tonight.

The vânător suddenly jerked my arm violently to the side. I was torn between nausea, pain, and disbelief. The double whammy of having more flesh and muscle torn from my appendage had me clenching my teeth and hissing in pain. But when my arm popped free of the socket, and I saw it dangling in his mouth like a bone, I started crying like a baby.

Get it together Elena, or this bastard's going to have your arm for dessert.

Or bury it in someone's backyard for later.

Despite the pain, I found enough focus to raise my opposite arm and bring a clenched fist down on the top of his nose. Knuckles and fur connected, and a searing pain shot through my hand and up my entire arm as something went *crack*. More tears rained down my cheeks, but the Vânător only responded with a grunt. I probably only bruised him, which meant he was seriously kicking my ass.

I wasn't feeling so cocky now.

He jerked me to the side again, pulling me off my feet and further rending my flesh with his teeth. I'd had enough now.

With that spare hand, already self-healing, I grabbed the knife, ignoring the lingering protests of pain, and slit the wolf's throat. It was messy, but quick, and ultimately efficient. God only knew how many minutes had passed where I'd been nothing but a chew toy.

The vânător dropped to the ground, falling in a heap and taking me down with him, the life behind his eyes extinguished.

I dropped the knife all the while keeping an eye on the other wounded wolf. He kept glancing between me, his now dead pack-mate, and the internal organs sprawled out on the concrete beside him. I could almost smell his fear now.

I pried this vânător's jaws open and dislodged my badly chewed arm from between his teeth—it was a bloody mess and as limp as a rag doll.

Luckily my vampiric genes had already set to work on repairing the damage. In a few minutes it would be as good as new again, just like my shoulder. I couldn't say the same thing for my coat though. It was destined for the trash.

I pushed to my feet and collected the knife that was by my side. The silvered blade and leather hilt was smeared in blood.

I felt a rising tidal of self satisfaction wash over me, glancing down at the dead vânător at my feet and at the other one that was whimpering a few meters away. I revelled in that sound—it feared me now instead of the other way around.

'Do you want this to be over fast or slow, Vânător?' As I said this, I lowered myself carefully down beside it, the blade still held out in front of me—a gleaming tool for justice. It whimpered something unintelligible through its snout and then its head dropped across its front paws in a gesture of defeat. A twinge of sympathy fluttered through me as I looked at the helpless creature in front of me. He looked so … vulnerable.

But the moment was fleeting and I realised that, given the chance, this vile creature would have made the same mess of me as he had made of the night patrolman. Plus, I'd recently watched *Cujo*, and now had a semi-serious loathing for all things canine.

I rolled the knife around in my hand, feeling the hilt flutter warmly against my palm before leaning forward and finishing this vânător off with a swift slice across the throat.

It was by no means creative, but like before, it was final. Death always is.

'That's a good doggie. Now, stay down.'

I wiped the blade clean against the grey matted fur of its back and then re-sheathed it in my leg holster.

'Ahem.'

I spun around to see George, Susan and Lucas all staring at me in bewilderment and, dare I say it, anger?

'Hey guys,' I said calmly, rising to my feet. 'What's up?'

CHAPTER TWO: OBSTINACY

Lucas's lips turned up into an immediate grin. He crossed his arms in front of his chest and looked to each of his parents waiting, for the outburst that he knew was inevitable.

Susan stared at me in a mixture of horror and awe as she glanced at me, the two dead vânători and the horrible mess they had made of my coat.

George, on the other hand, seemed less than impressed as he surveyed the scene in front of him. 'What's up?' He echoed my comments, growling as he took another step towards me, his hands balling into fists at his sides. 'What's up?' Veins were popping in his forehead and his cheeks were mottled red with anger. I was definitely going to get it.

I held up my hands in surrender and took a step backwards. Lucas could barely contain his delight at my growing discomfort.

'What's up, young lady, is that *you* are in very serious trouble.'

I fought the urge to roll my eyes.

Like I don't already know that.

'What did I say to you in the car on the way here?'

I crossed my arms in front of my chest, the cold finally reaching out to me and enveloping my body with icy tendrils. 'You told me to stay behind Lucas and not to wander off.'

His eyes narrowed and his hands uncurled, moving

straight to his hips like an angry teapot. 'And what part of that *didn't* you understand?'

Apparently all of it.

I shrugged. 'Sorry.'

His face went red. Susan reached out a hand and touched his arm. 'Let's just clean up this mess, George, and sort out what to do with Elena later.' She turned to me. 'Are you okay?'

I nodded. My arm and shoulder were already healed, even though my bloody and ripped jacket made it look otherwise.

'Why don't you two head back to the car and your father and I will sort out this mess?'

By *sort out this mess*, Susan meant setting all of the bodies on fire and letting them burn until there was nothing left to identify. We couldn't afford to wait for sunrise to do the job for us. It was too many hours away and fire worked effectively against all members of the undead. I suppose that includes me. Besides, the next patrolman was due to start work within the next few hours and would undoubtedly start searching for his missing colleague. The dead patrolman was likely to be identified through dental records, but it wasn't *his* remains that needed to be kept hidden from the mortal world.

Humans were certainly not ready to learn about the existence of vampires and werewolves. Hell, I'd almost had a heart attack when they'd first told me what I was and what I would eventually become. I'd spent the better part of the conversation waiting for Ashton to jump out from behind the couch and tell me I'd just been punk'd.

Most humans were happier believing in what they could prove with science, or see and feel for themselves. To humans of the twenty-first century, vampires, werewolves, and magic are simply the fictitious ingredients that create a top-shelf horror film. People would defile their underpants the world over if they ever discovered that these supposed fictional characters were actually real.

George wagged a long, slim finger at me, his face still as red as a beetroot. Susan pulled him away from me, towards the pile of bodies.

'You are in such big trouble, young lady,' he spat. I always found it extremely amusing that he thought his theatrics scared me.

Ignoring him, I edged my way around the carcasses and fell into step beside Lucas who was already walking slowly down between the passages of containers from which they had come. I kept my head down and my eyes on the ground, slinking away into the night beside Lucas and wondering what punishment was heading my way. I may not have been afraid of George or Susan, but I was a little concerned about the impending status of my social life.

Goodbye, Saturday night.

'I mean it, Elena!' George shouted at my retreating back, his voice an angry torment on the wind. 'So much trouble.'

I rolled my eyes. 'Yeah, I heard you ... so much trouble, I get it.'

'Are you smart-mouthing me?' he bellowed as we disappeared from sight, slipping behind another converging passage of shipping containers.

'No,' I yelled over my shoulder, and kept walking. 'Just saying it like it is,' I muttered. I wasn't really badass enough to provoke the situation further. As it was, I was fairly certain I was going to be grounded again.

Susan was more easygoing than George. It was probably why I liked her more than I liked him. He was so unfeeling in comparison. Then again, it wasn't like I was a ray of sunshine either. I'd never particularly warmed to either of them. I cared about them, no doubt, but I never really saw them as parents, unless you could constitute my continual house arrest as a display of loving affection.

Lucas was sniggering beside me.

I slapped him on the shoulder, fuming. My own mouth would get me into enough trouble without him adding his own backhanded comments.

'You really are in deep shit, Elena,' he said in between outbursts of disjointed snorts and laughter.

I touched his arm in mock concern and put on my best surprised face. 'Really? Are you sure? I mean how can you possibly be certain when he only said I was in trouble, what, three times? Do you think I should wait for a fourth before I fall to the floor and pray to the Gods for absolution?'

He sniggered again. 'Nope, no amount of praying is going to stop you from getting punished this time.'

'You think?' I shoved him in the arm again.

'What were you thinking, going off by yourself, anyway?' he said, shaking his head. 'One vânător is bad enough, but two? That's suicide, E. How did you manage to fight them both at the same time?'

I smiled, remembering I'd stashed my cell phone nearby. 'We need to go and get my phone. I left it by one of the containers near the right hand side of the rear passage. That's how I separated them.'

'Ah, so that's why your text said to ring you. Using your mobile as a diversion?' He sounded impressed. 'Who was it that said technology equals rubbish?'

I grinned. 'I believe that was you when some nerd from Nebraska beat you at online Tetris last week.'

He gave me a sour look. 'That twelve year old shit cheated and you know it.'

'Sure he did.' I laughed, nodding and shoving my hands into my pockets to warm them up. 'You know, I think you're going to be the only one who thinks what I did tonight was a good thing.'

He let out a long, low whistle and kicked at a stone in front of his feet, but didn't answer me. I craved his approval in any shape or form. After all, blood or not, he was my older brother.

He kicked another rock. It hit the side of a metal hull with a short, sharp clang before bounding across the passage, settling against another container.

'I can't believe you killed two vânători on your own tonight—without the aid of magic!' He sighed, enthusiasm dampening a little. 'Despite the fact that you were pretty stupid to wander off on your own, I do have to admit that it's pretty cool that you kicked their asses all on your own, not that I'm condoning your actions.' He fingered the ripped material of my jacket. 'Good thing you can self-heal, huh?'

I nodded. 'I'd be in a truck load of pain right now if I couldn't.'

'Why did you do it anyway?'

My eyebrow rose slightly. 'Do what?'

'Run off on your own. What made you think it was a good idea? You know the IMI trains us to work as a team for a reason and going solo isn't a part of our charter.'

I shrugged. 'I didn't think. No one would listen, so I just followed my nose.'

'You could smell the vânători?' he said, touching my arm and drawing me to a halt.

'No,' I answered hesitantly, my eyes drifting from the ground to meet his powder blue ones. 'I could smell the blood.'

'Ahh,' he said quietly and started walking again.

I increased pace to catch up with him again. 'Do you think I should be able to smell vânǎtors by now? Is that why you asked?'

He shook his head. 'I don't really know, E. I've never met a vampire before either, remember? But from what mum and dad say, most of the vampires that are around these days are the turned ones, not born vampires like you. Turned vampires, as you know, do not have the same strength, speed and self-healing capabilities that a born vampire does. Maybe it is normal for you to be able to scent blood while you're still human, but not anything else.'

'Maybe.'

He patted my shoulder. 'Sure would be interesting to meet someone else like you, wouldn't it? I mean one that was born and has already turned. At least then we'd have someone to compare you with.'

He shook his head and dropped his arm back to his side. 'Even if we do have a secure alliance at the moment with the Vampires, I highly doubt they're going to bother straying this far north. It's too sunny.' He kicked another stone again.

'I'll probably never meet a vampire unless I decide to leave Cairns,' he mumbled.

He was right. There were no reported cases at the Institute of Magical Intervention of any vampires coming past the Queensland border, mostly because of the unending days of sunshine and harmful bouts of UV that still penetrated the clouds even on an overcast day. Sunlight still meant death for all vampires, whether born or turned. It was just the exposure that varied the severity. For example, a turned vampire could not tolerate the sun at all, emerging only at night, where as a born vampire could move around in the shadows of the day and remain unharmed.

But one old fallacy that still appeared in the movies as the true death of a vampire, was staking. From what I had learnt, you could only stake a turned one with any degree of success, unless of course the stake was made from silver— then any vampire would die.

I focused back on the conversation and Lucas's dejected expression. He'd never even seen a vampire before. 'Well I guess in less than two years you're going to have your chance at meeting one aren't you, Lucas?'

He smiled. 'At least you'll be on our side.'

I grunted. The Protectors always spoke of sides, even Lucas. It was highly offensive to me that they would expect me to choose. It shouldn't have to be that way. 'There's an alliance, remember? You're not supposed to take sides.'

'The alliance is only temporary,' he reminded me. 'One day, someone will falter and everything will change.'

I laughed. 'Yeah, if you can call a three hundred year alliance temporary.'

'As soon as we find a way to bring down the Vânǎtors indefinitely, the blood suckers are going down too.'

I went quiet. The alliance between The Vampires and The Protectors had come into effect almost three hundred years ago, yet there was still so much, ahem, bad blood between them. I had a feeling that although I had mostly been accepted into the fold at the IMI, I was still vulnerable to persecution if the alliance faltered.

I may owe the IMI a lot, but I wasn't quite ready to turn my back on my own heritage, not when I didn't know enough about them to form a truly decent opinion. What if The Protectors were wrong? What if some vampires were different and not bad at all? Surely the ones that were born had to be given some leeway. After all, they didn't choose to be a vampire. It was forced upon them, just as it had been onto me. If I was a good person and fought for the value of human life, then surely there could be others out there just like me?

I shook my head. What I think and feel in the grand scheme of things probably didn't matter all that much, even if it was important to me. To others, my opinion counted for nothing.

The only reason the Vampires and The Protectors had joined forces in the first place was because the Vânătors had proven to be more of a problem to either side than the other. In fact, they were now ten times more problematic to humans than vampires had ever been.

The Protectors, which were now considered warriors of magical justice for the IMI, decided it would be easier to eradicate one species at a time, starting with the most dangerous one first—the Vânătors.

Between the speed, agility, and deathly talents of a vampire, and the magical powers that The Protectors possessed, the Vânătors were now considered to be an endangered species—if you could count *thousands* as endangered. Unfortunately that theory was proving to be more and more difficult to confirm as time went on. The werewolves were getting better at blending into the general populace.

The Vânătors not only shared the blood lust of the Vampire and some of their skills—speed, agility, and strength—but they also had the power to replicate. The lurid acts were tantamount to rape, a vânător taking human form to complete the process. As far as we knew, no vânătors were born female, an oddity to be sure.

Vânătors were being detected everywhere now. However,

it was rare for them to stray to Australian shores. Packs were already established all over Europe, and our consistent sunny weather afforded the same threat of death as a vampire. But day or night, sun or no sun, the weather or location did not alleviate their mating habits—hence why it was vital to destroy them before they got down to business and infected the world with more of their spawn.

When a vampire is born, it is from the pairing of a male vampire and a human woman. A pregnancy always results from these unions. The seed of the Vampire is very determined. Even the most barren of women would not be able to avoid a vampiric pregnancy.

From this union, a regular human child would grow. The only difference would be that their system would already be laced with vampiric blood—the catalyst for the change that would begin on the day of the child's eighteenth birthday. They would also be born, like me, with the ability to self-heal, something George believes is an inbuilt survival mechanism designed to keep the species strong.

Just like me, this child grows as a regular human does. It will eat, sleep, breathe, and be otherwise completely undetectable as a vampire among the human populace until the day of turning.

Once the transformation begins, it takes roughly twenty-four hours for full conversion. It begins with the human portion dying, followed by the renewal of the body into full vampiric form. I often wondered if it would be painful.

In regards to a turned vampire, I wasn't so well-informed. I knew that they were created from some sort of blood transference, and that their powers were muted in comparison to their makers, but that was all I knew. Well, besides how to kill them. With a vânător however, the process is slightly different. I had read about it in the journals that covered the library walls in the IMI's secret hideout. According to the texts, the sex is almost never consensual. They force themselves upon their chosen victims with no mercy or regret. There is too much wild animal in them to revoke their hormones and understand that 'no means no'.

Their seed is just as strong as a vampire's, and pregnancy is instantaneous. In a period of just two days, gestation, growth, and the actual birth occurs. It is torturous on the human who has to suffer through the rapid growth and broken bones. The birth itself is deplorable and so far, every single vânător birth has resulted in the death of the human mother.

The Vânătors do not make passage into the world as a regular human does. They grow in their wolf form inside the womb instead of their human counterpart. Once fully grown, they tear their way out, breaking bones and drinking whatever blood is left inside the human carrier.

It is disgusting, murderous, and unforgivable. Even the Vampires consider their methods inexcusable, hence why the alliance exists.

The Protectors merely chose the lesser of two evils to side with. But again, what did that say about me and my intended fate if they considered vampires to be evil?

Lucas touched his hand to my shoulder again. 'You know that I didn't mean *you* specifically, right? I'd never hurt you, Elena.'

I shook his hand away and bent down to retrieve my mobile phone which was where I had left it. I had a missed call.

Kayla.

I tucked the phone back inside my coat pocket and started

fast-walking towards the car. In the air the sweet scent of blood was slowly being replaced by the bilious stench of burning flesh. Either that or the dried globule of vânător saliva on my chest was starting to burn my nostrils.

I really needed a shower.

'Elena ... wait for me,' Lucas called after me, jogging to catch up.

I kept walking, shoving my bloodied hands deeper inside my coat pockets and hunching my shoulders to deflect the cold wind.

'Elena, I'm sorry. What I said ... I didn't mean for it to come out like that.'

'Yes, you did,' I said quietly, trying to breathe through my mouth so that I couldn't smell the stink on my chest and the charred flesh in the distance. 'Sometimes you talk exactly like the IMI expects you to. It worries me that you can be that narrow-minded.'

'No, really,' he persisted. 'We may not be technically related by blood, but to me, you are still my sister and I would never dream of hurting you. And,' he said, pointing a finger in the air as if to prove a point, 'if anyone does try to hurt you I will personally kill them myself, regardless of the species.'

I smiled in spite of myself. 'That's sweet.'

'Sweet is my middle name.'

'Really?' I said, slapping him on the shoulder again, 'I thought it was dumb ass?'

He frowned. 'I hate it when you call me that.'

'I hate it when you call me dickhead.' Our pet names for each other were so charming.

'I haven't called you dickhead ... yet.'

'Just getting in first.'

'I'm not a dumb ass. Okay, so what I said before was

stupid, but I said sorry, so end of story. But if you really want to split hairs Elena, you seem to have the dumb ass corner of the market covered for this evening by taking on two vânǎtors by yourself.'

'Shut up,' I said, elbowing him in the ribs and grinning. 'I'm already in enough trouble without you rubbing it in.'

We passed the last container and headed directly for the car, which was located on the other side of the metal fence.

'Yeah, but you're not just in any trouble,' he chortled as he swung the gate back to allow me to pass, 'but *big* trouble.'

I rolled my eyes. 'I know … I haven't forgotten.'

When Susan and George finally made it back to the car, barely half an hour had slipped by. I leant my head up against the window and pretended to be asleep. Not that I was even remotely tired. I was still too highly strung to even consider closing my eyes and letting the sandman near me. Besides, I smelt too much like a wet dog right now to even get comfortable enough to sink into slumber.

In the distance, beyond the shipping containers, I could see the swirling clouds of smoke that still filled the air with the heavy stench of death. It was a solemn reminder of everything I had been through tonight.

The front doors opened and both of my parents lowered themselves into the car. It rocked slightly under their weight. George turned around to look at me.

I immediately snapped my eyes shut again, pretending to be asleep. I felt his eyes heavily upon me, but I didn't give into temptation. I kept silent.

Eventually he must have given up because I heard the

keys turn in the ignition and the car purr to life. He shifted it into gear, everyone silent except Lucas who emitted small snoring sounds. In another few minutes, those relatively quiet snores would turn into the ripping sound of a chainsaw coming to life. Even earplugs would be a lost cause at *that* stage.

In the distance I could hear sirens wailing. They were drawing closer; no doubt the fire department was coming to extinguish the flames. When they arrived there would be no evidence to suggest something supernatural besides *me* had walked the shipping yards this evening.

I cracked my eyes open slightly. Susan and George were both talking quietly, neither one of them paying attention to me. I took that as a good sign. But between the sound of the sirens and the racket coming from Lucas's snoring, I couldn't hear anything intelligible that they might have been saying anyway.

I imagined that they were probably tossing up between hot oil or the rack in terms of punishment, although realistically, grounding was the most likely choice. I'd come to expect this hindrance to my social life, but it was not an unsalvageable punishment, especially when the possibilities of my second story window were endless. If they really wanted to punish me, all they had to do was ban chocolate from the house. That really *would* kill me.

We had only just driven shy of the shipping yard's entry point and turned back onto the side road that led us here when the sound of the emergency vehicles grew louder.

The sirens wailed and tension mounted. I could see the lights on the top of the fire truck flashing brightly in the darkness ahead. Behind the fire truck was a single police car, its sirens flashing blue and keeping an easy pace with the truck.

They both blew past us in an instant, the sirens fading as quickly as they had come.

I let out a small sigh of relief, but soon regretted it when I heard the short, sharp burst of the police car's siren. Its warning sounded again, assumedly because the policeman had left the wake of the fire truck and had set a new course back towards us.

I resisted the urge to turn around. The blue, neon flashing lights reflected dimly on the underside of the roof of our car. The police were definitely behind us. The siren sounded again and George swore underneath his breath, still loud enough for me to hear even above the racket of Lucas's snoring.

George manoeuvred the car over onto the shoulder of the road and switched off the engine. 'Stay calm,' he said to Susan as he wound down the window.

She nodded, seemingly unperturbed by our current predicament.

I heard the slamming of a car door behind us and a flashlight beam glance through the rear window, filling the cabin with mottled light. It moved around the car and then disappeared from sight before flicking back on again and hitting me full in the face with its intensity.

I squeezed my eyes shut at the sudden brightness before I felt the beam move away and I cracked my eyes open again.

The officer, walked around the car very slowly with the flashlight, arcing the beam over every surface of metal and every face inside the car. The fingers of his right hand were stroking the butt of his gun in readiness of a draw. He seemed very wary of us, skittish even.

'Can we help you, officer?' George said calmly.

Lucas snorted loudly and then shuffled around in the seat until his face was pushed uncomfortably against the glass of his side window. God only knew what it looked like from the other side.

I suppressed my amusement in light of current events.

'Can I see your licence please, sir?' the policeman asked sternly.

George made no move to find his licence. Instead, he glanced up and looked in the rear-view mirror, studying something outside the rear window. 'Are you alone, officer?'

The policeman wrapped his fingers tightly around the butt of the gun and turned the torch on George's face. 'Step out of the car please, sir.'

George didn't even hesitate. He unbuckled his seatbelt, pulled the handle, opened the door, and stepped out into the cold night air.

Susan looked almost bored.

The policeman took a step back and refocused the flashlight on each of us sitting in the car. 'None of you move, please.' He focused his attention back on George. 'Sir, I'm going to ask you to turn around slowly and place your hands on the side of the vehicle.'

'May I ask what this is about?'

'Sir, I'll ask you one more time …'

George did as he was asked and rested his hands on the front of the bonnet and looked back at the police car parked behind us.

I hazarded a quick glance behind me and noted that the police car was empty. That was strange. I thought policeman always travelled with a partner for backup.

'Please. My family is tired and we just want to go back to our hotel. We took a wrong turn on the road up ahead and got lost.' George said all this calmly as he looked in the windshield at Susan. She gave him a brief nod.

'I would believe that story if your face was not covered

in ash, sir,' the policeman offered abruptly as he dropped his hand from his gun and fished around on his belt for handcuffs.

George spun around, hitting the policeman dead in the centre of his chest. The officer dropped to the ground like a lead balloon, surprise plastered across his features.

His flashlight dropped from his hands and hit the road, the arc of light illuminating the road's centre dividing lines. Air rushed from the policeman's lungs as he braced his hands behind him to stop falling further backwards. The smell of blood once again hit the air and assailed my nostrils—I glanced down and noted that he had scraped his palms across the asphalt upon impact. It stirred the same feelings of excitement and need that I had felt earlier.

I drew in another sharp breath, tasting the scent across my tongue and feeling the bloodlust rise within me.

George stepped forward, placing his hand out in front of him. Red flickers of light danced across the tips of his fingers like tiny sparks of electricity, steadily increasing in colour, intensity and energy.

The policeman watched in disbelief. He couldn't seem to move. He was completely transfixed by the seemingly unlikely possibility that magic could even exist.

His eyes widened in shock and awe as George took another step closer and touched a finger to the policeman's forehead. Light pulsed through the end of his finger and spread a warm wash of red over the policeman's entire face. It soaked into his skin like a tide of thick, red water that consumed his skin inch by inch until he looked as red as a tomato.

'*Defanacus*,' George murmured, before releasing his finger and squatting down in front of the officer.

The policeman was instantly still, his eyes unfocused as if caught in a trance.

'You will get back into your squad car, turn around and head back to the fire,' George said quietly. 'You are satisfied that we answered all of your questions, finding nothing suspicious or reasons to detain us. Do you understand?'

The policeman nodded.

George stood up and came back to the car, lowering himself into the seat and starting the engine.

I glanced back down at the officer, who was still sitting in a daze in the middle of the road and then continued to watch him as our car pulled away. I had only seen the Defanacus charm used once, and that was purely for training purposes. This powerful spell caused memory loss and transplanted memories over others. It was not dissimilar to the compelling or glamour techniques of a vampire. I wondered briefly if it had ever been used on me before.

Probably.

It would certainly explain all of the holes in my knowledge of my own life.

'Still pretending to be asleep, Elena?' George asked quietly as he pulled onto the highway, the car almost rolling up onto two wheels as he turned.

Lucas snorted again loudly and then sat up. He opened his eyes as if someone had just shaken him awake. 'What did I miss?' he said sleepily, rubbing his fingers across his eyes. There was a small trail of drool running down his chin and he quickly wiped it away.

'Nothing,' George countered. 'Elena and I are just about to discuss her punishment for tonight's stupidity.'

Lucas grinned and looked over at me, rubbing his hands together in delight. 'Excellent,' was all he said.

If I hadn't been such a good sister, I probably would have

smacked him in the face right now, just to wipe away the supercilious grin he was still wearing.

What a dumb ass.

CHAPTER THREE: SECRETS

The harsh Queensland sunlight streamed in through the open window and rapidly began to warm the swathes of fabric huddled around me, despite the winter chill in the air.

August was a fantastic time in Cairns. It was still cold enough to enjoy wearing jackets and jeans, but warm enough during the day that neither was exactly necessary. At least it was warmer here than it had been in Brisbane.

I pulled the blanket up over my head to shut out the light that was trying to break through my closed eyelids. I could have slept for a few more hours if it hadn't been for the fact that it was fast becoming a sauna under all these layers, and my alarm clock was no doubt going to go off at any minute.

I groaned loudly and flung the blanket off my slightly sweaty body and reluctantly pushed myself up off the bed.

Why hadn't I called in sick?

It was Saturday today, which meant I had to go to work. Not something I was particularly looking forward to given we'd only just arrived home again, late last night. Hunting those two werewolves yesterday had to be infinitely more exciting than fluffing pillows and arranging table displays at the furniture store where I worked. Not to mention that I was dead tired.

The trip had taken just over eighteen hours by road and

my ears were still ringing from the lecture I had received from both Susan and George all the way home. I had never heard them use the words 'irresponsible' and 'stupid' so many times in the one lecture, which was odd given the fact that I was susceptible to frequent bouts of irrational behaviour. For example, if Susan said I couldn't leave the house while they were out of town, I had a party at home. If she said I was grounded on a Saturday night, then I went out on Friday and Sunday night instead.

You get the point.

Susan and George called it blatant stubbornness.

I preferred to call it 'spirited'.

I opened the bedroom door, waltzed down the hall and into the bathroom to wash away the incoming wave of sleepiness. The cool water coming out of the faucet was divine. I cupped my hands and splashed my face and neck with it, washing away the remnants of sleep. I also pulled a brush through my hair, straightening out the ringlets, before tying it into a loose knot. Tic Tac's stock prices went down as I brushed my teeth with super strong peppermint paste, and Kleenex's stock prices went up when I went to the toilet—but at least I was now suitably primped and preened, ready to face the world without offending anyone.

The house around me sounded empty as I bounded down the stairs and into the kitchen. It was empty, and a quick inspection of the rest of the house indicated that no one was at home.

What time is it?

I went back into the kitchen and looked at the clock on the microwave. It was almost eight. Maybe they went to the IMI today?

From upstairs I heard my alarm clock blaring noisily on my bedside table.

I dashed up the stairs, into my room and switched it off. I was wide awake now.

I pulled my nightshirt over my head and tossed it onto the side of my bed. I padded over to my dresser, pulled out a bra, and slipped it on. Then I yanked down my black dress pants from the hanger and the unironed cotton T-shirt that were my uniform, a dress requirement of my job.

I stepped into my black slip on shoes after I had secured on the pants and pulled the ugly pink T-shirt over my head. I straightened the collar around my neck and then glided over to the dresser to apply some lip balm. All in all, the beautifying process took no longer than a few minutes.

I glanced at the clock—still plenty of time to have some breakfast. At least that was something I was still allowed to do without asking permission.

As expected, after eighteen hours straight of lecturing, I was grounded.

For a month this time.

It was definitely a little longer than usual, but nothing I couldn't handle or hadn't already anticipated. Needless to say my window was going to get a work out this month. I may have been grounded and had received explicit instructions that I was not to step foot out of the front door without prior permission, but no one said anything about the window.

I smiled. It wasn't really my fault if they left giant gaping holes open to side step their punishment.

My mobile phone trilled on the bedside table and I ducked around the edge of the mattress to answer it. It was Kayla.

'What's up?'

'Are you allergic to calling me back or something?'

'What? Not even a hello for me?' I said grinning.

She harrumphed. 'I only say hello to friends who call me back.'

I laughed. 'Sorry. We were on the road, I couldn't get very good cell coverage and it was really too late to call you back.'

She snorted. 'Bad cell coverage? Are you serious? You were travelling on Highway One. There's cell coverage everywhere. At least if you're going to give me a lame excuse for not calling me back, make it a good one.'

'Okay, truth?'

'Yes, the truth.'

'I was getting my ass chewed out by a couple of were-wolves. One of them slashed my shoulder and the other one nearly chewed my arm off. That's why I couldn't get to the phone.'

She snorted again and then laughed begrudgingly. 'At least the other story sounded more believable.'

I grinned. Kayla was human through and through. She had no idea about my heritage or what my 'family' did, and I was hoping to keep it that way.

'You still want me to pick you up for work this morning?'

I almost began groaning all over again. 'Yeah thanks, that would be great. My family appears to have gone AWOL.'

'Righto, well I guess I'll see you in about twenty minutes then,' she said, sounding bored.

'Hey Kayla?' I asked, just before she hung up on me.

'Yeah?'

'What were you ringing me for anyway? It couldn't have been just to scold me.'

'Nothing in particular. I just wanted to tell you about this really hot guy that came into the store yesterday.'

'That was it?'

She huffed. 'Can you think of anything more important than a hot guy?'

I laughed in spite of myself. I could think of a million things actually. Boys weren't exactly high up on my list of priorities right now. I had had one boyfriend in my whole life—his name was Stephen, and that turned out to be a total mistake—a waste of my time. The guy was a paranoid, possessive, delusional jackass.

Enough said.

'Okay. I guess you'll tell me all about it when you pick me up then.'

'No doubt,' she said, giggling as she hung up the phone.

I smiled as I slipped my mobile into my back pack and threw it over my shoulder before heading back downstairs.

I grabbed the Coco Pops from the pantry and a clean bowl and spoon out of the dishwasher. I made light work of my breakfast as I waited for Kayla to turn up.

I hated this time of the day on a Saturday. It meant that I still had eight hours left before the end of my shift. It wasn't that I didn't like my job. In fact, working in the little boutique homewares store was actually quite nice compared to other jobs out there. I certainly couldn't see myself handing out burgers through a drive through window or checking groceries at the supermarket. That meant far too much customer interaction for my liking, and a lot of unnecessary smiling.

It was bad enough that for eight hours on a Saturday I had to make believe that scented candles, vases, platters, furniture, and scatter cushions were the most important elements to making a house a home. Not only that, I had to lie to Kayla in every conversation that we had about everything that I did and about everyone that I knew.

She was a good friend, probably my best. But since she

was pretty much my only friend outside of the IMI, I treasured her dearly, and hated the fact that she had to remain ignorant.

But it was safer for her this way. Besides, if she ever knew what I actually was and the things I was trained to do, I couldn't guarantee that she wouldn't scream and run for the hills.

I took my empty bowl back over to the sink and washed it up and set it on the draining board. It wouldn't be long before Kayla got here.

I grabbed my back pack from the dining room floor and wandered into the living room. I plonked myself down onto the sofa, grabbed the remote for the television and switched it on.

Cartoons.

Ugh, I hate cartoons.

I flicked through the channels until I settled on the news. Nothing particularly exciting going on in the world at the moment. It was the same old thing—fighting, killing, global financial crises and terrorists. On reflection, all that stuff must have been pretty scary to the humans, given that terrorists were like their version of the supernatural. The UN would have an absolute coronary if they discovered there were worse things out there than suicide bombers and weapons of mass destruction. Not that those things weren't shocking. I'd watched the news, seen the damage that hate between humans could cause. But if they only knew that an army of vânători alone could pretty much wipe out the planet if they so desired it …

Ugh, who am I kidding? People always find a reason to hate and a reason to fight.

I switched the television off when I heard Kayla pull up into the drive way and beep twice.

I grabbed my bag off the floor, swiped my keys off the bureau by the door and then locked up the house behind me.

'Hey,' she said as I got into the car beside her.

I tossed my back pack over my shoulder and onto the back seat. 'Hey.'

She threw the car into reverse and swung back out onto the road. 'So how was your trip, anyway? You didn't really say too much about it.'

I grinned. 'Probably because you were too busy getting up me about cell coverage to listen.'

She smiled back, turning left onto the main road. 'You were only gone for what? Four days? What's the point of driving all the way down to Brisbane for only a few hours?'

'Susan and George had some work to do.'

'What? They couldn't leave you and Lucas at home?'

I shrugged. 'I guess not. But in case this vital fact escaped your attention, I'm not exactly trustworthy, am I?'

She grinned and then, refocusing on her thoughts, frowned slightly. 'Why didn't you all just fly down if it was for a job? Why drive all that way?'

'Susan's afraid of flying,' I lied, not exactly sure why. After all it was a legitimate question. But I couldn't tell her that we scoped out every major town along the way to ensure that the Vânători hadn't moved on from the suspected point of contact. It wasn't like we could do that if we had direct flights.

Kayla's eyes narrowed and she gripped the steering wheel a little tighter before glancing at me with disbelieving eyes. 'But all of you flew to Melbourne last year for the Christmas holidays.'

Ah, whoops. How did I forget that? I guess that's what happens when you spend all of your time lying to people.

I shrugged again. 'We had some pretty bad turbulence on that flight and she vowed never to get on an aeroplane again if she could help it.'

'Oh,' Kayla said, staring back out the windscreen. 'So what did you do when you got—'

'Hey!' I said, interrupting. 'You didn't tell me about that cute guy that you mentioned.'

She broke out into a grin. 'I didn't, did I?'

It was so easy to distract Kayla. All you had to do was bring up her favourite subject and all else would be forgotten.

I listened to her ramble on about this one particular guy for the whole twenty minutes during the trip into town. I nodded at all the appropriate sections and also chipped in a few words of encouragement when required. Apparently there hadn't been any interaction between either of them other than a brief moment of eye contact. This of course meant we had to spend at least fifteen minutes of the twenty minute conversation dissecting just exactly what it meant when he fluttered his eyelashes a certain way or smiled at her with slightly upturned lips.

I was mentally exhausted before I even got to work. Kayla always wondered why I didn't bother with boys. It was just far too much effort to expend on one species. Plus I didn't have the heart to tell her I was dubious about the direction her latest crush's sexuality swung in. I mean, the guy was wearing designer threads and was hanging around in a furniture and accessory store. He was more likely to have been checking out Glen the store manager than Kayla.

'So, to sum up, we think that by him giving me an almost wink, a quick, but also lingering glance in my direction … oh yeah, and the slight upturn of his lips into a smile, he was definitely interested?'

Yeah, in the Laura Ashley bed linen.

I sighed. 'I don't know, Kayla. Do you even know who he is?'

She frowned. 'What does that matter?'

She pulled the car into one of the car parks behind the store and switched the engine off.

I unbuckled my seat belt and reached around into the back seat for my back pack. 'Well, if you don't know who he is, where he works, if he lives in Cairns, or even what his name is—what does it matter if he was interested? You may never see him again.'

She was quiet as she got out of the car. Looking back at me as she rested her arms over the top of the car, a small grin formed on her face. 'You're right,' she said, smacking a hand on the surface of the roof.

'I am?' I said, looking back at her in bewilderment as I slung the back pack over my shoulder.

'Of course he liked me. How could he not?' she said, gesturing to her voluptuous frame. 'He was just shy.'

Gay's more like it.

I rolled my eyes and smiled before shutting the car door behind me. If he hadn't been attracted to Kayla's long blonde hair, tanned skin and long legs then it was really anyone's guess why he hadn't made plans to hook up with her on Saturday night.

I wandered into the loading dock, Kayla shuffling along behind me. Glen, the store manager, was sitting on an upturned milk crate smoking a cigarette. We both stopped and said a quick hello.

'Morning ladies,' he said cheerfully, blowing out a cloud of smoke.

'Hey, Glen,' we both replied in return.

'Going to be a busy day today, I think,' he said, taking

a long drag. 'Elena, you'll be on front counter today, while Kayla and I attend to the consults we have coming in.'

He stubbed out what was left of the butt underneath his shiny black shoes, pulled a mint out of his pocket, and then popped it into his mouth. Very considerate of him considering how sensitive my nose was to smells, not that he knew that.

Kayla was doing a traineeship in interior decorating as well as studying a correspondence course in interior design and furniture restoration. She'd been working at the store for well over a year now, having left school immediately after her year ten examinations to pursue a career in the furnishings industry. Glen gave her a lot of opportunities to perfect her craft. She was actually pretty talented and held a lot of promise of one day becoming a good designer.

That was how Kayla and I had met, here at work. While she worked full-time, I just worked here for the Saturday shift. It was long enough to earn a little bit of cash and yet not long enough to send me completely crazy—one day of mundane human activities was enough for me.

Sundays were generally my day off and that time I usually spent with Kayla. While the rest of the week I was at the IMI either studying skills for the field or fulfilling my requirements to complete my homeschooling education. Of that, I still had a year and a bit left.

Although I actually hated the schoolwork part, I loved being at the IMI, despite the fact that the people themselves weren't one hundred percent welcoming. Sarah, one of the ladies, was racist in every way possible. I'm not black, I'm not gay, and I'm not foreign, but I was going to become a vampire, so that was probably reason enough for her to hate me. Kim, Sarah's friend, was just a nasty bitch. The rest tolerated me because I think they believed I would one day aid them in the fight against the Vampires. Peter just ignored me when possible.

But despite the frosty reception, watching The Protectors perform magic and hone their skills was definitely exciting. It was just a shame that I would never be able to learn that particular craft, as magical skills were inherent and not learnt.

It was in the blood.

'Elena, did you hear me?' Glen asked as he stood up, straightening his tie and silk shirt.

I'd never noticed before, but he was actually quite hand-some.

I wonder why I only just noticed now?

He was tall, slim, but athletic, with blue-grey eyes and short sandy-blonde hair that curled around the sides of his ears. He was in his mid-thirties, an interior designer, a massive fan of Ralph Lauren, the application of stripes and spots, and also apparently liked long walks along the beach. Or so he'd told me at last year's Christmas party when he'd had a little too much to drink.

Still, he wasn't really my type, and if his immaculately cut physical appearance, personal hygiene, and exceptional taste in clothing were anything to go by, then he was probably batting for the other team. 'Elena?'

'Umm, yep. I'm on the front counter. Got it.'

I pushed the rear door open and headed into the staff room, leaving Kayla and Glen to discuss the upcoming consults and who would be assigned to what. I dumped my bag in the cupboard by the sink and then headed out to open the store. It was almost nine.

The day passed quite quickly in hindsight. Glen had been right. It was extremely busy.

Kayla and Glen had spent the entire day attending to one

consultation after another, and booking several others that would involve home visits.

I manned the front counter as instructed, being entirely on my own since everyone was too busy to help. I also spent what little time I had not serving, labelling the new batch of stock that arrived on Friday, and setting up shelves to house the new kitchen wares. By the end of the shift my mind was swirling around with the varied aromas from the scented candles I had also unpacked, and the assorted questions relating to mirrored cabinets and the latest Trisha Guild fabric collection. By six o'clock I was ready to split. I'd more than had enough of helping people match their pillows to their bedspreads and other such menial nonsense.

'You ready?' Kayla said to me as she turned the sign around on the front window and padlocked shut the front door.

I grinned and blew out a sigh of relief. 'It's like you read my mind.'

'You ladies have a nice weekend,' Glen said, patting me on the shoulder before heading over to the cash register and counting the till. 'Good work today—both of you. Kayla. I'll see you Monday.'

'Thanks, Glen,' she beamed, walking back to me. She had that supercilious look on her face whenever a good-looking male complemented her. 'Let's go.'

I retrieved my bag from the staff room on the way out and then followed Kayla to her car. I checked my phone for messages. There was only one, a text message from Lucas that said, *'Sucks to be you'*.

I deleted the message and shoved the phone back inside my bag.

Dumb ass.

We were cruising home again before I knew it, Kayla

chatting excitedly about her day. I didn't have the heart to tell her that I wasn't the slightest bit interested—eight hours of home design conversation and dusting furniture was more than enough for me. However, I faked listening to her every word, *oohing* and *ahhing* when required.

I could have jumped for joy when we finally pulled up in my driveway, which instantly plagued my conscience, making me feel like a really bad friend. Then again, as much as I loved Kayla, she was conceited, and probably wouldn't have noticed my lack of interest anyway.

'So I'll see you tonight then?'

'Tonight?' I said, looking at her bewildered.

Had I forgotten something?

She rolled her eyes. 'You know, what we've been talking about all day ... the rave?'

Realisation dawned, and I grinned. 'You do realise that I'm grounded, right?'

She shrugged and grinned back. 'Since when has that ever stopped you?'

'True,' I said, grabbing my backpack and climbing out of the car. 'I'll meet you in the usual place at eleven thirty tonight.'

'Done.'

I closed the door behind me, and she waved as she backed down the driveway and disappeared from sight.

I shifted my backpack over one shoulder and headed towards the house. The strange tang of Susan's cooking insidiously invaded my nostrils, automatically triggering my gag reflex. She was the worst cook in history. There was no doubt about it. The other Protectors in our faction had stopped coming over for dinner years ago. Their excuses were good, and varied, but there was no excuse for family. We couldn't escape.

Need I say more?

I retrieved my house keys and let myself in the front door. The smell of burnt meat, stewed apples and tomato sauce were stirring in the air. My nostrils practically closed themselves in revolt.

Lucas was sprawled over an armchair watching cartoons on Nickelodeon. Not really a shocker there. It was either the TV or the computer that generally consumed his spare time, but ever since he'd been whipped by a twelve year old at online Tetris, he'd been burying himself in Sponge Bob Square Pants instead.

George was sitting at the dining table reading a newspaper, and from Susan's absence from the immediate area and the god awful stench, she was probably in the kitchen.

I dropped my backpack onto the floor next to the bureau and then wandered over to Lucas and plonked myself down in his lap. I usually didn't pester him this way, but I was in a funny mood, and annoying Lucas suddenly felt like the best idea in the world.

'E!' he whined, as I wiggled around annoyingly in his lap.

'What?' I said innocently, holding back my laughter. 'I'm watching TV.'

'Get off me. You do this every time I'm trying to watch something important.'

I glanced at the screen and saw the terribly important Pokémon characters engaging in a battle.

'I do not,' I said, finally answering him and pushed even harder against his stomach.

'Yes you do. Now get off me before I wet myself.' He shoved me hard, sending me sprawling onto the floor.

I laughed. 'I only have minutes left to live and I want to make the most of the time I have left by annoying you.'

He snorted. 'Mum's cooking isn't that bad.'

I threw him a look of disbelief, while George cleared his throat at the table and tossed both of us a sideways glance. It was layered thick with warning promise of retribution should we follow this conversation to its end.

Susan wandered into the dining room. 'Dinner's ready!' she said, cheerfully placing a large mounded plate in the centre.

Lucas and I stood up and wandered over to the table. It was clearly a mistake, looking down at the brown, fudgy looking goo sitting on top of a mound of what looked to be something like mashed potatoes. 'What is it?' I asked.

'Spaghetti,' Susan said, smiling happily and pointing at her bizarre creation. 'Isn't it obvious?'

I choked back a laugh and George shot me another warning.

Lucas grunted and sat down. 'Only a blind man would think that was spaghetti,' Lucas said loud enough for only me to hear.

I bit my tongue.

George cleared his throat and surveyed the wreck of a meal in front of him, folding the newspaper up and placing it on the table beside him. 'Looks lovely, sweetheart,' he said, smiling politely at Susan.

What a brown noser.

She smiled broadly and then headed back into the kitchen to grab us some plates.

'I hope our medical insurance is up to date,' Lucas said, sniffing at the strange looking concoction of food. His nose wrinkled and he pulled back immediately.

'And why is that?' George said, eyeing him warily.

'Because if I'm going to get food poisoning tonight, I want to make sure I get one of the good rooms at the hospital, the ones with a TV and a decent view.'

I snorted, biting back the laugh that was bubbling in the back of my throat. George leant across the table and slapped us both upside the head.

Lucas and George had both been admitted to the hospital twice with severe food poisoning. At least I could self-heal from whatever bout of sickness was heading my way. I couldn't say the same for the rest of them.

Dinner was a mighty quick affair.

Lucas, George, and I chugged down the food with brutal efficiency. At least that way, we didn't taste it much on the way down.

Susan, of course, had taken that as a sign of appreciation which probably meant we'd get served her version of 'spaghetti' sometime again in the near future.

After dinner and a quick shower, I bid goodnight to everyone and then headed upstairs to bide my time until Kayla came to get me for the rave.

I switched the bedroom light off to make it seem like I had gone to sleep, and then climbed up onto my window sill, mounted the side of the newly replaced guttering, and climbed onto the roof. This was one of my favourite spots around the whole house. No one else was game enough to climb up onto the roof without a ladder, for fear of plummeting head first into the ground below. My self-healing ability robbed me entirely of any fear of falling, and as I'd already done it a million times before and had broken more bones than I could count I was immune to the pain. Anyway, it was the one place in the entire house that I knew no one would follow me to.

I sat down on the corrugated sheeting, and dangled my

legs over the side. I watched the happenings of the street and listened absentmindedly to the sounds of the night. The street was relatively quiet except for the usual traffic—a handful of cars that occasionally drove past or parked in nearby driveways. People were returning home from a hard day at work, a casual afternoon spent with their families, or from enjoying what was left of the weekend.

I closed my eyes and focused on my other senses. I could still smell what was left of dinner resonating in the air around the house, and my nostrils wrinkled in disgust. Across the road I could smell the neighbours having a barbeque, cooking sausages and charcoal steak. The aroma was exceedingly appealing compared to what I'd just ingested.

The smell of the raw meat they were yet to cook cut through the air. It appealed to my senses the most. The sweet stench of blood, tainted with salt and metallic undertones.

I wondered if it tasted exactly how it smelt—would it be different when I became a vampire? Why could I smell blood so vividly but I could not scent people? It didn't make any sense. People had individual aromas, I was sure of that. Yet I could not smell anything on anyone except whatever artificial smell attached itself to their skin, like perfume or aftershave.

I sighed. There were so many questions about myself that were always going to go unanswered. Susan and George were reluctant to discuss my past and I had no one else to turn to for answers.

I knew very little about my natural mother, except for her name, *Elena*, and even less about my father. I had no idea where I was born or how I had come to be the adopted daughter of a family of Protectors.

My father had to be a vampire in order for me to be

conceived, but Susan and George had sworn to me that they knew nothing of him. I still felt like they were keeping something from me. I had no choice but to believe them. I could do no research of my own into the truth of their words—my files were all located at the headquarters of the IMI in Bucharest, Romania. But even so, no one thought that requesting them for me was a priority. Susan always said that no good came from digging around in the past. Yet despite that fact, she had agreed to tell me everything before my eighteenth birthday when she and George deemed I was mature enough to handle the information. I just didn't know if I could wait that long. What harm could really come from knowing more about myself? If I wanted answers then I was either going to have to fly to Romania to discover the truth, or hope someone finally slipped up.

It would also stand to reason that if my father was a vampire, then there was a good chance that he was still out there. Didn't I at least have a right to that information?

I had been sitting on the roof for just over an hour, contemplating my life, when I felt the beginnings of pins and needles in my feet and bottom. I hadn't changed positions in quite some time and was starting to feel it.

I tried to stand, pulling myself upright and grabbing my sore legs. I hopped clumsily from foot to foot, trying to get some feeling back into my limbs while I tenderly massaged my backside. A few seconds later all feeling was regained.

I sat back down again, rolled onto my back and stared up at the stars. An icy wind sprang up around me. I wished that I had had the foresight to put on a jumper. But I was relatively comfortable now, enjoying the serenity of my isolation. I had a few hours to spare before getting ready for the rave, so why not spend them enjoying a few moments of peace and quiet?

I cringed as I heard the vicious scraping sound of the rear patio door opening. First the glass slider scraped and shredded the metal tracks on which it ran, then the security screen following up the rear with an even louder groan of protest.

So much for serenity.

Huffing impatiently, I rolled onto my stomach so that I could peer over the edge of the roof. It was strange for someone to be going into the garden to begin with. No one ever really went out there anymore except for me. It was too hard to get through the patio doors without hassle, yet no one could be bothered to fix them, so the garden had become an overgrown jungle of plants and weeds.

Sometimes, in the cooler months like now, instead of sitting on the roof I would sit out in the garden on a Sunday and read, or catch up on school work. What had me curious was who would want to come out here in the first place, and at this time of night?

I peeked quickly over the edge of the roof and saw Susan and George step out into the night, closing the two doors noisily behind them. They made their way over to the little metal table and chairs that were near the back door.

They took a chair each and just sat there silently for a few minutes not saying anything. They looked concerned. It was probably the tomato sauce in tonight's dinner coming back up.

'Do you think it is safe to talk out here?' Susan murmured as she touched a hand to George's. She was whispering so quietly that it was a struggle to hear anything at all. But I did catch both of them glance around the garden and then look up at my window.

Safe to talk about what?

I shimmied backwards on the roof, flattening my body

out completely on the cold corrugation. I knew that they probably couldn't see me, not unless they were really paying attention but I wanted to be sure. It was lucky that Susan and George appeared just as intent on staying in the comfort of the shadows to continue their conversation.

When they looked away, I crept slightly forward again.

'I would think so,' George said. 'The kids sleep like the dead and, besides, I saw their lights go off over an hour ago. We should still talk quietly though, just in case. Who knows whose ears are listening?' He pointed a thumb over his shoulder at the fence, indicating our nosey neighbour Bob.

'What should we do, George?' I heard Susan say in her hushed tones.

'I'm not sure,' he said, 'I don't think it's the right time to be talking about any of this.'

'Well, when are we going to? This problem isn't going to go away, that I am sure of. We have less than two years to prepare. You know he's going to ask for her soon.'

What?

'I know, I know. The years seemed to have slipped by ...'

'Maybe we should tell her?'

My ears pricked up as I made a concerted effort to listen to their hushed conversation.

'Which part? Once we start where do we draw the line, Susan?' George said.

'Tell her what we do know for a start. She might handle it a lot better than the rest of us did.' She paused. 'I can feel her slowly slipping away from us. I knew it would happen, I know it should happen, but I can't help feeling ...' She stopped again, shaking her head helplessly.

My heart started to beat faster within my chest. It almost sounded like they were talking about me. At least I hoped so. Maybe they'd let something slip about my past?

I moved in closer, trying not to breathe for fear that I may miss something important.

'Elena's a smart girl,' Susan continued. 'She's already asking questions about her abilities and her parents. How long do you think it's going to be before she demands the truth from us and how long before she runs into them and gets told everything, anyway?'

Oh my God. They are *talking about me. They know something more than they were telling—I knew it!*

So shut up and listen then.

I am. Why do you always have to argue with me?

You can't argue with yourself.

Well, if you can't, then why are we doing such a bloody good job of it?

'She wouldn't know what she was looking for,' George answered, interrupting my internal debate. 'Besides, we only have a few more months left.'

Susan shook her head. 'For God's sake George, look at her. She's growing into an extraordinary beauty with every passing year. She already attracts far more attention than a regular teenage girl. She may not recognise them, but they will sure as hell know what she is the second they look at her.'

Hey?

'They don't know where we are and they definitely don't know about Elena. That's why the IMI gave her to us. She'll be safe here and everything will still go according to plan.'

'Then why are they heading up the coast then? And why have they asked to meet with us?'

George shrugged. 'I don't know.'

Safe from what? What's going on here?

'I don't like it, George. You know what she's like. She constantly disobeys us. We can't protect her from them if she strays from the IMI or the house.'

'She's grounded,' he stated quietly.

Susan chuckled lightly and patted the top of his hand. 'Since when has that ever stopped her?'

He frowned and leaned back in the chair. 'Why do we need to protect her anymore? You saw what she did with those werewolves the other night.'

'That had to be a fluke.'

He shook his head. 'She had to have moved fast to slash at them like that. I'm mad at her too for taking such a stupid risk, but in the end we do have to realise that she isn't one of us. Besides, what makes you think they would want to hurt her?'

'You know why!' she hissed at him. 'If they caught scent of that inside her, it could turn out to be very dangerous for her and for us. It could ruin the alliance—it could start a whole new war, one far worse than the one going on now. If they knew we had her all this time and never said anything …'

Susan's voice quivered, rising in pitch slightly as she placed a hand on her chest. She began to sob gently and George reached a hand out and covered hers with his own.

'I don't want to discuss this any further. At least not until we have any more news. Right now this is all speculation. The best thing for us to do is to watch Elena and make sure that she stays close by. We stick to the plan.'

What on earth are they talking about?

Susan's sobbing died down as she wiped a finger at tear-rimmed eyes, but she nodded in agreement.

He pulled her gently to her feet and embraced her briefly before they made their way back into the house, closing the two noisy doors behind them.

I was frozen to the spot, unable to move. I had no idea what had just passed in their conversation. So much of it was too cryptic for me to decipher. Who were these people that were coming? Were they vampires as well? If that was true, then why did they need to keep me away from them?

It was abundantly clear that my parents were keeping a lot more from me than they were letting on, and too much information was now swimming around inside my head for me to simply let this go.

I would have to confront them and demand answers, just as Susan knew I might. And it had to be sooner rather than later. Tonight was not an option though. I still very much wanted to go to the rave with Kayla to divulge in ridiculous hormonal exploitations and dance until my feet were sore. It's all about priorities.

The best thing to do was to wait until tomorrow. At least then I could give this whole mysterious conversation a little more thought.

CHAPTER FOUR: RAVE

Time moves by quite quickly when you think about it, particularly if your mind is occupied or sleep encumbers all thoughts and creates pockets of transient images that are easily forgotten.

I was actually no further along with resolving what to do about the conversation I had overheard earlier. I'd spent an hour thinking about it in great detail, and the remainder resting my eyes.

Sleep had unexpectedly consumed me, creating one of those empty pockets of time that absorb approximately a third of a human's life. For two and a half hours my head was filled with unconscious thoughts and the passing whisper of dreams usually forgotten in the light of day. The shut-eye was an instant cure for my puffy eyes and gave me a glowing complexion and a renewed sense of energy.

Luckily I had climbed back down to the comforts of my warm bed instead of passing out on the rooftop. I'd avoided any possible confrontations between my face and the hard ground below. Yay for me.

I glanced over towards the clock. The ever vigilant red neon light was saying that it was 11.14 pm. In a quarter of an hour Kayla would be parking her little white Ford Focus down the end of the street to wait for me.

She had to park far away from the property, but close enough not to draw any attention. My two gatekeepers (otherwise known as the parentals) had an eerie ability to hear, smell, and see when I was up to no good—I always had to ensure that my escape was flawless. Parking in the driveway with lights on, music blaring, and car doors opening and closing was not exactly the poster child for subtlety.

I stood there for a brief moment, clad in my laced pink underwear and bra and glanced towards my dresser.

Now, what to wear …

I snatched my denim slim fit jeans that were hanging over the back of my chair and slipped them on. The pockets were a little worn and there were the beginnings of wear and tear on the hems, but they were my favourite, not to mention comfortable and warm.

I leafed quickly through my drawers looking for something that would be suitable to wear tonight on the top half. I considered a few of my turtlenecks given the chilly weather, but decided against it—too hot for dancing. I decided on a red three-quarter length sleeved T-shirt with a gaping neck line as a compromise.

I gave the red piece of cotton the once over before slipping it over my head and smoothing everything into place including a couple of stray ringlets.

I ran my eyes over myself in the mirror and smiled appreciatively.

Not bad! Now if only I could figure out what to do with this hair. Should I put it up or wear it down? No, keep it down. It'll hide the ringlets if I get hot and sweaty from dancing.

I quickly brushed the chocolate brown mass of hair that fell just below my shoulders, trying to iron out some of the more stubborn ringlets that had already begun to form and that my fingers could not tame.

My hair was generally pretty straight and did what I

wanted it to—unless of course if it rained, in which case I would then amass an annoying bundle of ringlets around my neck line. Sweat was also an issue. It tended to cause all kinds of havoc with said ringlets and I'd been tempted on more than one occasion to just chop the whole lot off.

I cocked my head to the side, looking at myself in the mirror to see what else could be done to improve upon the reflection staring back at me. Kayla would probably have a barrage of ideas right now, all of them involving more make-up and skimpier outfits to compliment what she called my 'rockin' body'.

I suspected as a trainee designer, Kayla was so used to slapping paint colours all over people's homes, that she felt the same skills could be easily applied to my face. I just wasn't comfortable with testing the theory.

But I had been fortunate enough to be blessed with great skin. I had a small trail of freckles that graced my nose and both forearms, but these were unavoidable thanks to the tropical Queensland sun.

I ran a brush through my hair a second time and then glanced towards the clock again.

Crap!

Kayla would be waiting for me by now.

I turned to my dresser and grabbed my shoulder bag and tube of strawberry lip balm. With my index finger, I glossed some of the delicious tasting balm over my lips and stashed it inside my bag for later use. I also grabbed my knife and put that inside the bag too—better safe than sorry.

I looked over at my window, my ever favourable escape point, and started to shake my head in a self-depreciating manner. Cold night or not, I shouldn't have closed the window after climbing back down from the rooftop earlier. It was a rookie mistake, and one I hadn't made in quite some time. The problem was that the window was just so damn noisy. It always had been, but I didn't have much choice but to use it.

I couldn't go out the front door, regardless of the angle of approach or my stealthy abilities—I always set off the sensor light. Plus, it operated on a one hundred watt globe. The light would always stream in through the living room windows like Fourth of July fireworks and straight through to Susan and George's bedroom, so my only chance of successfully escaping still weighed heavily on the first option.

The window. The window of course was more than fine for escaping, but getting back in again was an entirely different matter. I was going to have to enter via the laundry window when I got back.

I had tried climbing the guttering system outside my window once to see if I could get back into the house that way. It was a disaster. Not only was I wounded from the fall, if only for a moment, but the plastic piping dislodged itself from the main gutters, ripping away from the side of the house and taking some of the older timber boards with it. Needless to say my parents were not pleased, and that was putting it mildly.

The glass panes of my window creaked noisily as I opened them again slowly. I cringed and glanced nervously towards the door, waiting with the very real expectation that I was about to be busted.

A couple of seconds passed silently before I realised that I had been holding my breath. I exhaled nosily and sucked in some fresh air, keeping my watchful eyes on the back of my bedroom door.

Phew! So far, so good.

My ears pricked again as I listened for any trace of

movement in the house. It seemed that all was quiet in the Manory household tonight.

Satisfied, I swung my bag over my head, straightened the strap on my shoulder and then climbed up onto the painted timber sill of my second story window. Then I braced myself for what was coming.

This was the painful part, because regardless of the miraculous effects of my self-healing ability, I wasn't immune to initial breakages, cuts, and abrasions. And every time I jumped from this window, something inevitably went snap.

I clasped my fingers around the window frame and stepped into a position to jump from the opening. Afraid of chickening out, I started counting steadily towards three. I started at one, got to two, and then started breaking it down in eighths, quarters, and then halves.

I'd gotten to two and three quarters when the door behind me opened so quickly that it even bounced on the rubber stopper before swinging back.

Ahh, crap.

'Elena, what are you doing?'

I smirked. What else could I be doing—bird watching?

I turned my head around slowly and grinned sheepishly at the silhouette of my brother, Lucas. He was standing in my bedroom doorway with his arms folded in front of his chest, eyeing me suspiciously.

God, he looked just like George when he stood there like that, trying to look all authoritarian and threatening.

'Nothing,' I replied innocently. 'I was just opening the window for some fresh air.'

His eyes narrowed into slits before he threw his hands up into the air in exasperation and started towards me.

I jumped back onto my bedroom floor.

'I know you're trying to sneak out again, Elena. Don't even bother trying to deny it. I heard the bloody window open,' he muttered under his breath. 'And just for the record, if the window needs to be opened, you can do it standing on the floor. You don't need to be in one of your best outfits and standing on the ledge.'

I laughed. 'This isn't one of my best outfits.'

He rolled his eyes. 'You know what I mean.'

I paused for a moment, thinking. I didn't think he would be such a mamma's boy about this. Don't get me wrong—I loved my adopted brother, but he could be a real pain in the ass sometimes.

The only thing he did that was morally questionable was usually because he had tagged along with me and Kayla. It was only in these rare moments when he truly let his hair down (so to speak) that I caught glimpses of the fun-loving guy inside. Still, like me, he hadn't indulged in many of the things a teenager of his age could, hence why the closest he had come to rubbing up against a girl was falling asleep on top of one of his Playboy magazines.

I looked quickly back at the clock again.

I don't have time for this now.

'Okay, okay,' I said, pressing a finger to my lips in an effort to get him to keep his voice down. 'I was sneaking out, but come on, you know that I'll be safe and I can't miss tonight! I have to go! Kayla will be disappointed if I don't. In fact, she's waiting in her car down the street right now.'

I saw his eyes flick away to look out the window and down the street upon mentioning Kayla's name. Lucas had always had a bit of a thing for her, but had never plucked up the courage to come out and say so. I'd never pushed the issue either. It was just too 'icky' to imagine.

All I wanted to do was have a good time tonight which

was obviously going to be short lived if I didn't invite him along.

I sighed. I couldn't do it. Kayla would kill me if I dragged him along to another night out just for the sake of blessed silence. With all of the drugs, alcohol, boys, and steamy make out sessions at the rave tonight, I knew he would be like the big brother chaperone from hell.

Make room everyone, buzzkill coming through.

'Lucas. I'd planned to go to this rave over a month ago. I can't wig out on Kayla now, she'll end up just going by herself and that would be dangerous. I promise I won't get up to any mischief—strictly dancing only and no funny business. I promise that I'll come home no later than four or five.' I crossed my fingers behind my back.

His blue eyes locked onto mine again and he sort of smiled, expectantly. I'd seen this sort of smile before and I didn't like where his head was at.

He's not coming.

The last time Lucas had guilted me into taking him along on one of our nights out, it ended quite badly. Needless to say there was a wedding dress involved, a bottle of tequila, a stolen golf cart which later ended up in some random's swimming pool, a black eye, a couple of stitches, and to top it all off, a night spent at the police lock-up.

No need for further details.

'I won't stay out for too long, I promise.' I said, pouting lips. 'Oh, and please don't tell Susan and George, they'll kill me. I just want to have a little fun tonight. Please, Lucas … pretty please? I'll do your chores for a month.'

He snorted. 'You'll end up having to do those anyway when you get caught.'

Undoubtedly.

'Come on, It'll be fine.'

'It's not you I'm worried about, dickhead—it's the other people,' he said, still smiling. 'Where is this rave anyway?'

'Does it matter?'

'Only if you don't want me to tag along with you. Besides, someone needs to know where you are in case something goes wrong.'

'What could possibly go wrong?'

Besides you blowing my cover and getting me grounded for even longer?

I thought about what I'd just said for a second, my mind lingering on the details of my parent's conversation in the garden, and I shuddered slightly. Perhaps there was plenty that could go wrong?

His head tilted to the side and his eyes narrowed as he crossed his arms in front of his chest. I knew he wasn't going to let it go.

'Fine. It's just past Ellis Beach. But don't worry. I've got my mobile and my knife. I should be fine. It's just a dance party, not a blood orgy.'

He scowled and then huffed at me as I turned and prepared to climb up onto the window ledge again, not waiting for a reply. I could feel his disapproving look on my back but I didn't care. I just hoped that the little moocher would keep his mouth shut long enough for me to have some fun tonight because now the probability of getting caught had just gone up by seventy-five percent.

'Are we done? Can I go now?' I said, looking back at him.

'Elena, it's not a good idea, I think I—'

Need to shut up and go back to your room.

'Okay, thanks Lucas, I appreciate it,' I said, cutting him off.

My hands braced against the window architraves again

as I pulled myself up and prepared to jump down to the ground below me.

Cringing, I counted to three, throwing myself from the window opening with all the reckless abandonment I could muster. The air that whistled past my skin was bitingly cold, against my face and the uncovered section of my arms. I barely had time to shiver before my feet hit hard earth below. The predictable snap of one of my bones breaking was the auditory accompaniment to the profanity that slipped past my lips.

Sharp pain coursed its way through my limbs sending spasms of unleashed torment through my legs, bringing tears to my eyes.

I bit down hard on my tongue to suppress the scream that was burning at the back of my throat.

A minute later, and feeling more composed, I rose slowly from my crouched position, feeling my Vampiric genes set to work on my fractured legs. In a few seconds there would be nothing more than a dull ache, the severity of the initial impact all but subsiding now that my body was concentrating on reversing the damages. It was amazing that my 'battery' for this particular gift never seemed to run low or die. No matter what I did to myself, I always seemed to bounce right back.

A slow smile spread across my face as the pain effects dissipated.

I looked back up to my window and saw Lucas shaking his head at me, and then disappear, probably to stalk off back to his bedroom.

I waved at his retreating back, a small giggle escaping my lips. My healing ability really was a neat little party trick. It was just a pity I could never tell anyone about it.

I straightened the bag against my shoulder and quietly

manoeuvred my way through the overgrown back garden and down the front driveway, picking out pieces of grass seed from the side of my clothes as I walked. Once I knew that I was definitely out of earshot from the house, I started to jog to where I knew Kayla would be sitting in her car waiting for me.

'Hey E, looking good,' Kayla said, sweeping an approving glance over my body as I got in and buckled my seatbelt.

I took a quick minute to eye my friend over in return. This was typical Kayla—she was wearing a super-short blue sundress over her voluptuous frame. Her breasts were barely contained behind the strained material, but I had to admire her confidence, even if it did get her into compromising situations sometimes. Her long blonde hair was tied back into a neat ponytail, her brown eyes were lacquered with lashings of thick eye make-up, and her lips were painted a vivid scarlet.

She was walking sin.

'So did you bring your bathing suit?' she asked, breaking into my thoughts while she pulled the car away from the curb. She made a left shortly after, which soon intersected with the main highway leading out of town and towards the northern beaches. The Main Roads Department sign we passed declared that we were sixty-five kilometres away to our intended destination. This would usually mean a forty-five minute drive, but since Kayla was behind the wheel it'd probably only last half an hour.

'Should I have bought my bathing suit?'
Bit late now.
'No, you didn't have to. I just wanted a chance to test my

new bikini out.' She shifted the straps on her dress, letting them fall from her shoulders to reveal the makings of a sparkling midnight blue bikini. How she could walk around in that get up in this weather, I had no idea.

'Nice, huh? I got it on sale. Think this might turn some heads?'

'Like you needed the bathing suit to do that—have you looked in the mirror tonight?' As if to make my point clearer, I angled the rear vision mirror towards her face.

She stuck her tongue out at me, flipping me off all at the same time. 'Are you kidding? I'm going up against you—naturally gorgeous supermodel extraordinaire. I have to work twice as hard at standing out, even if I am a blonde with big boobs.'

I rolled my eyes and nestled back into the seat. I had never thought that I was as beautiful as she or my family made me out to be. Attractive, yes—gorgeous, no. 'Sorry, were you trying to achieve *naturally* gorgeous?' I said as she readjusted the mirror.

'Shut up. I don't have *that* much make-up on. Besides, I think I look hot.'

You look something, that's for sure.

She flicked me a satisfied grin and readjusted the straps on her dress. Kayla turned the radio on in the car and flicked through a few stations before finally settling on her favourite one. The sounds of Rhianna's *Umbrella* blared through the speaker system, and we both turned and grinned at each other before singing along in the best shower voices we could muster.

We were terrible.

We spent the next half an hour in idle conversation about the party, work, and any boys that Kayla was semi-interested in, as well as bobbing along excitedly to the various new tunes pumping through the radio. It would have been nice to contribute to this area of the conversation myself, but I wasn't interested in anyone at the moment. In fact, no one had caught my eye since I had dated Stephen, and that had been a little while ago now.

Stephen had been a cute guy with a deceptive bad boy appearance that I had met at another party similar to the one we were going to tonight. Unfortunately, my expectations for what role a boyfriend should play in my life were obviously distinctly different to Stephen's. While I enjoyed the physical stuff, I didn't like talking about my feelings and holding hands while taking long walks on the beach. Kayla said that I was mentally defective when it came to boys. I was starting to think that she was right.

We arrived at the rave in less than half an hour. I shouldn't have been surprised. Kayla had run a few red lights and blitzed the speed limit on more than one occasion. She was a dangerous driver normally, but when in the pursuit of a good time she put race car drivers to shame.

We'd brought a little mud map of the location to the rave, that was on a fluorescent yellow flyer that had been passed around at the last party we went to.

I grabbed it off the dashboard and had given Kayla directions as best as I could. I wasn't actually certain if I was leading us in the right direction or on a wild goose chase, but given that most of these parties were in the area I figured I couldn't go too wrong.

The turn-off down the winding dirt road was a little difficult to find in the dark, but Kayla managed to locate it after circling the area for the second time. After a short drive down the unsealed road, we could see that there were cars parked everywhere among the trees. It was apparent that no sense of order was necessary. Loud bass beats were cutting through the dense foliage that led down to the beach. I could feel my heart rate start to climb as excitement spread through my limbs—the beat of the music began to run through me like a steady pulse.

I absolutely loved a good party. The chance of meeting new people, the dancing, the music—it was all great—and particularly when there was supposed to be well over five hundred people crowding the sand tonight.

We found a spot as best we could behind a Ute. Its occupants looked like they'd be settling in for the night from the camping paraphernalia we could see in the tray back. So we pulled up behind them and switched off the engine. We stepped out into the night air, letting the soft sand at our feet slip between our toes and the music from the beachfront swirl around us like a ferocious wind.

'This is going to be great!' Kayla squealed with delight. As she locked the vehicle and shoved her keys in a small pocket on the front of her sundress, her dress drooped even further at the front, showing off even more of her bountiful cleavage that was already on display.

She ran around the car and grabbed my hand, dragging me down the path to the beachfront where the party looked to be in full swing.

There were dancing bodies everywhere and the swirl of neon glow sticks lit up the night. There was a little bit of light coming from the DJ booth, but apart from that and the sticks, the only other form of illumination on the sand was the faint glow of moonlight shining from above.

As a precautionary measure, I tilted my head up into the air and breathed deep, the biting cold breeze stinging my nostrils slightly. I could smell the ocean, alcohol, vomit, and the decidedly unpleasant smell of sweaty flesh—not to mention the overpowering stench of cheap perfume and little boys trying to smell like men by dousing themselves in supermarket brand deodorants. None of these scents were uncommon, and none of them had me worried. But it was hard to throw all caution to the wind and break habits that I'd spent the last four years building. I was trained to be wary of my surrounds regardless of where I was, and given that vânătors had arrived in Queensland only days ago, anything was possible.

Peter, one of my trainers at the IMI, always said that danger did not cease simply because we desired it so. I believed, in theory, that that was probably true. Just because I closed my eyes in a speeding car didn't make the possibility of crashing any less real.

Peter had always sought to make me more aware of my surroundings and to be prepared for the unexpected, and his lessons had an impact. I was always cautious now.

We passed a small group of three, relatively attractive boys that were huddled together under a mass of coconut palms, passing around a bottle of an unidentified liquid that I assumed contained alcohol.

I glanced up at the bunched and ripened coconuts hanging just above their heads and grimaced. Apparently relative good looks didn't stretch to intelligence in these boys. I thought everyone knew that at least one hundred and fifty people each year died from falling coconuts.

Obviously not.

They looked up from their bottle as they saw us passing them by and motioned for us to join them, much to Kayla's delight. I couldn't have been less interested if I tried. I just wanted to go and dance and maybe rub up against some Sam Worthington look-alike.

All three of them eyed us appreciatively. The one with the short blonde hair held the half empty bottle out towards us and Kayla answered by commandeering the bottle, flashing a cheeky grin and taking a generous swig. They all clapped and cheered loudly and she bowed graciously at their drunken adoration, and, of course, revealing a little too much flesh.

I moved myself some distance away from Kayla and the circle of boys and kept looking up repeatedly at the coconuts hanging precariously from the fronds above.

Kayla handed the bottle over to me, at which point I promptly forgot all about coconuts. I shook my head. The alcohol was not going to have the slightest effect on me. Also, I had no idea where their mouths had been and I wasn't real keen on sharing their germs.

Kayla and I had both experimented about twelve months ago with the notion of getting drunk. It was one of Kayla's less than brilliant ideas that, of course, only ended in us getting into trouble yet again. We may have both been relatively independent in a lot of ways, but we were both still under age and drunkenness was still considered unacceptable behaviour from our parents. Notwithstanding the revving that I got from Susan and George that day, I learnt that it was impossible for me to surrender to the effects of alcohol (or any drugs). My Vampiric genes were stronger than I had thought possible, effectively burning the alcohol straight out of my system. Fixing my cuts and broken bones was handy, but self-healing robbed me of the ability to get smashed with the rest of my peers, if I'd wanted to.

'Come on, Kayla, let's go and dance,' I said and started dragging her towards the dance pit and away from the alcohol. She loved her alcohol. Did I mention the wedding dress, the golf cart, and the bottle of tequila? You can guess which one of us was driving at the time.

'Come on, girls, stay here and have some fun with us.'

Fun doing what? Watching you lot throw up in the bushes later? No, thanks.

'Maybe we'll come back later if there's any of that left,' Kayla said, pointing a finger towards the half empty bottle. She grinned like an idiot and flashed a little more breast.

I was going to have to find her a hobby—and a sports bra.

A girl in a green midriff top and denim shorts walked past us, laughing with a group of her inebriated friends and shoving a neon glow stick into each of our hands as she passed. Most of the crowd had them wrapped around their necks, heads or wrists. We wrapped ours around our wrists a couple of times and then made our way into the centre of the dance pit, to dance near everyone else who wasn't on the fringes of either throwing up, drinking, or making out with random strangers.

A new remix track from Incubus pulsed through the speakers, and seemed to vibrate through the sand and up the length of my legs as I began to move.

We both laughed and wrapped ourselves into the fold of pulsing, sweaty bodies and joined the hundreds of others who were just as intent on having a good time. We let our bodies ride the beat of the music as we laughed and danced and ground against the continual mass of people that surged around us. It was heated, exciting, and oddly sensual.

I danced like that for what felt like hours—and then felt something change. I couldn't put my finger on what it was exactly, only that something was different. It was almost like I was being watched (hopefully by a total hottie). There was a hum of energy all around me, and a distinct smell of spices and sandalwood that I had not scented in the air before.

I tilted my face upwards as I felt a new man press himself into my back and place his hands on my hips. I could smell soap and the sweat coming from him mixed with the sweet scent of Kayla's perfume somewhere in front of me.

Looking over my shoulder, I decided this new guy was definitely not my type. I ignored his advances and shimmied away. I was more interested in this enticing scent, one that I could not pinpoint to any particular source.

'Kayla, can you smell that?' I shouted.

She laughed, twisting around and pulling me close. 'All I can smell is how badly I need to get laid tonight.'

I laughed loudly and cupped a hand over my mouth at the shock of what she'd just said.

No more alcohol for her.

I sniffed again. Drifting across the cold wind I caught all the familiar scents from earlier this evening and this new one again. It was stronger this time and very, very alluring. It could be coming from any direction. It seemed to swirl all around me in a thick, transparent cloud and completely overwhelmed every part of my being.

Where is it coming from?

I glanced around at the people near me and, although a fair majority of the men were angling towards me, I knew that the scent did not belong to any of them. I felt certain that this particular smell was coming from somewhere outside of the dancing mass of people.

I started to dance my way towards the outer limits of the crowd, twisting and cavorting through the clinging press of people. This proved more difficult than I first thought. Hands, arms and legs were everywhere, and they crowded around me, drawing me back within the confines of the dance pit. And at the same time, I still had the distinct feeling that I was being watched again. I didn't know for certain, but I had the impression that a particular set of eyes were upon me … I shivered.

Am I in any danger?

I reached for my knife, wrapping my fingers around it, feeling immediately comforted by the protection of having it near.

I reluctantly let the knife go, tucking it back where it belonged. I didn't want to stab anyone by accident, my wariness was still unfounded.

I noticed Kayla trying to make her way through the crowd towards me. 'What are you doing?' she yelled over the music.

I shook my head. 'Nothing, I just thought I saw someone that I knew.'

'Christian Bale?'

'I wish.'

'You want to keep dancing?'

'Yes,' I lied. What I really wanted to do was track down that scent, but Kayla could never know that.

I ignored my instincts and instead, plastered a smile on my face and began a slow gyration that was sympathetic to the rhythm of Nickelback's *Far Away*. I could let it go for now but the smell had apparently no intention of letting up anytime soon.

I looked up the moment the crowd in front of me parted.

Bodies rolled away from me creating a tunnel of empty space that led in a direct path from the outer edge of the dance pit to me in the centre. It was as if Moses himself had commanded it—and it was weird.

My hands continued to weave through the air around my

head in time with the music, my hips gyrating suggestively. I rolled my hips around and turned to face the gap in the throng, my eyes lifting from the sand as if commanded and resting upon a man in the distance.

That was the first time that I saw him.

He was leaning casually against a palm tree with one jean clad leg crossed in front of the other. Even from this distance I could see that his arms were corded with muscle, folded across his chest in a gesture of self-assurance. His head was cocked slightly to the side, emphasising the chiselled squareness of his jaw. He was watching me dance, the heat of his gaze upon me, all but melting my skin. He was still too far away from me to make out any more detail than that, but I knew that it was me that he was staring at.

The scent of sweet spices and sandalwood gripped my senses again and I inhaled deeply, letting the sweet masculine scent fill me entirely. He was definitely its source, but how? I'd never been able to smell a person's essence before. I usually could only smell the variety of scents that people layered upon themselves. But this was different. The smell coming from him was his essence, not manufactured. I felt certain of it.

The crowd surged again and I took the opportunity to creep closer to him while I had the cover of bodies to hide my advances. I didn't want to scare him off, but at the same time there was something a little off about him. I still did not sense that I was in any danger, though.

I could see a little better from here. I had never seen anyone in my entire life that looked quite like he did. His short dark hair, although a little longer around the top and fringe area, was stylish mussed as if he had just walked off a photo shoot. From this distance I could see that his skin was much like my own, pale and blemish free, but there was a perfection about it that made me wonder if it wasn't just a trick of the night sky or the poor illumination.

I couldn't take my eyes off him for a second. I might have been imagining it, but it felt as if there was a strange pull between us, an invisible cord that kept my eyes firmly locked on his. It was as if he was silently calling me to him, willing me with his eyes to weave my way through this crowd of people and go to him.

All pretence of any decent form of dancing stopped the minute that his scent enveloped me again. It descended upon me like a thick cloud that wrapped itself around my appendages and forced me forwards down the path. My mind clouded over, the dizzying scent disorientating me. I heard no sounds other than my own breathing and the people around me appeared to be moving in slow motion.

I shook myself free of the fog and snapped my eyes away from his—the spell was instantly broken.

The crowd started to move again, surging around me like a storm, and closing the gap between the strange man and myself. The smell dissipated too. Noise returned, catapulting me back into reality.

What the hell just happened, and who the hell is that guy?

Kayla came dancing towards me again, small beads of perspiration forming on her forehead and hairline. She wiped it away and sighed happily, as she flung an arm over my shoulder and dragged me back to where she was dancing. But I was no longer in the mood to dance. I had too much running through my mind to concentrate.

'Hey,' I shouted above the music, 'I'm just going to have a little break and grab a drink.'

'You want me to come with?' she shouted back, all concern.

I summoned my best smile. 'No, its fine. I'll come and find you again soon, just enjoy the party.'

She nodded and turned to dance with another semi-good looking guy behind her. Not that Kayla was overly fussy when it came to male attention, she just liked to keep her lips busy.

I saw an opening in the crowd again and snaked my way through. It took some effort, but I finally found myself outside the crowd near the trees where we had first come in.

I glanced over my shoulder and quickly perused the area of palm trees where the man had been leaning, but he was nowhere to be seen. I noted the absence of coconuts. At least he had some intelligence.

I wandered the beach for a short time, looping around the perimeter of the rave, trying to sniff out the scent again, but he appeared to have vanished.

I gave up after ten minutes of searching. It was clear that he either did not want to be found or that he had simply left and gone home. Why I thought he would be waiting for me to confront him I had no idea, and to be honest I wasn't really the stalker type.

I found a suspect looking group of guys and a few girls that had created a makeshift sign out of Styrofoam, advertising that they were selling drinks. They looked baked and were undoubtedly profiteering from the unfortunate lack of drinking supplies and I was left little choice unless seawater had suddenly become consumable.

I purchased a bottle of water off them, cursing lightly under my breath as the five dollar note that left my hand did not return any change. I checked the contents of the bottle just to make sure that what I was purchasing was in fact just water. With that sort of price tag there should have been an accompaniment of fries and a burger and a happy little person at a drive through window passing it all to me in a brown paper bag.

I stood there for a while, turning my back to the stoners, and watched the crazy procession of neon glow sticks waving wildly through the night sky while I sipped gratefully at my drink. The exorbitant price was all but forgotten as the cool liquid eased the dryness collecting at the back of my throat.

The wind blew gently through the trees and whipped through my hair, blowing strands of its length into my eyes. I blinked repeatedly and tried in vain to pick them out, bumping the water bottle against my nose and forehead in the process.

I threw my head backwards and brushed all of the hair from my face.

Slowly, I lowered my hands and tilted my head forwards again as the scent of sweet spice and sandalwood all but consumed me. I searched quickly and my eyes found their target. The man I had been watching earlier was standing not more than a couple of feet away from me now. My voice caught in my throat as he brushed his fingers across my cheek, collecting the stray strands of hair and tucking them gently behind my ears.

The air seemed to grow still around me as I stared, mesmerised by the emerald green depths of his eyes, shocked by his presence and touch. I was unable to formulate any words, let alone string a sentence together.

I slowly pulled the pouch of my bag around just in case I needed my knife. Despite how harmless he appeared, there was a hunger in his eyes that I had never seen in another soul before—it made me slightly uncomfortable. Besides, boys this good-looking should never be trusted, particularly boys that touch without asking.

'There, now, does that feel better?' he said in a deep, velvety voice that was rich in British inflection. He was obviously foreign. If he was a typical drunk Aussie teen then he would have gone for the obvious bum or boob grope first rather than an innocent caress. Still, British, Italian, Indian, or Aussie—it didn't matter. He touched without asking, and I wasn't sure how I felt about that.

The man's hand dropped to his side again as if he had somehow read my mind. He looked at me expectantly. His head cocked to the side, waiting for me to respond, a small smile playing at the corner of his thick, full lips.

The wave of scent hit me again like a punch to the face and it took all the self-control I had to stop my knees from buckling underneath me. 'Tell me who you are,' I said, feeling dazed as my eyes blinked and then opened again.

Focus Elena, I think he's doing it on purpose.

How?

I don't know.

'What kind of question is that?' he murmured, his gaze never leaving mine.

I forced myself to forget the haze of sweet smelling scent and focused on him instead. 'You're doing something to me and I want you to stop it.'

His eyebrow rose questioningly. 'Is that so?'

My hand slowly snaked into my bag, my fingers wound tightly around the hilt of the knife. Another wave descended upon me and it was almost too much to bear. It wasn't so much the smell itself that was overwhelming, it was the reaction that his scent caused inside my body. It was like he was setting off tiny fires in the pit of my stomach. Not painful exactly, but something else.

'I said stop that!' I spat out, staring up at him with angry eyes.

A small smirk tilted the corners of his mouth as he eyed me. 'You can feel me doing that to you?' he quietly asked, taking another step towards me. The surprise was evident on his face.

'That's close enough,' I said, gripping the knife tighter and slowly withdrawing it from the confines of my bag.

His green eyes studied me briefly, defiantly. 'Or what?' he said, taking another step towards me and instantly regretting the decision. The insolent look on his face was wiped away when he peered down at the knife that I now had pressed against his groin.

I tapped it threateningly against his pants a couple of times to reiterate my point. 'Or I'll do something that *you* might regret.'

Amusement flared in the depths of his emerald eyes and he took a step backwards. 'Far be it for me to argue with the lady who wields the knife.'

'A smart decision,' I said, as I too stepped backwards, lowering the knife to my side. His scent immediately melted into the air around me, leaving only a faint trace of the smell radiating from his skin.

'Who are you?'

'I might ask you the same question.'

I frowned. 'Hey buddy, I asked first and I'm not the one with the crazy smell.'

He chuckled and crossed his arms in front of his chest. Wow, those really were some nice muscles that he had.

'Yes, but I'm not the one carrying around a hunting knife in their bag either.'

'Are you going to avoid all of my questions?'

'It's highly probable,' he said, amusement lighting his eyes again.

Wow. Muscles or not, I could tell this guy was out to

annoy me. 'You're not being helpful,' I said flatly. 'If you're not going to tell me who you are, and to be honest I guess I really don't care, at least tell me how you did that to me.'

He considered my question quietly before raising a finger in the air. 'First … you tell me how you could sense that I was in fact *doing* something to you, as you put it.'

I shrugged. 'I could smell you. You overpower everyone else here. If you smelled like every other sweaty, drunk teenager in the vicinity our conversation would be over with by now.'

His eyes narrowed and he took a step towards me again. I gripped the knife tightly and held it steadily by my side.

'You could smell me?'

'That's what I just said, isn't it?'

'How?'

I shook my head and tapped my nose, as if the answer was obvious. 'Look, I answered your question, now answer mine. Who are you? Or should I say, what are you?'

'I'm William, William Granville,' he held his hand out for me to shake, 'Just your regular, sweaty, overly-hormonal teen.'

I looked at his outstretched hand for a few seconds and blinked. I was a Monkey's uncle if this guy was a sweaty, regular teen. My instincts told me to stay back.

He shrugged lightly and gave another barely concealed smile, crossing his arms lightly across his chest again. Up this close to him, there was no ignoring just how exceptional his looks were. Even for someone like me who wasn't currently interested in boys, I couldn't help but notice how attractive he really was. His jaw line was hard and masculine, and as noted earlier, there were no pimples, blemishes or freckles. He was at least a head taller than I was—putting him at about six foot something—and it was refreshing to meet a guy taller than me. He wore a white singlet which clung perfectly to his body, enhancing his toned chest and muscled arms. The rest of his body was encased in dark denim jeans and he walked barefoot in the sand just like me.

He was probably no more than my age, twenty at the most, but there was something about him that I recognised. His eyes held experience and wisdom, like an old soul trapped in a young body. I'd heard the expression before and it sounded lame, and I'd never really understood what it meant until now.

Inwardly, I cringed for the rest of the male population. It seemed every other man, regardless of how good-looking they actually were, might as well have been beaten with the ugly stick in comparison to him.

'Elena!' someone yelled out through the crowd.

I turned towards the sound of the voice. There was no doubting who it belonged to. *Stephen.*

He pushed his way through the crowd until he was standing right in front of me, and right in front of William. I shunted the evil thoughts that ran through my head. After all, I still had a knife in my hand and I wasn't afraid to use it.

'What do you want, Stephen?'

'I just wanted to come and say hello. It's been a while since I saw you.'

'And you think that was accidental?' I said dryly, trying not to roll my eyes.

He snorted. 'Why are you always like that?'

'Like what?'

'Standoffish. We could have been good together if you just gave us a chance.'

I resisted the urge to flick the knife to the left and relieve him of his manhood. It would certainly save other women the same hassle in the future. He'd tried to whip that thing out on me more times than I could count—his forceful nature was unattractive and was one of the reasons I'd slammed the brakes on our relationship indefinitely.

'Maybe if you hadn't tried putting so many demands on my time we might still be together.'

He shook his head. 'Wanting to spend time alone with you is not a crime.'

I flicked William an irritated glare as he fought back a smile. 'It is when it borders on me slapping a restraining order on you.'

'I wasn't—' he said, mouth open in shock. 'I just needed to know why you kept so many secrets from me and why you wouldn't … you know.'

My face went red with both anger and embarrassment.

'Everyone has secrets,' William cut in, turning and looking purposefully out over the crowd as if there was something more interesting in the mass of people.

I frowned at his intrusion into our conversation, wondering why either of them was still in my personal space. Stephen spun around on the spot and propped his hands on his hips, suddenly aware that there was another male challenging his rights at what Stephen probably assumed was still his territory.

Jeesh. Men!

William's eyes met with Stephen's briefly. He laughed lightly and looked out over the crowd again, purposely avoiding my gaze.

'Who is this guy?' Stephen spat out, waving a thumb at William. He looked at me in anger.

I shrugged. 'A guy I just met.'

He looked at me incredulously, his eyes zipping

backwards and forwards between William and myself. William appeared to be highly amused, despite the daggers that Stephen was shooting the both of us.

'So this guy is your boyfriend now, Elena?' Stephen said angrily, taking a step towards me and grabbing the top of my arm roughly. His fingers dug possessively into my flesh.

I looked down at his hand. 'We just met, you frigging stalker. Now get your hands off me.'

Stephen gave me that mocking smile that I actually used to find endearing. Now it just pissed me off. 'Or what?'

That's it. Now you've pissed me off.

I tucked the blade back into my bag again so I wouldn't do something totally reckless, and then ducked down low, sweeping my leg out to the side in one quick motion, knocking him off his feet.

I dropped down to one knee, I pressed one foot over the top of his arm and pinned it to his side, the other foot holding the other arm. I wedged my knee underneath his chin and firmly pressed the side of his face into the sand.

Shock and fear crossed his features as he squirmed underneath me, trying to catch the breath that had been knocked out of him.

'Don't ever touch me again, Stephen,' I said, grabbing his cheeks and giving them a gentle squeeze. 'What we had was supposed to just be a bit of fun and now that's over. What I do with my life no longer concerns you. Besides, get a grip, we're only sixteen.' I pushed his face away from me, and then got up and stood off him. A small crowd of people gathered around to watch.

'Anyone else want a piece of me?' I said to the small crowd of insignificants. It was probably overkill, a line stolen from an action movie, but my point was perfectly clear.

The spectators looked at Stephen, still lying in the sand,

and then hastily moved in another direction, as far away from me as possible.

Wise decision.

'Well, that was enlightening,' William murmured, as he finally turned back to look at me through narrowed eyes. Weird. They looked darker than before.

Free from my hold, Stephen scrambled to his feet. He shot me the stink eye and then took off into the crowd in a huff, showing me a perfect view of his erect middle finger.

'Do you usually threaten everyone that crosses your path?' William asked me, his brow slightly creased.

'Only the ones who get in my personal space without invitation.'

He nodded. 'You used to date that guy.' It wasn't really a question.

I shrugged. 'You're asking me about my love life? I hardly think it's a relevant topic to discuss with a stranger, particularly a strange smelling stranger.'

'You're right,' he said. 'Are you here with anyone this evening or by yourself?'

I frowned. Avoidance was obviously his forte. 'No, I came with my friend. Safety in numbers and all that.'

He smiled again, but just kept looking down at me expectantly, so I held my hand out and pointed towards the dance pit. Through the crowd of people I could see Kayla at the perimeter of the pit, mingling with the boys from earlier on in the evening. She was already holding another bottle of alcohol in her hand.

I grimaced. She really was a lost cause. 'That's my friend over there, the girl wearing the blue dress. You'll probably see her on the five o'clock news tomorrow night getting arrested for being drunk and disorderly.' I chuckled quietly at my own joke, waiting for him to join in. He didn't.

Tough crowd.

His gaze never left my face, even to look in the direction I was pointing. I found it oddly unnerving. Why even ask the question if you didn't really care what the answer was?

'So,' I said quietly, 'seeing as how you don't seem too good with important questions. Are you here alone? Or are you here with friends also?'

'Yes, I came here this evening with two other friends.' A smile cracked the corners of his mouth. 'They are off somewhere having a drink.' He chuckled to himself quietly—this was some private in-joke.

'Why were you watching me earlier?'

'Why were you watching me?'

'So we're back to that again, are we?'

He shrugged. 'Quite probably.'

'Whatever,' I said, throwing my arms up into the air and turning to walk away. I couldn't be bothered any longer. The mystery could go unsolved as far as I cared and I'd already spent a good fifteen minutes locked in a pointless discussion. That was fifteen minutes too long to spend with any guy, regardless of the delicious packaging.

He caught my wrist as I took the first couple of steps away from him.

I spun on the spot, automatically bringing my other hand down hard on his wrist, an instinctive reaction due to years of training in self defence. My attempt was merely to dislodge his grip, but it didn't quite work out that way.

My fist connected with his arm and the brutal impact sent a shock wave rebounding up *my* entire arm and into my shoulder. He didn't even seem to notice that I'd touched him.

I'd felt the bone in the side of my hand snap as my skin met his. His arm was harder than anything that I had ever felt before, harder than cement. I had to bite my tongue to prevent the scream of pain building in the back of my throat from escaping.

His eyes met mine and saw the pain and confusion that were written all over my face. I couldn't even speak, I was so shocked. He couldn't be normal. He was either a vânător in a skin suit, a vampire who'd wandered too far north, or some freaky offshoot of the undead realm—either way, it was disturbing.

He raised my hand—it was visibly shaking—and turned it gently from side to side, his fingers gently caressing the area that had been in pain only moments ago. I'd never walked unknowingly into a situation that I wasn't prepared for before, and I most certainly was not prepared for him.

Instead of quivering like a lost puppy, I snatched my hand out of his grasp and held it against my chest, pretending to cradle the injury. I still had to protect *my* secret.

'Elena, I think—'

'No. Just stay away from me.' I backed up a few steps and walked quickly towards the dance pit to find Kayla. It was time to go home.

I heard squealing coming from the edge of the water back near the rave and searched the crowd for its source. I was worried—was Kayla in danger? After all, the stranger had mentioned he had bought two other friends with him tonight.

I should have known better.

I could see her running towards the water's edge with a couple of other people, all boys of course. She was pulling her blue sundress over her head, revealing the skimpy bikini she was wearing underneath. A couple of the guys closest to her wolf-whistled in appreciation, drawing the attention of other boys within the dancing crowd.

She flung herself into the lapping waves of the ocean and dived under the water, coming back up shortly after to start splashing the guys surrounding her.

Soon there were at least twenty people thrashing around in the warm waters, yelling and laughing at one another. Kayla, of course, was smack bang in the centre of it all, exactly where she liked to be.

I took a few steps in her direction, still falsely cradling my hand and then spun around to look for William as a feeling of unease washed over me. I blinked and looked around me.

He was nowhere in sight.

CHAPTER FIVE: OUTPLAYED

'There you are! I've been calling out your name—why didn't you answer? Look, E, I'm all wet,' Kayla said, gesturing towards herself, a slightly goofy grin on her face.

'I can see that,' I said, amused but still searching for William. 'That's generally what happens when you go swimming.'

She gave me a wry look. 'Where have you been, anyway? You left the pit ages ago.'

It hadn't really been that long. Half an hour tops. 'I just went and got a drink, met a couple of new people, just the usual.'

'Anyone interesting?' She rung out her wet pony tail and then smoothed the water away from her legs and arms.

'The jury's still out.'

'Anyone good-looking?'

I rolled my eyes. 'Is that all that matters to you? A pretty face?'

She frowned and put her hands on her hips. 'Of course not,' she said defiantly, and then allowing a small grin to lift the corners of her mouth. 'They have to have a smashing body too.'

I picked her dress up off the sand and tossed it over to her. It landed in her face. 'I saw Stephen tonight,' I said as she grappled with the material and slid the dress back over her head.

'Stephen?'

I nodded. 'Apparently he just wanted to say hello.' It was hard to stop my eyes from rolling. We both knew that Stephen never just stopped at hello. He always pushed things further.

'Pity he couldn't leave it at that,' Kayla answered, smoothing her sundress back into place. 'The guy's a total loon. I'm glad you never got too close to him. He was clingier than Glad Wrap.'

I smiled. 'He won't be bothering me again.'

I think.

'And you know that how?' she answered, her eyes narrowing.

'I knocked him onto his ass and then pushed his face in the sand. Then I told him in no uncertain terms to rack off and leave me alone.'

She laughed and slapped a hand on my shoulder, shaking her head from side to side. 'You're such a crappy liar, E.'

'I swear to God that actually happened.'

She laughed again and wrapped her arm around my waist. 'Sure it did.'

I shrugged. What else could I say? At least if she ever found out what I really was she'd never be able to call me a liar.

'Do you want to go home now? Or do you want to head back and dance?'

She cocked her head to the side and smiled enthusiastically at the boys who were calling to her from the water. I could tell she really didn't want to leave just yet.

'I'm easy,' I answered as calmly as possible, even though I was still unnerved.

She snorted. 'Between the two of us, I'm the one who's easy. You're like Fort Knox.' She bent down and brushed at the jeans around my upper thighs. 'See ... cobwebs every-where, and under those ... steel undies.'

I slapped her hand away. 'Don't be disgusting. I'm just choosy.'

'If you keep being *choosy*, Elena, you'll never meet any-one.'

I sighed. Did we really have to have this conversation again? 'I just don't see the point in making out with a whole bunch of losers in the meantime.'

'Kissing the losers can be a lot of fun, Elena,' she said smiling widely. 'Consider it training for the sexual mara-thon that you might one day compete in if we ever find that key to your chastity belt.'

I rolled my eyes. 'Ha-ha. Why do I have to meet someone anyway? I mean, what's the hurry? I'm sixteen for God's sake, there's no bloody rush.'

'You're not getting any younger.'

I nearly choked on my own laughter.

Did I look forty or something?

'I'm not getting any older either.'

She frowned at me. 'Be serious.'

'I am!' I said, laughing out loud now. If only she knew. 'I'm in no hurry, believe me. Why don't you stick to what makes you happy and leave me alone to worry about my cobwebs and steel undies.'

She harrumphed. 'Fine, I just think you wouldn't be so uptight all the time if you just got laid.'

I flicked my best irritated glare in her direction. 'So are we dancing or going home?'

She glanced down at her watch. 'It's a quarter to two in the morning. We should probably get back before we get busted anyway.'

Thank god.

'Are you sure?'

She nodded. 'Yeah, there are no interesting prospects here this evening anyway.'

'You didn't find Prince Charming splashing around in the shallows?' I enquired with a sideways glance as we very slowly trudged our way up from the water's edge.

She smiled. 'Not tonight. Maybe I'm subconsciously holding out for your brother after all?'

I cringed. 'Never mention that to me again unless you want me to redecorate your dress with upchuck.'

She laughed, but wisely decided to keep her mouth shut, much to the appreciation of my swirling stomach.

We hadn't managed to get very far through the crowd when I realised that my life, as I knew it, was about to end. The thumping music from the DJ booth was abruptly halted and the screeching sound of a microphone being turned on echoed in the night air. Everyone grunted in earnest to the agonising sound of feedback that rang in their eardrums, covering their ears with their hands.

Disgruntled booing sounds and a few accusatory words could be heard.

I glanced up, my gaze drifting across the heads of the crowd and settling on the DJ booth in the near distance. I heard myself audibly groan, recognising the cause of the disturbance.

My parents.

And worse still, they had the microphone. 'Elena Manory—get your backside over here right now.' I swallowed and tried to remember that at least none of these people knew me personally. I'd never have to see them again, and in all likelihood they'd never remember me either. But, still, how could they do this to me? It was so embarrassing!

Kayla stood rooted to the spot beside me, her hand

clamped over her mouth, probably in shock, but I suspected it was more to partially cover her face from the onslaught of spectators.

She started to slap her hand against my arm when Susan announced the same message over the loudspeaker again. All I could think about in that moment was getting over to them as quickly as possible. Someone had to stop her from killing my social life.

Laughter and a lot of finger pointing began to erupt from the crowd as we walked through the sand towards my enraged parents. This was not going to be good. I'd be lucky if I ever saw the light of day again.

George spotted Kayla and me through the laughing crowd first, his long slim finger pointing directly at me. It was like the finger of death—a pointed accusation that I was the cause of all their problems. He was probably right.

They gave the microphone back to the DJ and started marching over towards us.

I watched as George's short blonde hair and Susan's long windswept hair, hair the colour of corn, bobbed up and down hurriedly through the mass of people in front of us. I thought about making a run for it, briefly imagining myself running down the beach and disappearing into the darkness where they could not find me. Silly, really, considering the sort of creatures that loitered in dark places. But right now, I would have taken anything or anyone over the wrath of my parents.

People started yelling out to put the music back on. The DJ happily obliged and the rave kicked back into full swing again. At least it was a new distraction for the partygoers other than finger pointing and public ridicule.

Susan reached me first—no surprise there, her legs were longer than George's—and her face spoke of murder. No doubt the effect she was going for, either that or her intent had slipped way past outward physical appearance and dipped into intended actions. I had to admit, she did look pretty scary.

She stopped in front of us and crossed her arms angrily across her chest. George was only seconds behind her, looking equally irritated.

I stifled a laugh. His problems were a little different from hers. It looked as if they'd left the house in a hurry because he was still wearing his pyjamas. Not exactly a good look for someone at a party full of judgemental teenagers.

'Just what do you think you are playing at, young lady?' Susan started. 'Do you think that it is acceptable to sneak out of your room in the middle of the night and go to parties?'

The question was surely rhetorical.

'Well let me tell you, your father and I are very, *very* angry with you right now and you are in *serious* trouble.' I'd heard that word a lot lately.

She paused briefly and glanced at Kayla. 'Does your mother know that you're here Kayla?' She shook her head not waiting for a reply. 'I'm betting she doesn't if you're half as wilful as Elena. She *will* be receiving a phone call from me.'

Kayla hung her head and dutifully nodded in agreement.

'Now, both of you get in the car. We are going home and I mean now!'

'Um … Mrs Manory,' Kayla stuttered, 'Elena and I came in my car.'

'Kayla, Lucas will be driving you home.'

Lucas. I should have known he wouldn't be able to keep his mouth shut. I'll have to remember to thank the dumb ass for this later.

'Still want to make out with him now?' I whispered in Kayla's ear, as George walked around behind us and pushed us roughly towards the pathway leading back into the temporary car parking area. His bony fingers applied some serious pressure on both our spines as we walked.

She shot me a look. 'I'd rather kill him.'

I snorted. 'Me, first.'

Once we were in the car park, I saw the green Subaru Forrester immediately. Lucas was sitting hunched in the back seat, looking sad and sorry for himself, though what he had to be so upset over I had no idea. He wasn't the one who was about to have Susan go all Kathy Bates on his ass—club his knees, and keep him chained to his bedroom for the next century.

He looked up as we approached. He unbuckled his seatbelt and climbed out of the car, keeping his head appropriately low to avoid eye contact. Smart move considering I'd more or less considered the idea of poking his eyes out if he even thought about smiling.

'Kayla, give your car keys to Lucas, please,' George said stiffly.

Kayla obediently pulled her car key out of the pocket and gave it to Lucas. It dropped into his palm with a slight jangling sound. He took the opportunity to look up and smile at her nervously.

Her raging, filthy look was what stopped my itching fingers from turning Lucas blind. The irritation on her face all but folded his non-existent tail between his legs.

Susan pulled out her mobile phone from her purse and asked Kayla to repeat her home number. She began dialling and after a few seconds of silence, and then apologies to Mrs. Johnson for calling so late, she engaged in a brief conversation with Kayla's mother about our whereabouts and what we had been up to. During all the character sledging and disdainful reports on our activities she forgot to mention what a good time we'd actually had.

Apparently that was of little importance in her version of events.

The call abruptly ended a few minutes later, after we heard a few iterations of 'Oh, I agree completely' and 'Yes, punishment is inevitable'. I'd heard that violin before.

Lucas began to shuffle uncomfortably from foot to foot, carefully avoiding eye contact with me. I was still surprised that I hadn't decked him one yet. I decided it was because there were too many witnesses to simply say it had been an accident.

Susan shoved the phone back into her purse, her lips pressed together in a thin line as she motioned for Lucas and Kayla to get going.

Lucas touched a hand to the small of Kayla's back and propelled her towards her car. She shrugged his hand away and then shoved him hard in the shoulder for touching her.

I smiled. I couldn't help it. At least it meant she wouldn't be sexually corrupting him anytime soon.

Ugh.

George opened the back door of our Forrester and motioned a quick snap of his fingers for me to get in.

I scrambled in and the door slammed shut behind me, barely missing my feet in the process. I waved sadly at Kayla through the passenger window mouthing the word 'sorry' as Lucas drove the car right past us and out onto the dirt road leading back to the highway.

She half-heartedly waved back and then she was gone.

'Tell me something—did you honestly think you were going to get away with this?' George said as the Forrester turned left onto the highway back into Cairns, following closely behind Kayla's Ford Focus.

I would have if I didn't have a brother.

'I wasn't aiming to cause trouble. I just wanted to go to this rave and I knew you wouldn't have let me go,' I said in a dull voice.

He laughed bitterly. 'You do understand what the word *grounded* means, don't you? Because I'm seriously beginning to doubt your intellect, Elena.'

'Hey,' I said defensively, 'I didn't take one step through the front door.'

I watched as George's face went beetroot red and his hands quivered with rage. My lips moved in sync with his as I silently mouthed his usual line of retort along with him.

'Are you smart mouthing me, Elena Manory?'

'No,' I answered carefully, shrinking into my seat as I watched his hands clench the steering wheel tighter. 'I was merely pointing out that I hadn't technically broken the rules of my grounding.'

George slammed his foot on the brake and pulled the car over onto the shoulder of the road.

Uh-oh.

He unclipped his seat belt and spun around in the seat to look directly at me.

I automatically pulled my legs in as far from slapping distance as possible. Though he hadn't actually smacked me since I was a little girl, I wasn't about to put it past him when he was in the middle of 'meltdown' mode.

Susan also unclipped her belt and turned in her seat to face me. There was disappointment written all over her face. I tried to figure out which expression was worse. Was it the beetroot man, the scary angry mum, or the general air of disappointment? Probably their disappointed looks. Those looks meant that I had failed at something and I didn't like failing, not when I was naturally so good at everything I tried my hand at. Well, except for obeying rules and maths. But who needed algebra anyway? And rules? Rules were made to be broken.

'Do you even understand how much danger you put yourself in sometimes?' George stated stiffly, though his voice was relatively quiet. 'Any number of things could have happened to you and nobody would have known where you were to help. Can you understand how foolish that is?'

I swallowed. 'I understand your concern for me, really I do, but it's misplaced. It's just a party. There was no lurking danger amongst that group of kids except the inevitability of intolerable hangovers and a slight fear of teenage pregnancy.'

'It's not a joke, Elena.'

'Who's laughing?' I said seriously, containing a smile. 'Unprotected sex amongst teens is becoming a real problem.'

He growled and looked over to Susan. 'You try talking some sense into her before I knock her block off.'

Ha-ha. You have to catch me first.

'Elena …' Susan said, softly but sternly. 'You can't keep sneaking out like this. You know that there are things in this world that could seriously threaten your existence, yet you continue to take risks. We don't mind you going out and having fun. We only ask that someone accompany you on said occasions.'

'Well, that just sucks the fun right out of it.'

'Elena!' she hissed, all semblance of patience gone. 'You have seen what the Vânătors can do to someone. You're not infallible. You may be able to heal from any injury, but you are still essentially human, for now, and therefore are vulnerable to their attacks. Not to mention the other creatures lurking around at night.'

'You mean vampires?' I said flatly.

George and Susan passed a look between them.

Yeah, that's what I thought.

George swivelled in his seat, re-buckled his seat belt and pulled the car back onto the desolate highway. Even after a five minute hiatus from driving, we'd still undoubtedly catch up to Lucas quickly. That boy couldn't drive for shit.

Susan, on the other hand, remained exactly where she was, blinking at me in confusion. 'What are you talking about exactly?'

I thought about slapping her forehead and saying 'you damn well know', but I resisted the urge. Instead, I just went with calm and rational—a massive leap for my personality, but it was the only way I'd get any answers. 'I'm talking about the conversation I overhead you and George having earlier tonight.'

She blinked again. 'How much did you hear?'

She isn't even going to deny it.

'Enough.'

She nodded and twisted back around in her seat, probably so she could avoid my eyes and figure out some brilliant story she was hoping I'd swallow. 'Right now we shall discuss just exactly what you *won't* be doing over this next month, and I guarantee that I will be specific enough that you can't twist my words to suit yourself.'

I sat forward in my chair and looked at both of them in confusion. 'I'm sorry—did you just hear what I said? I overheard your conversation.'

'We heard you.'

'So, what? We aren't even going to discuss this even though it clearly relates to secrets you've been keeping from me?'

Susan shook her head. 'When you learn to act like an adult then maybe we'll start treating you like one. Until then, we will keep these things to ourselves.'

'That's hardly fair.'

Susan's eyebrow rose slightly as she turned to look back at me. 'And you think that your blatant disregard for our house rules is fair?'

'It's not the same thing,' I said, sounding defeated. God, was that a whine in my voice?

'Shall we begin?' she said calmly, looking over to George and smiling.

Smug bastards.

I'd been outplayed.

'You're still grounded. Nothing is going to change that. I'm just going to make it a little clearer for you to understand. I'll even have a contract drawn up by Vincent if the fine print is something you feel is negotiable, which, trust me … it's not.'

Vincent was one of The Protectors at the IMI, and one of my many trainers, not to mention a kickass lawyer that very rarely lost a case. If Susan *was* getting him to draw up a contract then I was stuffed.

I sighed noisily and slammed my body angrily back into the car seat. I turned to look out of the window.

She continued, 'Grounding explicitly applies to the restrictions of your comings and goings that have not been pre-approved by either myself or your father. That includes the use of *every* exit and entry point in the whole house, doors and windows included. There will be no phone calls in or out to friends. No internet or MSN—the computer is completely off limits unless necessary for home studies. And Kayla will be forbidden to step foot in the house during this period,' she paused. 'Oh yeah, and the biggest rule of all … no parties.'

'But—'

'Don't interrupt me! I'm not finished,' she chided. 'You will go to the IMI everyday with us as usual, and when your studies are complete you will work on extra training with Peter and Vincent. Saturdays you may go to work, but we will drop you off and pick you up. Sundays are no longer a free day for you to do as you please—it will be the day you do some of the housework.'

'So I'm a slave?'

She shot me a look. 'If you defy us again, Elena, I'm going to padlock that bloody window of yours shut and you will face harsher consequences than you have today. Am I making myself clear?'

I scowled. 'Crystal.'

Neither I nor my parents spoke for the remainder of the trip.

When our car pulled up outside of Kayla's house, the lights were all on inside. I could see Mrs. Johnson pacing frantically, wearing a nightgown and hair curlers in front of her living room window, a lit cigarette in one of her hands.

We had arrived a few minutes after Lucas. Kayla was already storming off towards the house, leaving Lucas standing in the driveway by the car, his eyes on the ground and his hands buried in his pockets.

Damn shame. It would have been good to see him get his ass chewed out by Kayla.

The front door opened before she could use her keys to unlock it. Mrs. Johnson's hand shot out into the darkness to grab Kayla roughly by the arm, pulling her inside the house and slamming the door loudly behind them. I could hear their dog Rufus barking loudly from inside the house, trying to join in on the commotion, though I doubted that his barking was going to outdo Mrs. Johnson when she really got stuck into it.

Lucas walked around to the other passenger side door and got into the car. He buckled in and then sat staring out the window in stony silence. He had obviously not liked Kayla's outburst.

We arrived home just ten minutes later.

I was the first one out of the car and the first one into the house.

I raced up the stairs to my room and slammed the door behind me. My back slid down the smooth timber of the door's surface until I was sitting on the floor, my head buried in my hands.

How could they withhold information from me, knowing that I already knew they were keeping things from me? How could they use this knowledge as a weapon against me to make sure I obeyed like a good little girl? Didn't I have a right to know what was going to happen to me? How do you behave like an adult anyway? Was I supposed to start wearing tweed overcoats and loafers and comment on subjects such as rising interest rates and housing prices?

I rubbed at my eyes and sighed. What they wanted from me was going to be a tough gig. Obeying the rules was one thing, but keeping my mouth shut? That was another thing entirely. Being a smart ass was imbedded in my DNA.

I rubbed at my tired face again and then stood, deciding that the information that they had about my past was far more valuable than my current social life. For a while at least it'd be worth the effort of at least acting mature to get what I needed out of the situation. I could live without parties. I had done it before I had met Kayla, and since I was forbidden contact with her in the next month it shouldn't be too difficult to obey house rules. As for my mouth, I'd at least try to bite my tongue. I couldn't promise much more than that.

I kicked off my jeans and threw them into the corner of the room. The singlet, bra, and underwear I had been wearing soon joined them. Naked, I padded over to my dresser and pulled out a clean pair of underwear, a night shirt, and slipped them on quickly, just realising that the window was still open.

It was a good thing that no other neighbours had second story homes around us and that our garden was overgrown enough to provide plenty of coverage.

I quickly flipped the light switch off and hopped into bed.

I pulled the covers right up to my chin. The air blowing through the window was ice cold, but I was far too lazy to get out of bed again to close it.

I reached my hands up and cradled them behind my head, sifting through the details of the night. I cringed inwardly when I thought of Stephen again and quickly dismissed his image from my mind. God only knew what I had seen in that guy. Sure, he was good-looking—there was no disputing that—but he was also possessive and domineering and I was one bird that could not be caged.

I smiled. At least I'd gotten some enjoyment from squishing his face in the sand tonight. But what about that other guy?

What was his name again? Phillip? Walter? W-something.
William! That's it. William Granville. How could I forget?

He was without a doubt the most infuriating person I'd ever met. Not that I'd ever see him again, especially not since I told him to stay away from me, but who could blame me? The guy had the freakiest scent ever, beyond intoxicating, and his skin was as hard as a rock. He couldn't have been a vânător. Their skin was as soft as a human's, completely penetrable by any weapon, where as William's was cold and hard like granite. He had to have been a vampire. But I couldn't be certain, having never met one before.

I knew that vampires could not walk in direct sunlight, but were still capable of moving around during the daylight hours. I also knew that they had toughened skin that was only susceptible to injury from silver or the claws and teeth of other undead. They were lightning fast and had extremely keen senses, senses that made them even more deadly than the Vânătors. If all the stories that Vincent and Peter had told me about them were true, then it was smart for The Protectors to have formed an alliance with the Vampires. But did I know all the facts? Were there some facets of this alliance that had been kept from me, like my past? Did the IMI know enough about what I was going to become to satisfy my own curiosities? Or was I going to have to search out a vampire for myself to get the real truth? Had they simply been teaching me what they wanted me to know, but never truly equipping me with enough information to formulate an opinion of my own? And if that was true, had I met vampire this very night and not even realised it?

How very disappointing if that were so.

Why did I always attack first and ask questions later? Not that he was real keen on answering questions anyway. He seemed more intent on repeating my questions and answers like some sort of irritating parrot—he hadn't exactly endeared himself to my sensibilities.

I sighed. Perhaps he was just as wary of me as I was of him.

I yawned loudly, stretched my arms out behind me, and then rolled onto my side. I probably could have laid there all night thinking about how I *almost,* maybe, met a vampire, but that was just ridiculous. Regret never changed a thing.

I yawned again, my eyelids closing reluctantly with the weight of heavy burdens and weariness upon them. Sleep was practically knocking at my door. In fact, I could hear the gentle tapping in the back of my mind and I welcomed it.

Then I heard it again—a persistent pounding that was strangely rhythmic, yet quiet enough to make me wonder. But the knuckles of the sandman did not knock like that.

It was silent for a few moments and then the tapping started again.

I opened one of my eyes and glanced at the door.

'Go away.'

'It's me, Lucas. Can we talk?'

'Are you deaf?'

'Come on, E. I just want to explain why I told mum and dad. It wasn't my fault, not really. They came up to your room to check on you and you weren't there and then they—'

'Go away,' I said, groaning loudly.

'E, come on, please?'

'Would you like me to say it in French and German for you too? Or is English clear enough?'

'You don't speak French or German,' his voice was muffled through the timber.

I threw my spare pillow at the closed door. He seemed to get the message because he didn't speak again after that. Either that or I was too tired to care, and fell asleep anyway.

The sun came up again far sooner than I had expected. I'd put up a good fight, ignoring it for the last few hours, but the sun was always going to win. Even hiding underneath the bed sheets didn't seem to diminish the amount of light trying to creep between my closed eyelids.

I rolled over in the bed and studied the alarm clock. It was almost lunch time. Definitely time to get my lazy ass out of bed. Although the prospect of simply spending a day doing absolutely nothing certainly appealed, particularly when I'd only gotten to sleep sometime after three, it was time to face the music.

I kicked back the sheets and stumbled over the side of the mattress and almost head-butted the night stand. I was definitely all class first thing in the morning. Clumsiness wasn't usually a part of my vocabulary, but anything less than ten hours sleep meant that I was generally as graceful as a bull in a China shop.

Shaking off a yawn, I grabbed my outfit, hurriedly dressed, and then headed downstairs to get some food into my stomach. I half-expected to run into someone by now, but I guess they were all out of the house today. No doubt they were teaching Lucas the Hevannatara spell he was having a little trouble mastering.

Whatever.

I opened the fridge door and pulled out a loaf of bread and some breakfast condiments, laying them on the counter top behind me while patting my stomach to quieten the grumbling sounds erupting from inside.

As I grabbed a knife from the top drawer and grabbed the bread to make toast, I found a handwritten note that had obviously been meant for me.

I glanced down at Susan's neat handwriting and debated briefly about pretending that I never saw it. I felt certain that she was going to tell me to clean my room today, not exactly an activity I was chomping at the bit to get stuck into. I had a definite flair for being untidy. I never saw the point of making the bed when I was only going to sleep in it again anyway.

I groaned and picked up the note. If I was going to at least *attempt* to be an adult this month then I probably should start with subjugation and shut up, dealing with the consequences of my actions.

Elena,

*We have gone to the IMI. I have listed below the chores that you **will** have done before we get home. These are some of the punishments you will be incurring this month. Do not even think about sneaking out or calling Kayla over for a chat. There is enough listed here to keep you busy until dinner time and I expect them all to be completed.*

Underneath Susan's note was a long list of chores.

My eyes widened as I read each task: clean the garage, vacuum the floors, wash the windows, and so on, and so on. Right at the bottom in capitals letters was written predicably: CLEAN YOUR ROOM!

I sighed and threw the piece of paper back onto the bench. This was going to be a very long month.

I quickly finished making myself some toast with jam and stood there at the counter eating and spilling a few crumbs onto the surface.

Once I was done, I gathered all the breakfast dishes that the rest of the family had left on the sink for me, and, rinsing them beforehand, loaded them into the dishwasher.

One job down, a million more to go.

I ran back upstairs to my bedroom and surveyed the space with a critical eye. It wasn't *that* bad. It certainly didn't look like the aftermath of the bomb explosion that Susan constantly made it out to be. It was organised chaos as far as I was concerned. I knew exactly where everything was. How was tidying it going to change that?

But I figured from the capitalisation of the lettering in the note that she was serious, so I swallowed my pride and began folding the piles of clothes that were lying across the floor and furniture. She didn't even realise that she was suppressing my freedom of expression by making me clean a perfectly habitable space. How else was I going to show my typical teenage angst and deplorable habits if my bedroom was made to be neat and tidy? It totally defeated the purpose if teenage rebellion and sloppiness was constantly quashed at every turn.

It was a good thing that the rest of the afternoon slipped by quite quickly. I hurried through as many of the jobs on Susan's list as I could possibly manage before their return, and given that I only emerged from sleep just after lunch there were going to be quite a few chores that were marked as incomplete. Not that I specifically cared, but making an effort meant scrubbing scum off the bottom of the bathtub. It wasn't like I was exactly putting my back into it either.

At precisely six thirty, the Forrester pulled up in the driveway and I heard the closure of three car doors and then the jangle of keys at the front door.

'Elena?' I heard Susan call out. She must have been afraid I'd skipped out.

Where's the faith?

I wandered into the living room with a bottle of detergent in one hand and a cleaning cloth in the other. At least

I looked the part. Susan didn't need to know that I'd gotten the shits just over an hour ago by a stubborn stain on the shower screen and had thrown in the towel. Ever since I'd just sat on my backside and read the latest copy of *Wheels* magazine.

'Oh, good—there you are. Been working hard?' she asked.

I held the cleaning equipment up in front of me and shook them gently to answer her question. She frowned slightly and I stifled a shrug.

What? The question was stupid.

Lucas grazed past her arm and headed straight for the kitchen with some bags of Chinese takeout in his hands. I nearly dropped to my knees right then and there and thanked the heavens for a reprieve from Susan's cooking.

George threw his keys and wallet onto the bureau by the front door and followed eagerly after him. I was only a heartbeat away from running after Lucas like a lost puppy dog myself.

'Okay, so I see you're still not speaking to us. I was hoping a day by yourself would have improved your mood,' Susan said sourly as she shrugged her purse off her shoulder and placed it on the bureau next to George's personals.

I had no idea what gave her the impression I would have been ecstatic at being stuck at home for a month and forced to clean every room in the house. Did she even realise what Lucas kept under his bed?

'Well?' Susan said, her patience obviously wearing thin.

'Well, what?' I said.

'Are we speaking again? Or are you going to continue with your little temper tantrum?'

Temper tantrum?

Lady, you ain't seen nothing yet.

I looked down at my feet and gently toed the corner of the floor rug. 'I wasn't aware that I was throwing a tantrum. Granted, I'm irritated that you're keeping vital information from me. Actually more than irritated, I'm pissed off, but you both know I've never been one to wallow in self pity.'

Wallow, no. Complain, yes.

Susan smiled slightly. 'True enough. I just gathered from your silence that you were being uncooperative.'

I snorted and raised my head, grimacing slightly. 'I'm trying to act like an adult. You said to me once that if you can't say anything nice, don't say anything at all.'

Lucas rounded the corner back into the kitchen, sniggering, a plate full of Chinese food in his hands. 'She has tone. Can't you hear it, mum?'

I bit back the desire to deck him. That chow mien and plum sauce would sure look lovely on top of his head right now.

'No,' I said coolly, shelving my plans to rearrange his face with the plate he was holding, 'The only person I'm ignoring around here is Lucas.'

'Me? What did I do?'

'Seriously? Should I write you a list?'

'What would be the point? It would just say "Blah, blah, blah, Lucas is a dumb-ass".'

I grinned. 'Oh, good, so you *have* read it?'

He flipped me off and I happily returned the gesture.

'That's quite enough!' Susan yelled across the living room. 'Your brother did the right thing by telling us where you were. Now I don't want to hear another word about it. You were in the wrong, you were the one who snuck out and you have been punished accordingly. End of story! Now go and get yourself some dinner and pull your head in Elena before I do it for you.'

'Why are you yelling at *me* and not Lucas?'

'Oh, I'm sorry, Elena, did Lucas sneak out of the house last night as well?'

I grunted as loudly as I could muster. 'Point taken.'

Remaining cautious of my facial expressions, I went back into the kitchen and threw the cleaning products back under the sink. I washed my hands and then grabbed a plate of the delicious Chinese food off the kitchen bench and stalked off towards my bedroom. I didn't really want to look at Lucas smiling at me so smugly.

'Elena, please do not take food into the bedroom. You can come and sit at the table with the rest of the family,' Susan said as she turned and headed for the dining room.

Oh, goody.

I chewed my food in silence, concentrating on the flavours and mostly looking down at the plate in front of me. Occasionally I shot Lucas a filthy look, imagining what my fork would look like wedged up hard inside his nose. No one bothered to talk at the table this evening and I was grateful for the silence, particularly as I didn't have anything nice to say.

When I was finished, I rinsed off my plate in the sink, placed it into the dishwasher, said a stiff goodnight to everyone, and headed upstairs for a shower. It was too early to go to bed, but I didn't fancy spending the evening in front of the television with the rest of the family trying to make forced conversation. I guessed I was still in a 'mood', as Susan would call it, and it would be better for everyone concerned if I remained in my own company for this evening.

I took my time in the shower, letting the hot water work its magic over my body. I ended up washing my hair twice because I was daydreaming. I was picturing my life without my family, sometime in the future when time had passed and I was a vampire. I wondered if I would still be the same person or would I change as time drifted by, becoming something unrecognisable and deadly, a force beyond even my own control?

Vincent had told me once that he had met plenty of vampires that had forgotten their humanity. They were so consumed by bloodlust that they had no moral compass for wrong or right. Would that happen to me? Would I crave blood so badly that I forgot everything that my family had instilled in me? Would I not know the difference between a life that matters and a life that needed to be destroyed? Or was Vincent selling me scary stories just to be an ass? He certainly made a habit out of it.

I let the warm water wash over my face again. Surely not everything that the IMI knew about vampires was true? There had to be more to them than just pure bloodlust. If there wasn't, and they were just blood crazy, dangerous creatures, then an alliance would not have been formed in the first place. Vampires had to see reason. How else would they have mutually decided that the Vânători were a threat to one and all? Or was it simply because vampires were no longer the top of the food chain with the Vânători around?

No, I couldn't let myself believe that what I was destined to become was better off being destroyed than understood. If my family could attempt to love me, and the other Protectors in this faction could at least tolerate me, then there had to be common ground after the alliance had ended. But, then again, I was still human right now. Having never actually met a vampire before, I had no idea what sort of person I was going to become.

Perhaps when Susan and George finally had that conversation with me I would learn more. All I had to do was be patient, difficult given the fact I was not a patient person, but I had little choice.

The Manory's were all that I had. I knew no other family, and I had to trust in the fact that they would hopefully sometime soon reveal everything that I needed to know about my past, present, and future.

I sighed wearily. The day's cleaning activities had begun to take its toll on me and the heavy thoughts in my mind were weighing on my muscles like no physical activity ever could.

I shut the taps off reluctantly and forced myself out of the warmth of the shower, wrapping a towel around myself. It was a good thing Lucas would rather go blind than see me sprint for the bedroom in a terry towel. He knew me well enough to avoid this area of the house until I was safely tucked away in my bedroom, unless of course he wanted to cop an eyeful of sister as I dashed past.

It had happened only once before.

He claimed he had never been the same since. I told him it was because it would be the last time in his life that he ever saw a girl who was half-naked. He hadn't been amused by the prospect.

Before I made my exit, I stared at myself briefly in the mirror, looking at the reflection staring back at me and wondering just who that person really was. Was it possible to think that you knew the person that you are exactly, but at the same time constantly wonder if that person was a lie? Was I just a reflection of other people's projections and influences and only a small trace of true genuine character that was based on my own personality? Because that's what I saw staring back at me—a shell that was crafted by a vampire I had never known, a mind that was being moulded to conform, and a heart that was searching for acceptance.

Hopefully I wouldn't have to wait until I was sucking down pints of blood before I found the answer.

Time was running out.

I slapped at my reflection in the mirror and then turned away, opening the door slowly and peering out into the empty hallway.

I padded quickly towards my bedroom, taking care not to be seen by anyone, namely Lucas, and then bolted the bedroom door behind me. I was relieved that this first day of enforced slavery was finally going to be over, and also vaguely aware that there was still twenty-nine days to go.

CHAPTER SIX: IMI

'Good morning,' Susan said chirpily, as I rounded the bottom of the stairs and entered the kitchen.

'Is it?' I replied dryly, surveying the damage she was causing to a simple creation of what could be scrambled eggs.

Her eyes narrowed. 'Are you still cranky?'

I gave her a wry look. 'It's Monday. Isn't that reason enough to be sour?'

She smiled, tossing a mound of yellow, burnt-looking cotton wool onto a plate.

'Are there any eggs in that?' I said, pointing at the odd coloured pile of muck.

'Of course there is,' she snapped. 'What else would there be in scrambled eggs?'

I shrugged. I just wanted to make sure that I wasn't starting my week off with salmonella poisoning.

I took the plate from her outstretched fingers and headed into the dining room with everyone else. George was bent over the morning paper, reading some article about women up the coast that were going missing, along with a few ongoing homicides that had no leads.

The details were a little sketchy.

Apparently at least three women from Rockhampton had been abducted, followed by another four in Mackay, and one now in Townsville.

Perhaps that was why Susan and George were both going so mental about me sneaking out on my own on Saturday. It was amazing the clarity you could actually achieve if you switched perspectives and tried to look at a situation from the other person's point of view. Of course I had zero intentions of telling them I understood. Hell would freeze over before I ever disclosed *that* little piece of information.

And speaking of all things hellish, Lucas was seemingly unperturbed by the smell of breakfast or the fact that I was pulling strange faces at him, trying to get his attention. He was sprawled out in the living room, his legs draped over the side of his favourite armchair watching Sponge Bob Square Pants on the television. I should have realised that communication with him during his morning cartoons was about as likely as Susan and George wrapping me in a warm hug and saying, 'Just kidding, Elena, you're not grounded anymore. You can do what you like'.

George poked his nose over the paper as I lowered the plate of eggs onto the table. He sniffed at the air and then glanced timidly back into the kitchen at Susan's turned back. 'Is that scrambled eggs?' he asked me quietly.

'Apparently.'

'Anything else in there besides eggs?'

I shook my head. 'Not as far as I know.'

He smiled and then lowered the paper, skewering a piece of egg with his fork and raising it to his mouth, before he changed his mind. I was waiting for the verdict on the taste test before I dug in.

'It's burnt, but not too bad considering,' he said, scraping a lump onto his plate and grabbing two pieces of buttered toast from the centre of the table.

I followed suit.

He was right. Considering what she could have cooked for breakfast, it was definitely edible.

Lucas trotted up to the table a few minutes later. The cartoons he had been watching were now finished. He picked at a piece of toast that was now cold, and then toyed briefly with the idea of eating some of the eggs, but apparently changed his mind. He settled instead for just the cold, buttered toast only and a glass of orange juice.

Pussy.

'I think we'll have you mastering the Hevannatara spell today,' George said to Lucas as he slapped him endearingly on the back.

'You think so?' Lucas sounded doubtful.

'Of course. You are the son of two Protectors. These things will just come naturally with time and a little practice.'

I snorted. 'I think Lucas was hoping to nail the spell *before* his seventieth birthday,' I said, shoving a forkful of eggs into my mouth and grinning. I didn't really mean it. If anything, Lucas deserved praise. He was smarter than I gave him credit for, learning spells far more quickly than everyone else at the IMI.

'Shut up, E.'

I pointed my fork at Lucas and looked at George innocently. 'Do you see what I have to put up with?'

He scowled and then picked the newspaper up again, abruptly halting our conversation in its tracks. But that didn't stop Lucas from flipping me off and mouthing something that should have ended in having his mouth washed out with soap.

I grinned. 'Right back at you, bro.'

'How's breakfast?' Susan asked as she glided into the room and took her usual seat at the table.

'Actually it's—'

'Excellent, my darling,' George answered quickly, interrupting me mid sentence and tossing me another one of his 'keep your mouth shut' looks. How was keeping quiet ever going to help improve her cooking? Isn't it called constructive criticism?

She grinned happily. 'Well, good. I was thinking tomorrow if I had time I would whip us up a batch of waffles.'

I choked on a piece of rubbery egg that I had been trying to chew for the last few minutes, in between the crunching of shell.

'From scratch?' Lucas chortled, glancing at his plate.

She frowned at both our reactions. 'Of course.'

'Where did you get the recipe?' I asked.

'I'm not using a recipe. I saw someone on TV make them and I'm just going to do it like that.'

Lucas and I looked at each other. That was not a good sign.

'I'm done,' I said, tossing my half-eaten piece of toast back onto my plate. I'd lost my appetite. 'I'll just get cleaned up and then I'll be ready to leave.'

'I'll drop you off at the IMI this morning,' Susan said, stuffing some egg into her mouth. 'But after that I need to head over to the store to do some bookwork. Your father will take you both inside. Martha will be instructing all of your academic lessons for today.' She swallowed. 'I should be back in time for afternoon training.'

Phew. At least it wasn't Sarah running classes today.

The woman seriously had it in for me. For some reason, Sarah had always disliked me. I think it had to do with the fact that she was strongly religious, and that my very being was a concept that evoked images of demons and devil worshipping.

Poor clichés aside, she was the worst kind of bigot possible. It wasn't just the Vânǎtors and the Vampires that offended her sensibilities, but also any person of mixed race or variation in religious beliefs. I felt tremendously sorry for the Jehovah's Witnesses that came knocking on her door every Saturday afternoon. By the time they'd be allowed to leave, she would have bullied them into switching religions or pummelled them over the heads with her precious bible.

I dashed back up the stairs leaving the rest of them to debate about whether or not Lucas would be shown the Light of Mellar spell today. I hoped so. Despite how much Lucas could irritate me sometimes, I really enjoyed watching him and the other two Protector children, Karina and Lisa, learning magical defence. It was just a shame that I would never be able to partake in magical bidding. I was not born a Protector and therefore did not inherit magic of any kind. I wanted to learn, I really did. But instead, I had to be satisfied with watching the others and learning tricks of my own that would hopefully equip me for the long future ahead.

Alone.

Everyone was ready to go by the time I came back downstairs again. I shouldered my back pack and headed out to the car, Lucas following right behind me.

George and Lucas hopped into the passenger seats of the car while I stood to watch the usual morning ritual Susan was about to perform. No matter how many times I had seen it, I never got sick of watching the magic.

She raised her hand in front of her, pointing towards the car with her fingers, and then gave me a quick wink. She concentrated on the parked car in front of her and then uttered '*Revatarus*' quietly under her breath.

Green light licked at her fingertips and danced across the air, smothering the car in its energy, pulsating over the metal surface like green glowing slime.

I watched as the Forrester slowly began to disappear from sight as the pulsating green slime oozed over the surface of the metal. The visibility of the car decreased exponentially and soon became all but invisible to the human eye. The only people who could see through this magic were The Protectors themselves. It never ceased to amaze me just how powerful these people truly were.

Susan took my hand and led me over to the car. She knew I didn't have a hope in hell of finding my way inside unless we had a while to play Marco Polo. But at least once the car door had been opened, I could quite easily see inside the cabin. It was this particular cloaking spell that was going to allow us to gain entry to the drive-in, and still remain undetected by unknowing humans.

The Institute of Magical Intervention had branches located all over the world, with the main headquarters situated in Bucharest, Romania. There were only six in Australia, in total.

There was our faction that was comprised of eleven members, including my parents and Lucas. It was a small group in comparison to the other states, but apparently all that was necessary for our overly sunny neck of the woods.

Susan and George were the directors, or leaders, of this particular branch and the entire state of Queensland's security was maintained under their command, just as George's father had done before him.

There were other branches also located in every other state in Australia, the largest being located in Melbourne with well over sixty five members and counting.

Each branch was in charge of protecting their own area

from vânător invasion and possible vampiric activities that were considered less than savoury or in direct violation of the treaty. Our faction was the smallest in the country, but also did not require anything larger given that Queensland was the sunshine state. Vânătors and vampires were more than a little reluctant to stray into areas where the sun shone down brightly for almost three hundred and sixty-five days a year. But just because our faction was small did not mean that we were without resources. In fact, our faction was often called in to help reinforce other territories such as Melbourne, or Adelaide, when the situation required.

Hence our Christmas holidays last year.

The drive-in, where we were heading to now, had been chosen as our faction's site because of its obscurity.

It had not been used for a good many years, and now remained relatively unoccupied, unless of course you counted misguided youths and homeless people who were occasional tenants. Even then it was mostly left abandoned, brandished with graffiti and covered in knee-high long grass. It was the most circumspect location that anyone could think of, and even if developers decided to flatten the place in years to come it would not matter. The branch was located under the ground and had several other visitor entrances that could be used.

I glanced out the window and caught sight of the familiar movie screens. Susan turned the car onto the side road that ran parallel to the highway and led directly to the front entrance of the drive-in. There was a six foot chain link fence that surrounded the entire perimeter of the area and had rolled barbed wire stretched across the top to daunt intruders from proceeding further. The owners of this land were trying to discourage vandalism to the property, but they unfortunately remained unsuccessful. They would have to fix the gaping holes in the fence first before the barbed wire became any real threat to an intruder. Not to mention the fact that an entire secret society had managed to manufacture an underground compound without the owner ever being aware.

Susan pulled the car into the short driveway in front of the fence and quickly looked around to see if anyone was watching. The place was practically deserted. People were too busy racing down the highway to work and school to notice our activities. Not that they could see any of us anyway, but if they had been looking they would be able to see what was going to happen next.

She looked at the fence, held her hand out in front of her and uttered the word '*Entriatus*'. I knew that she spoke the words for Lucas's benefit so that he could learn and remember the charms, as once a Protector was accomplished enough at a particular spell they no longer had to speak the words but merely think them.

I watched as the padlock and chain that was wrapped around the gated entry quickly undid itself and then danced around in the air. The gates pulled open and swung inwards as if the action was performed by invisible hands.

I turned around in the seat to watch the finale as Susan drove through the gates and down the gravel and bitumen driveway towards the restaurant building and car parking area. The gates closed silently behind us, the metal chain weaving quickly through the air in a silent song and securely fastening itself with the padlock again.

Amazing. I love magic.

'They're already all here,' I heard George say as I swung back around in my seat.

I glanced out of the window, but the place looked absolutely deserted to me. There was not a single car in sight, but given that I couldn't see through the magic, I was going to have to take his word for it.

Susan pulled the car up a little way away from the restaurant building and we all stepped out, leaving Susan in the driver seat.

She smiled thinly at me and started tapping impatiently on her watch as I began my usual hokey-pokey of placing one arm in, and the other arm out and then shaking my invisible bits all about. For some reason, playing silly buggers with the invisible car never got old to me.

'Okay, are you finished playing around now? Or do you and the car need some more time together?' George asked me, tapping on my shoulder.

I looked eerily at my half-amputated arm and then laughed as I pulled it free from the confines of the magic. 'No, I'm good,' I said, waving goodbye to Susan and then shutting the car door behind me.

Lucas shook his head and took me by the hand so I didn't hit any of the other invisible cars on the way inside. I did have to wonder, after I had rammed into the third vehicle with my knees, whether or not I should have asked for another guide. I was fairly certain that Lucas was trying to injure me on purpose.

I dropped his hand the second we reached the entry, marked only by two aluminium doors that were well-beaten and doing little in the way of shielding the interior from the weather. The windows here had been smashed in by vandals, as were many of the other windows that surrounded the small building. Small shards lay scattered across the floor, crunching underfoot as each of us entered the premises.

Inside, some of the old booths still remained, but were ripped by knife wounds and mistreatment. Graffiti marred almost every surface. The tables had not faired any better, some barely standing after being hacked at with knives, the counter tops ripped and burned from years of neglect and abuse.

George led the way through the battered restaurant. Nothing had changed since the last time we had been here on Tuesday.

I stepped over the old metal chain that led to kitchenette area, following closely on the heels of Lucas. The mirrored splashback that lined the old bar area was always the first thing that I saw, probably because I generally found myself warily watching my own reflection, somehow expecting it to jump out of the mirror and attack me. Ridiculous, I know.

The mirror itself was now cracked and broken in many places. There were rust spots that had accumulated in the corners and any other place that incurred damage over the years. What surprised me the most was that the mirror was still in one piece, as opposed to lying across the floor in shards, just like the rest of the glass in this place. Vandals generally weren't too picky when it came to tearing a place apart. Perhaps the old superstition about seven years bad luck for breaking mirrors kept it intact.

Glancing back at the counter tops in the kitchenette, I noticed they were laden thick with dust and graffiti and were littered with cardboard boxes containing old newspapers and mail out catalogues. Even though I was a strong advocate for only cleaning rooms—like my bedroom— when they became close to bordering on the hazardous, I couldn't imagine myself surrounded permanently by filth. This place was a cesspool.

George and Susan said it would look more suspicious and draw too much attention if we ever bothered to clean the place up. Their belief was that if we left it a wreck, then no one would ever look beneath the surface.

Pity they didn't have the same view about me cleaning my bedroom.

We all moved further into the small kitchenette where some of the infill of paper from the boxes was spread onto the floor like a giant cat litter tray. I looked a little more closely at the area where the trapdoor was located, but as usual I could see nothing. And as usual, George revealed it to me.

'*Revatarus!*' he said, extending his hand in front of him. The same green light that had danced upon Susan's fingertips this morning now appeared on George's. It slicked across his fingers and then weaved through the air like a pungent green fog until it found its target on the floor. The trapdoor, providing our first port of entry into the IMI, slowly came into view. It was as if someone with an invisible pencil had drawn its outline and was now colouring in details.

As if in slow motion, I watched as the magic revealed the well worn oak with its abundance of knots, indentations, and rippling character. The steel hinges that held it in place were rusted and in bad need of replacement, but so was the door itself.

When the door finally appeared after a few seconds, George opened it up for us and Lucas and I scurried down the steel ladder. George closed the door behind us, casting the lower room into relative darkness. At the bottom of the ladder he pointed his palm upward towards the trapdoor and said the same spell word again, meaning the trapdoor would once again be shrouded in invisibility.

This first entry room to the IMI was located roughly five metres below ground level. It was encased in thick concrete to support the walls and prevent cave-ins. The room was simple, plain, and had no adornments other than the secondary entry point located only a few metres away from me.

My eyes began to slowly adjust to the darkness—I knew my way well enough by now to know where the other door was. It was constructed from the same thick, solid timber as the trapdoor above with a small, centralised handle and latch in brass.

I walked forward, carefully running my hands along the concrete wall, treading carefully. The ground was uneven beneath my feet and the lack of light made it difficult to see anything too clearly, but I pressed on.

I could hear Lucas and George following closely behind me, their fingers also brushing against the wall. I often wondered who the bright spark was that built this room under the ground and neglected to install even just one light bulb—total dipshits.

Once I reached the door, I secured the handle in my grip, turned it clockwise and then pushed it inwards. I blinked a couple of times, my eyes now having to adjust to the new found brightness of the subsequent passage.

This area was also constructed from concrete, but the walls were finished in a smooth render of limestone or stucco and then painted gloss white to help reflect light and cut down on dust collection. You'd think they would have run the left over paint into the first chamber just to brighten the place up a bit—obviously not.

Set into the ceiling were some very ostentatious looking crystal chandeliers. They were strung roughly two metres apart from each other and cast pools of light upon the walls and floor, in complete contrast to the dark hole we had just emerged from and the dilapidated building back upstairs.

I walked down a set of oak timber stairs that led me further into the passage and took us a further two metres down under the ground's surface. I took the last step off the stairs and headed further in, my feet sinking into the thick, fire-engine red carpet that lined the concrete floors.

Persian runners were laid haphazardly over the top of the carpet that covered the entire area of the IMI, except for the training rooms which were lined in stone, probably for durability. Old and crumbling oil paintings depicting various battle scenes that I was unfamiliar with adorned the narrow walls, but there were no other adornments. Past this particular ornately decorated passage was a junction in which three other intersecting passages of similar decoration branched off.

I took the left passage, feeling the familiar slope of it heading downwards, until I came to another set of carved timber stairs that lead to the library passage.

This passage was no differently decorated than the other passages except that it led to the largest room in the entire complex—this was where we mostly all congregated and where our daily lessons were held. The library room was roughly the size of our entire house, possibly even bigger given how many books were crammed in.

The sumptuous red carpet and vibrant Persian rugs were strewn about the room. The walls themselves could not be seen as they were lined from floor to ceiling with journals and books, encased in a frame of stunning oak timber bookshelves. There were also organised seating arrangements and more books piled up on side tables.

The plush leather sofas had brass-studded detail and were arranged into comfortable groupings around coffee tables. In between each arrangement there were multiple brass reading lamps placed centrally on battered oak side tables, matching the shelves, stairs and coffee tables. It was these lamps that cast the warm glow around the cavernous room that created the feeling of a more intimate setting. There were at least six of these groupings set up all together and from previous experience I knew they could easily cram about one hundred people in this particular room quite comfortably.

I stepped into the library, giving Karina and Lisa a quick wave before throwing my back pack on the floor and sitting down on one of the sofas away from Sarah and her equally bigoted friend, Kim.

Lucas was greeted by everyone and then gravitated towards Peter, his favourite instructor.

Peter was a short, tubby man in his mid-fifties that some-how appeared charismatic in Lucas's eyes, but not so much to me. If anything, he kind of freaked me out a little bit. He always wore dark grey sweaters over similar coloured pants which were always rolled up a few times around the hems. His hair was dark where he wasn't balding and his eyes were chocolate brown. I thought that they were too closely set together to be able to see straight, but apparently not. He had no trouble seeing at all when it came time to whooping my ass in a training session.

He wore a deep, pink scar that started over his left eyebrow and intersected with the corner of his eye, distorting the edge of it slightly, and flowing down to the hollow in his cheek. He never talked about how he'd got the scar, but I liked to think by the way he taught me martial arts that it was from fighting bad guys and not a visual display on why children shouldn't play with knives.

He looked at me now with discontent, his lips thin and pressed together in a hard line that emphasised his wrinkles. His skin was deeply tanned and worn from both sun exposure and age, but it was not his appearance that freaked me out as much as his personality. He was cunning, devious, secretive, and always sneaking up behind me or watching me—his beady brown eyes held no compassion.

So I found his whole presence unnerving. Although I did have to admit he was an excellent self defence teacher, though I still found myself preferring Vincent or even Malcolm over him.

Vincent, on the other hand, was a polar opposite to Peter and probably, if I had to choose, my favourite adult at the IMI. At present he was sitting on a chair in the far corner of the room talking to Martha, our instructor for the day. He was only in his mid-forties, was over six feet tall, and slim but with a slight belly that he put down to drinking too many beers on a Friday night. He had a decent sense of humour, which he constantly flaunted by wearing hideous Hawaiian shirts, exclaiming they were the height of fashion, along with baiting me constantly in training with packets of blood maintaining that 'all good little vamps need their AB-negative'.

The guy was harmless enough, but like Peter, he was as ugly as sin. His slender build did little to hide his acne scars and a poor attempt at creating a decent hairdo by using what little of his blonde hair he had left resulted in a nineteen seventies style combover.

Ugh!

Malcolm, who was at least an ally to me here because I was *partially* friends with his daughter Karina, looked exactly like Peter except taller and thinner. They could have been twins except for the fact that Malcolm came from Spain and was moderately less creepy.

Sarah, of course, was the one person here that I really didn't like at all. No matter how much I tried, I couldn't bring myself to warm to her. Her attitude towards people was repugnant.

I flicked a quick look in her direction and noted that she was whispering something in Kim's ear, watching me. There was nothing particularly unusual about that. The woman always had her eye on me, though what she thought I was going to do was beyond me.

Sarah was short and quite plump. She was just on forty-six years of age, maintaining short strawberry blonde hair and blue eyes. Not an ounce of grey in those blonde curls. She wore a lot of pink and yellow ensembles, a bit glary for my liking, and was in complete contrast to the woman sitting next to her.

Like Malcolm, Kim wore a lot of black. She was scarily thin, almost twig-like in appearance and had similar short blonde hair and blue eyes like Sarah. Both of them were like two evil trolls, and I was glad that they spent most of their time keeping out of my way and out of my life. I didn't really have a lot of patience for people who were intolerant of other people's differences, particularly when narrow-mindedness was considered a noble asset by both of them.

I slumped down into the chair and waited for my morning classes to begin. I had a feeling Martha was going to run me through algebra today. She seemed to enjoy torturing me with mathematics.

'Morning, George,' Malcolm said as George lowered himself onto the sofa next to me.

'Morning, Malcolm,' he answered politely.

Martha and Vincent ended their conversation in the corner and came over to sit on the sofa in front of us.

'Malcolm tells me that young Elena here took down two vânători on her own last week.'

George frowned and then looked at me. I sank down lower into the chair and suppressed a smile.

'Oh yes, I forgot you've been away from the IMI for the

last few days, Vincent,' George said quietly. 'And, yes, it is true. Elena did kill two vânătors without any direct help from us.'

Vincent grinned at me and winked. 'I told you I'm a good teacher.'

'It was silly and irresponsible, Vincent,' George growled. 'Please do not encourage her antics.'

'But two vânătors on her own?' he continued, whistling. 'That's exceptional for a human.'

'She's not human,' Sarah piped in.

George leaned forward in the chair and touched my shoulder lightly. 'She *is* human, Sarah.'

She scoffed and then continued her whispering with Kim.

'So are we sending her out on more scouting missions?' Malcolm asked.

I looked up at George hopefully.

'No. She needs to learn the value of teamwork before she's allowed on the field again.'

'George,' I moaned, sitting up in my seat, 'that's not fair. What have you been training me for if you aren't going to let me use my skills?'

'Oh, boy,' Vincent said, standing up from the sofa, 'I feel an argument coming on. It must be time to leave.'

George shook his head. 'There will be no arguing. Until Elena learns that she doesn't in fact know the answer to everything, then she will continue to train and only hear about the missions rather than participate in them.'

I slumped back into my seat again and kicked the edge of the coffee table in disgust. 'That's bullshit.'

'I beg your pardon?' he said, turning to look at me with one raised eyebrow and a heavy set scowl on his mouth.

'I said ... that's bull—'

'Alrighty then!' Martha interrupted, her brown eyes silencing me. 'Time for lessons.'

She tossed her mane of curly red hair over her shoulders and then beckoned for me and the other kids to head over to the desks and chairs at the side of the room.

Vincent, Kim and a few of the others said a quick good-bye and took off for work. I watched them go.

Most of the Protectors had day jobs. Vincent and Kim were lawyers who jointly ran their own firm. Most of their associates ran the practice for them in their absence, bringing in the money and allowing them more free time at the IMI. Occasionally they had to stop into the office for a few hours at a time to sit in on consultations or even attend court hearings, but as they ran the practice together, it did give them both a little more freedom.

It was the same with the other Protectors. Malcolm taught Spanish at a night school, and Peter ran a martial arts academy in the city. All of the classes ran at night so that they both had free time during the day at the IMI training the rest of us how to fight.

As for Sarah, I didn't really give a rat's ass what she did with her time. She was probably the head of some sort of white supremacist party who spent all of their time plotting revenge against anyone who was even slightly different from them or dared to believe in Santa Claus. The woman was intolerable and annoyingly present.

Martha, on the other hand, was moderately nice. She was the reason I had my Saturday job at Cairns Fine Furniture and Accessories. Not only was she an interior designer like Glen, but she was also the owner, and I always thought it was nice of her to have offered me the job even though I was less than crazy about homewares. But if I was totally honest, it sure beat working in Susan and George's hardware store.

That was one job I would leave to Lucas. Give me scented candles and scatter cushions over pitchforks and shovels, any day.

I collected my backpack off the floor, waved goodbye to the other adults that were leaving for the day, and wandered over to my usual place at the long oak table in the corner of the room, avoiding the glare that George was directing at my back.

Lucas and Karina, who were both in their last year of high school, naturally sat together. Lisa and I took the opposing side of the table. She and I were both sixteen years old and still had our senior year ahead of us.

I liked Lisa. She never really talked all that much which suited me just fine. She was overtly shy and somewhat self-conscious. She had curly red hair like her mother, and the same brown eyes and smattering of freckles across the bridge of her nose and cheeks. She always made comments about how pretty I was, which I found flattering and uncomfortable, all at the same time, particularly when it was obvious that she seemed less than pleased with her own appearance. She was not unattractive, merely plain and a little on the overweight side. But once I had gotten to know her it was very difficult not to like her. She had a beautiful smile and perfect white teeth, and a laugh that made you feel all warm and fuzzy on the inside. I liked to remind her of those things when she called me pretty while nervously tugging on her curls and cursing her fiery red hair and freckly skin.

On the other hand, Karina was the exact opposite to Lisa. She was just as short, but rake-thin with voluminous, long black hair and vibrant green eyes. She was pale unlike her father Malcolm, who was deeply tanned, which had me wondering what her mother might have looked like. Since

I'd probably never know because the lady had run out on them, I'd decided her pasty pallor was probably because we were always holed up in the IMI with no windows to let the sunshine in.

Quite depressing, actually.

'Okay. Good morning, everyone,' Martha began, 'I will be taking your lessons for this morning. Lucas and Karina—you will continue on with your history assessments for the next few hours. Feel free to make use of the library for reference. Lisa and Elena—for today I think we shall work on biology.'

I stared at Martha open-mouthed.

Seriously—no maths?

'Is there a problem, Elena?'

I shook my head. 'No, Martha, biology would be great.' Well that was an over statement, but it sure as hell beat the crap out of having to do algebra.

Classes flew by, probably because I was so enamoured by the fact we were completely skipping over the mathematics part of the curriculum today. No doubt it was something that Susan would hammer it into me and Lisa tomorrow instead.

Something to look forward to.

Maybe I should get a head start on the maths tonight so I don't struggle tomorrow?

Like that's going to help.

I know but—

'Elena, you're not concentrating,' Peter growled, as he knocked me flat on my back for the third time in as many minutes.

I howled in surprise and sucked in a new breath of air to

replace that which had just been ruthlessly knocked right out of me. Why was I still thinking about school work when this was my favourite part of the day?

'Sorry,' I gasped.

'Don't say sorry, just concentrate and try and get the blade out of my hands.'

Peter held a fake wooden blade and was dancing around on top of one the foam mats we used in the training rooms, foam to prevent injuries. Not that the mats made any difference—Peter never took it easy on me. In fact, he'd broken more of my bones than I cared to remember. It was a good thing I could heal otherwise I might have started to think he was out to get me.

I rolled over on my side and scrambled back to my feet. I hopped lightly from one foot to the other, trying to get a bearing on my opponent. It wasn't easy since he seemed to predict every move that I was going to make.

I lunged forward, feigning a hit to the left and instead lashed out to the right.

He caught my swing with his arm and blocked me, taking a swipe with his right leg and kicking me hard in the left side, knocking the wind out of me. Again.

I dropped to my knees, sucking in air at the same time as trying to land a couple of blows to his flabby mid section. He blocked ninety percent of them, but I got one in just at the base of his ribs—but not enough to crack them.

He reeled backwards slightly, coming straight back at me with a roundhouse kick to the head. I ducked, smiling lightly as his foot sailed through the air just above my head, missing his target.

He grunted. 'Don't get cocky, Elena. That always happens. You get too brash and then all of a sudden while you're busy feeling smug you get kicked or punched in the face.'

I grinned, rolling away from Peter's feet.

Not always.

I danced around lightly in the space in front of me, watching for any sign from Peter that might give away his next move. I was feeling confident that I could beat him today. I hadn't really been concentrating until now, but I'd still managed to get away from him relatively unscathed, which was somewhat of a miracle. If I could just get that knife out of his hands then maybe George would change his mind, let me tag along on the next hunt.

Despite my vigilant stance and watchful gaze, Peter made no attempts to attack. He didn't move his eyes from me. I was going to have to make the first move, which would undoubtedly result in some kind of semi-painful counter-attack. I just needed to keep my focus and think ahead as best as I could.

In the next instant I lunged forward again, slamming a well-placed hit at the side his arm that was holding the wooden knife.

The pain registered briefly on his face, but I pre-empted his next attack and warded off several of the raining blows he'd aimed at my chest. My arms flailed around in front of me in sharp, blocking movements, our flesh slapping against each other as he slammed me with one attack after the other.

I felt my wrists and forearms beginning to hurt from the impact, but I was not going to relent until I had won. Lucas was kicking ass in the magic department, so the least I could do was excel at something. Plus, if there was bragging to be had around the dinner table tonight, it would be cool if it was about my accomplishments for a change.

He feigned a hit to my ribs which I managed to duck out of the way of. I was not quick enough to avoid the follow-up hit to the top of my shoulder. My knees buckled underneath me.

I hit the deck again, wincing momentarily at the pain in my shoulder, before my Vampiric genes set to work clearing up the problem. I rolled backwards and then flipped back onto my feet again, pursuing a roundhouse kick to Peter's head.

He caught my kick in his hands, spun me around in the air, forcing me to my stomach. I was prepared, though, and landed lithely on my hands. Then, rolling to my side, I scooped my legs around and up in one quick motion, sweeping Peter's legs out from under him and sending him sprawling backwards onto the floor.

I scrambled up off the floor and landed a punch straight to the middle of his chest, knocking the air right out of him. He grunted loudly, and I straddled his chest, pinning both of his arms to his sides with my legs. I took the wooden knife from between his pudgy fingers and waved it in the air triumphantly.

'Got ya!'

He shook his head from side to side in disappointment. 'Never celebrate until you are certain that you've won the battle.'

'But I have,' I said grinning. 'I've got the knife and *you* are flat on your back.'

'Are you sure about that?'

I nodded and grinned. He returned my smile with a particularly vicious sneer.

Uh-oh.

A second later, his legs flipped up behind me and slapped me on either side of the head, causing me to rock forward in shock and drop the knife. He shook his arms free and landed a good hefty punch in the side of my face, sending me flying through the air and sprawled out onto the mat behind me. My whole face sung with pain and I thought I saw stars behind my eyes. I tried to blink away the darkness that was threatening to engulf me.

By the time Peter had gotten to his feet and had started towards me again, my face was all but healed, just the memory of the hard-hitting punch burning in the back of my brain.

I too flipped to my feet, only to come face to face with a follow-up punch and a roundhouse kick to the head which sent me rocketing down to the mat for the final time. As I tried to shake loose from the pain shooting through every part of my head, I heard Peter chuckling lightly behind me. I wanted to return the favour, but I could barely see straight.

He crossed the mat, picked up the knife that I had dropped, rolled me onto my stomach, pulled both of my arms around my back and held them tight in his hand.

He pressed his weight against the back of my thighs and then with the other hand he held the wooden knife against my throat. 'See what happens when you get too cocky? Do you remember what I always tell you?'

I nodded, suppressing the urge to cry. I hated getting my ass whooped.

'Tell me,' he growled, jabbing the wood harder against my throat.

'Danger does not cease simply because we desire it.'

'Good,' he said, letting my arms go and taking a step backwards. 'Now what have you learnt from this exercise?'

I rolled over onto my side, sat up steadily and looked up at him, all seriousness. 'Stab you in the heart the first time I have you pinned to the ground.'

He blinked at me and then smiled sardonically. 'Not

exactly, but getting on with the job is, indeed, surely better than sitting about and gloating. But just remember, Elena—never celebrate the victory until you are absolutely certain the battle has been won. Or in other words, make sure your opponent is dead or inoperable before you start dancing around feeling proud of yourself.' He helped me back to my feet and patted me on the shoulder. 'Good work today.'

I forced out a smile.

'What did I miss?' Lucas said, re-entering the training room. Sarah, George, Susan and Malcolm trailed behind him. 'Did E get her face kicked in again?'

I shot him a look. 'What's it to you?'

Peter laughed. 'Leave your sister alone, Lucas. You shouldn't tease her so. You may be able to do magic, but if push comes to shove and you two were locked in battle, she could lay you on your ass any day of the week.'

Lucas slowly went red in the face and turned away.

I suppressed a giggle. The offhanded compliment from Peter actually made me feel a little better.

'Come now, Lucas, it's your turn to do some training.' He turned back to look at me. 'Elena? Would you mind stacking the foam mats back in the corner of the room?'

I nodded and started folding away the mats.

Susan and George were debating about some staffing issue at the hardware store. Malcolm made his way over to Peter to discuss Lucas's afternoon training session.

Sarah, on the other hand, made herself comfortable on the small metal grandstand that was for spectators while I busied myself clearing away mats.

There were only four large mats in total, so it didn't take me long to fold them in half and then drag each of them back to the corner of the stone room. I piled them out of the way, pulled my training robe off and then tossed it over my backpack and headed to the grand stands to sit and watch.

The training room we were all in was located down one of the passages that forked off from the main junction. The walls were constructed of concrete here also, but had been covered in heavy duty stone that ran over every other surface, including the ceiling and floor. The room was completely windowless of course as it was underground, but an extremely large timber chandelier hung suspended from the centre of the ceiling, spilling light in all directions. On the walls various pieces of armour and weaponry hung, ranging from medieval swords to daggers and hand guns.

I personally preferred to stick with my knife. I liked how it felt in my hand and the comfort it gave me. That didn't mean that I would not learn how to use each and every one of the other weapons on that wall—it just wasn't a priority. And particularly not when in less than a year and a half I was going to have killer instincts, sharp teeth, and razor sharp claws, far more deadly than things that go *bang-bang.*

'Shall we begin?' Peter said to Lucas, as I quickly darted out of the way and settled onto the grandstand, up high and away from Sarah. She seemed determined that we would be sitting together today, because she came up and sat down next to me.

I nodded a polite greeting and then turned to watch the proceedings, ignoring her presence as best as I could. It was difficult given that her perfume was pungent and smelt strangely like a cross between freshly cut roses and cat piss.

'Now the Light of Mellar, as well you know Lucas, is not about using spell words. To master this spell you need to be able to create an image in your mind that reflects your desired intentions.'

Susan took a seat on the lower grandstand to watch, while Malcolm quickly exited the room to go and help Karina with her training.

'George, would you mind?' Peter said, pointing at him.

George shook his head and stepped forward.

He held his hand out in front of him, silently studying his palm. A small glowing light began to appear, steadily growing bigger and burning brighter. It spun around, like a ball of white gas, across his fingertips, about the size of a basketball. He pulled his arm back and threw it across the room and at the wall, shrouding its entire length in darkness, regardless of the lighting from above.

'Wonderful. Thank you, George.'

George nodded and took a step backwards. It was better for Peter to take all of Lucas's field training classes. He was a lot more patient than George—he had a little problem with keeping his opinions to himself and avoiding anger management issues when he was in charge of training or lecturing.

'Now, Lucas,' Peter said patiently, 'would you like to have a go?'

Lucas nodded, although he looked nervous. He'd attempted this spell only once in the past, roughly just over a year ago.

It hadn't ended well.

George had chucked a mini tantrum about lack of focus and control, and consequently the lesson had ended with a rather shaken and apprehensive Lucas. It was hilarious for spectators such as me, but that little outburst from daddy dearest was exactly the reason that Peter now ran training classes with Lucas and me.

Lucas took a step forward, tucking a lock of his long blonde hair behind his ear, and then held his palm out in front of him in readiness. He appeared to be muttering something under his breath, but I couldn't hear what.

He focused on his hand, his blue eyes narrowing in on his palm, waiting like the rest of us for something to appear.

After about a minute of staring at empty space, he sighed in frustration and lowered his hand.

George grunted.

Susan shot him a look.

'Lucas, don't be discouraged,' Peter said sternly. 'Just concentrate and try again. Don't be distracted by the people around you.' Peter's scarred eye was directed specifically at George.

Hilarious.

'I'm trying,' Lucas muttered.

'Just try a little harder. Pretend the room is empty and then focus on the Light of Mellar appearing in your hand.'

'Okay.'

He raised his palm again, bringing all his energies to bear, concentrating hard. For a few moments nothing happened, and then, all of a sudden, white light began to flicker just above his upturned palm.

Susan and George both leaned forward in their seats, eagerness in their eyes.

Lucas focused in on it intently and the ball of light grew larger and larger, floating higher and higher, until it finally burned out.

George grunted again in earnest.

Susan shot him another look.

Double hilarious.

'Damn,' Lucas said, as he lowered his arm back down to his side.

'No, no, Lucas, you are doing absolutely fine. This time when you try to summon the energies, try focusing on the direction you want the spell to go in. Imagine, for instance, that the light is growing and expanding in your hand, and then throw it over at that wall over there,' Peter said, pointing behind him. 'Imagine, instead of it being ethereal, that it's a real object that you can touch and manipulate.'

'Okay, I'll try.'

He raised his palm again and continued the stare-a-thon at his hand. The small light flickered more quickly this time, growing exponentially until it was the size of a basketball, the same as George had created earlier. It hovered above his hand for a couple of seconds before he quickly turned and hurled the light at the wall with great force. It impacted without sound, shedding that section of the wall in total darkness, just as George had done.

'Excellent!' Peter cheered as he stepped forward and patted Lucas on the back. 'Try it again.'

He did. And then again and again. Lucas managed to conjure the spell successfully at least another ten times, the pride on our parents' faces clear for all to see.

'Now I know this might worry you, but I think we've practised enough now. I want you to now try this out on me. When the ball of light gets to full size, I want you to throw it at me. I will not resist.'

'But what happens if I hurt you?' Lucas asked worriedly.

'It shall not hurt me. You are ready.'

Lucas seemed hesitant, but he did as he was asked. The light began to grow on his hand again. I watched it morph and warp as it had done before, until, in one smooth motion, he turned and flicked it towards Peter, letting the ball hit him full in the face.

Peter staggered back slightly and then smiled. 'You did it, Lucas. I can't see a thing!'

'How long does it last for?'

'Only for around five minutes or so—then my vision will return. This spell has its advantages. It will allow you to disarm your opponent and give you time to either run or take action. I would hope that, of course, should the time come for you to face the Vânǎtors on your own that you would take action.'

'I will,' Lucas said almost instantly, and judging by the conviction in his voice he truly meant what he said. I had to admire him for that.

There was a disgruntled coughing sound coming from Susan and we all looked at her.

Peter shrugged. 'Well, that's if your mum *ever* lets you face them alone.'

I stifled a laugh.

Sounds familiar.

'Okay, I think my vision is slowly starting to come back. Do you think you have this mastered for now?' Peter asked.

'I think so.'

'Well, we can practice it some more tomorrow if you like. I would quite like to remain non-sightless for the time being.' He chuckled at his own joke and then fell silent when he realised no one else was laughing.

He coughed and continued. 'Okay, now pay attention to what I'm about to show you next. This spell is called Hevan-natara. It will make your opponent turn into a living statue and is quite useful when used in conjunction with the Light of Mellar. You have studied this spell in theory, but I want you to actually practice how to control its physical power.'

Peter stood still for a quick second before thrashing his

hands out in front of himself and uttering '*Hevannatara*'. A blue flash shot from his hand and flew fast as lightning across the room. The blue bolt crashed loudly into the stone wall.

Lucas looked on, eager with anticipation, waiting for Peter to do the trick again.

'He's very good, isn't he?' Sarah said to me. I'd almost forgotten she was there.

I nodded, not particularly interested in engaging in conversation with her. It usually ended in her calling me something nasty and then me having to bite my tongue.

'Pity.'

I'll buy it.

'What's a pity?'

'That you'll never be able to conjure magic, like him.'

I turned to look at her. 'I know that, but it doesn't matter. I have my own talents.'

'Yes, I expect that you probably do given that you're a *half-breed*.'

'Sorry? Did you say half-breed? I'm going to be a Vampire—that's *one* breed, not multiple.'

'If you say so, dear.'

I stared at her. 'Explain what you mean?'

She patted my shoulder and I shrugged her away. 'Pay attention, Peter is about to demonstrate something you'll never have.'

I resisted the urge to knock her backwards off the grandstand. Instead, I watched the arena as Peter walked to a small cage next to the door where we came in. I hadn't noticed it earlier. Perhaps one of the other adults had brought it in with them. Inside, I could see that it contained a couple of pigeons.

He pulled one of them out and threw it up into the

air. The bird took immediate evasive action as it fluttered around the room in a panic, looking for a way out.

Peter held his hand up in front of him, tracking the bird around as it flew. '*Hevennatara,*' he yelled and another blue bolt of lightning shot from his finger tips, hitting the bird perfectly in the breast. It froze in mid-flap and fell to the ground, landing with a loud *thud.*

Ouch, that's gotta hurt.

Lucas ran over to the bird and picked it up, tapping on its body with his fingers.

'Is it dead?'

'No. It's just immobilised for a short while. Put it back into the cage before it re-animates.'

Lucas obeyed, placing the pigeon carefully back into the cage, mildly distressing the other remaining birds in the process.

Peter sat down on the grandstand and gestured that Lucas should try this for himself.

His attempts were futile at first, as he repeatedly uttered the word and flicked his hands out in front of him. Nothing more than a small blue spark emanating from his fingers.

'Okay, Lucas, you're on the right track. The magic is already there—you just have to imagine the outcome as you did before. When you throw your hands out in front of you, imagine that you are gathering all the strength from inside yourself and focusing it in your hands. Then expel it from yourself with full force. The whole time you must picture the outcome, your opponent turning to stone in your mind. Of course, they do not actually turn to stone, or we would not be able to kill them. But they are rooted where they stand, unable to move for at least five minutes, just like the pigeon before. Now, it's not an exact science when it comes to the length of time. Age, weight, health, and power play definitive roles in the effectiveness of the spell. But generally a few minutes is enough time for you to kill.'

'Isn't there a spell that will just kill them instead of having to incapacitate them? It would save time.'

Peter shook his head and glanced quickly between Susan and George. 'That's dark magic, Lucas. We never use dark magic. It's not the way of The Protectors.'

Lucas nodded in apparent understanding and then began to concentrate on the task before him, more enthusiastic than before. A couple of small blue sparks erupted from his hand again, but then fizzled out in front of him as they had done previously.

I could tell he was concentrating pretty hard. His brow was slicked with sweat and his T-shirt was marred with the wet patches of heavier perspiration, but I admired his determination. This was even through the constant baiting he was receiving from the annoying man grunting down in the front row. If I had popcorn I'd throw the whole bucket at the back of George's head.

'Focus, Lucas,' Peter repeated.

George grunted even louder than before.

Susan slapped him on the arm.

I tried not to laugh.

Lucas struggled again, throwing his arms out in front of him with the full force of his physical strength and yelling 'Hevannatara'.

This time the magic worked. A massive ball of blue flames seemed to lick at his fingers as if they were coated in gasoline, before lashing out in front of him, like a flame thrower shooting forth blue fire. The fire slammed hard into the stone wall with a massive crash.

'Well done!' Peter cried, furiously clapping his hands in encouragement.

The rest of us jumped to our feet, yelling our congratulations.

Lucas breathed a quick sigh of relief, as he glanced at George and wiped the sweat from his brow with the collar of his shirt. He was looking rather pleased with himself. He tried the spell again, and this time success came more easily.

I was secretly pleased for him as I watched the blue light hit the wall repeatedly, watching his confidence grow. I continued to watch in complete silence as Lucas eagerly continued to practice both spells over and over, again and again until he appeared to have mastered them both.

Susan and George both looked proud as punch.

It started to get even more interesting when people began to duel each other, testing their powers. Peter and George won most of the duels and then waited patiently while Lucas and Susan regained their sight or the use of their limbs again. The most interesting part was when their magic intertwined. It would twist and contort in midair, the streams of light connecting and pushing against the other until one was victorious.

'So how are you taking all this new information?' Sarah said to me as I watched Lucas practising the Light of Mellar again.

'Sorry?' I said, shaking my head, barely listening to her. I sat transfixed, watching the duel between George and Peter down below.

'You know … your blood lines.'

'Hey?' I said, spinning around to look at her in bewilderment. 'What are you talking about?'

'Oh,' she said daintily, folding her hands in her lap and crossing one short pudgy leg over the other. 'Perhaps they haven't discussed that with you yet. It would certainly explain why you don't know you're a half-breed.'

'What? What are you saying, Sarah? Discussed what?' I eyed her suspiciously.

'It's probably a good thing,' she said, ignoring me. 'It's bad enough that you're going to be a vampire.' She shook her head, 'Deplorable creatures, really.'

I looked back over at my family as they practised their magic, hoping that Sarah would stop talking before my temper got the better of me. Sure she could turn me to stone and blind me if she wanted to, but she'd have to be quicker than a roundhouse kick to the face.

Lucas had stopped what he was doing and had started listening to our exchange. He could see my furrowed brows and the uncomfortable set in my shoulders, and had seen me try and distance myself from the hateful woman sitting next to me.

The other adults had stopped their duelling and now appeared to be embroiled in a mini-debate on whether or not to show Lucas the Defenacus charm. They were completely oblivious to the conversation I was having with Sarah.

Sarah forged on with her character sledging, regardless of the fact that she was clearly upsetting me. 'For now at least you are human. But later ... when you become a creature of the unknown, I should think you would take matters into your own hands, ensure that you don't become an emotionless blood drinker just like the rest of them.'

I stiffened.

Was she saying that she wanted me to kill myself?

'I don't want to talk about this with you, Sarah. My parents are the ones who need to answer my questions,' I said, staring down at the arena and trying not to let my agitation show. 'You're too biased in your opinions.'

'I beg your pardon? Tell me how *your* knowledge overrides

my vast experience with the Vampires?' she asked with a slight mocking tone, as she tapped her foot on the back of the stand in front of her.

I could tell that I had pissed her off and that this conversation was going nowhere fast. Still, I never could learn when to shut up. 'You're a bigot, Sarah, who is too narrow-minded to have a rational conversation with about this subject. I'm sorry, but I have no intention of talking to you about anything about my life that does not relate directly to the IMI.'

I could see from the corner of my eye that she was watching me, ire on her face and no doubt dreaming up ideas of strapping me to a church pew and slamming me in the face with the Book of Revelations.

Her foot was still tapping impatiently on the chair in front of her, her arms now folded in front of her massively inflated chest, all defiance. She sure had big boobs for such a short person.

'Well, I can see that you are intent on tearing my character to shreds rather than heeding sound advice,' she hissed, her teeth clenched. 'But make no mistake, my dear, although the Vampires are indeed our allies at this point in time, this will not always be so. As a species they are somewhat of a virus, a plague to this planet much like their creations, the Vânătors. So you, sitting there, calling me a bigot when you are on a course towards a path of eternal damnation is indeed a sin. You should be *begging* me to save your soul.'

I bit back an angry retort. It was difficult because I didn't really come with a censor button. I really wanted to say to her—that she was a fat, nasty, big breasted woman, but that was the anger talking. Insulting her would change nothing, but smacking her in the head? Tempting.

I could see Lucas watching me from down in the arena.

He did not look pleased. His hands were balled into fists, blue light dancing across his knuckles.

I shot him a look, with a quick tilt of my head in her direction. I wanted him to rescue me from my current plight before I did something we both might regret, because my foot was sure as hell itching to have a meeting with her face.

He understood, because he nodded his head back at me, a small smile spreading across his face, as he yelled out 'Hevannatara!'

A blue bolt of electricity shot from his hand and hit Sarah square in the chest. She instantly went still, her foot still in mid-tap and her arms still curled in front of her chest.

I grinned.

Nice one, Lucas.

'Lucas!' Susan yelled at him. 'You cannot do that to other Protectors without asking their permission first—it's very rude. Anyway, we were practising the Light of Mellar.'

He lowered his head, trying to hide his smirk.

She clipped him over the back of the head. 'Silly child. Apologise to Sarah at once.'

I watched as he lifted his head again, the smile gone.

He shook his head. 'I'll apologise to Sarah when she apologies to Elena. She just called her a virus!'

God bless him. I take it back. He's not a total dumb ass.

'Sarah did what?' George asked, looking up at me and frowning.

Why did everyone always look at me as if it was my fault?

'It's fine, Lucas,' I said, smiling lightly and giving him a wink. He relaxed. 'Sarah and I were just having a little disagreement and Lucas was just being a gentleman and jumping to my defence.'

'Well,' Susan started, looking helplessly between me,

Sarah and Lucas, 'perhaps we can overlook the random spell casting, if you were defending your sister's honour. Quite admirable, really, but I must insist that you ask a Protector's permission in the future before using magic against them. Regardless of what has happened while our backs were turned, issues in here should not be resolved with magic, but with words.'

Lucas nodded to our parents before they both turned around and launched back into conversation with Peter.

I smiled widely at Lucas and he grinned back, winking in reply. The spell had done its job rather well.

I swivelled around on the spot so that she could quite clearly see me, and then raised my hand and rapped on her stiffened forehead with my knuckles as if she was our front door.

Knock, knock, anyone home?

I snorted lightly and bit down on my tongue before any laughter gave me away, though the huge smile on my face could not be mistaken. 'Oh, you *poor* thing,' I said, lowering my hand and patting her gently on the shoulder in an overly-condescending manner.

Her blue eyes swivelled around in their sockets to look at me.

'It must be awful when something completely unexpected happens to you, something that is beyond your control.' I touched a finger to my chin like I was deep in thought. 'It's a bit like you turning into a stiff just now. It is surprisingly just *exactly* like me being born a Vampire. It happened without my consent or my control and there was absolutely nothing that either one of us could do about it.'

I grinned again, watching her blue eyes staring at me from behind a fixed mask. 'It's also a bit like you falling backwards over this grandstand.' I paused, my smile widening as I saw fear enter her eyes. 'There was nothing I could do to stop that either.'

She squeaked something in rebuttal from in between her stiffened lips before I gave her an 'accidental' push backwards, her whole body toppling over the edge of the grandstand and landing with a loud *thump* on the stone floor behind us. It wasn't high enough to break anything, but she was bound to have a bruise or two, not to mention and even bigger grudge against me when she was fully mobile.

Lucas practically convulsed with fits of laughter as Susan, George, and Peter spun around in dismay and surveyed Sarah's rigid body in horror.

She was frozen in her previous sitting position with her arms across her chest and her legs up in the air, one crossed in front of the other. It was a good thing she wasn't wearing a skirt today otherwise we'd all be seeing a side to Sarah that we'd sooner rather forget.

I looked up from Sarah's rigid body lying across the cold stone floor and turned reluctantly to the awaiting jury. Three sets of accusatory eyes were pointed directly at me.

'What?' I said, shrugging my shoulders innocently. 'She's top heavy.'

CHAPTER SEVEN: ULTIMATUMS

'What are we going to do with you, Elena?' Susan said to me as she took my hand, leading me out towards the car.

'What? I told you already—she just fell.'

Lucas choked on a laugh and gave me an apologetic look, covering his mouth with his hand.

'That's not what Sarah said,' she continued, ignoring Lucas's theatrics.

I shrugged. 'As there were no witnesses other than Lucas, I'm going to just say that the alleged 'shoving' is merely hearsay.'

'That's not how Sarah described the incident at all.'

I clicked my tongue. 'In her version of events, was I wearing a white cape and carrying a flaming crucifix?'

She frowned at me and released my hand. I suddenly felt stranded in the sea of invisible cars. 'There really are no words to describe you, Elena.'

'I could think of a few,' Lucas said, grinning.

'Shut up, Lucas, and get in the car.'

I chuckled lightly at her agitation. We were so nice to each other in this family.

Susan and George both stormed ahead of me, quickly getting inside the vehicle and closing the doors behind them, once again shrouding the car in invisibility.

Okay, so they're going to play that game.

I knew the general location of the car, but Susan had dropped my hand a fair distance away and I was going to have to feel my way to the door handle.

Lucas, of course, was providing zero help, merely standing back and watching me play hide and go seek with the door handle. To the left of me Vincent, who had come back to the IMI a little after lunch, gave us both a cheery goodbye and then disappeared inside his own invisible car.

Kim and Sarah had long since gone, Sarah nursing a dislocated shoulder from her 'fall'.

Peter, Martha and Malcolm, as well as the two kids, were the last to enter the parking area.

Lucas gestured with his hand towards our car impatiently. 'Chop, chop.'

I poked my tongue out at him and took a few tentative steps forward, holding my hand slightly in front of me in case I unexpectedly hit something. Unfortunately a well-timed horn blast from Vincent's car as he drove past was enough to make me jump, sending me scattering straight into the side of the car door.

My forehead cracked into the glass window with a loud *thud* and my right knee cap banged against the rear door, sending me reeling backwards into a filthy, old steel drum. It didn't hurt much, but my pride was a little wounded.

Karina, Lisa, and Lucas cracked up laughing, my legs dangling over the edge of the steel drum as I, firmly wedged inside, waited for someone to pull me back out.

Nice …

'Sure, sure, make fun of the blind girl,' I muttered, groping at the edge of the drum and trying to heave myself back out again with little success. Lucas was practically coughing up a lung he was laughing so hard.

Bastard.

When he finally managed to get a grip on himself and everyone had finished having a good laugh at my expense, Lucas gripped my hands and yanked me out of the drum. I was covered in rust stains and dirt.

'Enjoy that, did you?' I said to Lucas as I scrambled for the car door again and got inside.

He nodded, still laughing. 'I just wish I had a camera on me.'

I groaned.

The rest of the night slipped by just as quickly as the day, and by nine o'clock I found myself yawning out loud before bidding everyone a good night and heading upstairs to bed.

I laid awake for a short while, thinking about what Sarah had said today and hoping that she was alone in her thoughts. I'd come to expect insults as a part of her nature, but I couldn't concur with her description of vampires as a disease, and I wasn't about to go and kill myself just because one day I'd prefer to drink blood over Diet Coke. My future turning was entirely beyond my control.

Surely my integration with the IMI proved that vampires could at least attempt to live peacefully with the human populace? Granted, I was not a fully fledged vampire yet, but I knew in my heart I would not and could not hurt the ones that I loved, even though my penchant for blood appeared to be growing stronger and stronger with every passing day.

The only thing that I could gather from her comments was that her feelings about vampires and vânǎtors were based more on personal opinions than actual fact. But then again, what if I was wrong and she was right about everything? What if the bloodlust I would feel after turning was stronger than my willpower? What if I could not control my urges any more than I could control my temper?

I grabbed at my pillow and punched it hard. I didn't know. I had no one else to ask about such questions. My family wouldn't give me the answers. The worst part was that I had a sneaking suspicion I was never going to truly know who or what I was. At least not until after I had turned.

Scary thought.

I sighed deeply. I didn't even know if all the information I had absorbed over the years was true or completely bogus. I was so used to being treated like a mushroom— being fed shit and kept in the dark, that I tended to listen to everything that was said and push together the missing pieces myself until I came up with a plausible answer. This included everything that I believed to be true about vampires. What if all the information I had gathered about vampires in the last four years had somehow been falsely fed to me, forcing me to view my own species exactly as The Protectors had intended?

As enemies?

Did any of them truly care for me or was I simply an experiment that they had reared from birth and moulded into a soldier for their own causes? Whether by choice or not, vampires were a part of my past, present, and my future and I could not ignore what was a part of me, even if the IMI desired it.

So there was no need to keep bitching and moaning, and wondering about things that were beyond my control. I just had to accept that the past was unchangeable, the future was undetermined, and the present was a gift. Anguish, regret and self-pity were for people who couldn't move forward and change their own circumstances for the better. And I had decided a long time ago that I was not going to be one of those people.

I shook my head and wondered how many other sixteen year olds lie in bed at night and think about drinking blood, fighting werewolves, and contemplating the delicacy of the human soul. Not many I imagined.

Argh! When did the questions end and the answers begin?

I punched the pillow a few more times to help ease my frustrations, as well as iron out the lumps that had formed, before I rolled over onto my side to get some sleep.

Sleep didn't last long.

I awoke sometime in the middle of the night, sitting bolt upright in the bed and rubbing at my tired eyes, trying to figure out what had woken me.

I glanced around, my sleepy eyes zeroing in on the darkness outside of my window. Without thinking, my hand retrieved the blade that I kept hidden underneath my pillow at night. You never could be too careful.

I yanked it out, the tip of the knife tearing quite a large hole in the side of my fitted sheet.

I poked my finger in the hole and cursed.

Those were my best Egyptian cotton sheets!

I encircled the handle of the blade tightly with my fingers and quickly looked back at the window, at the view of the garden and beyond. There appeared to be nothing going on out there—just the sway of overgrown grass in the evening breeze, and the rustling of leaves in the trees. So what had woke me up?

Probably nothing.

Perhaps I'd just realised that I had algebra tomorrow morning and had given myself a mini-panic attack in my sleep.

If I didn't get back to sleep again soon, algebra class

wasn't going to be the only horrific thing that occurred at the IMI tomorrow. The walking dead would soon follow— namely me.

'Why don't you understand what I'm trying to show you?' Susan said in frustration.

I slammed the math book shut in front of me. 'Because I don't understand how the alphabet can be added together! What the hell is wrong with just sticking to numbers?'

'Because algebra requires using equations that involve both letters *and* numbers, Elena.'

I scowled. 'Who made this crap up anyway? Does anyone even use algebra?'

Lisa giggled beside me. Sure, it's extremely amusing to everyone *else* who can fathom why A equals B plus C.

Susan sat down on the chair beside me. Lucas and Karina smirked from behind their English books.

'Okay,' Susan said, tapping on my math book. 'Would it help you understand better if I changed the letters in the equation to something else?'

'Would that help me spell out an answer?'

Lisa collapsed into a fit of giggles.

'Susan!' a voice yelled behind us. 'Could you come with me, please?'

We all spun in our seats to look at George pacing frantically in front of the passage door.

What was going on?

'What's wrong?' Susan said, rising to her feet. They were my sentiments exactly.

He frowned and motioned with his hand to come. 'It's important.'

She started pacing towards him and all four of us rose to our feet to follow.

'No, kids,' George bellowed from across the room. 'Stay here and continue with your studies, please.'

The others sat straight back down. I remained standing as I watched Susan and George quickly whisper something to each other and then disappear from sight.

'Come on, guys, what are we waiting for?' I said, pointing over my shoulder at the library door.

'Elena, you heard what George said,' Lisa said quietly.

I snorted. 'It sounded like an invitation to me.'

All three of them rolled their eyes. 'And you wonder why you're always getting into trouble,' said Karina.

I sat down again. 'Aren't you all just a little bit curious as to what is going on right now? I mean, didn't you see the look on George's face? He looked … panicked.'

'All the more reason to stay put,' Karina chided.

I looked over to Lucas, who was glancing between me and the passage door. If anyone would be up for a little snooping it would be him. 'Come on Lucas—how about it? Would you come with me?'

He glanced at the door and then back at Karina, who was shaking her head from side to side. 'Yeah, alright. I'm in.'

I grinned at him and he smiled back.

'Lucas, you can't,' Karina pleaded. 'You'll get into trouble.'

'Not if we don't get caught,' I replied.

She rolled her eyes again. 'Elena, this may or may not come as a surprise to you, but you *always* get caught.'

I looked back at Lucas and frowned. 'Only because people can't keep their mouths shut.'

He shrugged.

Karina sniffed. 'Whatever. It's your skins.'

'I won't say anything,' Lisa piped in.

I smiled and tugged on a piece of her long red hair. 'Thanks, Lisa. I knew I could count on you.' I glared at Karina. She really was a goody two-shoes.

Lisa smiled back at me as both Lucas and I rose from our seats and made our way quickly to the end of the room, leaving the two party poopers behind to continue on with algebraic equations.

We stopped at the door and glanced up into the passage. No one was there. 'Hang on,' Lucas said, tugging at my shirt sleeve.

'What?' I said, slapping his hand away impatiently.

'I've got an idea.'

'What is it?'

'Just don't move okay? I've never tried this on a living thing before, so I'm not one hundred percent sure if it will work.'

'Lucas, what are you talking about?'

'I'm going to make us invisible.'

I backed away. 'Hang on a second. What if you turn my insides into my outsides?'

He grinned. 'I'll try really hard not to let that happen.'

I slapped him on the side of the head. 'It won't work anyway, you dumb ass. Protector's can see through the magic, remember?'

He smoothed his long blonde hair back into place and scowled at me. 'Okay, so I forgot. No need to slap me.'

'Well don't say stupid shit.'

I grabbed his hand before he tried to argue the point and dragged him behind me down the passageway. We stumbled up the stairs and hurried down the short passage. Both subsequent passages leading away from this intersection led to the training rooms, as well as the sleeping quarters.

This was where we knew that everyone must have gathered. If they weren't in the library, then the training rooms were the only option left.

Lucas suddenly slapped a hand across my chest and slammed me hard against the wall, all before I had a chance to protest. Apart from scaring the crap out of me, the air rushed out of my lungs from the impact. I gave him a filthy look as he clamped his hand over my mouth and mouthed the words 'shut up' to me. I would have decked him one if that wouldn't have given away our positions.

He pressed his back up against the wall and kept his hand clamped around my mouth. We heard Kim and Sarah stalking up the passageway that ran parallel to this one and talking rather loudly.

'I can't believe George just let them in here,' Kim whined. 'This is the IMI, not a bloody safe house for stray vampires.'

Lucas and I looked at each other, our eyes widening in excitement.

'I know,' Sarah answered. 'It's bad enough we have Elena running around the halls, let alone inviting more of her lot down here.'

Lucas pressed his hand tighter around my mouth and warned me with a look to keep my temper in check. He knew me well. I nodded.

'I don't care if they were hunting vânǎtors up the coast,' Sarah continued. 'This is our territory. If there are more of those creatures invading our state then it is our job to clear up the mess.'

'Quite right, Sarah. I know we have an alliance with these creatures, but I simply can't stand to be in the same room as them. I know this is a slight subject change, but would you care to join me for afternoon tea?'

'Where? In the library?'

Lucas and I shot each other a panicked look. No matter how quiet we were being, if they decided to turn down our passage and head for the library then we were about to be busted.

'No. How about we get out of here?' Kim answered. 'We'll go into town somewhere and far away from here, while it's being infected by those creatures.'

Sarah chuckled. 'This branch of the IMI has been infected for the last sixteen years.'

I gave Lucas a droll look. It looked like I was back to being painted as a disease again. Looks like I didn't push her quite hard enough from the grandstand.

'Quite right,' Kim answered, laughing in return. 'But that infection might turn out to be useful to us in the future.'

'Perhaps. But let's not discuss this here. We shall go and have ourselves some afternoon tea where we can complain until we are blue in the face.'

Their voices faded down the passage and then the sound of a wooden door closing drowned out the rest of their conversation.

Lucas lowered his hand from my mouth and then set his palm to my cheek in a reassuring gesture. He smiled dimly, brushing his thumb across my jaw, making sure I was okay.

'I'm okay,' I muttered. 'It's nothing I haven't heard Sarah say before.'

He smiled and dropped his hand from my face so that he could gather my hand in his warm one instead. 'Next time, you should just kick her fat ass her off the grandstand instead of pushing her.'

I frowned. 'She fell remember?'

'Ahh, yes,' Lucas said chuckling, 'she fell. How could I forget?'

I shrugged. 'It was karma.'

Lucas sniggered. 'No. It was the double F-cups and a little shove that did it, but who's keeping score?'

'You, apparently.'

'Oh come on, E, you have to admit, it was pretty bloody funny.'

I grinned and winked at him. 'I'm admitting to absolutely nothing.'

He laughed again and then cupped a hand over his mouth to quiet the sound. 'Come on. Let's go and find out what's going on.' He tightened his grip on my hand and then, at first hesitating, led me around the corner and down the first passageway, towards the first training room.

'I don't think they're in this training room, Lucas,' I whispered.

'What makes you say that?'

'I can't hear anything.'

'Maybe they're all dead.'

'That's not funny.'

'Okay, then they're in the other training room. Let's go.'

We took off back up the stairs and through the passage again, coming to the junction and heading left down the last remaining passage.

As we neared the bottom of the stairs the voices grew more distinct. We flattened our backs against the wall again and stayed at least a good couple of metres away from the doorway. From this angle we could see the wall of armoury but nothing of the grandstand—but if we could not see any of them, then they could not see either of us.

'Lovely to meet you, Susan,' a male voice with a familiar British cadence said politely. 'These are my travelling companions, Thomas and Marianne Woodland.'

'Brother and sister?' I heard Susan enquire.

'Yes. Twins, actually.'

There was a pause. 'My husband tells me that you have travelled here from London, is that correct?'

There was a silence which I assumed entailed either a nod or a shake of the head. 'I'm English, born and bred,' the strange voice answered. 'My companions and I have been living in London for the past three years. During that time we'd been tracking a rather large pack of vânǎtors. Between myself and Thomas, we have slowly whittled away their number from fifty to about five.'

'It took three years?' I heard Malcolm ask in disbelief.

There was a slight pause. 'Yes. They are getting a lot more intelligent as time goes by. They learn, and they remember where the dangerous areas are to avoid detection. Plus, London, as I'm sure you can understand, is a very heavily populated place and the Vânǎtors are exceptional at blending in.'

'I'm sorry,' Malcolm interrupted again. 'Did you just say that the Vânǎtors were getting smarter?' He chuckled quietly. 'They are *just* animals.'

Lucas and I looked at each other again excitedly and took a couple of steps further down the passage. It was obvious that beyond the doorway of this training room there were three bona fide vampires talking to the adults, and both Lucas and I were dying to get a look at them.

'Forgive me if I sound rude when I say this,' the stranger continued, 'but living in Australia you are not aware of how the European packs are starting to mobilise, changing territories to avoid detection. Their breeding process may have slowed down over the last few years, causing less concern for minority branches of the IMI like yourselves, but I myself have seen how clever they can be. They may just be animals as you say, but these animals have had over three hundred years to evolve, learn and hunt.'

'If that is true,' Vincent interrupted, 'then why are you here? If the problem in Europe is as bad as you say, then what has made you stray to sunny Australia?'

'Vânătors—the rest of the London pack, to be precise.'

'We took care of that problem,' George countered.

'Again, please do not take offence, but I'm afraid that can't be true.'

'What are you saying?' Susan asked defensively.

'Have you read the papers lately?'

'Of course.'

'Then you would have noticed that women are going missing from every major town the entire way up to Cairns.'

'There is no proof that it's werewolves,' George answered, slightly agitated.

'You are right,' the stranger answered, 'but we have an obligation to see this thing through. Our noses have led us to Cairns. There has to be a reason for that.'

'What obligation?'

'To kill the rest of the pack.'

'You say there are five remaining?' Vincent asked.

'We feel certain of it.' He paused. 'The pack that we had been hunting in London dispersed once it learned that we were killing them off one by one. We're pretty sure that an alpha is leading this pack, hence why they've been able to stay just out of our grasp for so long. We followed their scent to the docks in London, discovered they had hitched a ride on a cargo ship heading for Australia. We intercepted at least three different ships on the way here, worried that they had split up or fooled us with false directional scents.'

'Are you saying they laid a false trail for you to follow?' George asked.

'We're not one hundred percent certain about that, but we think so. We found the scented remains of the two dead vânătors you killed in Brisbane and then located another live one ourselves in Rockhampton that we took care of. But from there we've simply been following their numerous trails, trying to locate the Alpha, but all of them so far appear to be bogus.'

'I don't believe it,' Malcolm breathed. 'They're smart enough to lay false trails?'

'It's certainly starting to look that way, though it appears that they leave all of the decision making up to their pack leaders—the Alphas. Hence why we've managed to deplete their numbers and why you were able to capture and kill the two in Brisbane.'

'Well that's something, I suppose,' Susan countered. 'It would be horrifying to think that they were *all* capable of co-ordinating a decent defence. At the moment, the Vânătors we have encountered have all been relatively easy to subdue and defeat, but we've never been witness to the efficiency of an alpha before.'

Lucas looked at me excitedly. 'Can you believe this?' he whispered. 'We're actually only a couple of metres away from real, live vampires!'

I slapped him gently on the arm. 'I'm a vampire, remember?'

He frowned. 'You don't count. You're not even a proper one yet, anyway.'

'Hello,' a soft, melodic voice said from behind us.

We jumped in fright and then turned to stare in pure, unadulterated shock at one of the most beautiful women that either one of us had ever laid our eyes upon. She was the same height as me, but a slightly bigger build and a few more curves that filled out nicely in all the right places. Her hair was the colour of wheat and was styled into a short collection of ringlets that fell just above her shoulders, almost like Shirley Temple. Her eyes were the colour of sapphires, deep, dark pools of navy blue that were both frightening and enticing all at the same time. Her skin reminded me of fine porcelain that was both fragile and beautiful, despite her pale pallor and the almost translucent appearance of her soft, smooth flesh.

Forcing us backwards, she stepped in front of us in one quick movement that neither of us anticipated until it happened, and then smiled cheekily as if she knew that her movements were making us uncomfortable.

We followed her carefully with our eyes, both of us a little too awed and too scared to even return her greeting.

She smiled at the both of us, purposely flashing a set of pointed white canines our way before darting back into the training room.

'Did you see that?' Lucas whispered. 'That was a Vampire.'

I nodded, still unable to formulate words. I had just had a preview of what I was going to become, and so far, I liked what I saw. Sure, I wasn't a fan of the pasty white skin, but the rest of her physical presence was mysteriously enticing.

'It might interest you all to know that you have two spectators standing in the corridor,' she said merrily to the group, as she looked back at us and winked.

Lucas and I both flinched again at the sight of her flashing teeth, and shrunk backwards towards the stairs before the screaming and shouting could begin. It would only be a matter of seconds before our parents busted us.

Oops—too late.

George popped his head around the corner in an instant, his hands automatically at his hips and his brows furrowing in ire. 'Didn't you two hear me when I said stay in the library?'

We both stuttered, searching our addled brains for a genuinely good answer. We didn't have one. We were both still grappling for a view of the other two vampires while at the same time trying to make our feet move backwards. The task was not simple.

George stalked forward into the passage like an angry bear. We tripped over our feet trying to get away from him and ended up falling in a pile against the bottom of the stairs. He grabbed both of us by the scruff of our necks and began dragging us upwards and back towards the library with considerable force.

I turned my head awkwardly around in his grip and looked back towards the training room so that I could get one last glimpse of the vampires. To my surprise, I ended up getting more of an eyeful than I had intended, because there, standing near the open door way, was William Granville. 'You!' I shouted in surprise while stumbling along in George's grip. 'I had a feeling you were a vampire!'

He smiled at me, revealing a set of perfect white teeth along with a conspicuous set of long sharp canines.

Cool.

George halted abruptly in his tracks, swivelled my head back around in his grip to face him and narrow his eyes at me. 'You've met this man before?'

Uh-oh.

I nodded slowly and took the opportunity to shake free from his grip on my neck. My affirmation seemed to send him into some kind of vein-popping, blood pressure inducing all out Elena inspired rage, destined to bring about a meltdown. I was going to have to choose my words very carefully if I didn't want George to break me or the vampire standing only a short distance away.

As he continued to stare at me, bug-eyed and confused,

I took a tentative step back towards the training room and towards the vampires to get a closer look.

He snapped out of his reverie almost immediately, stepping in front of me and effectively blocking my view of William and his companions. I tried to sidestep him, but he shadowed my every move. Why was he trying so hard to keep us apart?

'When did you meet?' George asked me, gripping my chin in his hand to hold my face steady, even with his.

I tried to look away, but he held on tightly, squeezing my jaw painfully between his fingers. I swallowed. 'I met him at the rave.'

He turned around to look at William and then slapped Lucas in the side of the head when he realised that he too was trying to head back to the training room for a closer look.

Lucas rubbed the side of his head, giving George a filthy look, but he said nothing and went no further down the passage.

'Did he hurt you?' George continued.

I only vaguely heard the question, as I suddenly became aware of William's smell, his essence of sandalwood and spice teasing at the corners of my nose. All I wanted to do at that moment was drink in the sight of him. I didn't care if I had spectators. It was the same strange sensation that had enveloped me at the rave.

I stretched up onto my tippy-toes so that I could see over George's shoulder, but all I got was a clip under the ear for my trouble and a rough shake of the shoulders.

'Answer me, Elena. Did he hurt you?' he said, sounding more desperate than angry.

I shook my head from side to side, trying to free my mind from the scent. 'No,' I said pulling a face, and remembering the vice like grip that William had placed on my wrist as I had tried to leave. 'Why would he want to hurt me? I'm going to be a vampire too, remember?'

He clamped his hand down hard over the top of my mouth, crushing my lips beneath his fingers as I looked back up at him in surprise. 'Hush now, Elena,' he continued quickly. 'You've said more than enough foolishness for one day.'

My eyes widened. Why would they be keeping my Vampirism a secret from others of my own kind?

I looked over at Lucas who also appeared slightly confused. He shrugged his shoulders as if to say, *Like I know what he means*.

George spun me around on the spot, keeping his hand clamped tightly around my mouth and tucking me under the crook of his arm so that I couldn't turn back around again, couldn't get away. I thought about biting down on his fingers, but then I thought better of it once he grabbed Lucas just as roughly. He held him around the neck and pushed him down the passage ahead of us. Lucas and I kept silent.

I tried to turn around to get another look, but George had me tucked so tightly underneath the crook of his arm that all I could do was stumble forward and up the stairs. He hung onto me like that all the way back to the library.

He suddenly released me and pushed the both of us inside the room. We staggered forward and came to a stop against the back of a sofa.

Karina and Lisa looked up from their studies, concerned, watching as George stepped into the room. He blocked the exit door, raising his hand in front of him in a threatening gesture. '*Levitartium!*' he bellowed, pointing his hand directly at me and Lucas.

In an instant our feet left the ground and we were both floating up, higher and higher, until our bodies were easily a good couple of metres above the floor, almost to the point where we could touch the ceiling if we stretched our arms above our heads.

'There,' George said, more calmly now. 'That ought to hold you until we are finished.'

'What!' I shrieked, cringing.

Note to self—do not shriek, you sound like a banshee.

I lowered my voice to a more acceptable level. 'Are you just going to leave us here, in midair, after what just happened?'

He nodded, his eyes narrowing. 'That's exactly what I'm going to do.' Without waiting for a reply, he spun on his heels and left the library.

I crossed my arms in front of my chest and looked over at Lucas. 'This is just brilliant.'

He looked uncomfortably at the ground, before looking back at me and shrugging. 'Hey, it's not my fault.'

'I didn't say it was. Don't you know a spell or something that could get us down from here?'

He shook his head. 'I only just started learning the practical application of magic. I've only been doing theory the past five years.'

I looked over to Karina. 'Do you?'

She held up her hands in surrender and grinned. 'Don't ask me. I told you both not to go snooping. I said you'd get caught.'

I snorted. 'We only got caught because a vampire heard us.'

She blinked in disbelief. 'There's a vampire inside the IMI?'

'Three, actually,' Lucas said, all smugness. 'You'd know

that if you guys hadn't been such pussies, and had come and had a look with us.'

I smiled inwardly at my brother's new found bravado.

'I'm sorry,' she retorted, 'but look who's suspended in midair right now?'

I looked at Lucas again and rolled my eyes. If she hadn't been Malcolm's daughter I would have flushed her head down a toilet by now. She was too self righteous for her own good.

'I can't believe you already know one of them,' he said, grinning. 'Why didn't you tell me you'd met a vampire?'

'I didn't really know that I had until just then. I mean, I suspected he was different, but I couldn't know for sure.'

'How did you meet him?'

'Like I said to George, we met at the rave. He was watching me dance.' I frowned. 'At least, I think he was watching me dance.'

'That's right,' Karina muttered sarcastically, 'because everything's about Elena.'

I pointed my thumb at Karina. 'What's her problem?'

'She's just jealous that all the interesting stuff happens to you.'

I looked down and saw Karina shaking her head as she immersed herself in her studies. 'Anyway,' I said, enunciating each syllable for her benefit. 'When he looked at me I started to get this weird feeling, like I had no control over my body, that he was somehow calling me with his eyes and with his mind. His scent washed over me—it was cloying, but sweet. I think he might have been trying it again just before George started questioning me. All I could smell was him and all I wanted to do was look him in the eyes. The lack of control was … weird.'

'I've heard about that,' Lucas said, nodding. 'Peter told

me that vampires can hypnotise their prey. They have the ability to completely incapacitate their intended victims with scent alone. Apparently it's supposed to seduce your senses, lull you into submission, and then wrap you up in a wave of pleasure that's impossible to resist.' He looked at me sideways, grinning like the Cheshire Cat. 'Were *you* wrapped in a wave of pleasure, Elena?'

If I could have reached out and slapped him I would have. 'No, not really,' I lied. 'It was just weird, like every part of me wanted to lose control and surrender. The only reason I didn't was because I figured out what I was feeling wasn't normal, and bailed him up on it.'

'Do you think he wanted to bite you?'

I shrugged. 'I don't know.'

'I wonder what would happen to you if he did.'

'Nothing, probably.'

He pursed his lips, sucking a corner into his mouth thoughtfully. 'Maybe. I wish we knew more about them. The IMI isn't very forthcoming with information, are they?'

I shook my head. 'Speaking of information, before I pushed Sarah from the grandstand yesterday she said some strange things to me. This encounter with the vampires has brought some of those things back to the surface. Did you hear anything before she fell?'

'Oh, so you are admitting that you pushed her?'

I frowned at him. 'Trust you to hear only my admission of guilt in that sentence.'

'It's just so rare.'

I gave him a stony look.

He grinned. 'Okay, okay. I heard her say that you were a sinner and a disease all that kind of nasty stuff too.'

I shook my head again, looking down at Karina and Lisa

again, and lowering my voice so they wouldn't hear us. 'No, before that.'

He scratched at his chin and then sniffed. 'Sorry, I don't remember.'

'She asked me how I was taking the new information. The new information I'd learned about my blood lines.'

'What new information?'

'Exactly.'

He looked as confused as I felt. 'Do you think there's something mum and dad aren't telling you?'

'Oh my God! You don't know? Shit, I forgot I'd been sour at you for the last two days. Before I went to the rave on Saturday night, Susan and George had a secret conversation in the back garden. They kept talking about telling me the truth and keeping me away from people who would reveal the things I needed to know. It was a little hard to understand, but the gist of the conversation? Susan and George know more about who I am than what they are willing to let on.'

'And you think Sarah knows something about this too?'

I nodded. 'The whole IMI probably knows more about me than they let on. At least Susan promised to tell me what I needed to know as soon as I could stop clowning around and act like an adult.'

'Not much chance of that happening.'

'I know, but I'm trying.'

He snorted his disbelief and then quickly changed the subject. 'You know, all this must have something to do with those vampires. It seems a little coincidental for them to show up now after everything you've been hearing.'

I looked at him, more into this line of conversation. 'I was leaning towards it.'

'Well, I think dad's actions pretty much confirm it.'

'You're right, it's just that I was so caught up in William's scent that I didn't even really make the connection. I mean, I thought it was weird, but you are definitely right. It must have something to do with those vampires, or maybe there is something about me that they don't want the Vampires to know—something more than just my vampirism?'

'Of course I'm right,' he answered smugly. 'I'm very smart, you know.'

I ignored him. I was too focused on making a connection between the Vampires' appearance and Susan and George's late night interlude in the garden. 'What should I do?'

He shrugged. 'What can you do? You're suspended in midair right now. You're not going anywhere.'

'You're right.'

'Wow, I've been right twice in one day.'

'I know—it's a miracle.'

George and Susan stepped back into the room. Susan looked worried. George just looked angry. 'What do you think you two are playing at?' George boomed angrily up at us. 'When I said stay in the library I bloody well meant it!' He looked over at Lisa and Karina, sitting meekly at the oak timber table, pretending not to listen. 'You two can gather your books and head to the training rooms.'

They both obediently gathered their things and headed quickly out of the library without saying a word. I didn't miss the look of satisfaction that was plastered all over Karina's face as she left the room.

Lucas and I remained floating above the floor like idiots in space. We were doomed to endure another lecture before we touched down again. Like it or not, we were going to have to watch as George puffed his chest, clenched his fists, and went beetroot red as we listened to another sermon.

Susan coughed nervously and crossed her arms in front of her chest.

'Now, how much of our conversation did you actually hear?' George asked, calmer than before.

Was that a trick question?

'All of it,' Lucas answered.

I frowned at him.

Way to play the bluff big brother.

'I see,' George answered and looked to Susan. 'How should we proceed?'

'I have an idea,' I said quietly, the two of them looking directly up at me. 'How about you tell us why vampires have come inside the IMI and why you didn't tell us about it. Then we can skip to the part where you tell us everything that the IMI has been keeping from me, including why you are trying to keep us away from the Vampires. We also want to know all about what you were discussing in the garden the other night and why Sarah seems to think we should have had a little conversation about my blood lines—oh, and the fact that she described me as a "half-breed".' I paused. 'It seems like a good place to start.'

Susan and George exchanged a look.

'Yeah,' Lucas countered. 'And while you're at it, I want McDonalds for dinner.'

We all turned slowly and deliberately to look at him, frowning.

'What?' he said shrugging, 'I'm hungry.'

George grunted. 'We do have more important matters to attend to right now other than your stomach, Lucas.'

'What could be more important than not letting your child starve?'

I hissed at him and he frowned. 'I think there is nothing more important right now than explaining what the hell is going on here,' I said. 'You know I'm never going to let this go, so you might as well come out with it. And if you don't start talking, Lucas is going to get hungrier and then we all have to suffer the consequences.'

'We don't have time to satisfy your teenage curiosities right now—there are other women's lives that are at risk,' George growled. 'We need to do what we can to help the Vampires track the remaining pack members and kill them before we have a new den on our hands.'

'And that can't wait until tomorrow?' Lucas commented. 'No offence, but I don't think the Vampires really need our help. They're probably here more out of courtesy than necessity. It sounded to me like we are pretty damn useless in comparison to them, with their keen noses.'

Our parents glanced carefully at us, neither one speaking.

'Come on,' I said, more urgently this time. 'I can't be patient anymore, not now that I know there are so many truths to be uncovered. And I definitely can't keep pretending to be an adult. I really suck at it.' I paused, hoping for a new wave of confidence, because what I was about to say next was probably crossing the line. 'But with that being said,' I continued, 'I'm sixteen, not too far off my seventeenth birthday, and I'm more than capable of taking care of myself, even should you decide that the information that I need isn't worth me living under your roof anymore.'

The look on Susan's face was something I wish I could forget. Her puppy dog eyes were starting to eat away at my conscience.

'Are you threatening us, Elena?' Susan said, steely determination in her voice.

I swallowed. 'No, it's not a threat, but a promise. You

both tell me everything or I walk. No more secrets. I have a right to know what you're keeping from me.'

Susan turned and whispered something quietly in George's ear. He said something back to her and she nodded. 'What if you don't like what we have to tell you? We can't take it back once it's out in the open.'

I could see a small spark of fear in her eyes, but I remained undeterred. I tried lightening the mood by smiling and shrugging my shoulders nonchalantly. 'Please,' I said sounding offhand, 'if I can get through my twelfth birthday after hearing, *P.S you're going to be a Vampire—* how much worse can it be than that?'

A knowing look passed between them.

Uh-oh. That bad, huh?

CHAPTER EIGHT: EXPLANATIONS

With our feet back on solid ground where they belonged, Susan and George had agreed to have the discussion that they said would change my life. Neither one of them looked too pleased about being bullied, but at the same time I sensed a tremor of relief in the air. Their burden, the carrying of this secret for so many years, was finally going to be alleviated.

Lucas and I sat relatively patiently on the sofa next to each other, neither one speaking. Susan sat directly opposite and surveyed us both. She was edgy, nervous. Her fingers twisted into knots in her lap as we anxiously waited for George to return to the library.

George had headed back to the training rooms, presumably to see the vampires out and explain to Martha, Vincent, and Malcolm just exactly what was going to happen in the library. He also wanted to keep Karina and Lisa at a distance from the proceedings. Even Lucas had been told to leave, but I had emphatically insisted that he stay. He may irritate me constantly, but there had never really been any secrets between us. He was the one person on the entire planet that I actually trusted, probably with my life.

I chewed incessantly at one of my fingernails, tapping my foot upon the carpet as I waited. More than anything, I wanted to run down the passages and straight back to

William. His scent was still resonating within me and it took all of my willpower to keep myself seated on the chair.

George stepped back into the room and we all looked up. Susan looked relieved. Lucas was rubbing a hand across his stomach, annoyed that he hadn't received a Big Mac yet. I immediately dropped the tatty and chewed fingernail from my mouth. My bouncing foot stilled.

He sat down next to Susan and wrapped an arm around her shoulder, placing a tender kiss on her cheek. She looked up at him and smiled half-heartedly, patting the edge of his knee with her hand.

He turned to look directly at me, removing his arm from around Susan's shoulder and sitting forward on the sofa. 'Elena, I'm not exactly sure where to begin,' he said anxiously, rubbing his hands and keeping his eyes lowered to the floor. I wanted to say something smart like, *Try at the beginning*, but I couldn't muster the enthusiasm for it right now.

'What about the vampires?' Lucas said, setting the wheels in motion. 'We both heard why they are here in Cairns, but dad, why did you freak out when Elena said that she had met that English vamp before? What was his name? William?'

'I didn't freak out,' George said slowly. 'I was merely trying to protect her.'

'No, you freaked out and I think even the vampires noticed. William gave both you and Elena very funny looks.'

George frowned at him.

'What were you trying to protect me from? That's what I don't understand,' I piped in. 'William is a vampire and I will be too in about a year and a half from now.'

'That is *mostly* true.'

I shook my head. 'You're not making any sense, George. You told me four years ago that I was going to be a vampire—that I was born one. If that's still true and you didn't lie, then why do you need to protect me from people of my own kind?'

'You were born a vampire, Elena—nothing changes that fact—but it's not your vampirism that I worry about them detecting.'

My brow wrinkled in confusion. 'Well then forgive me for sounding slow, but I really don't understand what it is you're trying to tell me.'

'I know that you have questions, Elena, and I will answer them for you. But first, I need you to answer a couple of our questions. There are worries that we have and your answers might put our minds at rest, help us to better understand where it is that we all currently stand.'

He paused and ran his fingers through his short blonde hair.

'You see the minute that you said that you and the coven leader William Granville had met, I have not been able to stop worrying if their appearance at the IMI does not have more to do with you than hunting vânătors. As your brother so brazenly pointed out earlier, they certainly do not require our services in that regard.'

'But how can that be possible?' Lucas interrupted. 'Elena said she only met them at the rave on Saturday night.' He turned to look at me. 'Did you mention The Protectors at all?'

I shook my head. 'Why would I do that with a complete stranger? I know not to.'

'See, that's a no,' Lucas continued. 'So they wouldn't have known to find her here. So they obviously didn't come here specifically for Elena.' He looked at me and held up his hands. 'No offence.'

I shrugged. The thought hadn't even crossed my mind.

'So if they didn't come for her, then why else would they have come to Cairns, if not to follow a trail that the Vânătors have left?'

'We don't doubt that they were following a trail Lucas,' Susan replied. 'We were just concerned that, because we had not detected any vânător presence in Cairns ourselves, that the Vampires might have lingered in the area for another reason. It would not be difficult for William to have followed us home the other night or keep an eye on her movements if Elena had piqued his curiosity.'

I thought back to last night when I had woken up with a strange sense of unease. Was it possible that he had been watching me since the rave? Wouldn't I have detected his scent if he got close to me?

'Can a vampire come into someone's house uninvited? Or is it like the movies where they must be invited past the threshold before they are permitted entry?' I asked.

Susan blinked. 'No, they can come and go as they please.' Her eyes narrowed and her brow furrowed deeply. 'Why do you ask?'

Shit.

I shrugged. 'Just curious, I suppose.'

She seemed unconvinced by my answer, but let the matter drop. That was probably a good thing. I was far too busy trying to hide my sudden discomfort—I always kept my window open. If it was true that he followed us home the other night, then I had basically just laid out the welcome mat for him.

However interested in William Granville and his companions I may be, I wasn't into having my neck chewed out for a night time snack.

George cleared his throat, dragging my attention back his way. He seemed uncomfortable, his eyes still pinned to the floor and his hands writhing around in his lap. 'When you first met William,' he said, raking a nervous hand through his hair, 'did you touch or get close to one another in any way?'

I frowned, not entirely sure why he was asking. 'Not on purpose.'

'So, you did have contact?'

'Well, he touched me here and here,' I said, pointing to my cheek and wrist, remembering him brushing the lock of hair away from my face and capturing my wrist. 'And I also remember touching him here with my knife.' I pointed to my crotch. 'Does that count?'

Lucas choked out a laugh beside me.

'You didn't let him kiss you?' George slowly continued.

I blinked. 'I'm sorry. Do I have "Try me, I'm delicious" stamped on my forehead or something?'

Susan went red. George looked away. Lucas, ever tactful, let rip with the full extent of his laughter.

'Look, the guy was watching me for a while, nothing I couldn't handle. Then we ran into each other a little later on. He brushed a lock of hair out of my eyes, stepped a little too close to me and I threatened the fate of his manhood with my knife. After that we kind of parted ways, if you know what I mean.'

'So he didn't do anything to you at all?'

Lucas gave me a sideways look, which I ignored.

'No,' I hesitated. 'Well, not exactly.'

'Explain.' George urged, his face grim.

'It was nothing really. At the time I was confused, but now that I know for certain he is a vampire, it all makes a bit more sense.'

'What makes sense?' Susan asked.

'Well, why he looks like he stepped off the pages of a

Menswear catalogue, why his skin is as hard as rock and feels like he'd just ran naked through a snow storm. Not to mention the fact that I could smell his scent all around me.'

Susan and George exchanged another look. 'You could smell him?'

I nodded. 'His scent was everywhere. Sandalwood and spices. Very nice actually.'

'And how did that make you feel?'

I looked over to Lucas again who was grinning at me like an idiot, wiggling his eyebrows up and down suggestively.

I shrugged and looked away. 'I don't know. Good, I guess.'

George looked at Susan. 'He was using his innate ability of compulsion to entice her,' he muttered.

'Sounds like it,' she breathed.

'You know what that means, don't you?' he said to Susan, ignoring us for the moment.

Susan nodded.

George glanced back at me, all seriousness. 'There are only two reasons that we know of why a vampire would use their scent to entice someone. The first reason is because they desire to feed, or make a kill. The second is to lure them close enough to force them to submit, to be completely vulnerable to whatever physical encounter they wish to pursue. I hate to say it, Elena, but I do not trust William Granville. If he used his compulsion on you then I feel certain it was because he wanted to have more than a little chat with you.'

I frowned. 'William was strange, I'll admit that, but I never felt like I was in any danger. If anything he just seemed curious about me. When I asked him to stop the compulsion thing, he did. He was more interested in knowing how I'd realised he was doing something to me in the first place.'

'So maybe he doesn't know yet,' Susan murmured. George patted her shoulder gently. 'Then we were right to keep them apart.'

'Hello, I'm still here! You know, neither of you have explained anything to me yet. Tell me why you needed to keep me away from William Granville?'

'Because of your blood, Elena,' George answered.

'My blood?'

'Precisely.'

I looked at Lucas, who appeared just as confused as I was. 'Is it just me, or are we back at square one again? I don't have any idea whatsoever what you're talking about.'

George exhaled noisily and then clasped his hands together in front of him again. 'Your blood is unique, Elena, in more ways than one.'

'Well I'm so glad we cleared that up,' I said, frowning again.

'Can you put a muzzle on your smart mouth for five minutes while I endeavour to explain?'

'I don't know, dad,' Lucas countered, leaning back into the sofa. 'That's a pretty big ask. Smart mouth DNA might be part of her unique blood.'

That certainly would explain a few things.

Both George and Susan ignored the jibe and glanced back at me. 'Before we begin, Elena, we just need you to know that no matter what happens we will stand by you, as long as we have a choice.'

I screwed my face up in confusion. What did he mean?

'I'm going to start right back at your birth, Elena. Perhaps once you understand who you are, then you will understand why we were trying to protect you not only from William, but any vampire.'

'Okay,' I answered reluctantly.

'What about me?' Lucas piped in. 'Can I still talk to vam-pires?'

Susan and George both looked at Lucas in surprise.

'What? I find them fascinating—scary as hell, of course, but fascinating nevertheless.'

Susan just kept looking at him blankly, occasionally blinking. George just gave him an odd sort of look that I could only describe as something that resembled disgust or disappointment. He wasn't impressed by his son's enthusi-asm to understand creatures that had been known enemies of The Protectors for centuries.

Lucas didn't take their silence well. He unknotted his fingers from behind his head and slumped down further on the sofa, folding his arms across his chest and staring moodily at the coffee table.

Lucas started to open his mouth, but I had a feeling he was about to say something he might regret later so I inter-rupted him. 'Please, George, tell me the story.'

'Okay, but some of this may come as a shock to you, Elena. We always told you that we were unfamiliar with the details of your birth. But here it is.' He paused, raking his hand through his hair. 'You were born in Corsica, a small French island located just off the coast of Italy.'

I blinked a couple of times. 'Corsica? Seriously?'

He nodded.

'So, given that I'm technically a French citizen, what am I doing halfway across the world?'

'It's a little complicated.'

'Well uncomplicate it. Explain to me how I ended up with you and under the care of the Institute of Magical Intervention.'

'When you were born,' he began, 'various Protectors from the IMI were present at your birth. This isn't a regular occurrence, us gathering for the birth of a vampire, but you were an extenuating circumstance. There was something very different about you.'

'And how did you know that?'

'Because, while an ordinary human child or even a vampiric child would have died from the injuries sustained to your mother, you still lived, despite the fact that it should not have been possible. That is why, at the time, the IMI seriously debated whether to let you live.'

He paused and glanced right at me, his powder blue eyes crinkling in recognition of the memory. 'As you can imagine, it was a difficult decision given that you would one day grow to be our natural enemy. But, of course, given your current state of well being, I should think it is obvious what our decision was in the end. Truly, though, we had no real choice in the matter.'

'What do you mean you had no real choice? Did my mother or father stop you? Is that why I was allowed to live?'

He shook his head. 'No. The IMI couldn't kill you, because despite what you are, you were the most beautiful, innocent looking child that we had ever laid our eyes upon.'

I wrinkled my nose in disgust. 'So ... if I were an ugly baby I would have been a goner?'

He laughed. 'It wasn't like that at all,' he said, shaking his head with amusement. 'Yes, your beauty was beyond that of any other child, but there was something in your eyes that spoke to us of innocence and fragility. But that was not the only thing that stopped your execution. Someone or something was watching over you, protecting you from harm.'

'What like a guardian angel or something?' I said, barely disguising my scepticism.

What a load of rubbish.

George shrugged. 'I honestly don't know. All who were present attested to seeing a white light form around you right after you were born. You remained completely untouchable during incubation and after your birth. It wasn't until The Protectors present decided, in conjunction with the IMI, not to try and cause you harm that you were released from that protective light.'

I snorted. 'That sounds crazy. Who or what would be protecting me?'

'I don't have an explanation for you, Elena. It could have been a higher being, or it simply could have been some hidden talent of your own.'

'Were you there when I was born?'

'No. Your mother and I were contacted by the IMI a few hours after and asked if we would consider taking you into our home. You see, one of the head researchers in Bucharest is a close personal friend of Susan's, and he insisted that the anonymity and seclusion of our home in Cairns would be better than keeping you at headquarters.'

'And you agreed?'

He cringed. 'Honestly, at first we were less than thrilled by the prospect. Lucas was barely a year old and we didn't feel comfortable allowing a vampiric child into our home.'

'So what made you change your mind?'

'You did,' he replied without hesitation. 'After the phone call from headquarters, I immediately hopped on a plane to Corsica with Vincent. We needed him to fabricate documentation that would allow you back into Australia. We had not made the decision whether or not we would adopt you yet, but we still had to at least go through the motions for the sake of our positions with the IMI. I know that sounds terrible,' he said, looking at me apologetically, 'but until we met you for ourselves, we just didn't know.'

He paused again, looking to Susan for reassurances. She urged him to continue.

'But when I saw you for the first time, I couldn't look away. You were so beautiful, Elena—you still are, even more so than a regular girl of your age—but there was more to you than that. When I looked into your eyes for the first time, I knew then and there that I had to take you home with us. I knew that you would be a part of my family no matter what because we all need you.'

'Need me?' I repeated with suspicion. 'Why the present tense all of a sudden?'

He shook his head, eyes suddenly wary and fingers twitchy.

'Umm, yes,' he reconsidered. 'We need you as a part of our family.'

The warning look Susan gave him meant he'd probably just lied. I thought about pursuing it, but decided there would be no point. If he was lying about the original intentions for taking me in, then he wasn't about to come clean now.

I looked at Susan, shifting the subject slightly. 'Did you feel the same way about taking me in?'

Her tension eased and she smiled, shifting her gaze over to Lucas briefly before meeting my eyes again. They lacked the warmth they'd contained only seconds previously when looking at Lucas. 'Having you as a member of our family is for the greater good.'

My eyes narrowed at the slightly mechanical response—again with the present tense, as if I still had some vital role to play.

She laughed lightly and glanced at Lucas again. He was

still staring moodily at the coffee table and kicking the wooden legs with his feet, but there was no denying the chill that swept across her face when she focused back on me again.

'And Lucas,' she continued, looking back at him again with what appeared to be a flicker of disappointment, 'he loved you from the moment he met you. He followed you around everywhere, from the time you could crawl until the time you could run. He shared all of his toys with you and never let you out of his sight. If you hurt yourself, cried, or were upset because we had growled at you, he would always be right beside you, defending you.'

I looked at Lucas with new eyes. His face was now flushed, completely red with embarrassment.

I didn't let my gaze linger upon him because the attention was obviously embarrassing him. Instead, I promised myself that I would lighten up on him a little bit, and maybe try to stop calling him a dumb ass all of the time.

Suddenly realisation dawned. Some very vital information was being left out of the puzzle. 'Okay hang on a second,' I said, my attention directed at George, holding my hands up in front of me. 'We need to back up a little bit. You both at, one time or another, have told me that my mother died in a car crash shortly after I was born. If that was true, then why were there Protectors present at my birth? And why were you receiving phone calls from the IMI only hours after I was born? I'm fairly certain that, just after giving birth, my mother would not have gotten into the car and popped down to the shops for some groceries while she left me in the care of Protectors. My mother didn't die in a car accident at all, did she?'

'No.'

'Then I have to ask—is she actually dead? Or did the IMI

just decide that they knew what was best for everyone and fabricate a story for their own benefit?'

Susan shook her head sadly. 'No, Elena, I'm afraid that your mother did in actual fact pass away. But you are correct. She did not die in a car accident. She died from severe blood loss. She was attacked by a vânător.'

'So why lie about it? I would have understood.'

She tapped a fingernail against her teeth and looked over at George again. 'I'm not sure how to answer that.'

George stepped in. 'You were seven years old when you first realised that you were not a true Manory. You took one look at yourself in the mirror and then another at the rest of us and then cleverly pieced it together yourself. This was on top of the fact that every time you hurt yourself you'd self-heal. Your powers of regeneration were certainly getting difficult to explain away.' He sighed. 'It was at that time we decided to explain the details of our adoptive arrangement to you, which you accepted rather easily. It didn't seem to bother you that we weren't actually your parents. It was almost as if you already somehow knew the truth and that you had just been waiting for someone to give you the details.' He shook his head. 'Your only request was to know where your mother and father were. How were we supposed to explain to you that your mother was murdered by a hungry werewolf and your father was a fly by night vampire? Certainly not at such a young age.'

Point taken.

'What about my father? Do you know where he is?' I continued.

'No,' George answered quickly. 'No one knows who your father is, Elena. Your mother never mentioned him to anyone on the Island before she died. She was a very private person, according to the records.'

'You have records about this?'

'Of course we do. We have to keep records for future generations of Protectors.'

'I want to see them.'

'That's not possible, Elena,' George murmured. 'We aren't even supposed to be revealing any of this to you. You weren't supposed to know that you were going to become a vampire, but your incessant questions regarding the taste of blood and your macabre desire to see how many times you could injure yourself before you didn't heal again changed all that. That's when we integrated you into the IMI and told you that you were going to be a vampire. For some strange reason you've always known that you were different and very accepting of that fact, but that didn't make you ready to hear the truth. But you're too damn inquisitive for your own good.'

'Oh, I'm sorry,' I said angrily, a hint of sarcasm marring my voice. 'Forgive me for wanting to know my past, and who I am. I'm terribly sorry if I've disrupted any plans that you and the IMI had worked out for me.'

George bowed his head. Susan leaned back in the chair and closed her eyes. 'I'm sorry, Elena,' he started. 'That was not how I intended for that to sound. I simply meant that your curiosity and desire to defy seems to be what lands you in trouble.'

I didn't answer. I didn't have anything particularly pleasant to say.

'So why you?' Lucas mumbled, finally looking up from the table, glancing at our parents. 'I mean, out of all of The Protectors, why send Elena to Cairns? Why didn't they send her to Bucharest, which is nearer, to train and live at headquarters?'

They suddenly both looked uncomfortable. 'Elena was

sent to live with us because it was as far away from Europe as possible. Headquarters knew that we already lived here with a few other Protectors, so it seemed like the most logical choice to place her. Australia has always remained fairly absent from the intrusion of both vampires and werewolves, being so isolated.' He coughed and looked into Susan's eyes.

'But why did the IMI need to do that?' Lucas continued. 'Elena's going to be a vampire. Protecting her from vânători I understand, but other vampires? That doesn't make any sense to me.'

'Because none of us had a clue as to how either species was going to react to her.'

'Why should that matter?' I asked, still a little irritated.

'Because what is in your blood could change everything.' He glanced over at Lucas and then looked back at me.

I suddenly had the feeling we were having two conversations—the one that we were saying out loud and the one that Susan and George were having inside their heads. And the way that they kept looking between Lucas and me was odd.

'What is it that's in my blood?'

Another emotionally charged look passed between Susan and George.

'Oh come on, you've come this far. Just spit it out.'

Lucas gave me a sideways look and touched his fingers to the top of my hand. He squeezed gently. His gesture was heartfelt and reassuring, and I found myself warmed emotionally by his desire to comfort me. I became aware that, suddenly, I was calming down, my anger and frustration for our parent's distinct equivocation ebbing away.

George cleared his throat, reclined backwards into the sofa and placed both hands stiffly on top of his knees.

'Perhaps I need to start the explanation back at the beginning. It may help you to understand why you are so unique.'

'I'm ready when you are, George.'

He frowned at my tone, but continued nevertheless. 'To be truthful, we do not know too much about your mother. According to the records, she showed up one day on the Island, looking for lodgings. She was at least six months pregnant and looked in relatively poor condition. Her clothes were tattered and carried nothing on her except the clothes on her back and a small wad of cash. Now, on Corsica there is no branch of the IMI but there were still three Protectors living there. One of them ran an estate agency, took pity on her plight and offered to lease his converted garage in exchange for her helping to clean some of the vacated rental properties. Just as she did not know that Olivier was a Protector, Olivier did not know that she was pregnant with a vampiric child. It was purely by coincidence that your mother and The Protectors crossed paths. According to the records, she was extremely diligent with her work, pleasant enough to get along with, but never went out of her way to speak to anyone or make friends. She was quiet, reserved and preferred to keep to herself. The only thing that anyone knew about her was her name … Elena. We just thought it would be nice to honour her memory in some way given what she went through—'

'What do you mean what she went through?' I asked. 'Are you referring to her being attacked, her pregnancy with me, or whatever relationship she must have had with my father?'

'The night that your mother was killed,' George continued, ignoring me, 'a Vânător had snuck its way onto the island. He'd seen your mother walking alone on a path near the ocean, out for an evening stroll, and chose that moment to attack her. Olivier, The Protector who had housed your mother, could hear her screams coming from the pathway near his home and went to investigate. He saw your mother being viciously clawed at and drained of blood by the Vânător. He took immediate action, hurtling the Hevannatara curse at the beast. It dropped to the ground like a stone, trapping your blood deficient mother underneath him. Olivier stabbed at the beast until he knew it to be dead. When the beast no longer grunted, no longer breathed, Olivier rolled the Vânător away. He quickly pushed the carcass into the ocean below and then began to tend to Elena.'

'So she was still alive at this stage?'

He nodded. 'Yes, but there was blood everywhere and Olivier had no idea if it was hers or the Vânătors'.'

'Why should that matter?'

'The explanation is coming, Elena. Just be patient for a little while longer.'

I nodded reluctantly. I wanted the answers right now.

'Olivier began to call for help. He was sixty years old and in no shape to carry Elena himself to a hospital and, unfortunately, his home was also relatively secluded from the main town. No one lived close enough to hear his calls for help.'

'So what did he do then?' Lucas asked.

'Well, he had every intention of running to get aid, but Elena grabbed him by the hand and made him stay with her until the end. She gripped him tightly and made him promise that no matter what happened to her, he would protect her baby.'

'She said that?' I asked quietly.

George nodded. 'She made him promise that no matter what you looked like or what you might try to do, he was not to let harm come to you, because you were going to be an innocent child that would eventually tread a path that could change the fate of everyone.'

The sceptical look crossed my face again. 'You just made that crap up.'

'No, I did not,' George said, sounding offended. 'It's all in the transcripts. That is exactly what she said to Olivier.'

I rolled my eyes and flopped backwards into the sofa. 'Whatever.'

'It's true, Elena,' he said softly. 'She insisted that an angel had come to her while she was sleeping the night before, and told her that her child was special and should be protected at all costs.'

'And you believe that?'

'Honestly, I don't know what to believe. I'm just telling you the events of that night.'

'Do the IMI believe that?'

He shrugged. 'Some of them do.'

I snorted lightly. 'Sounds like a load of bullshit to me.'

Susan huffed and George cocked an eyebrow, his lips tightening into a hard set line. 'Must you use that language all of the time?'

I frowned. 'I must. It sums up the proper inflection of my innermost sentiments in just two easy syllables.'

Lucas sat forward and grinned. 'Yep, sounds like bullshit to me.'

'Lucas!' Susan shrieked. 'Watch your tongue.'

Lucas and I rolled our eyes at each other, but quickly pretended to rub at some imaginary eye injury before Susan caught us dismissing her so openly. George's loud throat clearing sobered us up.

I took a deep breath. 'Sorry, George,' I said, thinking once again of my birth. 'Please, continue with the story.' George gave us a reproachful look before proceeding.

'After Elena had made Olivier swear to protect you, she started to fade fast. He wasn't sure if it was blood loss or her imminent death that was making her say such strange things, but she just kept repeating the same thing over and over again: "Please don't be like him, please don't drink of the blood".'

'Please don't be like him,' I repeated. 'Do you think she was referring to my father?'

'Precisely,' George breathed. 'It was the one aspect of her ramblings that Olivier seemed to understand with absolute clarity.' He paused and looked at me with sorrowful eyes. 'She died soon after that.'

I paused a moment to take in the manner and truth of my mother's death. Knowing the details of how and when she had passed seemed to make it easier for me to accept that she was gone, even though deep down, long ago, I had known that her life force was no longer tied to mine.

'Are you alright, Elena?' Susan asked me, leaning across the coffee table and patting the top of my hand.

I instinctively shrugged away from her. 'I'm fine.'

'You don't look fine,' Lucas said.

'Did you get a medical degree in the last five minutes that I didn't know about?'

He screwed up his face at me and then turned away, folding his hands over his chest again.

'Do you want us to go on?' Susan asked quietly, trying to reach out to me again.

I slid back further into the sofa, kicking my shoes off and curling my legs up underneath me so she couldn't invade my personal space again. I knew none of this was her fault, but I wasn't in the mood to be touched right now. I had to deal with this information in my own way.

I took a breath. 'Just keep going George. You still haven't

explained what about my blood is so significant or how I survived my mother's death.'

'Very well.' He paused. 'Upon your mother's death, Olivier knew right away that he had to get you out of your mother's womb before you died along with her. Until there was incontrovertible proof that you were a Vampiric child, he had to assume that you were human and that your mother's ramblings were due to blood loss or shock.'

'But he didn't believe for a second that I was an ordinary baby, did he?'

He shook his head. 'He wanted to believe that your mother was slightly crazed and that you were human, but the evidence that you were in fact a child of the Vampires soon became all too compelling.'

'How so?'

He faltered slightly as he began to speak 'Olivier tried to cut you free from your mother's womb, but he couldn't.'

'Why not?'

'We don't know how and we don't know why—perhaps it had something to do with whomever was watching over you or something you personally were capable of—but as soon the blade struck your mother's flesh, you sealed yourself off inside her womb. All of her skin from top to toe turned into something resembling the strength of stone and was completely impenetrable by any weapon, effectively encasing you within her like a tomb.'

'So not even silver affected me?'

'No, not even silver. That was when Olivier realised that not only were you not a regular human baby, but you weren't even a regular Vampiric one either. So he ran into the town to locate the other two Protectors to seek their guidance in the matter.'

'Wait. What do you mean that I wasn't a typical vampire child?'

'You know this, Elena—vampiric children are born human and only develop their powers after they have turned. As far as the records indicate, they don't seal themselves off inside their human mothers and wait for gestation to complete.'

I stared at him, a little too wide eyed. 'So what are you saying then? I'm a freak?'

He shook his head and smiled grimly. 'You're not a freak, Elena. You're ...'

The words escaped him and he fell silent. He went to speak again and then stopped, looking at me with heavy set eyes.

'Olivier found the other two Protectors back in town,' Susan carried on quietly. 'He brought them back to Elena's body and explained to them everything that had happened. They all knew this was not a case for the human hospitals, so they helped Olivier carry the body back to his house and contacted the IMI immediately. Within twenty four hours another five Protectors from headquarters arrived on the island to review the case.'

'And, in the meantime, I just stayed holed up inside my mother's dead body?'

Was that as sickening as it just sounded?

'Regrettably, yes.'

'That's sick,' Lucas murmured.

Susan shot him a look, but I was inclined to agree with him. 'How long was I left inside her?'

Susan's brow furrowed slightly. She pinched the bridge of her nose between her fingers before answering the question. 'You stayed like that for a further two days until her blood supply was completely drained.'

Ugh, I think I'm going to be sick ...

'Elena, are you alright?'

'Not really.' I put my hand over my mouth and swallowed back a mouthful of rising bile.

'Do you want me to stop?'

I shook my head. I just needed a minute to get my composure back.

George looked at me speculatively. 'We can stop, Elena. We can just pretend we never had this conversation and go about our day. There are some things that are just better left unsaid.' He looked at Lucas again with a strange expression on his face and then glanced back at me, his eyes unfocused and his face deadpan.

'This isn't one of them,' I countered. 'Tell me what happened next.'

Susan sunk back into the sofa again and allowed George to take the reins. Her eyes watched me constantly, concerned. George's face remained set into a tight mask of indecision. He finally shook off the silence, took one determined look at my face and hurriedly continued. 'Two days passed, each Protector taking shifts to watch over your dead mother's body while they wondered just exactly what was growing inside her womb. Constant monitoring by IMI doctors didn't give any answers as to why you'd be different from any other child. It wasn't until the two days had passed and your mother's skin started to return to normal again that they fully realised just exactly what they were dealing with.'

I swallowed another rising lump in my throat. 'Do I really want to hear this?'

He stopped and looked straight at me. 'Elena, it was then that you tore your way out of your mother's womb.'

Oh my god, this time I am going to be sick.

I got up and grabbed at a waste bin beside the sofa and hurled up the entire contents of my breakfast into it. Lucas jumped out of the way, covering his nose. Susan hopped up and pulled my hair out of my face, patting me gently on the back in sympathy.

I retched again and again until there was nothing left to give, my stomach now completely raw and empty of any sustenance.

What was I? A vânător?

'George, look at her! We shouldn't have told her!'

I held a hand up in the air to stop her protestations, not yet ready to talk.

I stood up, placing the bin over in the far corner of the room and as far away from everyone's nostrils as possible. I sat back down on the sofa and retrieved a water bottle from my backpack and had a long, steady drink of water. The wetness of the partially cool fluid soothed my raw throat.

Wow, what a day. First algebra, then vampires, and after that a quick forte into levitation before settling into *P.S—you're a freak.*

I motioned with a couple of impatient flicks of my hand for Susan to sit back down again. She was flittering around me uselessly, and right then, all I truly needed for comfort was an explanation as to why I wasn't normal.

George looked hesitant as he glanced a couple of times at Lucas and Susan. All Susan had to offer in return was a few protests asking him not to frighten me any further, and Lucas, well he was staring at me like I was standing naked in the middle of a public shopping centre. If he opened his eyes any wider in shock, they were bound to fall out.

'George' I said sternly, trying to ignore the gaping goldfish beside me. 'Finish it, so I know once and for all just exactly what it is that I am.'

He sighed wearily and then nodded. 'Like I said, you tore your way out of her womb. As you know this is not the usual thing for a human or Vampiric baby to do. But a vânător, on the other hand, births itself by tearing its way out of the womb, just as you did. There's still no explanation for the hardening of the skin or the fact that you came out in human form, not as a wolf.'

'So The Protectors thought I was a vânător?'

'Not exactly. You couldn't have been a full vânător because your mother had a regular pregnancy, a trait more typical of both humans and vampires. But that did not stop every Protector in that room being extremely wary of you. By your entry into the world, they half-expected to see a wolf or something like it. But you were nothing that anyone expected—you were human.'

'So did the IMI learn why I was born in such an unusual manner?'

He nodded. 'In a way. There are still so many unknowns when it comes to you, Elena. Particularly given that we aren't sure what will happen to you on the night of your turning. But we do have some answers. For one, the doctors took some blood from you to study after you were born and the results were certainly interesting.'

'What were the results?' Lucas and I said in unison.

Lucas looked at me and smiled uneasily. I hated that I could now see fear spreading across his features. He'd never looked at me like that before.

'Do you know anything about human chromosomes?' George said.

'A little.' I couldn't say much more than that. Biology, genetics and science-based studies were right up there on my list of hated subjects.

'Well then just to give you an idea, there are twenty-three pairs of chromosomes in each human being. In these chromosomes there are genes that determine everything from your physical appearance, athletic ability, mental capacity, so on and so forth. In a vampire there are twenty-four, the extra chromosome appearing during the transformation process. This is what gives them speed, agility, strength and above all, heightened senses. In your blood there was also twenty-four, an unlikely occurrence given that even a born vampire is still human to begin with and only later develop the gene mutation, but you, you had the extra chromosome right off the bat. It was blended perfectly into your body.'

'So what caused it to happen?'

'Well that's the tricky part,' he muttered. 'We know that when a vampire turns another human into one of them, it has to occur from the transference of blood. We aren't sure of the method, because our allies have never been willing to part with the information. We've conducted experiments at head-quarters pertaining to the injection of Vampiric blood into various subjects, but transformation does not occur. We've tried everything, but now we are wondering if the subject has to be bitten first before they can receive Vampiric blood in return. In your case, given that you were already expected to be a vampire, we can only draw one conclusion.'

'And what is that?'

'That you are in fact half-Vânător.'

I leaned forward in my seat and tried not to scream at him. 'Are you saying that I'm going to be a bloody were-wolf?'

'Whoa,' Lucas said, looking at me edgily. 'There aren't any girl vânători, at least none that we've seen or heard of.'

'And I don't want to be the first,' I snapped back.

He held up his hands in surrender. 'And that is why they call female dogs ... bitches.'

I punched him hard on the side of the arm. The last thing I needed right now was to be referred to as a dog.

He gasped with pain and rubbed at his arm, glowering at me.

George shot us both a look and Susan threw her arms into the air in exasperation. 'Elena, I know this is a lot to take in,' George muttered, throwing Lucas a look as he went to hit me back, 'but don't count your chickens before they hatch. You've shown no outward or behavioural signs of vânător behaviour. There is a good chance that, given how perfectly blended that extra chromosome is in your system and the pure quality of your blood, that you may only project certain traits of the Vânător, not actually become one.'

'What do you mean by the pure quality of my blood?'

He bit his lower lip as if he had said something he shouldn't have. 'Did I not mention that?'

I shook my head.

He coughed uncomfortably and looked away from Susan's annoyed expression. 'Well.' He hesitated. 'Upon further analysis of your blood we noted some interesting results. There are absolutely zero defects in your blood.'

'Yeah, what does that mean?' I said impatiently.

'For lack of a better word Elena, your blood is perfect, more so than is humanly possible.'

'Perfect,' I echoed.

'Yes. Everything about you is perfect. Have you never noticed before?'

I scoffed. 'Well I like to think that I don't have my head up my own ass, if you know what I mean.'

His body shook with derisive laughter before he smiled warmly at Susan, who still looked agitated.

'Seriously, I'm not perfect,' I said.

'Well your attitude isn't,' George agreed. 'But Elena, physically, inside and out you *are* perfect.'

I snorted and turned away, trying to hide the rising wave

of embarrassment that was washing my face in a cherry red. 'So the Vânător blood in my system—was that injected during the pregnancy or was it a result of the attack on my mother?'

'We're pretty sure from the attack. Your mother was bitten while she was still alive and while you were still alive and growing inside of her. When the Vânător was stabbed by The Protector, some of its blood must have mixed with your mother's flesh wound on her neck, travelling into her bloodstream and dispersing through her to you. After all, you were a Vampiric baby. It only makes sense that you ingested it.'

'But given that a vânător bite does not spread the disease and nor does the injection of their blood, how is it possible?'

'We can only assume it's because your body was feeding off your mother's to sustain your life. In the two days you spent inside her womb, you absorbed every ounce of her blood into your body. Her blood was mixed with vânător blood, and given that you have the Vampiric gene, there is an excellent chance it merely bonded with your own perfect blood.'

I kicked my legs out from under me and rose to my feet. I needed to move around.

'Where are you going?' Susan asked me.

'I think I need some air.'

'Don't you want to stay and finish the conversation?'

'What else is there to say? My mother is dead, my father is AWOL and I'm a vampire that could possibly turn into a werewolf at any stage and devour everyone around me. I think that pretty much sums it up.'

'It won't be like that, Elena,' Lucas said quietly. 'You'd never hurt anyone intentionally.'

I stepped around the coffee table and collected my back-pack. 'But none of you know that for sure. Let's face it, even the IMI want to keep me close because they are afraid of what I might become.'

George and Susan exchanged relieved glances. 'That's not true,' George answered, almost mechanically.

'Don't lie to me, George. I heard Sarah and Kim talking in the passages earlier. They said I might become useful one day. That's why I've been training for the last four years. It was because it was easier to keep an eye on me if I was close. Then you could train me to be a weapon against both vampires and vânători because, in the end, I would never fit in with either of them. I'm neither human, Vampire, or Vânător. I'm a mixed breed and therefore an ideal piece of arsenal for the IMI.' I paused, looking at the shock on all three of their faces. 'I'm just an experiment to everyone here, aren't I?'

'Elena, you need to stop this,' George growled. 'Surmising the intentions of the IMI will get you nowhere. We trained you so that you could defend yourself. We knew that you might never fit in with the Vampires and possibly end up becoming one of the Vânători, so we wanted to arm you with as much personal defence as possible. There is no other reason other than that.'

And the air grew thick with lies.

I just didn't believe him. I stared back into his sombre face. 'Is that why you tried to keep me away from the Vam-pires just before? Were you worried they would scent the Vânător in my blood and try to kill me? Or were you more concerned that they might accept me as one of their own and take me away from the prying eyes of the IMI?'

George and Susan exchanged a panicked look that came and went quickly as my eyes narrowed upon them.

Choosing his words carefully, George continued. 'Elena, can you imagine what the Vampires finding out that you were a half-breed would mean for mankind, and for you? Sure there are enough of us here today to bring them down if they discovered your secret and decided to attack, but what if they got away? What if they told every vampire they knew about you and then all of a sudden, every coven conceivable rained down upon us? And what if they all died and then others came looking for them? What then? They hate the Vânătors as much as we do. They would not accept you as we have done. They would attack and consider this a violation of the alliance.'

For once, I had no witty comeback.

Susan stood up, walked around the coffee table and placed her hands on my shoulders. 'We aren't hard on you because of some strict IMI regime. We are hard on you because we want to protect the interests of the human race. Exposing you to vampires could mean an all out war.'

'I want to believe you,' I said, looking down at my feet. 'But I just don't know. I always feel like both of you are lying to me. I have to try and figure this one out on my own.' I looked back up her again and I swear that I saw regret in her misty blue eyes.

'Do you know what the sad thing is?' I whispered as I watched her face for a reaction.

She shook her head and blinked back what I thought looked like unshed tears. 'No, what's that?'

'If it turns out that you are lying to me, and the IMI do have an ulterior motive for keeping me alive, then there's absolutely nothing I can do about it. Because despite all my threats, smart mouthing and obnoxious attitude, I have absolutely nowhere else to go. I have no choice but to trust you. My life is literally in your hands.'

Something inside of her broke. 'Oh, Elena,' Susan murmured as she wrapped me fiercely in a bear hug. She hadn't touched me like that since I was a little girl.

I pulled away slowly. 'I don't need a hug, I just need some air.'

'I'll come with you,' Lucas said, jumping to his feet.

I shook my head and smiled. 'No. I want to be by myself for a little while.' I adjusted the backpack to sit more comfortably on my shoulders. 'I'm going to walk home if that's okay. I'll see you all later.'

I didn't wait for a response.

I spun on my heels and made my way quickly out of the library, stumbling slightly on the staircase as I took the stairs two at a time. After that, I all but ran down the passages, through the junction, past Kim and Sarah's surprised faces as they re-entered the IMI, and back to the trapdoor where I knew I would finally be alone, be able to breathe again.

CHAPTER NINE: INTRUSION

kicked at a stone by my feet, scattering it a few metres into the distance before I came back up to it for the umpteenth time and kicked at it again. Cars roared past me on the highway, some of the traffic from the after-school rush finally starting to disperse as it neared four o'clock. Hundreds of people flew past in their cars, completely ignorant to the fact that they were passing by someone that could one day soon be a very real threat to their existences.

A car horn honked. A pimply teenager leant his head out the window as he passed and wolf-whistled at me. I wondered if he'd still be doing that if he saw me turn into a hairy wolf with sharp fangs before his eyes, with breath that reeked of blood and death.

I sucked in another deep breath. It was slightly tainted by the smell of exhaust fumes, but still a welcomed reprieve from the stifling air of the IMI. I'd needed to get out, needed the time to think and gain some perspective about what was important. I didn't want to wallow in self-pity and I didn't want to give it all too much thought either. I always knew that I was different, and I had so easily accepted that I was going to be a vampire, but this? This was something else entirely. There was no manual for how to be a half-breed freak, and I wasn't exactly sure what to make of it either. There was no one to turn to.

I was completely alone on this path, with no guide rails for support.

I'd reached the rock again. I kicked it harder this time, sending it flying out onto the highway and underneath a passing car. It was truly an accident. I guess I didn't know my own strength at times.

The car's passengers honked their horn loudly as they passed and threw me the one finger salute out of the window.

I took a left into a road that I'd never particularly noticed the name of before, and still didn't, while continuing to follow the familiar footpath that led all the way back to our street and straight to our house. It would take no longer than ten minutes before I got home. Not that I was in any particular hurry to get there. But trudging around kicking rocks at passing cars could hardly constitute a favourable activity, even if it did make me feel slightly better. What would really make me feel better right now was a good sparring session with Peter or Vincent, but I didn't want to go back to the IMI today. And most of all, I wanted to avoid the pity on everyone's faces.

I turned to the side as an older model red commodore sedan approached me and tooted its horn. During my teen years I had gotten used to the attention that my looks sometimes drew, but I was never quite comfortable with such brazen public displays of appreciation that usually followed a drive-by hollering. It left me feeling both flattered and at the same time objectified. Go figure.

The whole left side of the car was dented from some kind of accident, and the mirror was no longer serviceable—it was left dangling down by the side of the car door from a few wires. It rattled noisily against the door, swinging from side to side as the car drove slowly past me, the yahoos whistling for my attention again.

Music blared from the open car windows, a sure sign of attention seekers. It was a garbled mess of electric guitars and drums. The words were incoherent and the melody indeterminable. It was the same sort of music that all teenage boys seemed to listen to, and invariably went hand in hand with driving beat up old cars that had far too much muffler resonance. Not to mention the fact that these seemingly uncouth boys thought that they were God's gift to women.

Burn outs, fast driving, loud music blaring from the windows, and insidious sexual comments, all said the same thing to women like me: 'Look at me, I'm an attention seeking Neanderthal who thinks he's top shit'. But seeing how teenage boys seemed to be about as thick as two planks, it was probably never going to sink in. I'd always had the burning inclination to tell them, *Get a personality, get a job, get a convertible and you're in with a chance*, but I'd never actually done it.

I shook my head. They were still watching me, still predictably honking the horn, and still had their heads hanging out either side of the windows like dogs that were barking for attention. Where was a can of dog food when you needed it?

I waved as they passed by, a small smile playing at my lips as I realised just exactly what was going to happen next. For a brief moment they both looked confused by my response, until a second later their vehicle careened directly into a street lamp, with a loud crash and a hiss of radiator fluid.

It certainly pays to watch where you're going. Perhaps I should have reminded them of that when they told me what a nice rack I had.

I turned left down another side street, glancing only once over my shoulder as both men opened their car doors and fell out, shaking their heads in confusion, the car sending up a torrent of steam from underneath the newly-buckled bonnet. The neighbours across the street were already dashing across the road to come to their aid.

I walked on, uncaring, the sounds of the panicked neighbours fading in my ears and allowing myself to smile at the karmic retribution of the situation. But just to be certain, I tilted my face back and sniffed at the air. The pungent aroma of a barbeque and someone cooking a roast dinner danced across the wind, entering my nostrils. I could smell plenty of other things around me too, but there was definitely no blood. Both of the men were fine—at least physically.

I rounded the corner and headed down the side of the local high school. Some of the students whose parents had forgotten them, or were running late, were sitting along the top of the fence patiently waiting to be collected. Most of them sat quietly talking to some of their friends. Others read books, and some of the more eager students had already started their homework, all of them just regular kids with regular human lives. In a small way, I envied them. Not because they were human, but because they had choices. All of mine had been taken away from me.

I smiled down at a little girl wearing the trademark blue on blue uniform of the grade school across the street. She was standing next to a boy who I assumed was her older brother, based on the protective way he kept an eye on her while reading his book. He wore the maroon and cream uniform, probably of the nearby high school, and pretended not to notice me as I approached. He dipped his nose further behind the pages of his novel.

The little girl waved at me as I drew near. She had little blonde piggy tails and large brown eyes, reminding me of a younger version of Kayla. 'You're pretty,' she giggled, bouncing excitedly from foot to foot.

I wished I had that much energy at four o'clock in the afternoon. 'And you are absolutely adorable,' I said, tugging on one of her piggy tails and smiling.

Her brother apologised, stuttering profusely. He went red in the face and then clamped his hand down over her mouth and led her away in the other direction. She continued to wave at me anyway, and I continued to smile. She was so small and so innocent—had I ever looked that way myself? I somehow doubted it.

I had never been a normal child, never been a normal teen, and if I was being honest, I would never be a normal adult either. So 'innocent' wasn't exactly a word I could use to describe myself, particularly not now that I knew that I was just a temporary human shell for both vampire and werewolf behaviour. What was going to be the trigger for my first uncontrolled bloodbath? Could I turn at any minute or would the first inklings of vânător behaviour only manifest after my maturity? Probably the latter. But seeing how no one knew for certain what was going to happen to me, it was all just speculation.

I shook my head. I had to think about this logically. What were the basic characteristics that defined a vânător? And how did they relate to my bloodsucking nature?

Well, for one, they were fast moving, like the Vampires. But as far as I was concerned, that was not actually a bad thing. I would love to be able to run fast, jump high and feel the wind in my hair. There was nothing particularly disagreeable about that gift at all. Okay, so running fast was a plus.

Two—they drank blood. Well, I wasn't exactly amenable to that idea just yet, but blood was going to be what I craved for in the years to come. The only difference between the two species was that the Vânătors also drank vampire blood. I could probably live with that too, especially if every one of them I ever met turned out to be an asshole. But if they turned out to be as intriguing as William Granville, then I was going to have to learn some self control. But what if I couldn't control my urges?

I chewed on the corner of my lower lip nervously as I crossed the intersection and headed up our street, the driveway coming into view in the distance. If I couldn't control my urges then there was really only one option. I'd have to turn myself into the IMI. I could not be trusted around the public. It certainly wasn't my first preference, but given the alternative, I really had no choice in the matter.

Okay, now that that's sorted, what else?

Three—vânătors didn't heal. Well, that was certainly not an issue for me. According to George, that extra chromosome was already well blended into my system, allowing that portion of my Vampiric genes to take effect.

Four—they didn't like sunlight. No problems there either. Vampires liked the sunlight about as much as I liked Algebra. What else?

Five—they could shapeshift. I wasn't really sure if I was keen on that idea. One minute I'm me, regular Elena, and then the next, I'm a big hairy wolf. Not a good look. But I suppose I didn't really have a choice in the matter. As long as I didn't get a hairy lip, bushy side burns or excessive armpit hair I could deal with going canine. But would I moult?

I shook my head and laughed. I quickly sobered, though, when I remembered the most important aspect of Vânător life that separated them from the more sane nature of the Vampire.

Their mating habits.

That got to me.

Surely it wasn't plausible for me to be endowed with a truly animalistic and insatiable sexual appetite? As it was now, I got less action than a nun. If I didn't specifically have an interest in men now then I certainly couldn't fathom feeling any differently about the subject after my turning. But perhaps that was the point? Just like I'd had no control over my Vampiric tendencies, maybe I'd have even less over the Vânător ones? Although if I started rubbing myself up against every man's leg that I saw like a rabid dog, I was going to have to shoot myself.

So what were my biggest fears then? Was I worried that I'd be horny all the time? Or was I worried that I would want to eat absolutely every single person that I looked at? No exceptions?

Neither.

I was scared that I had no idea what would happen to me, and even less of an idea about whether the other immortal beings would accept me. Eternity was an awful long time to be an outcast. I mean, look what happened to Edward Scissor hands. First the guy was preyed upon by an Avon lady, everyone's worst nightmare, and then the entire town turned against him because he was different. What chance would I have if I became a woman with fangs and a hairy back?

I huffed in frustration and grabbed my keys from my backpack. The phone was ringing inside the house, probably Susan and George phoning to check up on me.

I opened the front door and dashed inside. 'Hello?' I said, out of breath as I picked up the receiver.

'Hey, it's me.'

I frowned. I hated it when people did that. How were you supposed to guess who the caller was from just a few short words? Did I look like some kind of bloody mind reader?

'It's Kayla,' she answered for me, hopefully realising that vagueness would get her nowhere except a hang up.

I scratched at my forehead and brushed my hair back from my face, channelling calm and attentiveness. 'What's up?'

'What's up?' she shrieked. 'What's up? You do realise that you have not called me back, right?'

I pinched the skin on the bridge of my nose and bit back an angry retort. It wasn't her fault I was having a crappy day. 'I'm sorry, I wasn't aware that you'd called.'

'But I've been leaving you messages and texting you since Sunday.'

'My cell got taken off me, Kayla. I'm grounded.'

'Oh, I guess that explains it then.'

'Did you want something?'

'Wow, you sound kinda testy today.'

'Sorry, had a bad day, that's all.'

'Want to tell me about it?'

'Not really.'

'Oh,' she said, sounding put out. 'Well I just rang to find out why you dropped off the face of the Earth. Do you want to do something this weekend?'

I let out a long sigh. 'Kayla, I just finished telling you that I'm grounded. I'm not allowed to do anything. I'm not even supposed to be talking to you right now.'

'Where are your parents?'

'Out.'

'So I'll come over. They'll never know.'

I shook my head even though I was vaguely aware that she couldn't see the motion. 'No, I just need some alone time at the moment. I'll see you at the shop on Saturday.'

I was just about to hang up the phone when I heard her yell out, 'Wait!'.

'Yeah?'

'Elena, I have to tell you something.'

'What is it?' I said, pressing the receiver back against my ear again and rolling my eyes.

'Well, it might be nothing, but I thought I should just tell you anyway. It's one of the reasons I've been trying to contact you.'

I pulled a chair out from the dining room table and sat down. I had an inkling this was going to take longer than five minutes and after the day I'd had I felt particularly weary. 'Go on.'

'Well I tried calling you a half-dozen times because I wanted to see if that guy had gotten in contact with you. Of course, now I understand why you didn't call me back. Just as well, I was starting to feel a little cranky with you for not returning my phone calls and—'

'Kayla,' I said, interrupting her. 'What guy?'

'You don't know? Oh.' She paused. 'He seemed like he knew you.'

'Kayla, what are you talking about?'

'Well I was working yesterday and this absolutely gorgeous guy came walking into the store. He came up to the counter, and Glen asked him if there was anything we could do to help him, but he asked specifically for you. Glen said that you only worked on Saturdays and could he take a message for you.'

I strangled the phone cord with my fingers, pressing the receiver harder against my ear. 'Did he leave a message?'

'Ah-huh. He said could you please call him when you get a chance.'

'Did he leave you a number to contact him on?' Even to me, I sounded desperate.

She chuckled. 'He sure did.'

I leaned across to the centre of the dining table and grabbed a sheet of the newspaper that George had been reading at breakfast. I tore a piece of the corner off and grabbed the pen that he'd been using to do the crosswords. 'Okay, give it to me.'

She read the number out to me and then repeated it again, just to be sure.

'Did he leave you a name?' I asked, my voice sounding far too shaky not to be noticeable.

'Absolutely. He said his name was William Granville.'

I nearly dropped the receiver on the floor. I already knew she was going to say his name, but the shock of it still thrilled me. I fumbled the receiver in my shaking hands and stared down at the number on the piece of newspaper in front of me.

'Elena? Are you there?'

'Huh? What? Yeah, I'm here. Look, Kayla, I've got to go okay?'

'Hang on, you haven't told me who this guy—'

I hung up the phone and stared back down at the paper again. He wanted me to contact him. George's little covert operation to keep me quiet, and away from him this afternoon, must have piqued his curiosity, especially now that I knew he was a vampire and there was a good chance he knew I was going to be one too.

I stood up from the chair and wandered over to the kitchen. I needed a second to think about this.

I opened the fridge and grabbed a can of Coke. I popped the lid, downing some of the contents. The gassy liquid burned the back of my throat, which was still a little raw from retching earlier.

I took another gulp, hoping the answer to whether or not I should just call him was located somewhere at the bottom of the can. Susan and George had been adamant that he would want to hurt me once he figured out what I was, but I wasn't sure that I completely agreed. He'd had the opportunity to hurt me at the rave and he didn't, he was just curious, probably as curious as I was about him and his friends.

I downed the rest of the contents hastily and held the opening up to my eye.

Nope, still no answer there.

I tossed the can into the rubbish and headed back to the table. My stomach felt gassy and slightly distended and no more settled than it had been before.

I sat back down on the chair. My fingers tapped absently against the timber surface of the table. I was nervous.

Should I call him? What did he want?

Tap, tap, tap went my fingers on the table top.

I looked down at my hand and tucked it in my lap. I was irritating myself.

After a few minutes of quiet deliberation, I shakily picked up the piece of paper, holding the number in front of me.

What could it hurt just to call him?

Susan and George said not to.

Yeah, but was that an order *or a suggestion?*

I'm pretty sure that was an order.

I moved to the phone, my fingers dialling the number without my full consent. It was like having an 'out of body' experience. I saw myself doing it. I even felt the press of keys under my finger tips. But I could do little in the way of stopping myself, even though part of my head was scream-ing in protest.

There was a short silence before the ringing started. Once, twice, three times. I promised myself I'd hang up after five unanswered rings.

'Hello?'

I slammed the receiver back onto its cradle and stepped away, horrified.

You bloody chicken shit!

I paced a few steps back from the phone on the wall and stared at it. Why had I hung up on him? What was wrong with me?

And the phone started to ring.

I jumped and squealed with surprise. I caught the edge of the sofa with my hand, steadying myself as I looked back up at the ringing phone. What was I afraid of? It was probably just Kayla ringing me back.

I took a few steps towards the telephone. My fingers skimmed the ringing receiver as I slowly picked it up from the cradle. The ringing ceased immediately and I raised it up towards my ear. 'Hello?'

'Elena?'

I recognised the British accent immediately—toyed with the notion of simply hanging up again. I couldn't though. He knew it was me. But how?

Caller ID, you loser.

Several heartbeats passed. My mouth moved up and down, but no words came out.

'Elena? Is that you?'

I still couldn't answer. I was still debating about hanging up. It was my stupid fingers that weren't playing along with the directions from my brain.

'Elena. I can hear you breathing.'

'Is this, William?' I asked, cringing, my voice barely recognisable. What a stupid question to ask. I already knew the answer.

'Yes, it is. I am so glad that you decided to call me back.'

'I didn't,' I lied, closing my eyes and cringing again. Why

did he make me so damn nervous? I've killed vânătors. Talking to one little vampire should be easy.

'Okay, so you called me, and then I called you back. Technology is quite amazing these days, when you think about it. They have these caller ID functions that allow you to take note of the number dialling you and then you can return the call—quite ingenious really.'

I swallowed the lump in my throat. 'Are you vying for a job with a telephone carrier, or are you going to tell me what you want?'

He chuckled again. The sound was soft, masculine and very inviting. 'I wanted to make contact with you, so that we might talk.'

'I'm listening.'

'I was really rather hoping it would be face-to-face.'

I'm sure you did.

'Why don't you give me an outline of what you want to talk about and then I'll decide if this goes past a phone call.'

'Very well.' There was silence on the line for a couple of seconds. He cleared his throat lightly and began speaking again. 'I've scented what you are, Elena and, to be perfectly frank, I'm very curious as to how you could be possible.'

I held my breath, unable to answer.

'Given your current age there should be no detectable vampiric blood in your veins—yet there it is. This is somewhat of an anomaly for our kind, as I'm sure you're well aware since you seem to be rubbing shoulders with The Protectors. Not to mention the fact that I can smell the essence of your blood which seems completely clean of all defects and diseases, which is very rare given that you are still currently human.' He paused. 'You are still human, aren't you?'

I exhaled. 'What would you like me to say?'

There was another pause. 'The truth I guess. But I expect, as you don't know me very well, that you don't specifically owe me anything. But that was why I was calling. I was hoping that we could get to know each other a little better.'

'To what purpose?'

He laughed as if the answer was ridiculously obvious. 'Must there be a reason? I simply find you fascinating.'

He's lying.

'I'm afraid you're going to have to do better than that,' I said sternly, holding my ground.

'Well, how about this … I'll be perfectly honest with you. I'm attracted to your face, body, smell, and your no-nonsense demeanour that I've so far observed as quite a contrast to your delicate, feminine appearance. But I also want to know what makes you tick, Elena, and I definitely want to understand what's pulsing inside your blood … amongst other things.'

There was an extremely long pause where I didn't answer.

Is he trying to freak me out?

'So how did I do?' he said quietly, my silence began to verge on the uncomfortable, the same note of amusement in his voice ringing down the phone line.

I paused. 'Terrible. I'm hanging up now.'

I replaced the receiver back on the wall and, for some strange reason, I smiled. What an odd sort of reaction. But even I had to admit that there was something undeniably charismatic about him. Presumably it was impossible for him to entice me over the phone, so feeling strangely flattered by his compliments was because I must have enjoyed hearing them, and hence the reason I now smiled. It wasn't like I hadn't had men tell me they were attracted to me before, but it was different when he said it.

I shook my head.

No way. I can't let myself be pulled in by his charm. I have to keep my wits about me with this one.

A knock sounded loudly on the front door, and for the second time that day, I jumped back in fright.

Well, aren't I popular today?

I crossed to the door and swung it open. When I saw who was standing on the other side, I shut the door immediately, replacing the deadlocks and the chain.

'Are we going to play that game again?' William called through the door as he rapped on it for the second time

I smiled unknowingly. 'Go away.'

'I don't want to.'

'I wasn't giving you an option.'

'I can stand here all night you know.'

'Well then,' I said, smiling, and called out as I walked away, 'let me know how that works out for you.'

I grabbed my bag off the ground by the bureau and headed off upstairs, hopefully to leave him standing at the front door like an idiot. He could sit out there all night for all I cared. But, sooner or later, Susan and George would be home again and they'd blow him to bits if I asked them to. Maybe I wouldn't even have to ask. Maybe they'd just do it for fun.

I took the last few steps two at a time and opened the door to my bedroom.

'You shouldn't leave your window open,' he said, grinning at me from the window sill. 'You never know who might be lurking around the place.'

He dropped down to the floor inside and leant back against the window, crossing his arms in front of his chest.

I, on the other hand, choked on a scream and clasped a hand to my chest to stop my heartbeat from entering warp speed.

He stood motionless by the window, whistling lightly and staring intently at me as I tried to calm myself down.

Meanwhile, I still had the good sense to start unzipping my bag, protection my first thought even in the midst of a good squeal and a race to developing angina. But as I felt around inside my bag, trying to be circumspect about retrieving my blade, the air around me stirred, and something cold brushed against my hand.

'Are you looking for this?' he asked politely as he lowered his sunglasses. He pulled something from behind his back and held it out in front of him. My knife.

'Where did you get that?' I choked out in fear and in shock.

'From inside your bag.'

Holy crap, this guy's fast. I don't stand a chance.

I looked at my blade in his hands and then back at my bag, which I was gripping by one of the shoulder straps. I let it fall to the ground. There was nothing inside that I could use for defence, unless of course he was as allergic to algebra as I was.

'Give it back to me. Now.'

He pulled the sunglasses away from his face and tucked them in the front of his shirt. 'Are you going to stab me with it?'

'I honestly haven't decided yet.'

He clicked his tongue as if in thought, shaking his head from side to side. 'Then perhaps I should hang onto it.'

'I don't see how that's fair.'

He raised his left eyebrow slightly. 'Is that so?'

I nodded. 'You're the one breaking and entering here,

and to top it off, you're faster than I am and have sharper teeth. I think you should level the playing field and at least hand me back my knife.'

'Touché. Perhaps you have a point.' He deftly tossed the knife at a point above my head. I ducked, the blade splintering the wood of my door and lodging deep inside. He grinned. 'If you can get it out before I get to you, it's all yours.'

Shocked, I rose quickly to my feet and spun around, grabbing the hilt of the knife and trying to dislodge it from the confines of the timber. In the next instant, I was spun around and thrown up hard against the back of the door. William's fingers, cold and uncompromising, gripped my hands tightly. He held them securely above my head, and with great strength—there was little protesting to be done.

I looked up into William's face, his emerald eyes staring back at me as he pressed his cold, hard body against mine, pinning me more firmly against the door. He negotiated a wider stance, his hips now level with mine, his legs crowding me.

My breathing quickened and my pulse rate skipped ahead, but I was determined to show him that I was neither afraid nor slightly hot by the notion of his body being pressed so intimately against mine.

He leaned in close to me, his face only inches away from my own. His scent drifted across my skin and stirred the air between us.

I licked my lips at the taste of his essence and his gaze automatically dropped to my mouth. With his free hand, he brushed a lock of hair away from my face and tucked it tenderly behind my ear. It was something I had not expected. I had foreseen teeth, blood and my empty carcass soon to be sprawled across the floor—not the initiation of unwanted foreplay. 'You'd better not kiss me,' I said.

He pulled away, a strange expression crossing his face, almost as if the thought had never even occurred to him.

I cursed silently.

Of course it didn't occur to him. He's a bloody vampire, not a randy teenager.

'Kiss you?' he said, now suddenly amused. 'Why would I kiss you?'

'Well then, what are you doing?'

He leaned forward again. I didn't dare move.

His smooth face skimmed briefly past mine, his cold nose coming to rest on the pale flesh of my neck. 'I was merely trying to get some answers,' he said as his cool breath fanned my heated skin. 'And since you're not exactly co-operative, I thought I might as well enjoy myself while I took them ... with or without your permission.'

Uh-oh.

I felt cool air race across my skin as he drew in breath. I closed my eyes, waiting for the moment when he ripped out my throat—it was bound to happen any minute now. Several seconds passed before I opened my eyes again. His nose was no longer at my neck. His hands still held me securely in front of him and his body was still pressed against mine, but he was looking straight at me now. His face was completely expressionless and I suddenly felt more scared than I'd ever been in my entire life.

He knows.

His skin was more pale and translucent than it had been before, a transformation that I had not seen take place until my eyes had re-opened. His skin was streaked with faint lines of blue and when I looked closer, I could see that they were pulsing just under the surface. His eyes were completely black, no trace remaining of the magnificent green that I had previously beheld. In fact, there was nothing but darkness, not even the whites of his eyes present. They were like empty pits of obsidian, completely soulless and expressionless.

I sucked in a sharp breath, trying to calm my frantic nerves. I was not afraid of the sight in front of me or the transformation from man to beast, and I was not fearful that my life may soon be ended. What I was most fearful of was not being accepted by the one creature that I was supposed to become. I was so afraid that the first vampire I had ever met, that I somehow felt connected to, was about to turn from me with disgust and loathing.

I held my breath and closed my eyes again, waiting for judgement.

'Impossible,' he murmured under his breath, 'absolutely impossible.'

My eyes instantly flicked open at the sound of William's voice. It was soft and confused, but I sensed no disgust or hatred. But the man in front of me was a predator and a killer and I was still nervous. He still held me close, his body hard against my own and unrelenting in its hold. His eyes were undeniably dark and dangerous, and his canines were slightly extended and ready to tear flesh.

'When you kill me,' I said in a voice barely above a whisper, 'please make it quick.'

He blinked. It was the first real sign of animation I had seen in his face in the last few minutes. 'Kill you?' he whispered, releasing my arms and taking a few steps backwards. 'Why would I kill you?'

I looked up at him in confusion. I watched the black of his eyes slowly begin to fade, returning to the brilliance of green and his pale skin turning back to a more acceptable opaque covering. His teeth retracted.

'Because of what I am,' I replied quietly, bobbing my head

down in front of me. I wanted to avoid seeing the distaste in those vivid green pools. At least in the blacks of his eyes I saw nothing except for my own reflection.

I looked up when a few moments had passed and he had still not reacted. He had neither moved nor spoken.

I faltered slightly as he took a quick step forward, his hand reaching slowly towards my face to stroke the skin of my cheek. 'Elena. I—'

Then we both heard the front door slam shut from downstairs. 'Elena, it's me. Are you home?' Lucas's voice drifted up the stairs and I heard him throw his bag on the floor by the bureau and start to make his way up the staircase.

My gaze drifted back to William. His hand dropped back to his side. 'I should go,' he said, turning on the spot and heading over to the window.

He grabbed the sunglasses from the front of his shirt and slipped them over his eyes. I stayed where I was, still pinned against the door. Although there was no one holding me there any longer, I still couldn't move.

I heard Lucas almost at the top of the stairs, the thudding of his footsteps drifting down the short hallway to my bedroom. 'Elena? Are you home?'

William turned to look at me. A faint smile tipped the corners of his lips. He nodded at me and then leapt over the framing and disappeared into the garden below.

At that point, Lucas walked into the room.

'Elena? What are you doing?' he said to me in a slightly breathless tone. 'Who were you talking to?' He looked at me from head to toe and then zeroed in on the knife still protruding from the splintered wood of the door. 'Um, what's your knife doing up there?'

'Can you keep a secret?' I whispered. He couldn't keep a secret if his life depended on it, but I had to tell someone.

'Depends. Does it have something to do with the knife?'

I nodded.

'Does it have something to do with why you're as white as a ghost?'

I nodded again.

'Does it have anything to do with the Vampires?'

I nodded a final time.

He grinned. 'Then, hell yeah, I can keep a secret!'

CHAPTER TEN: MEETING

Lucas stood on the spot, rooted in shock. He was gaping at me like a goldfish, his cheeks puffing and his lips curving, trying to formulate words. The shock must have worn off fairly quickly because he was soon slipping backwards onto the bed, gripping the mattress to steady himself. 'He was here?' he said, pointing at the floor, and then randomly pointing to portions of the room around him. 'He was right here, in this room, with you?'

'Ah-huh,' I answered absently, finally managing to yank the blade out of the door after a steady succession of half-hearted attempts.

I ran my fingers over the indentation that it had left behind. The wood was badly splintered and was going to be difficult to patch proficiently, particularly given the door was unpainted timber. There was no way that the damage would go unnoticed and explaining how it happened in the first place was certainly going to be a little complex to justify to both Susan and George. I'd already started circulating through excuses in my head. They were all lame. The best one I'd come up with so far was 'I thought I saw a vânător', but that was so stupid that I couldn't believe I'd thought of it.

I pushed the splintered timber into the hole, hoping to fill the groove with what had fallen out of it. It wasn't working. The door still looked like it had been knifed.

'We have to tell mum and dad,' Lucas mumbled, breaking into my thoughts. 'We don't know enough about vampires to make this decision on our own. You heard what they said about killing us all and ending the alliance.'

I turned around on the spot and stared at him in horror. What the hell was he thinking? 'No, no, no, Lucas,' I said, hastily coming over to join him on the bed and shaking my head wildly. 'Susan and George would flip out if they knew he had been here. It'd ruin our chances of ever truly understanding vampires, and me of ever being able to leave the house again.'

'Yeah, but they wouldn't be angry with us, they'd be angry at him. He's the one who came here uninvited. You didn't do anything wrong.' He paused. 'For a change.'

I rested my hands on his shoulders and resisted the urge to smirk. 'Think about what you're saying, Lucas. If we tell Susan and George about William's visit, they'll run the vampires out of town.'

'What's your point?'

'We live in Cairns, Lucas. How often do vampires come to Cairns?'

He scratched his chin. 'Never.'

'Exactly. If our parents drive them away, when are we ever going to get the chance to talk to and learn about vampires ever again?'

He looked at me like I was crazy. 'Um, aren't you the least bit concerned that this guy might be after a little bit more than pleasant conversation?'

'What? Like afternoon delight?' I answered and then promptly began to frown when I remembered that William had considered the idea of kissing me as patently absurd.

Lucas snorted and then squeezed my knee. 'Yeah, delight in taking all of your blood.'

I shrugged. 'I guess I should be worried, but I'm not. Not now anyway. I've been thinking about this. He had his chance to kill me and he didn't take it. That has to say something, doesn't it?'

He snorted again. 'Yeah, Elena, it says he wasn't hungry at the time.'

I groaned and flicked him in the ear. 'Seriously—think about it.' I listed the points on my fingers one by one. 'He said he was curious about what I was and yet didn't kill me. He got a good whiff of my blood and then just stood there shocked, but still didn't kill me. When I asked him to make my death quick he seemed genuinely shocked by the request and he still didn't kill me. His exact words were, "Why would I kill you?". That's important, don't you think?'

'I guess so,' he answered, glancing out the window and then looking back at me. 'So … what are you going to do?'

'Honestly, I have no idea. I guess we have to just play it by ear and see what happens.'

'You mean wait for him to jump through your window again?'

I smiled. 'Do you have any other bright ideas?'

'Yeah,' he said, nodding emphatically. 'We go to the shed right now and grab a hammer, some nails, an electric drill, and some screws, and we bolt the bloody window shut.'

I slapped him lightly on the shoulder. 'I thought you liked the idea of meeting vampires.'

He nodded again. 'I do, but have you noted how close my bedroom is to yours? It's across the hall. That's exactly three footsteps away. And just for your reference, you're quite slim, Elena, hardly a decent meal at all. Once he's finished draining you, who do *you* think he's going to come after?' He pointed to his own chest. 'Me, that's who. He only has to take three minuscule steps before he's chowing down on yours truly.' He was silent for a moment before he spoke again. 'Yep, it'll just be me in that room alone, me and my yummy tasting blood.'

I laughed loudly and wrapped an arm around his shoulder. 'You're such an idiot, Lucas.'

He frowned. 'I am not. I'm just too beautiful to be eaten.'

'Relax. I think if he was going to hurt me or you, he probably already would have. Besides, now that he knows I'm part Vânător, there's a good chance I'll never hear from him again anyway.'

'I doubt that, somehow.'

'What makes you say that?'

He looked at me like I was daft. 'Didn't you notice the look on his face this afternoon at the IMI?'

I shook my head. 'I couldn't see much at all actually. I kind of had our father standing in front of me, remember?'

'I remember that, but I also remember how he looked at you, E. It's the same way I look at the chicks when I'm surfing through the late night porn channels. There was hunger and curiosity in his eyes.'

My face screwed up in revolt as he smiled at me and winked. 'Now I don't know for certain if his kind are attracted to your blood or not, given what's in it,' he continued regardless of the fact that I was trying not to imagine my brother watching lurid acts of fornication while I slept innocently across the hall, 'but he looked like someone determined to get what he wants and he looked like he wanted you.'

I got over my disgust long enough to choke back a laugh of disbelief.

'I'd watch your back if I were you,' Lucas said, more

seriously. 'It's no wonder that mum and dad are trying to keep you away from him if his intentions are based more on stroking than choking—if you know what I mean.'

My smile was extinguished. 'You're gross.'

He nodded in acknowledgement. 'That's the problem with home schooling. There's not enough contact with the outside world.'

I grimaced. 'You worry me, Lucas.'

He nodded again in agreement.

Jeesh.

The front door opened from downstairs and the noise of people entering the premises floated up the stairs. There was a rustle of plastic bags and the smell of take out wafting across the air.

I breathed in deeply.

Oh, good. Noodle Box.

'Kids? We're home. Are you here?' There was a decidedly uncertain tone to Susan's voice.

'Coming!' Lucas shouted, almost immediately.

He pushed himself off from the bed and tucked his hands inside his pockets. He opened his mouth to say something and then thought better of it.

'Lucas?' I said, grabbing his arm as he turned on the spot and headed for the door. 'You promise not to say anything, right? At least not until we are sure that William is dangerous.'

He looked down at the floor for a minute, as if he had found something distinctly tantalising to watch amongst my pile of dirty clothes.

'What if it's too late by then?' he said suddenly and quietly, taking me by surprise. 'What if by the time you realise that William and his friends are dangerous you are already dead?'

I smacked my lips together and made a popping noise. 'Then I guess I won't have a chance to be upset about it. Will I?'

'That's not funny, E.'

'Okay then, how about this? We keep this to ourselves for now. If William contacts me again, then you and I will go and meet him together and then we can decide between us whether or not he's dangerous. I promise I won't do anything on my own.'

'Seriously? You're not playing with me right now?'

'Why would I? Admit it. You are just as curious about them as I am.'

'I'll admit that, but if we get caught, Elena, you're taking the full wrap for this. I'm going to plead complete ignorance. I'm too young to die. At least you'll be able to heal from whatever punishment mum and dad dish out.'

I shook his outstretched hand. 'Okay, it's a deal.'

Lucas scratched his chin again and pointed to the splintered wood of my bedroom door. 'What are you going to do about the door?'

I looked up at where he was pointing. 'Oh that,' I answered, smiling at him. 'That's totally your fault.'

He frowned 'Say what? I wasn't even here!'

'Oh come on Lucas. If I'm eventually going down for associating with vampires, because let's face the facts, I will, then you can take the rap for a damaged door.'

'Like hell I will,' he said, defiantly shoving his hands in his pockets.

'Go on Lucas, take one for the team.'

'What team?'

I grinned. 'The team that's going to pummel your ass if you don't.'

He kicked at the pile of my clothes on the floor with his

sneaker and stared at me moodily. 'What am I supposed to say when they notice it? I was playing with knives and I missed?'

'Yep, that'll do it. At least it's a totally believable story. Why do you think Susan gets up you every time you touch her knives in the kitchen?'

'Because I don't use the bread board?'

'No, because you can't be trusted with sharp objects. Now go downstairs, suck it up and take it like a man.'

'You know they're going to make me pay for a new door right?'

'It's a good thing we own a hardware store then, isn't it?'

A good couple of days passed without any contact from William, not that that surprised me. It was exactly as I had suspected. That one sniff of my blood had obviously turned him off me for life. Not that I blamed him. What vampire would want to know a half-breed like me? I was technically half his enemy, half of a creature that he hunted. He hadn't killed me when he realised the truth, but he'd obviously decided that I was way too much of a freak to try and contact me again.

The alarm clock beside me started beeping loudly, jogging me away from my inner turmoil and reminding me of the responsibilities that came with 'pretending' to be normal. Sometimes, I truly hate my life.

I groaned, rolled over and slapped the alarm's off button with a heavy thud of my hand. I didn't feel like going to work today. Actually, come to think of it, I never felt like going to work. But I'd have to get over that quick smart seeing as how I had to learn to support myself for, gee, let me think … eternity?

I rolled off the mattress, my feet touching the cool floor-boards. For an instant I just considered ducking back under the covers and pretending I was sick. That was never going to work. I'd never been sick a day in my life, all bar the exception of Tuesday, where mentally, I had made myself physically ill.

I sighed. I needed the money anyway, and given I only worked for eight hours a week, I couldn't really afford to miss even one day. I only had about two and a half thousand dollars to my name and that wasn't nearly enough to buy myself a decent motorbike. If I hadn't taken out half of the guttering system on the house late last year, it would be closer to four. That Ducati 1198S Superbike I wanted seemed further and further away.

I reluctantly pushed myself off the bed and scooted over to the dresser with heavy feet to find my work outfit. It was going to be another cool day today judging by the way my skin goose pimpled under the caress of the morning breeze, so I grabbed my black cardigan as well.

I dressed hurriedly, aware that the house was already filled with the noise of breakfast being started downstairs. I couldn't loiter around today. Susan and George were determined to fulfil their parental duty of upholding my grounding and driving me to work. At least if Kayla were taking me, I could have a more leisurely, *edible* breakfast.

An odd smell was emanating from the kitchen as I bounded down the stairs. My nose wrinkled in disgust. What were we all doomed to suffer through today?

'Good morning,' Susan said, relatively cheerfully as I entered the kitchen.

'Is it?' I replied.

She frowned at me heavily. 'Is that your stock standard answer? Can't you just say *good morning* in return?'

'Well, when it is a good morning, then I will.'

She flipped over something brown in the frying pan and then settled one hand on her hip, looking me over intently. 'So then tell me, Elena, what's wrong with today that prevents you from just responding like everyone else?'

I looked at her as if the answer was obvious. 'Well, for a start, it's still morning and I'm out of bed. I'm suspicious of anyone remotely chirpy before ten o'clock, and its Saturday today. I have to work. Does that cover it?'

'Oh, heaven forbid,' she answered dryly as she shoved me towards the dining room table. At least she and George appeared to have gotten over their acting weird towards me. They'd spent Tuesday night and all day Wednesday treading on the proverbial eggshells. I think they thought I was going to spontaneously combust from learning that I was a veritable genetic fruit salad.

In hindsight I was actually okay with learning that I was half-vânător. . . As people sometimes say, there was no point getting upset over spilt milk. I was what I was, and there was nothing anyone could do to change that. The only thing that really upset me was that William seemed to be ignoring me. Not that I really expected any different, but I had hoped that he would see past my freaky genes and explore the reasons why he'd sought me out in the first place. It seemed grossly unfair that he had had his curiosities satisfied by a whiff of my blood, yet I was left wanting and annoyingly unsatisfied that I might never see him again. I suppose that meant that the very simplest notion of all was to move forward and deal with the rejection like an adult, but it's hard when the shoe is on the other foot.

Well how about that? I'm actually acting mature for once. Go figure.

The phone on the dining room wall started ringing. I

looked up as soon as it started ringing. I couldn't help it. I'd been doing that all week, wondering if I'd ever hear from William Granville again.

'I'll get it,' Lucas said, jumping out of his chair and snatching up the receiver. 'Hello?' There was a short pause before Lucas held the phone outstretched to me. 'It's for you.' He grimaced. 'She's still not talking to me yet.'

I frowned. 'Who is it?'

'Who do you think? It's Kayla.'

'Oh.' I could hear the disappointment in my voice. Hopefully no one else did.

George gave me one of his disapproving glares.

'Hey, it's probably something to do with work.'

He seemed to calm down a bit, but still scowled like no one else's business. Given what Susan had just dumped on a plate in front of him, I understood the reason for his tension. He was simply projecting his disgust at a shitty breakfast onto me.

Lucas handed me the phone. 'I hope you realise she just called me a jackass.'

I smiled. 'Well if the shoe fits.' I took the receiver off him and he rolled his eyes at me.

'Kayla, what's up?'

'Your brother is such a jackass,' she hissed.

'He did mention that.' Our eyes met across the dining table and he shook his head from side to side, picking up a fork and tapping the food in front of him. I turned away. 'What did you call for?'

'I'm ringing to let you know that I'm not coming into work today. You'll have to get your parents to take you.' She coughed a few times down the line and then sneezed with a shriek that hurt my ear. She sounded awful. And she'd obviously forgotten that my parents were driving me to work for the length of my grounding.

'You don't sound too good.'

She coughed down the phone line again, answering my question. 'Yeah, got the flu I think.'

'I'm sorry. I hope you feel better.' I briefly wondered what it must be like to have the flu. Luckily, I'd never have to find out.

'Me too. My nose feels like sandpaper at the moment.'

'Well, I guess I'll see you next week then.'

'Yeah, you will.' She paused. 'Hey, did you call that guy back?'

I looked at Susan and George who were both watching me. 'Ah-huh.'

'What did he want?'

'Not much.'

'Are you seeing him?'

'It's not like that.'

'Are you into him?'

'I don't think I can answer that.'

'You can't talk right now can you?' she said conspiratorially. 'Your parents are listening.'

'That is correct.'

She sneezed. 'Okay.' She blew her nose so loudly I had to pull the receiver away from my ear. 'I'll talk to you about it next Saturday then.'

'Okay. Feel better.'

'Thanks.'

I hung up the phone and sat down at the table. Susan and George were still watching me, questioning looks on their faces.

'It was Kayla,' I said, motioning with a dismissive wave of my hand as I glanced down at the round, brown, thick piece of something on my plate. 'She's sick. She just wanted to let me know that she couldn't pick me up for work today.'

They both nodded and looked away.

I stared down at the plate again. Was this the waffle creation thing Susan had talked about making on Monday?

I picked up a fork and tapped at the concoction like Lucas had done a few minutes ago. It was apparent he was still deciding how to negotiate his food, as he tried to make stabbing incisions across its surface, to break it up. Mine made a hollow, but hard sort of *thwack*ing sound that suddenly had me concerned about the structural integrity of my dental care. I didn't know whether to eat it or play Frisbee with it.

Instead, I picked up the maple syrup from the centre of the table and smothered it on. It might soften the hard exterior slightly, allowing me to bypass the flavour that I was positive was unique to Susan's cooking. The less I had to taste of it the better.

From the corner of my eye I saw Lucas and George watching me. It was obviously my turn for the taste test. 'You guys going to the store today?' I asked as I tried to skewer a piece of the now slightly softened creation onto the end of my fork. It was still like trying to spear a piece of concrete with a toothpick.

'We are, but don't worry. One of us will come and collect you at six.'

I shrugged. 'No problems. I could catch the bus if you prefer?'

Susan shook her head. 'No, no,' she answered quickly. 'We will come and get you.'

I tossed a piece of the waffle into my mouth and began to chew.

Lucas watched with intense interest.

I had to stop myself from letting my lips shrivel up and pucker inwards. She must have used salt in the recipe instead of sugar—and lots of it. I put my fork down and pushed the plate away. That was enough for George, who promptly picked up the newspaper, and feigned a stomach ache. Lucas claimed he simply wasn't hungry and, amazingly, Susan didn't seem the slightest bit put out. I decided then and there that her taste buds had to be inoperable because she ate every last piece on her plate and then helped herself to the rest of mine.

The woman has a cast iron stomach.

When I arrived at work, Glen was already busying himself inside the shop, dusting shelves and arranging a few of the accessories. Apparently Martha, my algebra instructor at the IMI, was going to make an appearance today. She had book-work to catch up on and a few important clients that spent ridiculous sums of money that were coming in specifically to see her sometime during lunch. Glen didn't seem offended that his design services were not required during the meetings. He said that he was happy to have a reprieve from the consults so that he could work on the store's displays. The fact that Kayla was off sick today meant that I was roped into helping him, but asking me to decorate was like asking a man to remember to put down the toilet seat—impossible.

I listened to his ramblings good-naturedly, though I wasn't specifically listening to the details. My head was drifting back to my brief interlude with William. It had been three days since I had last seen him last and looked into his widened eyes and read the shock and confusion in them—seen what I was dawning upon him. During those three days, I was ashamed to admit, I'd thought of little else.

Between learning to accept what I was, trying to trust my parents, and dabbling with the notion that I might be one day soon be wandering eternity alone, I hadn't made room inside my head for much else.

True to my nature, I hadn't wandered around the house feeling sad and sorry for myself as Susan and George had first expected me too. Instead, I'd thrown myself into my training at the IMI. I wanted to do all that I could to arm myself against any enemy that may soon be upon me, enemies which could possibly include William Granville, and sadly, as the realisation had struck me on Wednesday, my parents. Though they seemed to care about me, I always felt a little on the outer circle, just out of reach of their embrace, just enough so that they didn't have to feel anything too deeply for me.

'Did you hear me, Elena?' Glen said, reaching down from the ladder he was standing on and touching my shoulder.

'Huh?' I said, looking up at him in a daze.

'I said could you please pass me that blue lamp behind you?'

I turned around and grabbed the lamp. 'Sorry, must have been in my own world.'

'I can see that,' he said, frowning heavily at the red cushion that I had just passed him. He carefully climbed down the ladder, walked around behind me, tossing the red cushion back onto the bed display and grabbed the blue lamp that he'd asked for.

I should have stayed in bed. What's wrong with me today?

'Why don't you go and grab yourself some lunch, Elena? It's quiet today. I can manage the store on my own for an hour if you want to step out.'

I glanced at my watch. One o'clock. 'Thanks Glen. I might just take you up on that.'

I left him sorting out the display of blue accessories, or red ones, I couldn't really remember which, and headed to the staffroom to grab my backpack. I toyed with the idea of walking over to the shopping centre and grabbing myself some sushi for lunch and then quickly dismissed it, remembering that I had left my wallet at home.

I cursed silently. It looked like I was going to have to pray there was something edible for dinner tonight or there was a very good chance I was going to die from starvation.

When I got to the staffroom, I saw that my backpack was sitting on the table instead of tucked into the cupboard where I was sure I'd placed it earlier that morning. Given that it was just Glen and I here this morning, and he wasn't the type to riffle through other people's belongings, I could only conclude that someone was trying to get my attention.

I crossed the room, pulled my backpack closer to me and studied its exterior. There was nothing abnormal going on there.

I grasped the zips in my fingers and pulled them back slowly, peeking into the gaping interior lining. Just inside the opening was a small folded piece of white paper. I plucked it out, unfolded it and then read the tidy script written inside.

Elena,
A thousand apologies for how I reacted the other day. You must understand that in all my years I have never encountered another such as yourself. I do not fully understand what I have learnt yet, but I would like you to know that my offer still stands. I would very much like to get to know you better.

W.G.

I re-read the letter a further three times, the words not fully sinking in until the fourth read. I held the stiff white paper in my hands and stared at the letters until they all blurred into an inky mess. It took several attempts to remoisten my eyes. Rapid blinking and lid rubbing were what eventually cleared my vision. And when I could finally see again, the words looked strange—harder to translate than Egyptian hieroglyphics. Or perhaps that was merely the surprise talking. How had this happened? How had he found the moral constitution to look through the horror of what I could potentially turn into and still find enough resolve to want to get to know me better? Was he simply curious now that he knew the truth? Or was this just an excuse to get to know my weaknesses, instead? Or did he sympathise, understanding what it means to be different?

I shook my head and folded the piece of paper back up, a small sliver of happiness rippling through me. Maybe I was as insane as he was, but I wanted there to be truth in his words. I wanted to know him just as much as it appeared that he wanted to know me.

'So can we start getting to know each other now?'

I started and looked up to see William standing by the staffroom door. His sudden appearance had knocked the wind right out of me and sent my heart into a panicked rhythm.

Why does he have to keep doing that?

'What are you doing here?' I demanded, just realising I worked in a store that was owned by one of The Protectors, a Protector that was due to arrive at any moment now.

'I came to see you,' he answered, smiling playfully. 'Your boss mentioned the last time that I came here looking for you that you worked on Saturdays.'

I heard the jangling of the front bell and the door closing

noisily, followed quickly by Martha greeting Glen. I could also hear her asking where I was. 'You can't be here right now,' I hissed. 'My boss is a Protector.'

He folded his arms in front of his chest, the muscle in his forearms and biceps bulging slightly. 'So?'

I frowned. 'So? How can you say that? I'm forbidden from talking with you. If Martha finds you here with me she's going to tell my parents.'

'I'm still not certain I foresee a problem.'

'Seriously? You've met my parent's, right?' I didn't wait for a response. 'Well, if they find out that you and I are speaking, they're going to tear me a new one.'

He cocked his head to the side and frowned. 'Tear you a new what? I don't believe I've heard that expression before.'

I blinked at him. 'It's a pretty common turn of phrase for people our age, you know.'

'Our age? Elena, I'm four hundred and forty-four years old. Give or take a few years.'

'Ah sh-shit,' I stuttered. 'You're like the Crypt Keeper or something.'

'Elena?' I heard Martha call out from somewhere near the front entry. The bell from the door was still jangling from her arrival.

I looked at William in a panic. He just smiled. How could he be so calm? I knew why. It wasn't his ass on the line here. It was mine.

'Hide!' I hissed at him.

'I'm sorry? Did you just tell me to hide?' he replied, amusement lighting his voice.

'If you don't hide, I can promise you there'll be no getting to know one another, because I'll be dead.' I gave him a pleading look.

'Elena? I hear voices? Are you back there?'

'Yeah, Martha, I'm in the staffroom.' I dived into my backpack, looking for my MP3 player and made shooing motions at William at the same time. He grinned at me, and then, crouching down low, sprung up towards the ceiling. He landed with a gentle *thud*, splayed out flat on the roof above me.

Cool, he looks like Spiderman.

'Elena?'

I immediately looked back down again. A second later, Martha stepped through the door. 'Hi there,' she said enthusiastically. 'Thanks for coming in to work today, even though there isn't too much point. We're a lot quieter than I thought we'd be for a Saturday. Everyone seems to have this flu at the moment—even Glen thinks he might be coming down with something. He said you weren't your usual productive self today either.'

'I um … it's no problem Martha. I need the money.'

'Who were you talking to?' she said, glancing around the room.

I crossed my fingers behind my back and prayed that she didn't look upwards. 'I wasn't talking to anyone,' I said, holding my MP3 player up. 'I was singing to the music.'

She looked at me suspiciously and then swept the room with her eyes. 'Well that's some kind of baritone you've got going on there. I could have sworn I heard a man in here with you.'

I shook my head and laughed nervously. 'What part of that sentence sounds right to you? Since when have you ever seen me with a man?'

She looked at me, seemingly unconvinced, and then shook it off with a wide smile. 'You're right, sorry, I did come in here for a reason and it wasn't to disturb your lunch break. But I thought, given how quiet we are today and that I had to come in anyway, that you might want to go home and enjoy the rest of your Saturday.'

I resisted the urge to look up. 'Umm, are you sure?'

She nodded. 'I already called Susan. I hope that's okay? She's sending Lucas over to come and get you.'

'Oh, okay. I guess I'll see you Monday at the IMI then.'

'Okay, sure thing. Enjoy your weekend, Elena.'

After that she left.

I looked back up as William flipped backwards like an acrobat and dropped down quietly from the ceiling. His feet impacting with the linoleum floor barely made any sound at all. 'So I guess that makes you free to talk then, doesn't it?' he said, straightening the collar of his shirt.

'Shhh.' I placed a finger to my lips to emphasize the point. 'Keep your mouth shut, will you? I don't want her coming back.'

I dumped my MP3 player back in my bag and zipped it up. Tossing it over my shoulder, I made my way to the staffroom door and peered around the corner. Martha was greeting some clients that had just walked through the door and Glen was still busying himself with the accessory display.

Oh would you look at that—it was definitely blue.

'Okay, go,' I said, motioning with my hand for him to duck past me and head out through the backdoor. His blank face was a good indication that he wasn't real good at charades.

William stepped up beside me and looked out over the front of the shop. 'Go where?' he asked innocently.

'Oh my God!' I said, slapping my forehead. 'Are you always this obtuse? How have you not been staked to death by now?'

He shrugged.

'Look, my brother is going to pick me up soon. You have to scram.'

He leaned back against the door frame casually, like he didn't have a care in the world. He crossed his arms back in front of his chest and then proceeded to cross one leg lazily over the other. 'You are on a mission to get rid of me today, aren't you?' He chuckled, the lilt of his British accent rich and thick with amusement.

'Well your timing isn't exactly fabulous.'

'I take time where I can. I am busy trying to track down some rogue vânători at the moment, or had you forgotten?'

'No I had not forgotten,' I answered testily. 'But there is little proof that there is a pack in this area at the moment. My parents are pretty good at what they do. Just in case you had forgotten. If there were any vânători here then they would know about it.'

I paused and looked at him intently. I had no idea why I had suddenly felt the need to defend their actions so strongly. 'At the moment they're more concerned that you and your friends are here for … other reasons.'

His eyebrow rose marginally. 'Such as?'

I swallowed, wondering how I could answer without sounding full of myself. 'Well, umm … me.'

He chuckled again and turned away. 'That couldn't be further from the truth.'

'Then why are you still here?' I said, challenging him.

'I just told you. We're here to hunt the rest of the pack. There are still five of them out there, Elena. Five. That's a lot for such a small area.'

'There's no proof.'

He tapped the side of his nose with a finger. 'This is all the proof that I need.'

'Are they in Cairns right now?'

'I think so, but I'm not one hundred percent certain. We're trying to run down each of their scent trails, but it's not easy when there are so many.'

'Oh I'm sorry, I thought this,' I said mockingly, tapping the side of my nose, 'was all the proof that you needed.'

'Elena!' Martha trilled from the front of the store. 'Lucas is here.'

I glanced out to the front and saw the Forrester pull up in a disabled parking space just by the front door. Through the glass I saw Lucas drumming his hands on the steering wheel, nodding his head and singing to himself.

I looked back at William who was no longer looking at me. 'I gotta go,' I said quietly, as I stepped around him and headed for the front door.

He grabbed my hand before I disappeared around the corner. His fingers were cold and hard. I looked down at them, his flesh so pale against my own. 'Meet me later,' he said quietly.

'I can't.'

'You can do anything you want to, Elena.'

I shook my head. 'I've pushed my luck too far lately. I was serious about the wrath of my parents, you know, and I like my backside just the way it is.'

He frowned in confusion. 'Will you try?'

I looked at his fingers enclosed around my own and sighed. It felt good. Safe. 'Where?'

'Let's keep it close. How about the high school oval just down the road from your house? There's a small skate ramp there and some benches in the shade of some trees. Find those bench seats. That's where I'll be waiting for you.'

I nodded and pulled my hand out of his stony grip. The skin of my fingers felt cold and kind of tingly where he had touched me, and there was a definite warming in the pit of my stomach. I turned away from him before my body decided to throw another weird sensation at me. The tingling I could handle. It was the odd feelings deep inside my body that I wasn't prepared for.

I pushed those thoughts aside and headed through the store, refusing to glance back just in case he was still watching me. I didn't want to give him the satisfaction of seeing how he had affected me.

I waved goodbye to Glen over my shoulder and pushed through the front door, the bell announcing my exit. Lucas was still bobbing away excitedly to music in the car when I hopped in. He was really into all that alternative, techno-style dance music. I personally preferred something you could really listen to, something that you could actually sing along with.

'Hey,' he said to me as I closed the front door and threw my backpack onto the rear seat.

'Hey.'

'How was work?'

'Boring.'

'Yeah, me too. Mum's got me going through the storage room and counting how many bags of nails and screws we have. It's a belated stocktake or something like that. At least we're finished for the day.'

'What? The hardware store is closing for the rest of the day?' Why was I panicking? I could always meet William another day.

He shook his head and turned the music down. 'Nah, I'm finished for the day, but Mum and Wesley are staying and keeping it open. Dad's been picked up by Malcolm, though, and they're heading over to the drive-in. Apparently they're getting a little concerned by the number of girls going missing in Townsville and Mackay. They're going to try and work out what to do next.'

So they won't be home for a while …

'Do you think the Vampires were right and the Vânǎtors are to blame?' I asked.

He shrugged. 'I don't know. It seems likely though given that the Vamps are still in town.'

'Speaking of vampires,' I said, glancing sideways at him. 'Are you still up for a little co-mingling?'

'What did you have in mind?'

'How about a little rendezvous at the skate ramp?'

He looked at me abruptly, the car wavering on the road. Just in case, I grabbed onto the door handle and checked that my seatbelt was secure.

'You saw him again didn't you?' he said nervously.

I nodded, still gripping the handle with my fingers as his careless driving continued. 'Ah-huh. He came into work. He wants to meet me this afternoon sometime.'

'He came into Martha's place?'

I rolled my eyes. 'I know—don't get me started. He didn't even care that I might get in trouble by his presence. I swear to God that vampire will be the death of me.'

'That's not funny, E.'

I grinned. 'Sorry. I didn't mean it literally.' I swallowed. At least I hoped so.

'Does he know about our little arrangement?'

I snorted. 'I don't care if he does or doesn't. I'd feel much safer knowing you were there.'

He switched off the radio and looked at his watch. 'Dad's been gone for an hour already and Mum said I don't need to pick her up for at least another couple of hours yet, so we can go now if you want to.'

I screwed my face up. 'Can we go home first? I want to

get out of these clothes and into something I can better conceal my knife in. I also need to eat. In case, you didn't notice, I didn't exactly eat much this morning.'

The tires squealed as he rounded a corner a little too sharply and then over-corrected. 'Neither did I. Now that you mention it, I'm starving too.'

I closed my eyes briefly and prayed to a higher being as he swerved the car dangerously past some pedestrians who weren't even off the crosswalk yet. 'Besides,' I said, opening an eye and watching the speedometer drop to near zero, 'I only just left him at work. The sun's high in the sky at the moment and it's more difficult for him to get around. I imagine he might be thinking of meeting us sometime after three when the afternoon sun isn't so intense.'

'If we leave it too long, Elena, Dad might come home and then we won't be able to leave again, especially not with you being grounded and everything.'

'What are you suggesting then?'

He smiled. 'Let's get changed, get some food into us and then we can go. If we're not at home then no one can stop us.'

'What about your cell phone? They might try to call us and find out where we are.'

'Oops,' he said, covering his mouth in contrived surprise. 'I must have forgotten to turn it on this morning.' He reached into his pocket, retrieved his cell phone and switched it off.

I frowned. 'I think I'm starting to rub off on you.'

'Bullshit. I've always been a badass. I'm just way better at lying, sneaking out, and pretending to be a saint than you are. But if anyone ever asks, particularly any tall, gorgeous, overly inflated blondes—then I taught you everything you know,' he said. He winked at me and then accelerated.

My mind boggled at this latest revelation. My brother obviously had more going on than I gave him credit for. Perhaps we weren't so different after all?

'How are we not blood relatives?' I said, laughing at the irony—our misbehaviour might bring us even closer together.

He grinned. 'It's a frigging mystery.'

CHAPTER ELEVEN: BLUSHING

The quickest and less obvious method of getting to the agreed upon meeting place was by foot. Taking the car meant trying to find a parking spot close to the grounds and fighting with the sporting fans packed into mini vans and utility vehicles all vying for coveted parking.

So Lucas and I ran down to the end of the street, dashed across the road and jumped the four foot fence into the high school grounds. We were excited by the prospect of our imminent meeting with William, if not just the tiniest bit apprehensive.

We paused for a moment, straightening our clothes and wiping away the beads of perspiration that had began to form across our skin. There were plenty of people here on the high school grounds today which meant lots of witnesses. Not that I expected anything other than conversation to occur.

In the centre of the oval a soccer match was in full swing. To the side, track and field athletes were using the long narrow strip of grass to run their paces. Surrounding both parties was a smattering of family members and plenty of small children playing happily in the winter sunshine.

I had to ask myself why he had chosen this place. He'd said it was easier for me to get to. That was true enough, given I only lived down the street, but why here? Was it because the place was so littered with spectators? And if so, did that mean he selected the neutral location to ease my apprehension or his own?

My gaze drifted across the groupings of athletes and bystanders, searching for the skate ramp that William had been referring to. Given that I didn't attend a regular high school myself, I'd never wandered here before. Sure, I'd walked past the fence, but I'd never ventured inside.

And then I found it.

It wasn't far but you could hardly call it a decent skate ramp. It was no bigger than our driveway. It was a half-pipe concrete construction semi-recessed into the ground and offered very little in the way of excitement or newness. The ramp, or should I say, concrete dip in the ground, was practically deserted. There were only two young children in the vicinity, rolling their toy matchbox cars down the ramp rather than skating.

I smiled at them as we passed. They smiled back and then continued to argue about whose car could go the fastest. There seemed to be a tie between a little black hummer and a sporty red corvette, although the yellow convertible was most definitely still in the running.

I left the sound of their eager chatter behind us and headed towards the bench seats William had described.

They were closer to the basketball courts than the skate ramp and were completely covered in shade—thus the appeal, I supposed. The large overhanging mango trees were dense and closely packed together. Their branches spread like gnarled arms far and wide creating the perfect canopy for a vampire out wandering around in the afternoon sun.

'There they are,' Lucas said mechanically, his arm extended in front of him.

I saw where he was pointing and spotted three vampires

instead of just one. He'd brought his two companions. Why? I was suddenly grateful for the crowded park and Lucas standing by my side. Though we had not made any specific arrangements regarding our meeting, I had expected him to come alone.

'He's not alone,' I said quietly.

Lucas shook his head. 'Did you expect him to be?'

'Honestly? Yes.'

'Well lucky you brought me then.' He grabbed my hand in a reassuring gesture and tried to smile. I could see the fear in his eyes. I couldn't blame him. If it came down to push coming to shove, we were toast.

We pushed forward anyway. We were both too stubbornly curious for our own good. It was like opening the refrigerator door and seeing a rich chocolate cake with thick butter cream frosting. It was impossible just to look at it and imagine its sweetness across your tongue, only to close the door again without the courage to taste it.

It was the same scenario. We were both anxious to learn about what we'd been trained so proficiently to one day kill. And now an opportunity had presented. These three vampires were our chocolate cake.

Despite the mounting tension in the air due to the presence of his travelling companions, William, clad in a pair of jeans, a black, long sleeved shirt and with his trademark sunglasses, reclined comfortably on a seat behind them. He draped an arm casually over the back of the chair, his long legs spread out in front of him, one foot resting lightly over the top of the other. Behind the sunglasses I knew he was watching me.

I could feel it.

His presence was all-encompassing, impossible to ignore. Not only was he exquisitely handsome, but he was downright alluring, seemingly oozing confidence. His scent of sandal-wood and spice penetrated the air like a thick cloud and bathed my skin from head to toe in warmth. It was not overpowering like it had been at the rave, merely a pleasant aroma that seemed to wrap me in a cocoon, testing my resolve.

His two companions were less than enamoured by our approach, and contrasted with William's outwardly calm appearance at our imminent arrival, they leapt forward into half-crouch positions, like lithe jungle cats defending their young. I watched as their lips curled back slightly over their perfect white teeth. Small snarls erupting from the backs of their throats, followed by the hiss of a warning.

What was with the hostility?

'Kind of testy considering they called the meeting, aren't they?' Lucas whispered to me.

'Maybe they just caught a whiff of that microwave burrito you ate for lunch.'

He jabbed me in the side with his bony elbow. 'Better safe than sorry.'

I smiled. He'd only eaten it because the ingredients on the back of the box said that it contained garlic. Despite all the truths we knew about vampires, Lucas was still adamant that some of the crap you saw in movies had to be true.

We slowed down a little, realising that each step that we took closer was making them more and more uncomfortable. The last thing we wanted to do was cause a scene. The blonde girl we'd briefly encountered at the IMI with the Shirley Temple hair hissed at us like a rattlesnake. The other one, the male, was certainly wary of us, but not going as crazy as his sister was. He looked uncannily like his twin, except he was a head taller, extremely muscular and had soft curls of blonde hair that rested on top of his

shoulders, just like Lucas. He smelt faintly of raw masculinity and a touch of lemon myrtle, while his sister smelled
like citrus sorbet.

*I wondered if that's what their compulsion smells like. Or
am I simply in tune with the individual aromas of vampires
because I'm going to be one?*

To ease tension and show that we meant no harm, I
raised my hands in front of me in surrender, Lucas following suit. If nothing else, it was to simply appease the delicate
nature of the blonde who couldn't keep her fangs inside her
mouth.

'Easy now,' I said quietly, as if talking down an over-
excited thoroughbred. 'We're just here to talk.'

They both hissed at us again, an ominous sound rum-
bling from the back of their throats that halted the both of
us in our tracks.

I looked to the right. The two kids playing with the
matchbox cars back near the skate ramp looked over at us
warily. The hissing was quite loud compared to the relative
silence at this end of the field and it was clear that the children were more than a little frightened by what could have
made such a menacing sound.

I forgot about the welfare of the kids and focused back
on the scent that William was still wrapping around me.
Whether it was purposeful or not, my knees went weak and
my stomach filled with riotous butterflies. I didn't like it,
and I certainly didn't like being snarled at by his two vampire friends.

'William, call off the guard dogs please or we're out of
here,' I said breathily.

They both turned around to look at him, as if waiting for further instructions. He said nothing at all, simply
gave them a quick nod. They altered their stance slightly,

straightening up a little and putting their teeth away, but neither one stopped watching us.

William stood up, stepped around in front of them and placed a reassuring hand on each of their shoulders to calm them down.

'What do you want?' the male companion asked me. I couldn't remember what his name was, or his sister's, who was looking at me as if I was contaminated.

I looked at him, perplexed. 'What do I want? William's the one that invited me here, not the other way around.'

The male looked to William for confirmation, confusion clearly evident in his eyes.

William patted his shoulder again and he seemed to relax a little. 'It's okay, Thomas. I asked Elena here so that I might get to know her a little better.'

'Why?' the girl said pouting. 'She's doesn't look particularly special.'

I scowled, taking an instant dislike to her.

At least I don't look like a four year old.

'What about him?' Thomas said, looking Lucas up and down. 'Why is he here?'

Lucas held two fingers up in front of him and smiled nervously. 'Peace man. I'm just a spectator.'

I interrupted. 'He's my brother and a Protector and I wanted him here,' I said as I yanked his hand back down and shot him a look. 'No doubt my reasons are the same reason that William brought the two of you here today.'

William shook his head. 'I did not ask Marianne and Thomas to come here, Elena. I apologise. They followed me here without my consent.'

'Is mistrust common for vampires?' I asked.

Marianne snorted. 'It's not him we don't trust. It's you.'

I nearly laughed. They were afraid of me? What a lovely

notion. I instantly felt more secure. 'Well, I'm here now. Either you want to talk or you don't. But if we talk, William, it's just between you and me. I didn't agree to a group discussion.'

'Like hell it is!' Marianne hissed.

Lucas also looked less than pleased.

The silence that followed seemed to hang in the air as I looked from one face to the other, unable to gauge any idea about what they were all thinking. Their expressions remained icy as they looked to William for guidance, pursing their lips together in a hard line. It didn't help either that I couldn't see any of their eyes underneath the protection of the sunglasses. It was difficult to tell what they were really thinking, having only eyebrows and mouth movements as an indication.

'Okay,' William eventually answered.

Thomas turned to William. 'Do you think that's a good idea?'

He patted his friend on the shoulder again. 'It's alright, Thomas—we're just talking.' He turned to me. 'Shall we?' he said, gesturing with his hand towards one of the benches at the far end of the mango tree allotment.

'William. I think we should come with you,' Marianne said, pouting again.

We're just talking, Blondie, not planning marriage.

William held up his hands in front of him, which seemed to stop both Thomas and Marianne from approaching. 'It will be fine.' He gave his friend's a long look. 'I need to know for sure.'

'William will you please just think about this for a second,' Marianne murmured. 'The family that cares for her are not the sort of people we want to be up against.'

'Think about who I will be up against if I don't follow this through,' he answered her quietly.

Thomas and Marianne snarled at me.

'Look, I'm not going to hurt him, if that's what you're both worried about.' I almost laughed at the insanity of the idea. Instead I settled for shaking my head indignantly. 'Besides, if there's anyone here that you should be worried about, it's my brother, Lucas. He wields magical capabilities above and beyond any Protector of his age.'

All heads swivelled to Lucas standing beside me. 'Thanks for that,' he muttered in my ear, 'I so love having a giant red target stamped on my forehead.'

I jabbed him in the ribs. 'Man up, badass.'

He grunted in earnest.

Marianne redirected her attention to me, her fingers curling into fists at her sides. The vein in the side of her temple was pulsing and I could tell by the way that her skin was slowly becoming translucent and her canines extending, that she was seriously considering whether William's conversation with me was worth all the drama. Thomas was now looking at me with genuine interest as opposed to hostility.

'Look, I understand that you're all a little bit wary of me and that's okay,' I rushed on, a little more sympathetically. 'But I promise you that I won't hurt, William, if you don't hurt my brother.' It sounded like I was pleading, and I wasn't surprised that when I looked up at Lucas he was shaking his head at me.

'Why don't you just cut my legs off so I can't run away either?' he whispered.

I grimaced and gave him an apologetic look. Hopefully he would just understand that I was nervous.

'What? Are we supposed to just take your word for it?' Marianne answered, her lips pulling into a vicious sneer.

'No, but you can take my word for it,' William answered

quietly. 'And I'll hear no more about this. You know this must be done.' He turned his back on both of them and motioned with his hand for me to start walking.

I looked at Lucas and suddenly had a real twang of guilt in the pit of my stomach. Besides being completely exasperated by my words, he suddenly looked like he was about to pee his pants.

I turned to him and placed a reassuring hand on his arm. 'Now remember,' I said, trying to make it all better again. 'If they try anything, you can use your magic to incapacitate them, but otherwise play nice, okay? You don't want to accidentally kill them like you did to that pack of werewolves last year.'

I bit my tongue to hide my smile, hoping they would buy the lie. It seemed to make Lucas feel better because he nodded.

Both Thomas and Marianne took an almost imperceptible step backwards. It was good to see they had a healthy respect for the power of The Protectors. 'I'll be back in a few.'

I took a few steps backwards before turning around and following quickly after William. He hadn't gotten far. 'Where are we going?' I asked, even though I'd already surmised we were heading to the furthest bench seat under the shade. I just wanted to fill the silence between us with something. That way I could distract myself from the weird jittering that was occurring in my body just from the sheer proximity of him.

'It doesn't really matter where we go,' he answered. 'We won't get any privacy, anyway, so I just thought somewhere so that you can sit down.'

'I'm fine. Do you need to sit down?'

He shook his head. 'Not especially.'

'Why is that?'

He looked at me oddly. 'I would have thought that you would know everything that there is to know about us.'

I shook my head from side to side. 'I know most things, but given that I only found out I was a born vampire four years ago and I live with Protectors,' I grimaced. 'Well, my knowledge is limited. Tuesday was the first time they even bothered to tell me I had werewolf DNA. And that was only because your sudden appearance at the IMI raised questions that couldn't be ignored anymore.' I shrugged, realising that I was rambling a little bit. 'Relevant information is very difficult to come by when the IMI decides that it's need to know only.' I laughed bitterly. 'Apparently I didn't need to know.'

He smiled and motioned to the bench seat. I sat down and he took a seat right beside me, our knees briefly touching and energy surged between us.

'Well, in that case then, let me educate you.' He smiled and I briefly wondered if there had ever been a woman who had resisted him in the past. 'I don't need to sit down because I don't get tired. It's simply out of habit from our human days that we do it. There's also the necessity to blend in with the rest of the human populace. It's the main reason that we maintain these common practices. For instance, we don't need to breathe, swallow, blink, scratch or perform any other instinctive human reaction to physical stimulus, but we still do. It would alert the unknowing to what we were if we didn't.' His smile suddenly became slightly lopsided. 'It's bad enough that we're stuck with cold skin and a pasty complexion. We don't want to make it too easy for humans to guess what we are.'

'Do you sleep?'

He nodded. 'Sometimes, but it's not at all necessary

because we never get tired. But it can be nice to black out for a while. If I didn't shut my eyes occasionally and block out all the madness of the world, then I feel positive I would go mad from sensory overload.'

That made sense I supposed. 'Do you like being a vampire?'

He frowned. 'I never had a choice.'

'So you are a born vampire, like me?' I was so eager to learn what could not be learnt from those around me, that I was hurling questions at him even though we were not properly acquainted just yet. 'I'm sorry,' I quickly added. 'I don't mean to pry, I'm just tremendously curious.'

He nodded again and smiled. 'Don't apologise. This is the reason we met—so that we can understand each other better. And yes, in answer to your question, I am a born .'

'Do you know who your father is?' I was doing it again. Did I have no buffer between my brain and my mouth?

'Yes.'

'Was he always around? Did he know when you were born? Did he love your mother? Are you close?'

He chuckled lightly. 'That's a lot of questions, and a no to all of them.'

'What about your mother?'

He looked away and stared at the soccer match in the distance. 'I'd rather not talk about that.'

A mystery. How interesting.

'What about Marianne and Thomas?'

'Yes, they too are born vampires.'

I sat quietly for a few moments before speaking. 'I've never met another vampire before.'

His eyebrows showed his surprise. 'Never?'

'Nope. You three are the first.'

'Actually, I probably shouldn't be surprised. Given where

you live I imagine it would be rare for you to encounter us.' He seemed to look down at the ground as if suddenly lost in thought.

I shrugged. 'It doesn't help that Lucas and I have been sheltered from the truth our entire lives. We're both very confused at the moment.'

He looked up again. 'Confused?'

'Ah-huh,' I said, looking over to Lucas who appeared to have gotten over his stage fright. He seemed to be having a particularly animated conversation with the others, even if it was apparently one-sided. They were merely watching him while he talked with his big, expressive hand gestures. I wondered briefly what it was that he could be speaking about.

I focused back on William again. 'Lucas and I don't know whether or not you want to get to know us for the sake of friendship, or for the sake of bleeding us for information, pardon the pun, or just to kill us.'

He chuckled lightly. 'How about we save the killing for the Vânătors? Besides, I wouldn't want to stop your brother now. It appears he is giving Marianne and Thomas a full descriptive lecture about the benefits that garlic has on the immune system.'

'You can hear them talking all the way over there?'

'Of course.'

I blinked a couple of times. 'How far away can you hear a conversation?'

'No more than five or six kilometres I should think.'

'That's quite amazing. So Thomas and Marianne can hear what we are saying right now?'

He nodded. 'If they are listening, which undoubtedly they are.'

Marianne chose that exact moment to turn and look in

our direction which immediately cleared up any doubt. I may not be able to hear her across great distances, but if she could hear me that would be karmic. 'So if they can hear me now,' I said, looking at her hateful gaze across the park, 'then Marianne would know that I think her hairstyle looks like it belongs to a preschooler.'

She snarled at me and snapped out her teeth again, as if daring me to say something to tip her over the edge.

William chuckled lightly. 'I think she heard you. She's quite sensitive about her hair you know.'

'So I gathered. Is that because it doesn't grow and you can't change it?'

He nodded. 'How we look on the night of our turning is how we are destined to look for eternity.'

I looked at William's short dark hair and frowned as a flash of images shot past my eyes that didn't make any sense. William's image blurred in front of me and I saw a version of him with soft, wavy shoulder-length brown hair and green eyes that were tinged with grey and silver, not the short dark hair and plain green eyes that I had come to recognise. It was weird. It was almost like I was looking at someone else for a moment, someone that I had met once before, someone who wasn't William.

'You'd look good with long hair,' I said, in a daze as the image of the dreamlike apparition disappeared and William's face came back into focus again.

He frowned. 'No I wouldn't.'

I held up my hands in surrender, but decided to keep future thoughts regarding his appearance to myself. Obviously it wasn't just Marianne who was touchy about her locks.

'Can I ask you something?' he said, trying to change the subject.

'You may.'

He leant back on the bench and crossed his legs again. 'How did it happen?'

'How did what happen?'

He lowered his glasses and peered at me over the rims. His green eyes were devastating and I wondered why I had earlier thoughts of grey and silver tendrils running through them. 'How did Vânător DNA get into your bloodstream?'

Be careful, Elena, you don't know what his intentions are.

'Oh that,' I said, now staring down at my sneakers. 'That's kind of a long story.'

'I've got time.'

I shook my head. 'I don't. I shouldn't even be here right now.'

'Because you aren't allowed to associate with your own kind?'

I smiled with relief and a sudden surge of happiness belted through me. Despite the fact that I was in fact half vânător, he still appeared to consider me a vampire above anything else. It made me feel a little bit better about my circumstances and the future ahead of me.

'No, that's not it,' I answered. 'I mean, don't get me wrong, Susan and George would kill Lucas and I if they knew we were talking to you right now, but that's not the reason. I'm technically grounded.'

He raised an eyebrow. 'Grounded? I gather this means that you are being punished in some regard?'

I frowned. 'Do you even remember being a teenager?'

He motioned to his body all over. 'I am technically still a teenager. The only part of me that has aged is my mind. My physical being is forever frozen in time. Unfortunately that also means that I'm eternally challenged with teenage

… urges. It's quite unfair really.' He flicked me a devilish grin.

I giggled in response.

What the hell? Did I just giggle?

You totally just did. What a loser.

My face flushed red with embarrassment and I turned away before he could notice.

'Oh, Elena,' he said suddenly, panicked and rushing out of his seat. 'Please try not to do that.'

'Huh? Do what?' I looked back over at him, my face still the colour of crimson.

He was no longer sitting beside me, but several paces away.

I stood, suddenly feeling awkward.

I looked over to Lucas. He was no longer standing in animated conversation, but standing particularly still beside Marianne. All three of them were watching our exchange intensely. I saw the blue light dancing across the tips of Lucas's finger. All three of them could sense that something was wrong. 'What have I done wrong, because I have no idea?'

'I'm sorry, I didn't mean to frighten you, it's nothing,' he answered dismissively, taking a small step back towards me, visibly tense.

I snorted. 'I'm not scared, but it's obviously something. Just tell me. I don't like playing games.'

He took another few steps forward, his eyes hidden beneath the lenses of his sunglasses again. 'This is not a game to me either, Elena, believe me, but this is what I am.' He reached up and lowered his glasses, giving me a quick view of his midnight-coloured eyes.

I glanced nervously at Lucas. Thomas had a hand resting on his shoulder. Was he restraining him? Whatever the intended result, Lucas couldn't have cared less.

William halted, stopping at the edge of the bench seat again, and replacing the sunglasses back over his demonic eyes.

Instead of attacking me, as I had expected, he ran his fingers nervously through his short thicket of stylishly mussed black hair and then gripped the edge of the bench seat for support. His knuckles flexed automatically with the strength in his fingers and he took a deep breath in, calming the creature within. His fingers left behind indentations, biting into the edges of the wood as if he'd just pressed his hand into something no harder than a lump of butter. And as I stared at the newly formed grooves, I couldn't help but wonder what those fingers could do to my body if he ever lost complete control around me.

'I'm sorry, Elena,' he said quietly and calmly. 'It was your blushing that took me by surprise.'

'I wasn't blushing,' I said, shaking my head. 'I don't blush.'

Well, at least not until I'd met you.

He looked upwards as if asking for help, then took a deep breath and sat back down, motioning for me to join him.

I took a few wary steps back towards him before I sat down again, my curiosity ticking into overtime. Before he had a chance to do anything, I leaned forward, slowly reaching out and touching the rims of his glasses, lowering them down to the end of his nose as he had done just before. I wanted to see his eyes. I wanted to see if I was once again sitting next to the man or the beast.

He stared back at me with all the beauty and the clarity of his usual emerald eyes. There was absolutely no trace of the darkness that had prevailed before, but in its place was an almost restless desire that seemed to stop him from breathing and his lips to form a tight line of imposed self control.

I swallowed deeply when I realised that I was staring,

and what had started out as innocent curiosity to watch his shift in form had suddenly become a wordless exchange that made my entire body tingle.

I started to slide the glasses back up his nose, trying in vain to end the awkward pause and my sudden shyness, but he caught my hands in his. They were cold and hard against my own, but I barely noticed it. All I could feel was the warmth of our connection as it spread like fire from his skin straight to mine, then down into a portion of myself that I barely recognised.

I sniffed discreetly at the air. He was not enticing me. I could smell his captivating scent, but was not overwhelmed by it. It was his touch. The tightening I was feeling way down below and the butterflies that played havoc in my stomach were a reaction purely of my own creation.

Swallowing again, I guided the sunglasses the rest of the way up his face until his eyes were completely covered again. I tried to pull away after that, but his hands did not let go and I suddenly felt those butterflies building.

Is this feeling normal?

He cupped my warm hands gently in his own, running his fingers along the flesh of my palm and touching the skin with tenderness and care. Heat stirred underneath his touch, scorching my flesh with need, and filling my mind with unwelcome thoughts of an intimate union.

I shook loose of whatever magic he was trying to fill me with, pulled my hands out of his grasp and tucked them back into my lap. I couldn't afford to let my emotions rule me. It would be dangerous to let these new feelings he had unearthed off the leash right now. I didn't know anything about him. I didn't know what he was capable of and worse—I had no idea what he wanted with me.

'Why did you ask me here?' I said quietly, keeping my

eyes on my hands in my lap. 'And don't tell me it's because you want to know me better because that just doesn't make any sense to me.'

'What do you want me to say?' he answered, his voice a little more gravelly and deep than before.

'Tell me the truth.'

'But Elena, I have told you the truth. I do want to know you better.'

'Why?'

'It's a whisper in my heart and a message in my head that is not to be ignored,' he answered, as if that explained everything. He must have seen the look on my face because he continued. 'It's not just your genes that fascinate me or your beauty, or even the fact that you even exist.' He muttered the last part more to himself. 'It's also the unnerving effect that your blood has upon me.'

'My blood? So it *does* appeal to you?' I shifted away from him, putting some distance between us. 'Lucas was right. You don't want to get to know me at all. You're trying to find a way to will me into submission so you can take your fill.'

'No, Elena, you've got me all wrong,' he said vehemently. 'I would never touch your blood. I haven't drunk human blood for practically my whole undead life. I'm not about to start with you.'

I pointed to his glasses. 'Then why the black eyes before? Is that why you wear the sunglasses, so that you can hide your thirst from everyone?'

He shook his head and tried to reach for my hand. I slid further away from him.

'No. We wear the sunglasses because the sunlight hurts our eyes. As for my brief transformation before, that was simply because you blushed.'

I started to hesitate.

He held up his hands. 'Deny it all you want, but it happened. Blood surged through every vein under your skin and lit up your face like a Christmas tree. I'm not saying this to scare you. I'm trying to be honest. Although I have been able to resist drinking human blood for just about my entire life, I'm not without my weaknesses. Your blood is irresistible, Elena. It's so clean and pure, completely untainted. When you blush, the vampire side of me finds it extremely difficult to ignore.'

'Oh,' I said. I didn't have a more intelligible response to that. 'What about at the rave where we first met? Could you smell my blood then?'

He nodded. 'I can smell everything around me, some things with more detail than others. If I choose to focus on a particular scent, it will become stronger to me than the others in the air nearby. When I met you, I could smell that you were human, smell the sweetness in your veins and smell the purity of your life force. But, until I was right up against your neck, I could not smell the werewolf in you or the vampire part of your blood.'

'Then why did you single me out from everyone else there? You were enticing me, I know it.'

He turned to the side and smiled lightly. 'Ah, now that is a question for another day.'

But I was stubborn, eager to know. 'Were you planning on biting me that night?'

'No, I just told you I don't drink human blood.'

'Did you know I was training with the IMI?'

'No.'

'Then what? Why were you trying to glamour me?'

He turned back to look at me, his lips still upturned in a smile. 'Need I remind you that I have the body of a teenage boy?' he said, gesturing to his long, lean body again.

I felt a renewed sense of heat fan across my face. So he was attracted to me. And that just made things infinitely more complicated.

He stopped smiling and pinched his nose. 'Blushing—again? Are you trying to punish me?'

I pushed myself to my feet and glanced over at Lucas. All three were still watching, and no doubt listening. 'I should go,' I said, doing my best to cover my burning face with my hair. 'Thanks for the chat. It was … enlightening.' I turned my back on him and headed off to rescue my brother, although he didn't look particularly bothered at the moment by his current company.

'Elena, wait,' William said, reaching out and taking my hand again. 'When will I see you again?'

I looked down at his hand in mine, the same feeling of heat instantly stirring something in the pit of my stomach. *Damn him.*

I shrugged, trying to feign nonchalance. 'When we cross paths, I expect.'

'That's rather vague.'

'Yes, I suppose it is, but given that both of us are resourceful people it will probably be soon.' I shook free of his grip and turned away without a backwards glance. He was simply too dangerous to be around right now and it wasn't his teeth that were the problem.

It was me.

I was attracted to him too, and those feelings that were stirring something deep inside of me were more dangerous than either of our darkest natures could ever be. I'd always prided myself on my focus and determination. Granted, I did enjoy partying with Kayla, but I still cared most about excelling at skills that would equip me for immortality. My main objective for the past four years had been to train hard and prove to the IMI that I was capable, somewhat emotionless, and ready to rise to the challenge of hunting without fear of retribution. I didn't have time to mess around with boys. There would be plenty of time for that later on when I was no longer human. But then again, where did I fit in? What if William turned out to be the only vampire that ever accepted me for who and what I was? Was I just about to walk away from something that could be good?

The only problem was, I still didn't trust him, and I certainly didn't trust my bodily responses around him either. So if I had to walk away, then so be it.

'Lucas, let's go,' I said, grabbing his hand as I walked right past the other two and tugged him back towards the fence line.

'Nice to meet you guys,' Lucas yelled over his shoulder as he waved to Thomas and Marianne. I had no idea what their reaction was and I didn't look.

'What's the rush?' Lucas said as he fell into stride next to me and shook his hand free. 'It seemed to us that you guys were just starting to get along.'

'Listening in were you?' I spat out.

He grinned sheepishly. 'Only after the part where you frightened him off.'

'I did no such thing.'

He touched a finger to my cheek and I slapped his hand away. 'I didn't know that you could blush,' he murmured. 'I thought you might have been missing that girly gene.'

'Shut up, Lucas.'

He threw his hands into his pockets and hunched his shoulders forward. 'Why are you upset with me? It's not my fault you have a crush on the Vampire.'

I lurched forward and clamped my hand over his mouth. 'Be quiet, they can hear you!' I hissed.

'I know,' he mumbled through my clamped hand. 'Great, isn't it?'

I took my hand away and punched him lightly in the shoulder. 'No, it's not. So just shut up before you say something really stupid.'

'But you do, don't you? Have a crush on William, I mean.'

I didn't answer. I was too busy deciding whether to punch him or just knife him instead.

He nodded and smiled. 'Marianne said that you liked him. She said that you giggled.' He laughed. 'It must be true. You never giggle.'

'You know what else I never do?'

'No. What's that?' he said eagerly.

'I never kill humans, but with you I'm willing to make an exception.' I patted the knife blade in the pocket of my pants just to make my point even clearer.

He looked at me, smiled and then bobbed his head forward, keeping any further thoughts to himself.

We neared the fence, sprinted forward, and then jumped it easily. I checked my watch. We'd only been gone for about forty-five minutes, but that definitely could have been enough time for George to come home, find us gone, and devise an even more hellish punishment.

I picked up speed, Lucas managing to keep pace easily as he fell into step beside me.

When we got to the driveway, we noted that the house appeared to be unoccupied. We both breathed a sigh of relief and then smiled at one another. At least that was one hurdle we didn't have to jump this afternoon.

Lucas unlocked the front door and let us into the house. We both collapsed on the lounge, wiping away the sweat after the brief jog. I twisted my hair in my fingers and wound it around the back of my head, pulling it off my heated neck. Lucas tucked his behind his ears.

'Well, I had fun. What about you?' he said, throwing his legs over the arm of the chair and spinning around in the seat.

'Fun?' I said, narrowing my eyes at him. 'For the first ten minutes I thought you'd swallowed your tongue and messed your pants.'

He scoffed. 'You did leave me alone with two vampires remember? Not just one, but two. I think I did okay considering.'

'So what are the health benefits of garlic, anyhow?' I said sarcastically.

He flipped me off and then leaned back against the arm of the chair and closed his eyes. 'Marianne's very pretty, isn't she?'

I snorted. 'If you like that sort of thing.' I sat up in my seat and Lucas flipped his eyes open as we heard a car pull up into the driveway.

'Dad?' Lucas asked, straightening himself up.

'I don't know.'

I got up from my chair, crossed the floor and glanced out the living room window. A white Mitsubishi Pajero was pulling into the driveway. Malcolm's car.

I dashed back to my seat when I saw George jump out the car and head towards the house, a grim expression on his face. The keys rattled in the locks for a brief second before the door was pushed open and George pressed his way inside. He looked at the both of us sitting tensely on the sofa. We must have looked guilty but he didn't appear to notice. He looked worried and a little frazzled.

'Hi dad,' Lucas said nervously.

'Kids get your stuff,' he said, dashing into his bedroom

and then coming out with his backpack in his hands. We sat there looking at him for a brief moment, not understanding.

'Did you hear me?' he said, grabbing the car keys off the bureau and tossing the backpack over his shoulder. 'I said get your stuff.'

'Dad, what's going on?' Lucas said, jumping to his feet. I was a second behind him.

'We have to go to Mackay immediately. There have been recent sightings of wild animals and numerous attacks specifically targeting women.'

'You think it's the Vânătors?' I said slowly.

He nodded. 'It appears the Vampires were right. We have to leave immediately. Malcolm, Vincent, Peter, and Sarah are leaving straight away. I promised we would not be far behind them, so hurry up and get your stuff together, because we need to leave.'

'What about William and the other vamps?' Lucas asked. 'Are they coming too?'

George gave Lucas a stern look, his eyes narrowing. 'Why should that matter?'

Lucas shrugged, trying to appear nonchalant. 'I just thought their heightened senses and fighting skills might help.'

George's eyes closed off, looking like nothing more than angry slits. 'We've always managed on our own and we will again. We don't need *them* to do our job efficiently.'

'George is right,' I said as Lucas gave me a funny look. 'We don't need the Vampires. You've got me.' I tapped the side of my nose. I could smell werewolf blood from miles away.

'And you,' George said, smiling lightly and pointing at me, 'will be staying in the car.'

'What?' I barked. 'Staying in the car? How can that be helpful?' I saw Lucas biting back a laugh from the corner of my eye.

Dumb ass.

'It will be helpful because it means we don't have to keep an eye on you while you run around by yourself like G.I. Jane.'

'I won't.'

'I know you won't, because you're staying in the car.'

'George—'

He shook his head. 'Don't George me. Just go and get your stuff and both of you get in the car. I promised your mother we'd pick her up ten minutes ago.'

I flounced out of the room and dashed up the stairs behind Lucas. We were going on a hunt and I was going to miss the best bits. What possible good was I going to be to anybody sitting in the back of the car?

Bored. That was what I was going to be.

Bored and completely and utterly useless.

CHAPTER TWELVE: BLOOD

///

kicked at the back of the chair in front of me in frustration and began to draw patterns in the fog of my rear window. Susan, George and Lucas had been gone for almost an hour and they'd left me in the car like a pet poodle. They'd even wound down the windows a quarter of an inch so that I could get some air. All I needed was a leash, some dog food, and a water bowl and I'd be set.

Ooh and a chew toy!

I scowled. At least then I'd have something to keep me entertained.

I wrote a couple of curse words on the steamed up window to mask my growing irritation at being excluded, and then wiped them clear again, feeling slightly foolish. I was still jacked off that my growing talents, not to mention my ability to self-heal, were going entirely to waste.

I stared, somewhat deflated, through my greasy finger marks and out into the alley where they had parked. It was completely deserted. I hadn't seen a single soul walk down this alley the entire time that I'd had been here—not even a lone vagrant asking for some pocket change. It was strange to say the least.

It was a Saturday night. People should have been out, crowding the streets. But perhaps, given that the local paper had reported two mysterious sightings of large forest wolves and three local women going missing, people may have been a little reluctant to venture out. If The Protectors had just listened to the Vampires on Tuesday instead of procrastinating, the town's residents might have had zero sightings of wolves in Mackay and only one missing woman on their hands instead of three.

I glanced at my watch. It was almost midnight. The trap would be set by now. I just prayed that, after an eight hour stint in the car getting here, the usual plan would work. We couldn't afford for this new pack getting out of hand. If that happened, we'd have to call in reinforcements from other states and in all likelihood, enlist the help of vampires. But that was always going to be the last resort for the IMI. They were stubborn and narrow minded right to the very end.

Despite being left alone and desperately bored out of my mind, I hoped that the bait was going to work. If vânători were in fact in the area as everyone believed them to be, then it wouldn't be long before the scent of blood that was weaving its way through the night air found them. Even I could smell its sweet, yet metallic undertone gliding down my nostrils. It was not as strong as it had been forty minutes ago, when they had first poured the warmth over Sarah (the bait for this evening), but there was no mistaking the somewhat enticing scent that flowed from her direction.

Her role in tonight's hunt would be simple. I had seen it executed many times before and it generally worked. Her task was to sit alone at a bus stop or at a park bench, her clothes drenched in the blood that we specifically kept on reserve for situations such as this from a company known as Synth Corp. With warm blood covering her from head to toe, she would pretend to be injured or hurt. A vulnerable human was hard for a werewolf to resist, particularly a weaker female.

While she waited patiently for their appearance, The Protectors on the hunt would be hiding nearby with their cloaking spells, waiting to attack, with their individual aromas cloaked by the heavy scent of blood in the air. No matter where the Vânătors were in the town or city that they were hiding in, they would inevitably follow the scent until they'd found exactly what it was they couldn't ignore—food.

A hand rapped on the side of my window. I squealed out in terror.

What was with everyone sneaking up on me lately?

'Whoa, Elena, it's just me,' Lucas said. He opened the car door and I punched him hard in the side of the arm as I climbed out.

'You scared the crap out of me.'

He winced and rubbed at his arm. 'Sorry, just thought I'd let you know that there's no sign of them yet. We could be here for a while.'

'Well that's just lovely,' I mumbled, closing the car door behind me and leaning against it. 'I was worried I wasn't going to have enough time to finish being bored.'

He grimaced. 'I'm sorry you're stuck out here by yourself. Hopefully mum and dad will let you join in on the next hunt.'

'We're you trying to cheer me up?'

He nodded.

'Well, stop it. You're doing a crappy job.'

He smiled and tugged at my ponytail. 'If it makes you feel any better, it's twelve degrees out here this evening and Sarah is sitting in the bus stop over the street covered in wet blood. She has to be close to freezing by now.'

'You're right,' I said with a dazzling answering smile. 'That does make me feel better.'

'I've got to get back. I just thought I'd keep you in the loop. Do you have your knife on you?'

'Always,' I answered and patted my pants pocket. 'Why?'

He shrugged. 'Just in case. Mum and dad might not believe the Vampires when they say that the Vânătors are getting smarter, but I'm not taking any chances and neither should you. Just be careful, yeah?'

'Ah-huh. I'll keep an eye on those shadows over there. They look a little sinister.'

He tilted his head to the side and frowned. 'Don't be a smart ass, E, I'm being serious. You just never know.'

I waved him off and opened the car door again. 'You better get back. The excitement is going to be over there, not here at the car. There's no point both of us missing it.' I kicked at a loose stone and sent it sailing against the brick wall on the other side of the alley, trying not to let him see my disappointment.

'Sorry, E,' he said again before patting me on the shoulder and jogging back down the other end of the alley. He darted around a corner, disappearing from sight.

I let out a short sigh of frustration and leant back against the opening of the door, searching the end of the alley where Lucas had just disappeared, and the rest, just to be certain that I was still miserably alone. I was. Even the darkest of shadows looked devoid of danger and as harmless as a fluffy bunny.

And then a set of cold white hands circled tightly around my waist, tugging me back hard inside the vehicle. My head banged viciously against the metal door frame as my body flew backwards like a rag doll into the rear passenger seat of the Forrester.

I let out a strangled cry of surprise before one of the cold, hard hands left my waist and clamped down firmly over my mouth. Instinctively I reached up with shaking hands to protect my head. It was throbbing dully.

What the hell?

I took a deep breath in through my nose to steady my racing heart, my mouth still kept mute by the cold, white hand. Spice and sandalwood slowly suffused the cabin, overwhelming the scent of blood that was still hanging in the air.

William.

I let go of my head, briefly rubbing at the spot that had hurt not less than ten seconds ago, and turned around as best as I could to stare at William.

He placed a finger to his lips to tell me to keep quiet and then slowly released the hand that he had over my mouth. 'Sorry about your head,' he whispered, gently brushing his fingers across my crown.

'Are you stalking me?' I hissed, slapping his hand away.

'Shh. Keep your voice down. There's a vânător just outside.'

I pulled my dangling feet inside the car and then turned around to glance into the alley. I couldn't see anything, just brick walls, concrete, trash dumpsters, and more concrete. I listened. I couldn't hear anything either. When I sniffed at the air again all I got was the heavy scent of blood and the more pronounced scent of William's essence circling around me.

I wish I could smell vânătors.

I gave up the search and spun around again. 'What are you doing here?' I whispered.

He was still wearing the same clothes I had seen him in earlier today but his sunglasses were nowhere in sight.

'I'm hunting, the same as you.'

I managed an indignant snort. 'Hunting? I wish. I'm the designated driver for this evening.'

He smiled in reply and then shuffled closer, his thigh resting against my own. My breath caught in my throat as he leaned across me slowly, washing me with another bout of his essence.

His head dipped past my face and peered out into the alley beyond. All I could see was the smooth, pale skin of his neck and his profile—the long, dark lashes that fanned his eyes and the tufts of soft hair that curved sinuously around his ears. The depth of his beauty was alarming.

I sank back into the seat as far as I could go, creating as great a distance between our skin as possible. Even if my eyes were closed I still would have known he was there, that he was only a heartbeat away from me. His skin may have been cold, but his body appeared to emit heat and phero- mones that were just as powerful as if he had been touching me with his bare hands.

I mentally slapped myself and then concentrated on where he was looking. He appeared to be transfixed by some- thing down the far end of the alley. I looked but couldn't see anything except the well lit buildings surrounding the car— fluorescent bulbs hung in sporadic locations from the brick walls outside the shop's back entrances. Even the shadows that clung to some of the walls and corners of the alley held no secret hiding places for the beasts to hide.

He stayed like that, only for a couple of seconds, his head only a short distance away from mine. After more silent seconds passed, he leaned back in again, turning to look at me and caught me gawking at him. 'He's close.'

'Who, the Vânător?'

He nodded. 'He's about one hundred metres away, sitting on the roof of that bakery.' He pointed.

'Well then what are you doing in the car with me? Shouldn't you be out there hunting him down with everyone else?'

'I can't,' he said quietly.

'And why is that?'

'Because he's hunting you.'

I snorted quietly. 'And why exactly would he be bothered doing that when there's a buffet of blood just over there?' I pointed in Sarah's general direction.

'You can smell that?' he said, amazed.

I frowned. 'How can you not?'

He grinned. 'That's true enough for vampires and vânători, but you're still clearly human, Elena, a fact which has not escaped the werewolf that is scenting your blood at this moment, and is now hunting you.'

The trap isn't working.' I whispered.

He shook his head and leaned forward, his eyes muddying slightly in colour. 'It was never going to work. I tried to tell your parents that these ones are too smart.' His breath was sweet and incredibly enticing, sweet like chocolate, apples, cinnamon, and every other yummy thing I could think of.

Whoa, cut it out, Elena.

My fingers started to shake slightly as a sudden image of them running through the thicket of his hair flashed through my mind. Only I kept imagining him in that different way for some reason, with the shoulder-length hair stylishly framing his face.

I sat on my quaking fingers to prevent me from doing something stupid. 'Are you trying to compel me again?' I breathed.

'I am.'

'Why?' I murmured, glancing at him from under my lashes. 'Why would you need to?'

'Because I need you to stay in the car and I don't think that you would if I simply asked you to.'

'So your answer is hypnotism?' I said drowsily.

'If that's what it takes to keep you safe.'

I laughed lightly. 'You, protect *me*?' I laughed again. 'I don't need protecting. I'm more than capable of looking after myself.'

'I believe you,' he said quietly. 'But I don't want to test the theory with an alpha.'

The fog that had been circling around inside my head vanished the second my interest in the conversation piqued. 'Alpha? There's an alpha hunting me?'

So much for his compulsion. Looks like I'm not fully susceptible after all.

I stuck my head out the door again and glanced into the distance. I could see it now, perched quietly on the edge of the bakery rooftop, looking down at me with black, beady eyes.

William sighed and touched my hand. 'Please, Elena, stay in the car.'

'Nah-uh. Not while there's an alpha just outside. I haven't seen one before.'

'You're quite impossible,' he murmured under his breath, shaking his head. 'Ever heard of curiosity killing the cat?'

I nodded and glanced out the window again. 'Yep, but I still have nine lives left so no probs.'

The Vânător was gone. I automatically reached for my knife, pulling it from my pockets. I had a feeling I was going to need it.

'You're not invincible, Elena. Please try to be smart and let me handle this. I have aeons of experience in these matters.' He hesitated. 'You're still just a child in a lot of ways.'

I snorted. 'You sound exactly like George, and that's not

an attractive trait, believe you me.' I started to slide out of the car.

William grabbed at my hand and pulled me back inside. 'Where are you going?'

'Let go,' I hissed, pulling my hand free. 'He knows I'm in the car. In or out, it doesn't make much difference, does it? At least if I'm out of the car I can see him coming.'

'You can't go up against an alpha, Elena. You'll be no match for him. He'll snap you like a twig.'

'Good thing this twig can grow new branches then, huh?'

'Are you always this stubborn and pigheaded?' he said angrily.

I smiled. 'You say that like it's a bad thing.'

He growled and then leant across to slam the door shut again. 'No wonder you're *his* mate. You're exactly the same.'

'What?'

'Nothing,' he grumbled as he tried to grab at the seatbelt next to me.

'What are you doing? If there is an alpha out there then we need to hunt it. We can't let it just wander around.'

'Elena—'

I grabbed the handle and swung the car door open again. 'Don't Elena me. You and I don't know each other well enough for you to tell me what to do. Besides, even if we did, I'd still do what I want to do anyway, so just deal with it. Everyone else has to.' I got out of the car and slammed the door shut behind me, twirling the blade around in my hand as I did so.

He stood at my side a second later, his arms crossed angrily in front of his chest.

Geez, he's fast.

'So what's your big plan then? I'm assuming you have one?' he said sardonically.

I shook my head. 'Don't be an ass. I don't have one. I'm more of a fly by the seat of my pants kind of girl, if you know what I mean.'

He mumbled something unintelligible under his breath, something that sounded a lot like what I'd been writing on the window of the car earlier. He pointed behind him. 'He's on the shoe shop roof now, about twenty paces above us. If you were planning on doing something, then now would be the time. I'm just *dying* to see what you have buried in that little bag of tricks of yours.'

'Aren't you already dead?' I answered just as sarcastically in return. 'So you can't be dying.'

He waved a hand at me in dismissal. 'I'm waiting …'

I sneered at him. 'Okay then wise guy, what's your big plan? Leave poor little Elena in the car like a useless damsel in distress and then run off to fight the big bad wolf all on your own?'

He didn't answer, just glared at me.

'Oh, good plan,' I muttered as I shook my head. 'Then what happens? You kill the wolf, come back to the car victorious, gush about how you brought him down with your super strength and sharp teeth and then expect me to swoon and bat my eyelids at you? Sorry Prince Charming, you've got the wrong century.'

A howl exploded from the rooftop above us and I spun around. The Vânător dashed across the edge of the roof, leaping through the air and landed with a light *thud* in the middle of the alley a few metres away from us.

I gripped the knife tighter in my hands and stretched out the muscles on either side of my neck, waiting for the *crack* I knew would ease tension I was feeling.

This werewolf was bigger than any of the other wolves I had ever seen. He was closer to the size of a large lion than of a wolf. His fur was long, dark grey, and matted, but his teeth were just as pointed and sharp as any other vânător. His eyes were black as pitch—a similar darkening I'd seen in the eyes of William, earlier that day. Its dark eyes made it difficult to differentiate just exactly who the wolf was looking at until his head was turned and pointed in your direction.

I turned and looked at William standing beside me. He was transformed. The change had been instantaneous and because I'd been distracted, I had missed it. He had removed his shirt and tossed it onto the roof of the car. As a human he'd be well-muscled and pleasing to the eye but in his Vampiric form there was no denying that I could not take my eyes off him. William's skin was as pale as the snow, verging on transparent. Blue, blood-filled cords entwined their way around his muscles, encircling his entire body, including his face, the veins eerily visible just beneath the surface of his flesh. His fingernails had grown and were now long stiff talons, as black as the very depths of his eyes. His canines were drawn, like sharp white knives that brushed against his lower lip. He was the Devil Incarnate, but he was beautiful, even as more monster than man.

The Vânător took a step forward and William echoed that step, shooting his arm out to catch me in the chest, pushing me back hard against the car.

Who did he think he was?

He quickly looked at me with his dark eyes. I could see no inference of words or meaning behind them. They were empty, like big lumps of coal embedded behind his lids. I still had a feeling that he was going to slog me if I thought about moving a muscle.

He really doesn't know me at all.

I tried to move back beside him, but he hissed at me and pushed me back against the car with more force than before. I winced.

What an ass.

The Vânător, taking advantage of a distracted William, leapt forward into the air.

William was faster.

He let go of me and leapt forward, a blur that hit the wolf straight in the chest, sending it flying backwards through the air and hitting the brick wall at the far end of the alley. The landing was clumsy and the wolf crashed heavily into the metal waste cans. William landed lightly on his feet, immediately ducking into a defensive crouch. He held his claws out next to him, his teeth bared. A hiss escaped from his lips, louder than a steam engine.

The Vânător quickly flipped himself back up onto all fours, tipping one of the trash cans over and spilling rubbish into the alleyway. The clatter of a glass bottle rolling across the concrete floor was the only sound for almost a minute, slightly musical and ending with the crescendo of a *ping* as it touched the brick work. The werewolf kept looking at William for the entire performance without moving, his muzzle drawn back, revealing every single sharp tooth in his arsenal.

A gurgle escaped from the back of his throat, erupting into a howl of warning. It was shortly followed by a secondary howl coming from another wolf somewhere in the nearby vicinity.

The alpha looked to me. There was an unexplainable emptiness in the darkness that stared right back at me, absorbing every detail and no doubt memorising my scent with ardent determination.

I gripped the knife tighter and held it ready and waiting at my side.

William stalked back towards it, the wolf glancing back to its primary target. Another hiss exploded from William's throat before launching himself through the air again, moving so quickly that I had to quickly double-check.

The Vânător immediately jumped up onto the waste bins and jumped back onto the roof of the tobacconist shop, disappearing from sight. They were both moving too quickly, but William must have chased after him because I was standing alone in the empty alleyway again. I could hear their scuffle on the rooftops above and I could still smell the blood on the air, but that was it.

I glanced around the rest of the alley, looking for signs of life. I had heard another vânător howling just before. It had sounded close and I wasn't prepared to drop my guard just yet.

I scanned the rooftops where the alpha and William had disappeared—still nothing. There was only the soft caress of the wind upon my face and the sound of a couple of passing cars in the next street over.

I padded forward slowly, occasionally spinning around on the spot and checking the areas behind and above me. I felt my chest burning with anxiety and it wasn't from the fear surrounding me. I could only put it down to concern for William. Strange considering I'd been angry with him minutes ago.

A distressed howl sounded from somewhere far behind me. It was further away than before. It resonated clearly, tainted with pain, the howl turning into a faint whining sound and slowly into a whimper.

Must have come from the other vânător with The Protectors.

I took off in a quick jog, running past the car and down to the opposite end of the alley where I had seen Lucas leave earlier. An empty street loomed in front of me. No one in sight, not even a passing car.

I stopped for a moment, sniffed at the air and then followed my nose towards the scent of blood.

I ran down to the end of the deserted street, stopping only briefly to gain my bearings, turning right and heading down another street. The street consisted of a couple of restaurants and bars that appeared to be closed for business.

God, how far away were they?

And how far away can I scent blood?

I ran across the street, amazed that I had been running for a few minutes and still smelt the blood with the same unbelievable clarity that I had before. I approached the next corner and then stopped again. The blood was definitely getting stronger now.

At the T-intersection I took a left. In the distance I could see a bus stop and a small crowd of people gathered around something lying in the centre of the street. It was The Protectors—the huddled mass in the middle would have to have been the secondary vânător.

I took a step forward and then halted immediately when a fury grey mess stepped out from a side street to my left and padded in front of me. I raised my knife in warning, calming myself. I prayed that the beast could not hear, smell, or sense my fear.

I shook my head and took another few steps back, only to have it mirrored by the alpha. I shouldn't be afraid. I could do this. I'd been training for four years so I could kick vânător butt. Just because this one was a little bit—okay, a lot bigger than the other ones—did not mean that it was invulnerable.

Then it hit me.

If the alpha was here with me, then where was William? Was he hurt?

God, please, let him be okay.

My backwards footsteps brought me back around the street corner and down the street littered with the closed restaurants and bars. The huddled mass of Protectors, of safety, disappeared from view as I rounded the corner slowly.

The Vânător followed me, unrelenting in its pursuit. It made no sound or effort to attack. It simply followed me like a lost puppy.

'What do you want?' I asked. 'If you're going to eat me, then just do it already.'

The alpha did not answer me.

'Can you talk in wolf form?'

He let out a small, choked barking sound from his throat.

Hmm, guess not.

'I'm getting a little sick of all this backpedalling. If you're going to attack me, then do it now before I turn you into a pin cushion.' I held up my knife to make my point perfectly clear.

The Vânător barked something in return and shook its head from side to side. It pulled its muzzle back tighter across its teeth. It looked like it was smiling—either that or it was preparing to chow down on me at any second. I didn't want to give it a chance. If the choice came, I'd kill first and ask questions later.

'Stuff this for a joke,' I said, stopping abruptly and taking a step forward. 'I'm getting dizzy and I'm tired of walking backwards, so game on, wolf.'

I lunged forward, flicking my blade quickly in my fingers

and slicing the blade across the alpha's snout. His muzzle opened and then snapped shut with a deafening crack as he snapped at my quick moving hand. Blood from the wound dripped onto the pavement, and pooled in little red splotches of liquid crimson.

A gurgled growl of protest ripped out from between the wolf's clenched teeth as he lunged forward, snapping at me again with his razor sharp teeth.

I ducked to the right as he tried to bite my knife wielding arm. He missed and another deafening crack echoed through the night air. His teeth crashed together like an iron vice. As I moved, I made another quick swipe at his neck line, but he was faster than me and had already moved out of the way.

He lunged at me again, this time keeping his head lowered, his eyes fixed on me, swiping his sharp claws at me. I ducked the first blow, a blow that would have taken my head from my shoulders, and stumbled backwards. I regained my footing and tried to flick another cut at his neck. I missed again.

He was fast, almost as fast as William.

He struck out with the same clawed paw, taking me by surprise and slashing the side of my face. The hit sent me sprawling backwards across the pavement in anguish, my left ankle twisting as I fell.

I cried out in pain, moisture automatically filling my eyes and blurring my vision. My hand went to the side of my face where blood was steadily pouring from the deep penetrating cuts his claws made against the delicate flesh of my cheek.

The Vânător sniffed, its attention drawn to my bloodied cheek and hands, its tongue suddenly running along it's snout in one sweeping movement of pink flesh and warm drool. Repulsed, I pushed the pain to the side and wiped away the tears. I'd show George just how valuable I could truly be.

He came at me, his jaw now fully open, his teeth bared and ready for the kill.

I rolled backwards and kicked myself up to my feet. He hit me again, he was too fast, but this time I managed to lodge my knife in his shoulder blade before I fell to the ground. The howl that erupted from his throat ripped across the night air like an air raid siren. It was loud, ominous and wrought with pain.

Good.

I fell to the ground for the second time, my hands reaching out behind me and scraping savagely across the concrete pavement. I brought them back up to my face. Between my own blood, and the blood from his shoulder wound, my hands were a monochromatic canvas of arterial red.

My knife was wedged deep in its flesh. I could smell the fresh blood oozing from the gaping knife wound. I sensed that it was undoubtedly warm, thick and sweet even though it appeared to gush forth like a small fountain of ruby-coloured wine. Despite the wound, he came at me again, like a bulldozer, barely unhindered. I had to give Fido points for persistence.

Before I could think, he was upon me again. He sprang up onto my chest and pinned me down hard against the pavement, my legs wedged underneath his massively clawed paws. He was so heavy I wondered if my bones were going to break under the sheer weight of him. William had been right. He was going to snap me like a twig.

I struggled uselessly, trying to roll him off me—no such luck. One free hand punched at the side of his face and neck, while the other hand grabbed at the blade in his shoulder, twisted it and then pulled it free.

He growled in pain again and then lowered his muzzle to my neck and sunk his teeth down hard into the soft flesh there. I cried out in agony, a strangled sound that escaped my throat more out of shock and surprise than fear or pain itself.

His teeth seized me from the neck all the way down through my collar bone and down to the top of my breast. I could feel my actual collar bone grinding against the sharp points of his teeth, and any minute now I half-expected it to snap under the strain of the bite.

I struggled, the blood draining from my body making me weaker by the minute. I couldn't even grip my knife anymore—it lay limply in my hand. The bite must have severed a few of the tendons.

Immobile, I waited for help to come. That was all I could do. Screaming out for help seemed impossible. My throat was dry and my body felt consumed by weariness. I couldn't even move my lips.

In the distance I could hear the pounding of footsteps on the pavement. At least I thought that was what it was. It could have been the sound of my heart pounding in my ears too, but I couldn't be sure. I was so close to losing consciousness now that it probably didn't matter. All I could smell was blood all around me.

My blood.

His blood.

The Vânător licked at the flesh of my shoulder with his tongue and dug in deeper into my skin, slurping at the blood that continued to pour forth from the wound. It was strange that I could still feel him there, feel him biting into my flesh and draining the life out of me, but the initial pain of the experience was starting to ebb away. A haze was starting to build around me that was blanketing coherent thoughts, numbing my physical response.

I swallowed absently, an ever increasing dryness in my throat.

Why am I so thirsty?

My mouth was parched and rough. I needed some water, something that could satiate my growing thirst. Worse than before, swallowing felt like a chore. Even the act of breathing seemed to evaporate any moisture left behind.

I swallowed again trying to abate the feeling of thirst and ignore the Vânător clinging persistently to my neck and shoulder, draining me of every last ounce of fluid.

He shifted his grip and moved further forward, repositioning himself directly above me. I turned my head to the side to keep my face away from the side of his muzzle, unconsciously breathing through my mouth instead of my nose so I could avoid the fetid smell of his drool.

I swallowed again, and a warm, unrecognisable sweetness dribbled past my lips, rushing across the surface of my tastebuds, like liquid syrup. It eased the persistent ache of my throat and the unrelenting dryness.

My prayers had obviously been answered. Someone must have found me, scared off the alpha, and then eased my thirst with some kind of liquid heaven. Whatever it was that they were feeding to me was absolutely delicious.

I tried to concentrate as I drank down the warmth, but everything seemed so far away in my mind. I tried to remember what was happening, but I couldn't see or think clearly. Everything was so hazy and distant. Maybe I was dead? I was caught in a fog so dense that there seemed to be no way out.

I swallowed greedily. It tasted like a cross between

condensed milk and hot, liquid milk chocolate. Its syrupy sweetness filled my veins with a growing fire, my conscious surging back from the dark.

I suddenly became aware of the alpha, the bulk of his weight resting across my chest like a four storey apartment block, his sharp teeth planted in my neck like a wrecking ball with spikes.

I should have stayed in the car.

Pressure was released from my neck and my shoulder. The hideous heaviness of the apartment building resting upon my chest was gone. I heard a howl. It was short and unassuming and sounded very far away inside my mind.

The sweet tasting syrup that I had been lapping up had stopped and I was instantly saddened. There were voices now—lots of them. Snippets of murmured conversation between people I recognised, but words I could not make out.

I lay very still.

The voices got louder and louder. I heard the word *demon*, closely followed by the word *blood* and a few cuss words from somebody else. It was still a little difficult to discern what was happening. I still hadn't fully decided if I was dead or alive yet.

'Elena? Elena? Oh my God, George, look at her.' I heard Susan mumble through the fog.

Something shook at my body. My head wobbled from side to side. I wasn't ready to wake up just yet. I felt tired. I felt drained.

A second later a hand slapped at my face and I cursed. *That wasn't very nice.*

'What!' I gurgled angrily, slowly opening my eyes and trying to focus on the blurry images crowding around me. The first person I saw was Susan. She was leaning over me, fluttering her fingers over my body and brushing my hair from my face.

'Are you okay?' she whispered, bending down and kissing my forehead.

Dazed and confused by her motherly concern, I tried to sit up. My body felt so weak. I looked down at my shoulder. My shirt was soaked with blood and there were holes all through the cotton where the Vânător had taken hold of me.

I brushed the destroyed fabric aside and ran my fingers over my shoulder and neck. There were no imperfections in my skin, just the destruction of my T-shirt. Apart from that, I appeared to be in perfect health.

Susan helped me to my feet, and I staggered slightly. Lucas and George were reaching out to me with their shaking hands and worried expressions. I'd seen those looks before.

Sarah, not surprisingly, gave me a disgusted look, even though *she* was covered with blood. Malcolm and Vincent merely stood there, both of them looking like they'd seen a ghost. If I didn't know any better, I might have thought they were all truly concerned about me.

The moment passed.

'Did you get him?' I asked groggily, becoming aware that blood covered my hands. I looked at it for the longest moment, imagining the taste of it all, and then curled them into fists and tucked them inside my pockets.

'Yes, we got him,' George said quietly.

'Good. It would have been terrible to let the alpha get away.' I looked around by my feet. 'Um, where's the body?'

No one answered me for the longest time.

I turned around on the spot, searching the street for the alpha's remains. There was none. Over the trees and looking towards the street where they had laid the trap, I could see spirals of smoke winding up high into the air.

I pointed to the smoke over my shoulder and Lucas began to shake his head. 'We got one of them,' Lucas answered. 'We didn't realise there was a secondary one until we heard the howling.'

'It was an alpha,' I stated. 'It must have gotten away before you found me.'

Sarah folded her pudgy arms in front of her blood soaked chest. 'And how do you know that it was an alpha? We didn't see anything.'

I looked at Lucas for guidance and he nodded his head at me. I took it as a sign. 'William Granville, the Vampire, told me.'

'The Vampire!' George roared. 'You've been associating with a vampire?'

I shook my head. 'No, not exactly. He came here tonight because he too was hunting the Vânători. He found the alpha and realised it was hunting me. He was trying to protect me from getting hurt. He told me to stay in the car where it was safe and then chased after the alpha and just disappeared.'

'He was trying to protect you?' Malcolm said in disbelief. 'Why? Vampires generally only look out for the members of their own coven.'

'Look, it's the truth. I was staying in the car like you told me to. Ask Lucas if you don't believe me.'

They all looked to him and he nodded.

'When the alpha started his attack, William defended me, and after they disappeared from sight I did the only thing I could think of which was try and find you guys. Only problem was the alpha must have slipped away from William somehow, or killed him, I'm not sure which, but then he attacked me.'

'I see,' George said calmly, touching the side of my neck with his fingers and then letting them fall to his side. 'How did you know where to find us, Elena? I parked the car down an alley that was far enough away that you wouldn't be able to get yourself into trouble, and yet here we are, yet again. You're caught up in the very middle of it all. So tell me how you found us so quickly?'

He already knew the answer, I could tell just by looking at his face. 'You know how I found you George. The same way I found the last vânătors.'

'I told you she's not right in the head, George,' Sarah said, stepping forward in front of me like I was invisible. 'I don't care about future plans. She's not safe to have around the IMI anymore. Look at her! She's becoming more like a beast by the minute.'

'Calm yourself,' George retorted. 'We must hear Elena's side of the story first. We know that she has always been able to smell blood but—'

'Yes, she smells the blood,' Sarah continued, interrupting George, 'but drinking it! That's crossing the line! She's supposed to be human right now. Headquarters needs to know about this. It could change things.'

Sarah's face was going red, her voice tinted with frustration and anger. I really didn't like this woman. Next time I was going to have to push her off a higher grandstand.

Drinking blood? What was she talking about anyway?

'Sarah, you need to take a step back,' Vincent said calmly. 'You're saying things that shouldn't be said and you're not looking at this from any other perspective except your own. Elena was being drained of blood. Perhaps this was her body's natural response in order to save itself?'

'She drank Vânător blood!' she screamed.

I took a step back in shock.

I did?

'Does this not worry any of you? She lives with you, George, in your home with your family! Think of what she might do to Lucas or Susan while they are sleeping!'

'I said, that's enough!' George roared. 'One more word out of you Sarah and I will have you dismissed from your position at the IMI. You know I have the power to do it.'

She sniffed. 'I will report this, George, mark my words.'

'Do your worst, Sarah. I run this faction and it is by direct orders from Bucharest that Elena is still a part of the IMI, so if you have a problem with it, then you can take it up with them.'

'I might just do that.'

He waved his hand at her in dismissal and then pushed her to the side to get a better look at me.

I glanced around at all the faces staring at me in concern, all of them zeroed in on my face. 'I didn't drink any blood,' I mumbled pathetically. 'I've never drunk blood before. It's not possible. I would remember if I did.'

Susan took a step forward and brushed her fingers across my lips. When she pulled her hand away she held them up to show me that they were indeed stained with red.

I ran my tongue across my lips, tasting the last remnants of the imaginary chocolate concoction. It still tasted divine. I was instantly repulsed.

I cupped a hand over my mouth and wiped at the blood that was covering my face and lips.

How ... when did this happen? How could I?

'When we found you Elena, your face was covered in blood. Vânător blood,' Susan continued. 'I'm afraid that, somehow, some way, you have successfully ingested the alpha's blood.'

I shook my head. 'No, it can't be. I didn't bite him, I don't have the teeth. It must have been something else. It tasted sweet like chocolate. It was delicious. It couldn't have been blood. Blood smells salty and metallic.'

I was reaching and I knew it. In all likelihood, I *had* swallowed the Vânător's blood.

Susan touched my cheek with her hand and shook her head from side to side. 'I'm sorry, Elena, but the evidence is incontrovertible. It's all over your face, lips, and inside your mouth. You drank blood tonight.'

I dropped down to my knees, my hands splaying on the pavement in front of me. 'Jesus, what am I?' I said, dazed, looking back up at everyone and knowing what pity looked like for the second time this week.

'I assure you the lord Jesus Christ had nothing to do with it,' Sarah muttered under her breath. 'He has much better taste.'

Lucas bent down next to me and tugged at my ponytail. 'You're my freaky sister, that's what you are. Blood drinker or not, Elena, I still love you, nothing will change that.' He draped his arm around my shoulder and pulled me slowly back to my feet.

I looked up at him, my eyes brimming with tears. 'But, Lucas ... I enjoyed it.'

Sarah gagged and Vincent and Malcolm turned away to hide their disgust. I got the impression, as Susan and George looked back at me, that they had somehow expected tonight's events would eventually unfold. Their reactions were mechanical, clinical, and observatory.

Lucas was the only one who smiled at me with any degree of warmth. 'Of course you liked the blood, dickhead,' he said, using his pet name for me. 'You're going to be a vampire, remember? It's what you're supposed to do. Don't feel bad about what you are.'

I gave him a little shove and smiled weakly in spite of myself. Susan and George lingered briefly to check I was alright before they turned and started heading back towards the car.

'Thanks,' I said quietly to Lucas as we walked behind them. His arm was still draped casually around my shoulder. It was warm and comforting.

'For what?' he replied, stroking the side of my arm.

'For trying to make me feel better.'

Lucas grimaced. 'Hey, I never said it wasn't gross, I just reminded you it's in your nature.'

I punched him lightly in the stomach. He buckled over and gulped in a breath of air. 'Geez, Elena, did you have to punch me so hard? I was only kidding you know.'

'Don't be a baby, I barely touched you.'

He sucked in another breath and then looked up at me in dismay, his golden hair dangling in front of his eyes like a halo. 'Well then I'd hate to see what you could do if you were trying.'

I laughed and helped him up. 'Come on, stop whining. We have an alpha to catch and that means no time for self-pity.'

He rubbed at his stomach and gave me a crooked smile. 'It's good to see that blood sucking hasn't changed your *radiant* personality.'

I laughed with him, inconspicuously swallowing the last remnants of blood still inside the crevices of my mouth. I shuddered, remembering the sheer pleasure of its taste.

Something inside of me had changed. I still wondered exactly what that was.

CHAPTER THIRTEEN: STRENGTH

The week had been tumultuous to say the least. Everyone, including Karina and Lisa had been avoiding me as much as possible and to say that the air was thick and fraught with tension at the IMI was the understatement of the century. My family were the only ones that treated me with any semblance of normalcy, though it was abundantly clear that Susan and George were more concerned by last Saturday's events than they let on.

Malcolm and Vincent remained as civil as always, but both found it relatively difficult to look me in the eye. Even Vincent's generally vivacious personality had seemed subdued after witnessing my blood drinking debacle. He'd teased me about it often enough, but obviously being confronted with the issue firsthand didn't have the same hilarity as dangling a tetra pack of Synth blood in my face had in the past.

Peter, of course, was just as distant as always, so I was grateful that he was at least fairly consistent in his behaviour. He was the one instructor at the IMI that actually managed to remain fairly civil towards me, even if our training sessions were totally counter-productive. It was safe to say that, at present, I was learning about as much martial arts training as a five year old would watching a Bruce Lee movie. It was becoming increasingly apparent that he was avoiding any physical contact with me. But at least he was still talking to me. That was more than I could say for Karina and Kim.

Due to the buzz circulating relentlessly about my latest party trick, my job appeared to be in jeopardy too. Martha had made it clear that I was not required for work on the Saturday that had just passed and she'd made no indication about when my services would be required again either. I'd honestly thought she would be one of the last people to judge me, but it appeared that I was wrong. To every one of them now, in one way or another, I was even more of an outsider. I'd be lucky if I soon wasn't banned from entering the IMI altogether. It was only by orders from headquarters in Bucharest, Romania, that I was still permitted entry and allowed to train.

Sarah had made good on her promise to report me. She'd made it perfectly clear that night that I was an aberration in her eyes. I'd always known that any amiability she had displayed towards me was gone the second I'd ingested blood. Detesting me came easier now than before. I had to give her points for consistency.

Her latest pastime, besides wearing mismatched fluorescents and sporting more chins than a Chinese phone book, was to constantly quote passages from the Bible at me and make the sign of the cross every time we accidentally crossed paths. This was followed by a kiss to the tiny gold crucifix that hung around her neck which sat somewhere, lost between the mountainous watermelons she dared to call breasts. The tableau wasn't complete, however, until she'd finished the entire production off with a good dousing of holy water straight in my face. The woman was a complete lunatic. She had even suggested to Susan that an exorcism be performed by the church to consecrate my soul and rid me of the evil demon within.

Thankfully, Susan concurred that the woman was totally crazy. Otherwise I would have been strapped to a gurney right now with a creepy old priest touching my head and chanting: '*The power of Christ compels you*'. I may not have been a saint, but I certainly wasn't possessed.

Sarah, despite the rocks rolling around inside her head, had been right about one thing. I had changed. There was definitely something different about me, I just hadn't pinpointed any notable physical difference yet. But I did feel stronger at least mentally, and more capable than I had been in a long time.

Despite my protests to everyone that I was feeling completely fine and totally normal, it was requested by headquarters that I was to undergo immediate testing. They wanted confirmation as to whether or not the Vânător bite and the blood that I had consumed had re-structured my DNA. George had taken a vial of my blood and posted it to Romania to have it tested the night of the incident. We still hadn't received any results back yet as far as I knew and I figured that everyone would remain distant until there were some definitive answers about my supposed developing condition.

It was growing clear that no one felt safe around me at the moment, and everyone would have been more comfortable if I didn't turn up at the IMI at all until the results were in. Susan and George, however, were adamant about life continuing on as normal, and as George was the leader of this faction, the others had no choice but to follow along. I was pleased to say that even Sarah's complaints about my presence had fallen on deaf ears in Romania.

In the meantime, while everyone took their time deciding whether or not to associate with me, I was free to ponder just how deeply the effects of my blood drinking had run.

I had enjoyed it, for one, which was totally grossing me out in so many ways that I couldn't even list them all. And, two, there was a light thrumming in my veins ever since the night in question. And finally, I'd also spent a good portion of my time contemplating what could have happened to William.

So, in between meditating on why I was suddenly drinking blood like it was creaming soda, obsessing over just exactly what headquarters had install for me, and debating about whether or not William was still alive, I hadn't had time to consider whether or not I cared that everyone detested me right now.

The whole scenario, despite some minor setbacks such as the recent twenty-four hour a day parental guard duty, proved to work out brilliantly well for keeping both Sarah and Kim as far away from me as possible.

I saw Karina coming towards me in the passage. She gripped her spellbook tightly to her chest and tucked her head down to avoid eye contact. It was amazing how their fear made them all forget that they could pin me down in an instant with just one simple spell.

Lucas was right about one thing—I was going to have to watch my back, but not around vampires or werewolves. I'd have to protect myself from the very people I had spent my whole life surrounded by and had grown up with.

I thought about yelling '*Boo!* at her as I walked past, but decided against it when I saw an asthma puffer curled tightly in her left hand.

Damn shame.

She ignored me completely as she walked on by, even after I greeted her politely. I guess I shouldn't have been surprised. She never really liked me all that much before I started chugging down the blood.

When I got to the junction, I shifted my backpack to my other shoulder and headed towards the first training room. Lucas was just finishing up with Malcolm for the day. I'd already had my 'supposed' training earlier in the morning, and since then I'd spent the rest of the afternoon trying to wrap my head around the English assessment that Susan was expecting from me by the end of the week. The IMI's library was fantastic if you were researching the supernatural or anything remotely paranormal, but when it came to studying Shakespeare or Robert Frost the reference material was inadequate. Later on this week, when I could be bothered and the deadline drew nearer, was when Google and I were going to get better acquainted.

Lucas waved to me as I entered the training room. He was packing up the last of his floor mats while Malcolm, Vincent, and George huddled together in the corner discussing his progress.

Sarah, who had been sitting on the grandstand watching, decided to split the second she saw me. She stood, made a hasty exit towards the door and, as she passed, began to recite the Lord's Prayer and flick at me with her vial of holy water.

Having already been doused three times today, I wiped the droplets from my eyes and then sucked on my fingers. 'Thanks Sarah, I was kind of thirsty.'

There were a couple of moans and a 'Jesus save us,' as she backed quickly out of the room and disappeared down the passage.

I smiled. The only thing Jesus needed to save us all from was stupid questions, cucumbers, country music, and her.

'How's your day been?' Lucas asked, slinging his backpack over his shoulder.

'Pretty crap. What about yours?'

He shrugged. 'Same old.' He tugged at my hand and pulled me down into the passageway. He leaned in close, whispering: 'Have you heard from the Vampires yet?' He asked me that question just about every hour on the hour.

I shook my head and looked around conspiratorially as Lucas de-cloaked the trapdoor that lead to the outside. We both ascended the ladder.

'No. Not a word. I'm really starting to worry.'

'You think the Alpha got him?'

'I really don't know, Lucas, but I hope not. William is very fast. Faster than me and I still managed to get a couple of good shots in.'

Lucas reached the top, pushed the trapdoor open and climbed out. He leaned back down, offering me his hand. 'Then why hasn't he contacted you? I thought he liked you?'

I took his hand and climbed the last ladder rung and hauled myself out of the hole. 'Well, I kind of yelled at him the last time that we spoke.'

He raised an eyebrow. 'You yelled at a vampire?' He re-cloaked the trapdoor again. 'Geez, Elena, you really do have big brass balls, even for a girl.'

I gave him a light shove that sent him stumbling backwards and into the edge of the dirty kitchenette counter. He rubbed at his hip and frowned at me.

'What's wrong with you lately, Lucas?' I said, hefting my backpack and helping to steady him with my other hand. 'I know you're skinny and everything, but lately every time I touch you, you seem to stumble, fall over, or cry like a baby.'

'I don't cry,' he said indignantly and frowning. That was true. I just couldn't help myself. 'Besides, it's not like you're being gentle or anything. You just shoved me pretty hard then.'

I screwed up my face. 'Hardly. I barely touched you.'

'I'm not the only one, you know. Even Peter has a couple of bruises from where you've landed punches on him during training last week.'

'What? Our training hasn't been up to his usual standard. We've been doing more martial arts theory than practical application, and when we do Peter has been showing me in slow motion. I've been more of an observer this week than I have been the entire time that I've been with the IMI.'

Lucas scratched at his head and frowned. 'So there's been barely any physical contact?'

'Nope. We tried it last Monday after we got back from Mackay. After a few minutes in, Peter called a timeout. We haven't tried again since. At first I just thought he was being a total pussy, but now I just think he doesn't want to touch me.'

Lucas led the way out of the restaurant area and across the parking lot to the gaping hole in the fence that we sometimes used as a shortcut to get home in a hurry. He held the wire to the side for me, and I ducked my way under. I waited for him to join me but he seemed to be pondering something. His brows were heavily furrowed and his eyes were darting backwards and forwards across the ground, as if there was something deeply disturbing about the grass.

We walked for a short while, leaving the drive-in and cutting down past the side of the convenience store. He still hadn't said anything.

'What are you thinking about?' I said finally, when I couldn't take the silence any longer.

'I'm just piecing a couple of theories together in my head.'

'Such as?'

'Well, they're just theories of course. They probably mean nothing, considering your test results were inconclusive.'

'What?' I yelped, my voice raising an octave. 'How do you know about my test results?'

He gave me a sly grin. 'I listened in on the conversation that Malcolm, Vincent, and dad were having this afternoon before my training session. They thought I was in the other training room with Martha, Kim, Karina, and Lisa, but I wasn't.'

'So tell me!' I hissed. 'What did they say?'

He dragged the moment out for a little bit longer than necessary and I resisted the urge to punch him. 'It was all very hush-hush,' he continued. 'Apparently headquarters did a full work up on your blood. They couldn't find any notable changes in your added chromosome and your blood test gave the same result as when you were born. It appears that your blood is still as perfect as it was the day you were born. According to dad, they said it was like nothing had even happened to you.'

'Then why did I drink the blood in the first place?'

He shrugged. 'I don't know. Why is the sky blue? Why do vampires even exist? I don't have an answer for you and neither does anyone else apparently. But I do know that dad's been ordered to watch you and check for any other changes. They all seem to agree that you drinking of blood helped you survive, replenishing your own.' He suddenly looked confused all over again.

'But you're not convinced?' I stated.

He shook his head from side to side. 'You have changed. I may be skinny, Elena, but I'm not exactly a push-over. I think the blood that you took may have altered your physicality.'

'What are you saying? I haven't noticed any difference physically.'

'Are you sure about that? You *were* born with the extra

chromosome, born with perfect blood. What if by you consuming some of what is already embedded in your system you've somehow awakened certain traits that are supposed to remain dormant until you turn?'

'Lucas, are you saying that I'm going to want to drink blood from now on?'

He shook his head again. 'Not necessarily. You're still human right? Your body is still technically alive and growing, so you still need nourishment in order to survive. So my theory is that maybe some of your other Vânător and Vampiric senses might be starting to come to the surface. What if by drinking that Vânător's blood your strength has increased?'

I laughed nervously. 'Seriously?'

He nodded. 'How else do you keep injuring me so easily?'

'I told you, you're not eating enough protein.'

'Elena, I'm being serious. I think the blood may have altered your abilities slightly.'

I frowned and then threw him a sceptical look.

'Think about it,' he continued. 'You were born with a self-healing power and that hasn't changed, otherwise you'd have teeth marks in your collar bone right now. You've also been able to scent blood since you hit, um, puberty, and now it seems that you're capable of greater feats of strength than you've ever had before. Why do you think Peter's resorted to theory instead of practical application? They must know something has changed within you, despite what the results of your blood tests say. If dad's been ordered to watch your development then the IMI must have an inkling about what you're capable of.'

'Do you think it's permanent?'

'Maybe. Who knows? Perhaps that's why everyone's

keeping their distance from you at the moment? Maybe they hope that with a little time it might just go away.'

'So they've had suspicions since my training lesson last Monday, but no one has thought to tell me that I'm the subject of an internal experiment?'

Lucas snorted. 'Since when do the IMI ever reveal useful information to us? We're just kids to them and you, well, you're something else entirely. If I were you though, Elena, I'd try to keep this to myself.'

'Why?' I asked, my eyes narrowing.

'Because I reckon that if headquarters ever found out what you could be capable of, now, *before* you turned, they might want to ship you off to Bucharest for further study.'

'Bloody hell, are you serious?'

'Deadly. Mum and dad talk to Chester, the head of the lab there, all the time. You would definitely be of interest to him if your powers unleashed themselves ahead of schedule.'

'Lucas, you don't even know if we're right. I gave Peter a few bruises, nothing I probably haven't given him in the past. So what? And as for you, you're so skinny you'd blow over in the next wind.'

He puckered his lips in disapproval. 'Care to test the theory then before you refute the evidence?'

'What did you have in mind?'

'How about a little exercise?'

'Ugh, don't you know I'm allergic?'

'Yeah, but this will be fun.'

We crossed the road after the traffic had cleared, made our way onto the footpath and picked up the pace until we got home. By the time we reached the driveway, I was already starting to sweat. It wasn't winter anymore. It was early September now, the third day in to be precise, and although the nights were still relatively cool, the days were not so forgiving.

I dropped my backpack as we entered the house and headed directly into the garden behind Lucas. The patio doors made their usual scraping sound of protest, the glass door whining along its aluminium tracks.

Lucas disappeared into the backyard and told me to wait where I was. I stood on the patch of dirt just below my window, waiting for him to reappear from behind the jungle of bushes, weeds, and trees.

He returned a few seconds later, his palm extended out in front of him using the same magic spell that George had used on us in the library a fortnight ago to levitate a bar bell and several weights from the shed.

'What do you think?' Lucas asked, letting the weights float gently onto the ground in front of me.

'Are you going to get into trouble for using magic like that?'

'Dad shouldn't have showed me the levitation spell if he didn't want me to use it.'

'He didn't show you, he used it on you. There's a difference.'

He smiled at me and gestured towards the bar bell. 'You'd be surprised what dad tries to show me when no one else is around. Now why don't you give it a go?'

I looked down sceptically at the barbell. Lucas had stacked four, twenty-five kilogram weights on either end, two hundred kilograms in total, plus the weight of the bar.

Was he high?

George had gone through a phase about six months ago where he wanted to look like Bruce Willis from the *Die Hard* movies. He'd bought the barbell and all the weights expecting that a couple of repetitions and a few protein shakes would transform his lean body into a muscle machine. He'd tried it once, tore a ligament in his shoulder and hadn't touched any of the equipment since.

'Come on, E. What are you waiting for?' Lucas grinned.

'A forklift.'

He rolled his eyes and grinned. 'I don't see one, do you?'

'Thank you, Captain Obvious,' I mumbled under my breath. 'Just what do you think this is going to achieve besides severe muscle strain and a brain aneurysm?'

He laughed. 'We're trying to prove whether or not your experience has given you greater strength.'

I looked down at the bar bell again. 'It looks freaking heavy.'

'Well, *duh*, that's kind of the point.'

I screwed my face up at him. 'It's too heavy, Lucas. I'll strain something just trying, it's going to hurt.'

'So does constipation, but we all suffer through it at some point.'

I stared at him blankly. 'I'm not sure I see the connection.'

He grinned. 'Come on, just do it. If you can't lift it, then we'll rule out the whole extra strength thing and just go inside and watch Sponge Bob.'

'Sponge Bob? Why didn't you say so?' I said, clapping my hands together and pretending to be thrilled by the prospect.

Not.

'Couldn't we start with something a bit smaller?'

'Shit, Elena, will you stop procrastinating? I could have cured cancer by now.'

I frowned at him and then studied the weights in front of me again. It was almost four times my own body weight.

I wiped my hands and then circled them around the cool steel of the bar. It flexed gently as I tightened my grip and pulled upwards. At first nothing happened, mostly because I was too scared to pull any harder in case my spine snapped.

'Come on, Elena, give it a bit more.'

'Want me to toss you over the fence?'

'No.'

'Then shut up.' I closed my eyes, counted to three, took a deep breath, opened my eyes again and then heaved. The barbell left the ground with surprising ease. Yeah, I could feel the weight of it, but I couldn't exactly call it heavy.

I raised it to my knees and then lifted it up to my chest and then over my head.

'That's so freaking cool,' Lucas murmured as he watched me spin it above my head.

I grinned. 'I know, right?'

There was some rustling of tree leaves over near the fence and a couple of branches on the jacaranda tree bobbed up and down and brushed noisily against the fence post.

Ahh, crap. Why did Bob always take neighbourhood watch so seriously?

I lowered the barbell from over my head and placed it back down on the ground before Bob, our nosey next door neighbour made his daily appearance over the fence. His bald head, cracked through the shrubbery a moment later. 'What's going on over here?'

'Hi, Bob,' Lucas and I said in rehearsed unison. He must have propped a ladder up against the fence so that he could peer into our garden as the fence was well over six feet tall and there was plenty of dense foliage crowding his view of our backyard. You think he'd get the hint that we weren't communal people when we erected the fence six years ago and let the shrubbery grow wild. He must have really wanted to know what all the fuss was about.

'You kids causing trouble?' he asked gruffly.

'Not today,' Lucas answered politely.

He smacked his lips together and rubbed at his grey bearded chin. 'What are you doing with that exercise contraption there?'

I slapped Lucas lightly on the shoulder and smiled. He buckled forward and stumbled to the ground. 'We're trying to buff Lucas up, Bob,' I said, smiling politely. 'As you can see, he's about as strong as a fart in the wind.'

Lucas scrambled back to his feet and shot me a look.

Bob huffed and scratched at his chin again. 'I think you're aiming too high, boy,' he said, pointing to the barbell. 'Maybe for someone of your stature you should start with some small hand weights instead.'

'Thank you, Bob,' Lucas muttered through gritted teeth as he flipped me off behind his back. 'What an excellent idea.'

Bob frowned and looked at the weights again. 'Just try and keep it down. Your hollering interrupted my TV time— Antiques Roadshow's on.'

I sniggered quietly to myself and nodded.

He leaned away from the fence and swatted at something crawling over his arm. 'You might want to take a look at the green ant's nests that you've got building along this fence here while you're at it. The little buggers really have a nasty bite on them.'

'Sure thing, Bob,' Lucas said, waving at him and then, turning his back on Bob, rolled his eyes for my benefit.

Bob waved to us both and then disappeared back behind the fence again. I could hear him folding his ladder up and putting it back inside his carport, muttering loudly about how many times he had just gotten bitten by 'those bloody ants'.

'Can you believe that guy?' Lucas said, jabbing his thumb over his shoulder and pointing in Bob's direction. 'Trust us to move in right next door to the chairman of the Neighbourhood Watch committee.'

I laughed and then looked back down at the barbell at my feet. 'Do you want to take it back to the shed or should I?'

He paused. 'You know, things are going to be different now. You're going to have to be a lot more careful than you have been in the past.' He said this as he concentrated on levitating the weights back up into the air in front of him.

'Are you talking about keeping this secret from everyone at the IMI?'

He nodded. 'But not just them. You'll also have to be careful in the way you touch people or objects. It may just be a temporary side effect, but if it's not, you're going to have to relearn how to touch things and people with care. If you don't, you'll probably break someone. If that happens, then the secret will be out of the bag.'

I looked deeply into his powder blue eyes. 'Can I trust you, Lucas?'

He sniffed. 'As if you even had to ask. I don't want you to be shipped off to the other side of the world anymore than you do. However sad this is to say, you're not just my sister, Elena, but my friend. I know eventually that you're going to turn and then leave us, but until then, I don't want you to go.' He turned away from me before I even had a chance to answer or gauge a reaction from his face. He headed off down through the weeds, into the backyard and disappeared behind the shed.

That night the family congregated together in the living room to watch a few sitcoms together. This meant being together in the same room and acting like we were enjoying one another's company, even though the endless dialogue from the television negated the need for conversation.

My test results had not been brought up even once and it didn't appear like they were going to be. I saw the quick glances that were aimed in my direction and then the silent conversation that seemed to pass between Susan and George. At least Lucas was keeping up the pretence that all was normal.

After the shows had ended and the non-existent conversation appeared to stretch on into the silence, I excused myself and said goodnight to everyone. I headed to the bathroom for a hot shower, and from the murmured dialogue that was going on in the living room as I left, it appeared that everyone else had the same plan. Apparently dealing with Sarah's mutterings of satanic possession and Kim's threats of leaving the IMI if I stayed was starting to wear Susan and George down. Both of them had bags building under their eyes, and not the stylish Louis Vuitton kind that I'd love to get my hands on.

When I got out of the shower, I ran a comb through my wet hair and loosely folded it up with a clip.

I searched the room for my clothes and then slapped my forehead when I realised I had forgotten to bring my night clothes in with me, for the umpteenth time. As a compromise, I wrapped a thick towel around myself and darted for my bedroom as quickly as my feet would carry me. My family had already dispersed to their own areas of the house, and all the lights had been turned off downstairs. Lucas's bedroom door was closed as I sprinted on past.

I got to my room, gliding along with the stealth of an

assassin and the speed of a cheetah. There was only my own shadow that was stalking me along the wall beside me for company.

I shut the door silently behind me and then turned around, and switched the light on.

'What took you so long?' William asked, sitting perched on the edge of my window sill.

Bloody hell!

I had to cup a hand over my mouth to prevent a scream from escaping.

I steadied myself against the edge of the desk, took a calming breath and then looked back up at him. He couldn't have looked any more relaxed if he tried. I searched his face for marks, scratches or imperfections. There were none, and it was clear now, more than ever, that he was alive and well. Why had he not tried to contact me, to tell me he was alright? And why had he not returned any of the messages that I had left on his phone?

Geez, Elena, calm down. One thought at a time.

I tucked the towel more securely around myself, trying to be demure. Luckily, even after the scare and *almost* forward tumble down to my knees, everything appeared to be in its place.

So what the hell is he looking at?

I grew more self-conscious by the second, as his gaze appraised me, taking in the creamy, white expanse of my bare arms and shoulders, and the length of my naked legs, right to where the towel cut off the view neatly at the top of my thighs.

I reached over and switched the light off again. He began to chuckle at my growing embarrassment. 'Do you think turning the light off makes a difference to me?' he said, still laughing.

'Would you mind turning around please?' I said stiffly.

He continued to chuckle to himself, but effortlessly spun himself around on the window frame to avert his eyes.

I ran over to the dresser and quickly pulled out a pair of underwear and a bra, and studied them in the darkness by holding them out in front of me. I wasn't sure if the colours even matched.

Why are you worrying about your bra and panties, you dipshit? Just throw something on!

I shook my head at my girly behaviour, dropped the towel to the floor and slipped them on as quickly as possible. I grabbed my denim shorts from the top drawer along with a red turtleneck sweater that I hadn't worn in years. The excess fabric rolled warmly around my neck and ears, and the sleeves were long enough that the cuffs covered half of my palms. It may have been an overreaction on my part, but I thought the more of my neck and open vein sources that were covered the better.

I kicked the towel into the corner of the room and then walked over to switch the light back on again. William had already beaten me to it and my fingers gently brushed over his, in search of the switch as his hand was pulling away. His skin was as chilled as always, but it transferred to the flesh of my fingers as a welcoming heat that I both enjoyed and detested.

'What are you doing here?' I asked, breaking the silence between us, our hands slowly lowering. 'I thought something had happened to you. I left you messages on your phone but you never called me back.'

His eyes glistened with amusement. 'Have you been worried about me?'

'Don't flatter yourself. I was just wondering.'

He chuckled and touched a finger to my nose. 'I think you have been worried about me. How lovely.'

I groaned audibly. 'What happened to you? Do you even realise that the Alpha came after me?'

He took in my appearance with a quick glance of his eyes and then started to chuckle again, ignoring my question completely. He reached up and fingered the red fabric that was wrapped so comfortingly around my neck. 'Nice outfit,' he answered simply, lowering his hand and crossing his arms in front of his chest, a smug sort of smile forming on his face.

'It's not exactly the Vogue designer wardrobe in here, you know,' I answered sharply. 'What I really wanted to wear was the latest Versace number with Jimmy Choo pumps, but I guess you caught me on a laundry day—sorry about that.'

He looked at me for a second, expression neutral, before he tugged at my turtleneck again. 'What I meant was,' he said slowly, 'why the turtleneck? It's not winter anymore.'

I shrugged. 'Just trying to make things a little easier.'

'How so?'

I chewed at my fingernail for a moment, pondering the best choice of words. 'Well, when the alpha found me the other night, things didn't exactly go very well and the last time you and I talked you mentioned that my blood *is* mouth-watering and difficult to ignore. I just thought this,' I said, tugging on my sweater, 'would make things a little easier for you to be around me. You know, out of sight, out of mind?'

He bobbed his head in acknowledgement. 'I appreciate the thought, but there isn't anything you can do. The thirst is something that I need to deal with. It's not your problem, but as for resisting you, well ...' He trailed off.

'Well, what? Can you smell me all of the time regardless of what I'm wearing?'

'Yes.'

'Oh.' I was thoughtful for a minute. 'What if I roll around in a poo patty?'

His smile widened. 'Even then.'

'Oh, okay.'

He took a step towards me, the heat of his proximity instantly warming my skin. I could feel my heartbeat quicken at his approach. 'Don't be afraid of me, Elena.'

'I'm not,' I stammered.

He grinned. 'Yes you are.'

I'm not afraid. I thought to myself. *How can I tell you that my heart's beating faster because you're near? It's not my fault you're so damn attractive!*

'I'm most definitely *not* afraid of you,' I whispered as he took another step towards me, stopping directly in front of me and looking down at me with wickedly mischievous eyes. My heart skipped a beat and then proceeded to thud along at an even more ardent rhythm than it had before.

He placed a hand on my sweater, directly above my heart. It seemed to beat erratically inside my chest, trying to pierce through the flesh of my chest and leap into the palm of his hand. 'Then why is your heart beating so fast?'

I looked away. The heat of my embarrassment was clearly becoming evident on my face again.

Ah, crap. When am I going to get some control over that?

I could feel his eyes on my face and kept mine lowered to the floor, hoping that I hadn't inadvertently stirred the beast within.

'I see,' he said, taking another step closer, our bodies only inches apart now, his hand still resting gently against my chest. I couldn't look up into his eyes.

'Um, what are you doing?' I whispered as he pressed

himself against me, my body flattening out against the wall behind me. It seemed like we'd been down this path before. I had no choice but to look at him now, unless I fancied squishing my nose up against his chest and inhaling lint.

His eyes were slightly muddied, a mixture of green, black, brown, and white—all mixed up and swirled around together like food in a blender. 'I'm trying to get used to your scent,' he murmured as he leant forward, brushing his nose against my cheek and softly inhaling my aroma.

'Why?' I said breathlessly, trying not to move an inch.

'Because I have a feeling you and I are going to be seeing a lot of each other.'

'Why?' I repeated again, sounding like a four year old.

He chuckled. 'Because I like you Elena Manory and I'm pretty sure that you like me too.'

I sniffed. 'Someone's got a big head.'

'Am I wrong?' he asked, drinking me in.

I didn't answer. What was I supposed to say to that?

He pulled his head back from my face, opened his eyes again and looked at me. They were no longer the jumble of colours I had seen before. They were now completely and utterly black and I couldn't help but be a little bothered while he was standing so very close to me.

He breathed in again, letting my scent wash over him a final time before shaking his head and then looking straight back at me.

I watched in amazement as his eyes very slowly began to shift back to the emerald green depths that symbolised his humanity and more docile nature. 'Are you done now?' I asked shakily.

'Yes, that is enough for now,' he said, taking a step away from me and back towards the open window. 'It will get easier the longer I am around you.'

'Assuming I'll let you come back,' I mumbled under my breath.

He grinned. 'Do you want to get out of here?' he said, gesturing with a hand outside the window.

I looked over towards the bedroom door, remembering what had happened the last time I had snuck out. I was already technically grounded and sneaking out again was sure to lead to death and dismemberment, and not from William.

I quickly skirted through Susan's very specific terms of my grounding and I couldn't think of one rule that I could twist to suit myself. She'd made it very clear not to leave through any openings in house, including my window.

Hang on a second—was I actually considering this?

Being alone with him could spell trouble in so many different languages that even Google Translate would tell me to get a clue.

So should I or shouldn't I?

'Don't worry. I promise I won't bite, no pun intended, and I'll have you back before anyone even notices that you are missing.' William smiled at me, his white teeth lighting up every darkened crevice in the room.

How could his smile and only his smile alone have that effect on me?

He raised an eyebrow at my reaction but then smiled again as he turned his back to me, putting his hands around my wrists and placed my arms around his neck. His skin was cool, even through the thick fabric of the turtleneck, but not uncomfortable.

'Are you getting fresh with me?' I asked as he slid his hands down to clasp the back of my thighs. I didn't have the heart to slap his hands away, and it felt nice.

He laughed gently and hoisted me easily onto his back. 'I don't do fresh. I'm technically dead, remember?'

'Eww ... thanks for the mental picture.'

He laughed again. 'I'm simply being practical. If you want to get there fast and undetected then you'll have to let me carry you there.'

'Where exactly is *there*?' I asked as he adjusted my weight.

'It will be a surprise.'

'I don't like surprises.'

'Is that a fact?'

'Ah-huh. Every surprise I ever got ended in tears.'

He turned his head around and smiled at me. 'Yours or someone else's?'

'What do you think?'

Laughter came easily to him. 'You're a tough nut, Elena,' he said jovially. 'Are you ready?'

'Not really, this is kind of a new experience for me. I've never even ridden a horse before let alone a vampire.' I grimaced at how that entire sentence had actually sounded.

'All you have to do is hang on tight and I'll do the rest.'

And the innuendos keep on coming.

'I bet you say that to all the girls.'

Laughter convulsed through his entire being. At least he saw the funny side of unlife.

'How fast are you going to be running?' I asked, trying to change the subject as he jumped up easily onto the window sill.

'Faster than you can blink, so you better hold on tight.'

'Are we still going to stay in the state of Queensland?'

'Of course.'

'Just checking.'

He shifted me around effortlessly on his back so that he could get a better grip of my thighs. I tightened my hands around his neck, careful not to choke him, but then realised that it was improbable that I could kill him again.

I tightened my hold on him and nestled my chin into his shoulder. He smelt so unbelievably good that I repeatedly inhaled, letting his essence wash over my senses and tingle all the way down, deep into my lungs.

'Are you ready now?'

'Is that a trick question?'

He turned his head slightly sideways. I saw the corners of his lips upturn into a smile as he ducked carefully under the sill, careful of my head, and then jumped off the ledge. He leapt into the garden below without warning, fear or thought.

CHAPTER FOURTEEN: PUNCHES

What am I doing again? Oh yeah, that's right—I'm playing piggy back with a vampire.

As William jumped from the opening, with me clinging to his back like a giant parasite, all I could think about was when and how I had agreed to being toted about like a handbag. Didn't he have a car like a normal guy? Or was he just showing off?

Unlike me, when William landed on the ground just below my window, there was no reverberation. His body seemed barely capable of disturbing the earth beneath his feet. He was feather-light and nimble on his feet, despite having a body that was more solid than a cement truck.

As soon as his feet connected with the ground and he'd readjusted his grip on my thighs, he took off.

I felt as if I had been body-slammed into a whirling vortex. I had to grab on tight and nestle my head into his back to keep my head from being blown off my shoulders. My eyes could barely stay open and at not one point did I have enough time to focus on any one object or landmark that we passed. Even my hair, despite being contained in a clip, had found a way to fly free and mingle with the wind that gushed past my face like a raging tornado.

I managed to crack my eyelids open a couple of millimetres. That was the best I could do without blowing them into the back of my skull. I saw only the darkness of the night and the swirling lights of cars and buildings that fled past my field of vision like streaks of electrical currents. It was beautiful, cosmic, exciting and stomach churning, all at the same time.

I closed my eyes again. Far too much sensory overload for one night. I'd only just finished eating pizza an hour ago and I didn't want to see that again anytime soon.

'Nearly there,' he yelled back at me. 'Just hold on for a little bit longer.'

Holding on would not be a problem. My fingers were knotted so tightly around his neck right now that if I fell off I was definitely taking him with me. 'How can you see where you are going?' I yelled back at him.

'I'm using my eyes.'

'Well then mine are broken.'

A second later, he stopped. In fact, he stopped so abruptly that I ended up head-butting him so hard that I almost knocked myself out. Tiny white stars danced in front of my eyes, and I felt my hands slip from around his neck and my legs go limp under his grip.

That could not have hurt anymore if I tried.

'Elena? Are you all right?' he asked, sounding frantic as he caught my arms to stop me from falling off his back completely.

I shook my head, waiting for the confusion and the headache to dissipate. I rested my forehead on his shoulder.

'Can I have a little warning next time?' I muttered, as my vision very slowly began to clear.

He spun me around quickly, cradling me in his arms like a baby. I would have protested, but given that I was still seeing little green gnomes dancing around my head, I figured I'd stay put.

'Elena, you should be unconscious or dead right now,' he said frantically, running his fingers over my forehead and checking for damage. If there was any, it surely would have healed by now. Sometimes the internals just took a little while to catch up, and head injuries were the worst for me.

'I only head-butted you,' I said, blinking away the last little gnome and pretty white stars.

'Exactly.'

'Aww, have a heart, William. I just had my head bashed in and I'm seeing green people, I don't have a mental capacity right now.'

He cursed under his breath and checked my forehead again, his eyes dripping with concern. 'I can't believe how careless I just was. I'm not used to being around humans like this. I didn't think. I'm so sorry, Elena.' He shook his head again. 'I'm supposed to be protecting you not trying to kill you.'

'Huh?'

'It's nothing. I'm just frustrated.'

I wriggled around in his arms trying to find a way out. He wasn't having a bar of it. 'Don't worry about it, I'm fine.'

'Yes, but you shouldn't be fine. Any other human would have had their skull crushed instantly by the impact you just experienced. Even I felt our heads collide and a little bit of pain and that shouldn't happen. Self-healing capabilities or not, I can't understand why you're still alive right now.'

'Just lucky, I guess.'

'I think we both know that's—'

'Hey,' I interrupted him. 'May I suggest a saddle and some reins for the next time you decide to try that with someone? It might make it easier to hang on and slow down.'

His eyebrow rose marginally. 'Are you suggesting what I think you're suggesting?'

I smiled, grateful that the subject had changed so easily. 'That depends. Do you prefer giddy up? Or go horsey go?'

He let go of me instantly and I fell to the ground landing hard on my backside.

Ouch.

'Okay, I deserved that,' I said as I scrambled back to my feet, wiping the dirt from the back of my shorts. 'Where are we, anyway?'

'You don't recognise where we are?' he said moodily.

Note to self: don't compare overly sensitive vampire to a thoroughbred.

I took a closer look at my surrounds and noted nothing remarkable. It was just an empty parking lot in the city.

Woohoo! What a spectacular surprise. Not.

I did work out after a few seconds of surveying the area that we were in the middle of the business area. We were just down the street from the convention centre and fairly close to the harbour and shopping district. Across the road there were a few cars, a luxury apartment building that I'd never be able to afford to live in, and directly next to us was the National Mutual tower looming impressively above us—it was one of the tallest buildings in Cairns.

'I'll buy it. What are we doing here?' I asked.

'We're here to admire the view.'

I looked around. As I said, the street was still littered with quite a few parked cars and people happily walking the footpath on the way to the restaurants, coffee shops and nightclubs in the area. But I could not see this *view* that he was speaking of. Not unless he meant the blonde with the short red dress clacking in her high heels along the footpath on the other side of the street.

I leant back against the concrete wall and folded my

arms across my chest. 'There's nothing worth looking at here. Why did you really bring me here, William?'

He glanced upwards and pointed to the top of the tower. 'I told you, the view. I'm taking you up there. That's where the view is and that's where we will be able to talk without being disturbed or followed by unwanted spectators.'

I followed his gaze up to the top of the tower and almost fell over backwards trying to take in its full height.

Was he crazy?

'Ah … no,' I answered and took a few steps away from him. 'I'm not going up there.'

He grinned. 'Are you afraid of heights?'

'No, it's not the height that's the problem it's the sudden stop at the bottom.'

'You'll be safe with me, Elena. I won't let you fall.'

My brows furrowed. 'You'd better be joking. I'm not going up there.'

'Yes, you are.'

'William Granville, I *will* hurt you.'

'You have to catch me first,' he laughed as he lowered into a crouch and then disappeared in a blur of movement.

I looked around the parking lot and spotted him at the far end walking across a steel chain that resembled a tightrope, suspended stiffly between two timber stumps to stop cars from accessing some of the reserved parking spaces. Just to be a jackass, he flipped into a handstand and continued to walk along the chain with his hands, his feet balanced effortlessly in the air above him.

'Is there any particular reason why you're showing off?' I called out to him, internally awed by his theatrics.

He cartwheeled backwards onto the chain and stood with perfect balance. He smiled and gave me a quick wink. In the next instant, he blurred and then vanished again.

I searched the space for him again, but I couldn't see him anywhere.

He whistled to grab my attention and I swung around to see him standing next to the tower wall about halfway across the car park. He pressed his fingers against the smooth concrete and then watched my face intently as he climbed the vertical surface like a spider. He scuttled up the wall about twenty metres and then turned around and clambered quickly towards me in a blur of arms and legs.

I ducked when he reached me, but then he changed tact and backflipped off the wall behind me, landing soundlessly on the ground at my feet. After that he disappeared again, my eyes far too human to keep pace with his speed.

'You're still showing off,' I yelled into the empty car park, searching him out. 'It's not a particularly becoming trait for you.'

A blur of wind sent my hair flying wildly into my eyes like shiny brown tentacles. I picked them free and then swore in fright as William appeared directly in front of me again.

He slammed me up against the wall, claiming my hands in his and pinning them to my sides, his face only an inch away from my own. 'Do you think I've been showing off?' he breathed.

I nodded, unable to be articulate when he was standing so close to me.

'That was nothing,' he whispered. 'This is showing off.'

He dipped his head forward and brushed a quick kiss across my surprised lips before he released me and disappeared all over again.

What the hell?

Before I even had time to contemplate what had just happened, he blurred in front of me again, grabbed my arm, swung me onto his back, and leapt up onto the side of the building before I had a chance to protest. I was fairly certain that I spent the rest of the way up to the top squealing like a little girl. And there was nothing feminine or delicate about it—I swore like a trooper.

I chanced a look back down and nearly passed out, the cars were fast becoming the size of small matchboxes. That meant that we were really, *really* high up. 'Please don't let go of me,' I cried as I buried my head into his shoulder and closed my eyes.

I'm going to kill you as soon as we get to some solid ground.

A moment later we stopped. I couldn't open my eyes.

I felt William's hands pull gently at the back's of my thighs and turn my body around so that I was clinging onto his front now. My legs were now tightly wrapped around his back, my arms still around his neck, my head was buried deeply into his chest.

'It's okay. We're at the top now. You can open your eyes,' he said gently, as he helped me unravel my body parts from around him and lowered me to the ground.

As soon as I felt solid floor underneath my feet I let go of him and stepped away, but not before I threw the biggest and hardest punch I could muster directly at his face.

He stumbled backwards in surprise and cupped a hand to his now bleeding nose. I felt smug for just a second, but that was before I fell straight to my knees and screamed blue bloody murder for all the pain I was now feeling in my right hand. Each and every one of my knuckles had cracked as they connected with the toughened skin of his face. And yet despite the instant gratification from messing with his perfect features and taking him by surprise, I'd never felt more idiotic.

But, boy, what a punch!

I clutched my broken hand against my chest and bit back the tears of pain that were threatening to spill down my cheeks. I knew it wouldn't be long before my hand was healed and I didn't want him to see me cry.

When I looked back up at William, his face was restored. Even the blood that had covered his nose and lips had found a way back into his system. There was no facial swelling, no bruises, no anger or irritation, and no telltale signs that my fist had ever encroached on his perfect features.

I shook my hand and flexed the fingers a couple of times, just to confirm that the bones had set correctly. There was no pain at all anymore. Even the anger I had felt towards him had dispersed and had been replaced with a growing sense of satisfaction.

This was mostly because of the way he was looking at me now. It was like a light had exploded underneath his pale skin making his whole face radiate with energy, his gleaming eyes watching me with a mixture of awe and uncertainty.

'How did you do that?' he said urgently, his eyes wide and full of wonder.

I climbed back to my feet and smiled ruefully at him, giving my hand the final once over. 'I did say that I would hurt you. It's not my fault that you're apparently deaf.'

He gave me a forced smile in return. 'Yes, you did, but that explains nothing.'

'It tells you why you shouldn't show off and why you definitely shouldn't kiss me unless invited.'

He grunted in reply. I took his non-answer as a good opportunity to change the subject and find out where I was.

I did a quick little turn on the spot and deduced that the top of the tower was fairly ordinary in comparison to the view that it offered. The structure was near oval in shape, but with squared-off edges that did little more than drop right off to thin air below. In the centre of the roof there was a large, concrete construction that probably housed the air-conditioning compressors for the building. But I was only guessing.

There was nothing remotely attractive about the rooftop. It was dirty and plastered with bird droppings. But there was something magical about being up here, nothing to do with the construction of the building itself. It was the three hundred and sixty degree view we had of the esplanade, inlet, city, and southern industrial areas. During the day I imagined that it was possible to see all the mountains, thick blankets of green that bordered the city. You could probably see all the way down the coast, past the airport and out towards the northern beaches too. From this height I imagined that the sun probably made the ocean sparkle with the kind of green iridescence you see only in tourist brochures, and the sand would look like glistening sugar crystals as the water lapped at the edges. At night, however, the mountains were nothing more than looming dark shadows on the horizon, the water looked like ink as the moonlight highlighted its depth and continual movement, and the sand was practically nonexistent—even grey in the instances that I could see it.

Despite my method of transport to reach such dizzying heights, and lack of pre-safety instructional video for flying Vampire Air, the view was spectacular. I could see the casino, all of the hotels that littered the esplanade and the lagoon, as well as the shopping precinct and beyond. They were absolutely breathtaking at night. The lights of the city twinkled below—the breeze that blew across the rooftop reminded you that you were a little closer to heaven than everyone else.

'It's beautiful,' I murmured, turning again to look at him. He was still watching me intently.

He took a few steps towards me and offered me his hand. I looked down at it for a brief moment before shrugging my shoulders, and closed my hand around his. If he was going to maim me for punching him in the face a moment ago then he probably would have done it already.

He led me to a small concrete shelf that surrounded the central concrete shaft and shrugged free of the leather jacket he was wearing. He placed it down on the dirtied concrete and motioned for me to sit down.

How very debonair of him.

'So,' I heard myself saying as he sat down beside me, his thigh resting against mine. All the questions I'd had for him suddenly flew out the back door of my brain the second his body touched mine.

What was I going to say again?

'Now that we are alone and relaxed,' he said casually, as he reached up and tucked a lock of hair behind my ears, 'perhaps we can pick up from where we left off last weekend?'

I swallowed. 'Umm, okay.'

'I have so many questions for you, Elena,' he continued. 'You make me curious in a way that no person ever has. I hope you don't mind. I'd like to try to unravel some of the mysteries that have been circling around in my head since we first met.'

I shook my head.

What does it matter if he knows everything about me now, anyway? He already knows the worst of what I am and, after that, I'm still alive.

That's true, but don't drop your guard completely, not when you know so little about him.

At least he's doing all the talking.

God, he's just so … beautiful.

'How about, to begin with, we just start out slow. I want you to feel like you can trust me, so why don't we swap, take turns to speak. Does that sound fair?'

I swallowed and remembered I had vocal chords. 'Sure, but as for trusting you, that could take some time.'

He sighed. 'And time is what I have plenty of.'

'So I start first then?'

He nodded. 'As you wish.'

'Okay then, tell me where you've been for the last week. Why did you never once call me back?'

His face instantly upturned. 'So you were worried about me?'

I sniffed and looked away. 'Marginally. But I was mostly pissed because you spent ten minutes telling me to stay inside the car, and then you deserted me and the alpha ended up getting to me anyway.' I rubbed my neck where the Vânător's teeth had bitten deep only a week ago.

'I like that you've been thinking about me,' he said calmly, touching a cool finger to my cheek and brushing it across the skin, searing it. 'It says that not everything is written in stone, and that some things that are destined can be changed.'

'Okay,' I said, frowning and shrugging his hand away. 'Why don't you stop changing the subject and answer my question. What happened to you?'

He sighed and dropped his hand. 'The alpha and I got into a serious fight. Unfortunately he came out a little better off than I did. I'm assuming that you and the IMI realise that the alpha has gotten away?'

I nodded.

'So with that being said, Thomas and I have been doing everything that we can to find him and fix my blunder before he gets time to round up a new pack. For the past week we've been following the scent trails between Mackay and Cairns. It doesn't look like he's heading back south. There must be something in this town that takes his fancy.'

'How did he slip you in Mackay anyway?' I asked. 'Aren't you supposed to be stronger and faster than him?'

He grimaced. 'To some extent, but he caught me off guard. I was too busy listening to you running down the alley, wondering if the second werewolf would hunt you down. The alpha hit me so hard in the side of the face that he knocked me through the side of a building. By the time I pulled myself back together again he was gone and you were screaming.'

'So you couldn't trace him once he was finished with me? I wounded him you know. There would have been a trail of blood to follow.'

'I know,' he said quietly. 'But his scent was impossible for me to find when mixing with your own blood riding the wind. It drove me beyond all distraction. I had to get as far away from the area as possible before I did something completely unforgivable.'

'Unforgivable—as in, drinking my blood?'

He turned away from me and looked out over the horizon. 'Yes. That's why I haven't been in contact since. I thought it would be sensible to put some space between us as long as the scent of your blood was still at the forefront of my mind.'

'I don't get it? What makes my blood so appealing? I know you said it's defect free, but so what? Don't you vampires drink human synthetic blood anyway? What's the damn difference?'

'What's your favourite food?'

'What?'

'Just answer me,' he said calmly. 'What's your favourite food?'

I touched a finger to my chin. 'Chocolate, especially those ones with the little gold wrappers that have the nut in the middle. They're the best.'

'Well imagine there is a room full of candy, cakes, and deserts. Each of them is more delicious than the next. But right in the very centre of that room, on a golden platter, is a slab of the thickest, richest, creamiest milk chocolate that you have ever seen.' He smiled wryly. 'And the ones with the little gold wrappers are on top,' he added.

I nodded. 'Okay, I'm picturing it.' I licked my lips.

'So which piece of food would you choose amongst the millions of other items of similar taste?'

'The chocolate.'

'Why?'

I frowned. 'Because it's my favourite and because I know it's going to taste better than everything else in the room.'

He looked at me unblinking. 'Do you see now?'

'Are you saying that I'm *your* chocolate?'

He gave me another wry smile. 'You're not just *my* chocolate, Elena, but every other vampire's on the planet. And, judging by the attack last Saturday, probably every werewolf's as well. No amount of Synth blood will ever satisfy me enough to ignore the call of blood as tantalising as yours.'

I sat silent for a minute and then looked back at him again. 'How's your sweet tooth at the moment?'

He threw his head back and laughed. It was deep, masculine, and if it hadn't have been so warm and inviting I would have packed my bags and left town. 'I am fine,' he said. 'I fed just before I came for you this evening, just in case.'

'Okay, so now that we have established that my blood is

uber tasty, can we just assume that you will keep your fangs in check and never bring up this subject again?'

'I don't think it's wise to just pretend that I'm not dangerous to be around.'

'Yet you still came for me tonight, knowing that fact.'

He contemplated this, as if it hadn't occurred to him. 'You have a point.'

'I always do. But in this instance,' I said, looking up into his eyes, 'why don't we go with the old adage that ignorance is bliss.'

He chuckled. 'As you wish.'

We both gazed at each other for the longest time, smiling despite the strain of the subject of conversation, before turning away nervously and laughing. 'Okay, it's my turn to ask questions now,' William said.

'Okay.'

'How did you do that before? The only people who can injure me are other vampires, and obviously the werewolves, and you are neither of those things right now.'

I took a breath. I knew this was going to come up eventually, but since he was not part of the IMI, I figured it was safe to tell him. 'Lucas has a ton of theories floating around inside his head. And after what happened this afternoon, I'm beginning to think that he might be right. I seem to have gotten stronger since drinking the alpha's blood last week, and now I'm stronger than any normal human being has a right to be.'

'Is there any particular reason why the two things should be linked? Maybe you're coming into your abilities early.'

'Well, the encounter did kind of go beyond the normal realms of physical contact.'

His eyes narrowed in confusion, and then the skin they

seemed to tighten. 'Did it … ?' He looked down at my stomach.

I followed his gaze. 'Oh God, no! It's nothing like that,' I said, horrified. 'The Vânător didn't do … that. He bit me. He fed from my blood and then, in turn, I fed from his.'

William's head practically swivelled right off of his shoulders as he looked back up at me. His eyes held barely concealed horror. 'You drank vânător blood?!'

Why do I keep getting that reaction?

I grimaced and turned away from him. 'Don't be so judgemental, *vampire*. I didn't know I'd been swallowing blood until after The Protectors found me. I was blacking out at the time, and it just … happened.'

At my raised voice his expression softened, and he whispered, 'How did it happen?'

My lips tightened in a hard line. 'I wounded him with my knife. The blood from his shoulder injury must have been dripping into my mouth. I can distinctly remember being so very thirsty.'

I looked away when I saw him frown again. 'I wish I could say that I hated every minute of it, but I didn't. It was the most delicious thing I've ever tasted.'

He leaned in close to me and pressed his nose to the side of my face. I held very still. 'Haven't you done this already tonight?'

He took a deep breath, ignoring me. A second later he pulled away, eyeing me with furrowed brows and darkened eyes. 'You're exactly the same as before, exactly the same as the first time I met you too. How can that be?'

I shrugged. 'I was hoping you might know the answer. The IMI already took some of my blood for testing and they found nothing out of the ordinary. They even tested it against my original birth sample but came up empty handed.

I'm trying to keep this all between just Lucas and myself, so I would appreciate it if you kept your mouth shut.'

He nodded.

'I'm guessing from your silence that this has never happened before?'

'No. Not even alphas carry the ability to turn humans from a bite. I'm guessing it's because you are half werewolf—his blood awakened something within you during the exchange. If the same thing had happened between you and a vampire, regardless of your special talents, you would have turned into a vampire.'

'So there's really no explanation.'

'I'm afraid so.'

'Do you know of anyone else that might have answers?'

He shifted around, ignoring my question. 'So you haven't experienced any shifting or tendencies to want to taste human flesh since the exchange?'

I frowned, but understood the necessity of such a question. 'Not that I'm aware of, but the night is still young.'

Ah, crap, did I just say that out loud? I sound like Hannibal Lecter.

Inwardly, I cursed myself for my inappropriate choice of words. 'I meant, for the shifting thing. Not the other part.'

He seemed way more amused than he should have been.

'Okay, my turn to ask questions again,' I said as I laughed like a bumbling idiot. 'Let's start with a few easy ones, questions that have been bugging me for years.'

He smiled but did not answer me.

'Okay, how often do you feed?'

'Roughly once a week.'

'How difficult is it to resist human blood? I only ask

because one day I'm going to be like you, or at least something like you. I need to know.'

He clasped his hands together in his lap and looked down at our dangling feet. 'For Vampire kind, the desire to drink blood is constantly thrumming away in the back of our minds. The older we get, the easier temptation becomes to resist. For example, a born vampire who is over five hundred years old will be able to live in a house filled with humans and quite easily resist the call. A turned Vampire is not as lucky. They have to wait a full thousand years before the call of blood is not as strong. Their sire, or maker, whatever you prefer, is bound to stay with them at all times to prevent them from not only feasting off everyone in sight, but exposing what we are on a very large scale. This is why turning has been made illegal amongst us. It creates too much risk.'

'You have Vampire laws?'

He smiled. 'Humans have laws to prevent anarchy—so do we. To be honest, there aren't many. The number one rule is to avoid exposure and, if nothing else, to stop worldwide panic and a witch-hunt on a grand scale if we were to be exposed.'

'What about relationships between vampires and humans, like that of my mother and my father?

'Between vampires, there is no permission necessary, but when a human and a vampire fall in love, which is extremely rare, there are far greater consequences to consider.'

'You're talking about the resulting child?'

'Yes. Some of the older vampires went a little crazy at our race's beginning, hence the rules since.'

'Who makes up all these rules, anyway?'

He looked away and out over the view of the city. 'Someone I hope that you never have to meet.'

'Who?'

He shook his head. 'My turn.'

'No way, I'm still on a roll,' I said vehemently. I had so many other burning questions that I didn't care whether or not he'd answered that last one. 'Does it hurt? Becoming a vampire, I mean.'

'Yes.'

'A lot or a little?'

'A lot.'

'Care to elaborate?'

He shook his head. 'I don't want to give you night-mares.'

Well that's something to look forward to.

'Okay, what triggers your transformation? What shifts you to your other vampiric form?'

'Anger, thirst, or need—the rest of the time we remain in human form.'

'So ... if your eyes turn black when you are around me it's because you're either thirsty or pissed off at me?'

'Generally.'

'Okay, good to know.'

'Anything else?' It felt like he was trying to push the conversation along, bored by the details that intrigued me.

I nodded, staring at his lips. They seemed to twitch every time he noticed me looking. 'Actually about a million things, but I can't seem to think of anything else right now. All I have is these crazy vampire clichés about garlic, crosses, and coffins going through my head.' I licked my lips and kept staring at his.

'Are you feeling a bit distracted?' he said, touching the skin of my cheek, dropping his finger to my lips and then running it down my chin, my neck, my—

I folded my arms to avoid his advances, standing up to

stretch my legs. I needed a minute to think. He had to know that this wasn't normal for me, and just how easy it was for anyone, including me to be distracted by his presence. 'I don't get distracted,' I muttered under my breath.

Total bullshit.

I wandered closer to the edge of the building and peered over.

Ugh, not such a good idea.

I backed up a couple of paces and stared out over the harbour and inlet in the distance instead, trying to clear my mind of all things William—an impossible task.

'It's okay for you to like me, Elena,' he said from behind me. 'I promise you that your feelings for me do not go unwanted.'

Well, isn't he presumptuous?

I'd had this feeling building deep down in the pit of my stomach that William had brought me because he was interested in something far less innocent than just a generalised chat. I knew that he was curious about me and had questions of his own, but the way that he looked at me, the way that he touched me—these were not the questions of someone that simply wanted to be friends.

I closed my eyes and concentrated on the wind, as it whipped across my face and blew torrents of chilled breeze through the long brown tendrils of my hair. The air smelt thickly of the sea, as well as having an underlying aroma of Chinese cooking—probably from the yum cha restaurant at the end of the street. I could hear the sound of the cars driving by below. But, as much as I searched, there were no voices of reason or instructions from above that could help me to decipher just exactly why William was interested in me—or, for that matter, why I was excited by the thought that he was. I could only assume that it was blatant curiosity.

My mind wasn't fully equipped to process anything above and beyond that, but then again, shouldn't I try? If I had managed to make a little room for Stephen in my life, then surely I could do the same for a man even more sublime than my wildest desires? But then again, look what happened to Stephen?

He isn't for you, a calm voice whispered through my head.

What the—was that me?

There was no answer. I wanted to laugh. Of course there was no answer because no one had said anything. Okay, definitely weird, but I could surmise whether I was a lunatic or not later.

I turned around slowly and paced back towards William.

'Elena? Is everything all right?'

A variety of emotions ranging from confusion to fear quickly touched my already troubled expression. I pushed them all away and looked into his eyes, sensing the urge to protect and possess within them. 'I'm fine.'

When I was no more than a few feet away, he reached out to me and smiled, easing my tensions. It was as if his entire face had lit up every darkened corner and crevice on the rooftop, warming me to the core and melting my apprehension. I had to catch my breath. It hurt to look at him. How could I not give him a chance if that was all he was asking for?

He took my hand in his, that familiar aroma of sandalwood cutting through all the other smells of the night air, dominating each and every one of them until all that I could smell was him. The voice became a distant memory.

My knees gave out as I lowered myself down onto the shelf next to him, our gazes never parting. For the first time in my entire life I felt like I was as light as a feather, burden free. I was yearning for a taste of those lips that I couldn't quite seem to stop looking at. 'It's your turn,' I said shakily, as he slipped his fingers through mine and set them on his lap. 'Ask me anything you want.'

He gazed at me for the longest time before he spoke. 'Will you tell me the story of who you are? I want to know everything about you, Elena. I want to know where you were born, who your real parents are, how your blood got so mixed up, and everything else that you've been doing since.'

It wasn't *exactly* what I had in mind at that time, but it would do. 'That's going to take a long time.'

He smiled and brushed his fingers across my hand. 'I'm a vampire, remember? Time is all I have.'

I took another deep breath to steady myself and then launched into the full story of what happened the night I was born, and everything up until that day. It took awhile, but as he said, we had time.

He listened quietly, never interrupting me while I spoke and nodding occasionally to keep the story moving forward. He occasionally stopped and asked me questions, and I did my best to answer them as honestly as I could. When I was finished, he sat there in silence for the longest time, absorbing what I had just said and filling in all the missing details in his mind. He now knew more about me than any other person on the planet and, funnily enough, I was okay with that.

'That's quite a story,' he finally said. 'I'm honoured that you decided to trust me with it.'

'I'm assuming that you will keep this to yourself?'

'Of course.'

I paused. 'Can I ask you something?'

'What would you like to know?'

I looked down at my hand, still enveloped tenderly in his lap. 'Did you just want to be friends? Or were you planning on something more?'

He chuckled lightly and tapped the back of my hand. 'You really don't beat around the bush, do you? You get straight to the point. I like that about you. But as for your question ... yes.'

Huh? Yes, what? Yes, you want to be friends or, yes, you want to be more than that? This is exactly the reason I avoided getting too friendly with boys. You never get a straight answer.

'Well, now that we have that cleared up,' I said, shaking my hand free of his, 'maybe you could clarify one last thing for me. I was hoping that you could tell me the history of how the Vânătors were created, and maybe, a little bit more about yourself. You know everything about me now. It seems only fair that I know something more about you in return.'

'Alright,' he said calmly, making a play for my hand. I let him hold me again.

So he didn't want to be *just* friends.

That's all you can ever be. The same voice from minutes before whispered through my mind again.

Jesus Christ, I am going crazy.

William's story broke me free of my thoughts. 'The Vânătors were created from the blood of the Vampire, which I'm sure you know, and which I'm sure you've gathered after your recent dance with that alpha the other night.'

'Yes, I know that part,' I said, wondering if I was going to start hearing voices on a regular basis, 'but how, and why?'

'I'm getting to that. In the beginning, twenty vânători were created—twenty ordinary forest wolves that we vampires once kept as loyal pets and servants, suddenly turning into killing machines overnight. They were turned in the same manner that a human is turned. All blood must be drained from the recipient's body. Just before their very last heart beat, an offering of their maker's blood is used to revive the recipient before they can slip into the afterlife. Both blood transactions must occur through skin to skin contact and the bite is the catalyst. There is a venom in our teeth, and when we bite the near dead, it kick starts the entire process.'

I shook my head. 'But a vânător bite does not create new vânâtors. What's so special about a vampire?'

'The Vânâtors and turned Vampires have two things in common. One, they are both carbon copies of an original, namely a born vampire. And, two, neither party can stand out in the sunlight. So they do not entirely possess the same powers that we do.'

'So what you're saying is that only a born vampire has the power to make more vânâtors and more vampires?'

'Through blood transfusion, yes, but the Vânâtors have learnt that procreating with a human is the next best step to initiate continuation of the species. The Vânâtors take without remorse and do not follow rules. They are still animals in a lot of ways and do not see reason the way a vampire can.'

'So does a turned vampire have the power of procreation?'

'A male-turned-vampire can create a child, yes, but that resulting child does not always become vampiric. Only a born Vampire can create another like us with any certainty.'

'But where did it begin? Who was the first?'

He paused. 'I don't know.'

He was lying. I don't know how I could tell, but I just did. It must have been some sort of vampire trade secret that I wasn't allowed to know until after I turned. Well, I could wait.

'And the sun, you mentioned that vânǎtors and turned vampires cannot venture into the daylight?'

'That is correct,' he said nodding. 'Both must hibernate during the daylight hours. The reason born vampires are free to walk through the daylight hours as compared to the werewolves is still unknown, although we must still stick to the shadows to remain unharmed.'

'What happens to you if you stray into the sunlight for too long? Do you burst into flames?'

He grinned. 'Eventually, but not straight away. It takes quite a lot of sunlight to cause any lasting damage.'

'But something I don't understand is why did you vampires make the Vânǎtors in the first place?'

He laughed. 'Do you want to stop for some air or something?'

'No way. I want to know everything. I have no idea what to expect from my life once I turn and so far you've given me more information in the last half hour than I've been told in the last four years. So don't stop now.'

'Alright, but just remember it's my turn next and you can't refuse me anything I ask of you.'

'Yeah, we'll see.'

He picked up my hand and turned it around in his so that my palm faced upwards. He spread my fingers out and then placed the palm of his hand directly over the top of my own, lacing his fingers through mine. 'You're so warm,' he murmured as he stared down at our entwined fingers.

In comparison to his cold skin, I was a raging furnace. 'William …'

'Okay, okay. The Vânătors were created out of our fear and lack of understanding.'

'Fear?' I said. 'Fear of what? The Protectors?'

He nodded. 'Times were very different then, Elena. The legend of the blood drinkers, the Vampires, was feared by many, and as a species we had lived untouchable for centuries. We were the top of the food chain and we took what we wanted, when we wanted. We killed many without remorse. This changed when a small village in the Carpathian Mountains of Transylvania decided that they were no longer going to be subject to our wanton ways any longer. As I'm sure that you are aware, they educated themselves in all forms of paganism, witchcraft, and any other magical or religious influence that they could get their hands on. These were the first Protectors.'

'They were fighting something beyond the realms of the ordinary. So they had to use the extra-ordinary to fight your kind.'

'That is correct.'

'So out of fear of being destroyed by The Protectors, the Vampires decided to transform their pets into something to help in the fight?' I asked.

He nodded. 'The wolves and vampires had been companions for many years. Wolves have always been the one animal that has never feared us and, as such, we have lavished them with adoration. Such was our arrogance that it took the mistake of only one coven of vampires to transform a creature that was once our beloved ally into a mortal enemy. Now, because of that coven, we have a planet roaming with creatures that feed just as we do, breed just as we can, but have no moral compass in order to guide them. They do not care for rules. They care only for blood and domination.'

'What happened with that particular coven of vampires to make them turn in the first place?'

'Those Vampires thought they could dominate the changed wolves as they had once done when the werewolves were just animals. But once they took their first sip of human blood, they became filled with a consciousness and the ability to communicate like never before. In their human form they had expected to be treated as equals, but the coven had little patience or desire to look on them as anything more than animals. Once the Vânătors became aware that we Vampires intended to keep them locked up and trained like house pets, they began an uprising. They annihilated nearly every member of the coven. It was left to some of the rest of us to seek out the escapees, make an alliance with The Protectors, and try to destroy the mistake that had been made.'

'So what happened to other living coven members? Were they punished for their actions?'

William turned away. 'No, they got away. There was nothing but a bloody mess by the time reinforcements came in.'

I blinked. 'Reinforcements?'

'Legionnaires from the Roman Guard, the main faction of vampires that act as a body to govern us—they decide our rules and our fate.'

'And were you a member of this governing body?'

He looked back at me. 'A long time ago. Things don't necessarily work out that way now. The world has changed in the last three hundred years. Human populations have exploded and you are less wary of outsiders now. It's much easier for us to blend in now, and the need for the Roman Guard is not as strict or necessary.'

'So you were there on the night that the alliance was signed between Protector and Vampire?'

'Yes.'

'Wow. I have so many more questions now that I don't even know where to begin.'

'Perhaps we could save some of those questions for another night? I'm not really comfortable with diving into some areas of my past just yet. There are a lot of things I have done, Elena, that I'm not proud of.'

'Like kill other vampires?'

He sighed. 'Yes.'

'What about humans?'

'No. I draw the line at harming humans,' he said tersely.

'What about me? Now that you know what I am and what I could one day be capable of, am I someone that the Legionnaires, your Roman Guard, would hunt?'

'I won't let that happen,' he answered, resting a hand on my shoulder. 'I will protect you, Elena. I have to.'

I frowned at his choice of words. 'Why would you protect me? What do you have to gain from keeping me alive?'

'Everything,' he breathed, letting his hand snake around to pull me close. 'You are so much more than you are willing to see in yourself. There is something very pure about you that makes me want you in more ways than to simply satiate my thirst. And though I should not say, there are some that would travel the length and breadth of time just to ensure they could be with you.' His face darkened ever so slightly as he said this.

I closed my eyes and swallowed.

Uh-oh, now we're getting heavy.

'When I saw you for the first time, Elena, I couldn't take my eyes off you. It wasn't just your scent that drove me wild. You were the most beautiful woman I had ever laid eyes on.'

'Now you're considering me a woman?' I said, eyeing him

sideways. 'Last week wasn't I just a little girl to you?' I had to throw that in. Men could be so fickle sometimes.

'Mentally, in a lot of ways you probably are, but physically—physically you are a woman in my eyes.'

I scoffed. Typical. 'Well, that's bloody convenient, isn't it?'

'I'm just trying to be honest.'

I could feel heat rise to my face at his words and I tried to push it away, knowing that it stirred his hunger. 'So what are you saying?' I whispered, looking up into his eyes. 'What are your intentions?'

'I'm saying that I'm very bad for you, Elena. I'm the most dangerous and present threat to your life, but I don't care. I know that sounds selfish. And I know that I should not be doing this, but I can't help myself. I want to be with you whether I should be or not. In four hundred and forty-four years I have never met anyone like you. And I can't let ...' He trailed off, his hands curling into fists at his sides. 'I can't let fate get in between us. That's not fair.'

I closed my eyes, letting his words emanate through my entire being as I processed their implications. 'You need to get out more,' I said shakily, 'broaden your horizons and what not. I can't be the only one out there for you.'

He shook his head. 'Perhaps I should,' he said, his finger reaching up and tracing the line of my cheek. 'But I have a feeling that I'd still only want you.'

I swallowed. Some of my walls may have been knocked down tonight, but was I ready to clear out the rubble of their destruction? Could I swallow my fear at the chance of being hurt and take a step forward with him knowing that one day he might leave me, just as my real parents had done?

I drew in a slow, deep breath and then opened my eyes again, and letting them fall to the fullness of William's lips once again. I knew that as soon as he pressed them against mine that all reason and common sense would fly directly out of the window. If I wasn't going to go down this path then I was going to have to make a decision fairly quickly.

'Elena,' he said gently, his lips moving seductively as he formed the sound of my name.

I melted as he picked up my hand and pressed it against the side of his face, breathing in my scent and emitting a satisfied rumble from his throat. It was music to my ears, hearing his pleasure from that simple act of touch. My palm warmed his cool skin as he guided it to his lips, my breath catching as his eyes held mine. His hand closed tighter around me, my seemingly confined fingers now itching to trace out every plane and angle of his body. He was like a sculpture of perfection, hard, but strangely smooth and supple underneath my touch. He was a paradox.

His eyes closed as I let my fingers gently trace across the planes of his cheeks and then travel further down to the fullness of his lips. They were cold, slightly pink, and very smooth. I drew a picture in my mind of how they would feel pressed passionately against mine.

He opened his eyes again and wrapped his hand around the back of my head, pulling me closer to him. His eyes were still green, but only just. Tendrils of brown had started to creep in from the corners and I knew it wouldn't be long before he was pushed to his limits.

'Stop,' I said calmly, rising to my feet and pulling away from him.

He grabbed my hand and spun me back around to look at him. I could feel his presence, my desire for him encircling me like a thick cloud. I began to feel giddy. All I wanted was to throw myself at him.

'Don't stop now,' he murmured.

'I just don't know,' I said, my voice trailing off like my doubt, away in the wind like a puff of smoke.

He smiled. 'Well, I do.'

He tugged on my hand and pulled me back into him, dragging me onto his lap before I had a chance to protest. He wrapped his fingers around my ringlets that encircled the nape of my neck, looking at me with his ever-changing eyes and then pressing his lips hard against mine.

I gasped as his scent enveloped me completely. I could feel the weight of need pressing against me and the sound of my heart beating rapidly within my chest. His smell filled my lungs completely, the cloying sweetness and sting of desire filling my heart. I could feel the chemistry between us spread throughout my blood like liquid fire.

He moved his lips against mine with a passion and a need that I had never felt before. I was drowning but not wanting to come up for air.

Was all kissing supposed to be like this?

A moment later he stopped, my lips still aching for more of his. I opened my eyes as he pulled away. His eyes, hard to see, were blacker than the night, and his skin was marred with the tiny blue veins that marked him as a changed being. He held onto me tightly, his fingers still gripping the back of my hair.

I could see in his eyes that he was struggling against the hold his thirst had over him. But this new and exciting passion that I felt for him roared inside of me, blocking out the sound of my racing heartbeat and any words of warning.

I threw caution to the wind and, hormones or not, pushed myself against his lips again. Satisfaction filled me from within and it wasn't long before his stiff physical response softened and melted.

I brushed my tongue gently across the surface of his

closed lips and waited for them to part for me. They would. They did. He met my enthusiasm head on, his lust matching mine and drowning me in the need I felt for him. A small gasp of pleasure escaped my parted lips, the intensity between us building.

His hands stilled in my hair and he wretched himself free of my hold over him. 'No!' he panted, forcefully pushing me off of his lap and leaping quickly into the air. He clambered up the side of the central ducting system and climbed quickly to the top, leaving a good few metres between us. He was breathing in and out very heavily, his chest expanding and contracting at a rapid rate. His canines were fully extended, his eyes were blacker than obsidian stone.

I stayed where I was, watching him, my lips still buzzing and slightly swollen from the last few minutes of bliss.

'Just give me a minute,' he choked out, breathing ragged as he stood up from his crouched position and inhaled. His breathing slowed slightly, as his chest began to expand and contract in a more relaxed manner.

After a few minutes of silence and deep breaths, he jumped down.

'Are you okay?' I asked tentatively as I took a step towards him.

'I will be,' he said, looking up me again. 'I underestimated you.'

'How?'

The sides of his lips lifted into a smile, his canines retracting. 'I thought it would have taken much longer for you to kiss me. I helped it along by enticing you. I just never expected that you would enjoy it so much.'

I sniffed. I hated it when men just assumed that they'd get their own way. 'You kissed me, remember? And who said I enjoyed it?'

He looked at me slowly from head to toe and smiled. 'If you could see what I see right now under your skin, you wouldn't be in denial.'

I smiled in spite of myself. 'I'm not blushing.'

'Oh, I'm aware of that. This is a *different* heat that marks your skin. I suggest we practice constraint in the future.'

I grinned. 'In the future? Aren't we being presumptuous?'

He smiled like a kid in a candy store and then stepped forward to wrap both arms around my waist and pull me in close again. He brushed his fingers across my cheek, lowering his lips down to mine again. 'It's inevitable.'

I scoffed and slid a hand in between our lips to stop any more presumptuous behaviour. 'The only things that are inevitable are death and taxes.'

He gave me a funny look.

'Okay, so maybe not death in our cases,' I said, tugging at his hand behind my back, 'but definitely taxes. Now, how about you get me off this building and take me home before you decide to assault me again?'

He finally found his voice. 'Assault you? Wasn't I the one with a broken nose this evening?'

'Would you like another one?'

William tilted his head to the side, his lips twitching in amusement. He touched a finger to my nose, winked at me, and then promptly tossed me over the side of the building, which he no doubt found highly amusing.

I wish I could say the same.

CHAPTER FIFTEEN: ALONE

As William shrugged the leather coat he had stolen from the wardrobe upstairs from his shoulders and dropped it onto the bureau by the front door, he knew that Thomas would be waiting. Without even further entering the house they were currently 'borrowing' he knew that his long-time friend was standing in the adjoining room.

Thomas would have his arms crossed, and brows furrowed heavily—the same expression Thomas had given him earlier when he'd mentioned the intended rendezvous with Elena. Thomas had already voiced his thoughts about the two of them pursuing a relationship. So what would he think now that Elena's scent was all over him?

William could already feel the mounting tension in the air. He considered heading straight upstairs to the bedroom—avoidance better than confrontation. He knew exactly what Thomas was going to say to him and he didn't want to hear it all again.

'William,' Thomas said evenly from the next room. 'Could you come in here, please?'

As sure as William knew that Thomas was there, Thomas knew that William had returned. The front door was the final signal of his arrival, but if he had been listening for him, Thomas could have heard William running further away, along the coast road and through the mountains.

He fingered the coat for a second longer, glanced longingly up the stairs. 'I'm coming.'

William rounded the corner and stepped into the white living room, decorated with sumptuous sofas and strewn with colourful cushions. He flopped down onto the one opposite Thomas, shaking his head at the predictable nature of his friend. Sure enough, he stood with his arms crossed over his chest and frowning heavily.

'William, what are you doing?' Thomas said quietly.

'I'm sitting.'

Thomas frowned deeper. 'You know exactly what I'm talking about.'

'Thomas, this doesn't concern you.'

'William, you and I have been friends for almost three hundred years now. I have always watched your back and you mine. I'm doing that for you now when I tell you that getting romantically involved with that human girl is a mistake.'

'Elena.'

'What?'

'Her name is Elena, Thomas, and it's too late. I think I'm falling for her.'

Thomas groaned and dropped onto the couch opposite him. 'What have you done? You told me yourself that Araqiel did not ask this of you.'

'Araqiel told me to protect her, and that is what I will do.'

'Yes, protect her,' Thomas said tersely, 'not fall in love with her. She's not for you. You know that.'

William could feel his temper rising. 'What I know is that Araqiel said to protect her and keep her safe from harm and—'

'He also said that you needed to deliver her to her

family—to her true partner. Who is *not* you. You're not supposed to love her, and she is not supposed to love you. She belongs to someone else and you damn well know that, William.'

'I make my own destiny, Thomas. I will not let my future be dictated to me by you or anyone else.'

'I did not come to you with this request!' Thomas shouted. 'Araqiel did! Are you going to deny an *angel*, one that could eventually give you a free pass into heaven? An angel that made it very clear that Elena is very important to coming events and must be returned to Sebas—'

William thumped his hands against the arm of the sofa, lips pulling back into a feral snarl. 'Don't say his name to me.'

Thomas recoiled, sliding further back into the chair.

'Araqiel may be an angel and may hold dominion over Earth,' William continued with a growl, 'but he cannot tell me who to love.' He moved his hands around dismissively. 'Where I go when I finally leave this place is of no consequence to me. Hell, heaven—it's all the same. I just want her.'

Thomas shook his head. 'You're treading on very dangerous ground, William. By keeping her from her real family you may be endangering her life. She's already been targeted by an alpha. That might not have happened if you had followed orders and taken her away when you first received the message.'

William rose to his feet and ran a hand through his hair. 'We're just dealing with the vânătors, Thomas, just like we always do. Elena is different. Araqiel said to keep her safe, and by keeping her away from *them* I believe that I am upholding his word.'

'No, Will, what you're doing is twisting his words to suit yourself.'

William's hands balled into tight fists at his side. He couldn't believe this—after almost three hundred years of friendship, his best friend would choose the opinion of an angel over him. They weren't even supposed to be interfering. Just like Lucifer himself, they were supposed to mind their own business and stay in hell or heaven, respectively. Something major was happening if angels were breaking the rules to protect enemies.

'I want Elena. I need Elena in my life. I've waited far too long for someone like her. I will do as the angel says, I will protect her, but I'm going to do it *my* way.' He paused and looked at his friend. 'Are you going to stand by me on this, Thomas?'

Thomas looked worried, defeated. He knew arguing with William was pointless. William had always been stubborn, and had always been too narrow-minded for his own good. It was just like him to not open his eyes to the bigger picture, and the same reason he was no longer with the Roman Guard or associating with his own family. He couldn't see past his own foolish pride.

What Thomas should do was take her, now, take her back to her family as Araqiel had requested. But the last thing that he wanted to do was push his friend away. What choice did he have?

Thomas slowly rose to his feet and walked over to his friend, resting a hand on his shoulder. 'I will support you my, friend, but please do not pursue this thing with the girl. It will only see you get hurt.'

William shook his hand away. 'I won't get hurt.'

Thomas shrugged. 'I'm just saying—fate has a funny way of eventually bringing people together who were supposed to meet. Don't stand in the way of what should unfold.'

I awoke the next morning to warm sunshine streaming through my bedroom window, caressing the bare skin of my arms with early spring warmth. I had an unexpected smile plastered across my face, seemingly permanently entrenched on my features. I was smiling so wide my cheeks hurt from the effort.

I touched a finger to my lips and giggled at the memory of the night before like a naughty school girl. Then I buried my face into the pillow to shut myself up.

When had I turned into one of those people?

I buried my face deeper into the polyester filling and screamed loudly, before bursting into a fit of giggles once again. I must be high. It was the only rational explanation for my ridiculous behaviour. Maybe Susan had unknowingly slipped some magic mushrooms onto the pizza I ate last night.

I shook my head.

Too convenient.

The pizza last night had tasted too good to have come from Susan. This crazy, completely uncharacteristic behaviour looked like it belonged solely to me.

I laughed again and then rolled onto my back. Maybe I needed to think something horrible to be able to wipe the ridiculous smile off my face? If Susan and George saw me like this they'd know something was definitely different.

God, what had William done to me?

I clamped a hand down over my upturned mouth and set to work on conjuring up the most repellent thing I could think of. It didn't take me long to gather the ammunition. The absolutely most disgusting and truly undesirable vision I could conjure up was Peter and Sarah bumping uglies. Unfortunately, the main image was of giant bouncing boobs and piles of sagging old flesh slapping and grinding against one another in a big, sweaty heap.

Yuck.

I immediately shut down the rolling film in my head, trying to stop the gagging and the burning at the back of my throat.

A short knock on the door announced the determined entry of my brother, as he stepped in, plonked himself down on the bed next to me and smiled.

'Morning. Geez, you look nasty. Are you sick or something? You're all white.'

I shook my head and smoothed the bed hair away from my eyes. 'I think I just unearthed the best form of teenage contraception ever.'

'Hey?' he said, sounding confused.

'It's nothing,' I said, shaking my head at the vivid images I was trying to dispel. 'Did you want something?'

'I just came to give you the good news.'

'What good news?'

Hopefully it's a confirmed appointment for my lobotomy.

'The IMI is closing down until the adults figure out how to capture and kill the alpha. They don't have time to train us while they have vânǎtors to kill.'

'We don't have school for the rest of the week?'

'Ah-huh. Malcolm, mum and dad are driving to Townsville this morning to survey the area. Vincent's staying behind to run the law firm, while Kim joins Sarah and Peter in Mackay just to ensure that the alpha has left the area.'

'What about the kids and Martha?' I asked.

'Karina and Lisa are staying home too. Martha's going to be watching over them. Mum was hoping that we could stay with her too so she wouldn't have to leave us alone, but ...'

'But Martha's too freaked out by me to let me stay in her own house.'

He grinned. 'Bingo. So you and I get to stay home alone.'

'I hope our house insurance is up to date.'

Lucas cackled. 'Planning on burning it down while they're gone were you?'

'Nope, but with you and I left to our own devices, anything's possible.'

He laughed in short quick bursts, stopped and then looked back at the door. 'You know, I was thinking—after mum and dad leave, we could try and contact the vampires again.'

I shook my head. 'Lucas, they're too busy trying to hunt to stop and play with us.'

'How would you know? Talked to them recently?'

I looked at him guiltily and tried to conceal my grin.

He shoved me hard in the shoulder, at least I think it was meant to be hard. He could have been dusting fairy kisses across my skin for all the pressure I felt from him. 'How could you!' he growled. 'You know I wanted to come along if you saw the vamps again! What did you do? Where did you go? When? Was it last night? Did he come through your window again? Did he—'

'Lucas, calm down,' I said laughing. 'He came for me late last night after everyone went off to bed. I didn't want to come and wake you up because, to be honest, there was only room for one with his method of transport.'

'Where did you go?' he said, eyes wide with curiosity.

'Into the city. You won't believe this but we sat on top of the National Mutual tower for hours and hours just talking.'

And kissing.

He blinked. 'Did you just say on *top* of the tower?'

I nodded and grinned. 'I can laugh about it now, but at

the time I seriously thought I was going to need a change of underwear. He threw me on his back and just climbed up the side of the building like King Kong.'

'What did you talk about?'

'Everything and anything. Did you know that he was witness to the signing of the alliance between the Vampires and Protectors?'

'Really?'

I nodded again. 'Yep, he didn't really want to talk too much about his old life, but he said that he was a legionnaire in the Roman Guard.'

Lucas frowned. 'What's the Roman Guard?'

'Apparently they're a military contingent formed by the Vampires. Their purpose was to uphold their laws and sort out any major issues between the covens. William's not sure if they still exist or not, but how cool is that? They have their own laws too. There's a head vampire who dictates all matter of crime and punishment amongst the Vampires, but he didn't tell me who. He also told me about the Vânǎtors, how they were made, and how turned vampires are created.'

He scowled at me and crossed his arms in front of his chest. 'This is the kind of thing I would really like to have heard in person. Is there anything else you two did that I wasn't a part of?'

My face went red and I was suddenly awash with that goofy style grin again.

Lucas surveyed my reaction for a moment, noted my change in colour and no doubt the look on my face—he burst into hysterics. 'I don't believe it!' he chortled, as he gripped his stomach and I once again I buried my face into the pillow in embarrassment. 'Elena Manory finally got hot and heavy with a guy!'

I grabbed the pillow and beat him over the head with

it. It sent him flying off the edge of the mattress, but he kept on laughing anyway. 'What's so funny about me liking someone?'

He gasped for air in between bursts of laughter and laid his head back on the bedroom floor, trying to calm himself. 'It's funny because for the first time in your entire life you took an emotional enema and fell, not for just the closest horny teenage boy, but for a four hundred year old dead guy. You're severely unhinged, I hope you realise this?' He burst into laughter again. I threw the pillow at him.

'He's still … fresh.'

That just sent him into another fit of hysterics and I couldn't help but join in.

'Kids? Will you come downstairs please?'

Lucas and I abruptly stopped laughing and I helped him back to his feet. All serious now, we padded quickly down the stairs and into the living room where Susan and George were. They had gathered together a few weapons, as well as two overflowing overnight bags that were sprawled across the sofa.

'Now, just a few quick rules before we leave,' Susan said, waving her finger at both Lucas and I. 'We are going to be gone for probably the entire week and you're going to have to fend for yourselves. Your father and I have only two simple rules for you to follow while we are away. Elena, the first rule is for you—no leaving the house. Lucas, the second is for you. Make sure Elena doesn't leave the house.'

Lucas frowned. 'Am I that predictable that my only rule revolves around enforcing Elena's punishment?' His hands went his hips. 'I can be a badass too, you know.'

Susan patted the top of his head. 'You're always such a good boy. We don't have to worry about you the same way that we have to worry about your sister.'

Lucas shot me a filthy look and I grinned.

'Now, remember, don't open the door to strangers. I've stocked the fridge full of food so you shouldn't have to order any takeaway, but if you do, there's money in the tin above the microwave. We'll call you every night for an update and make sure that you are both okay. I still expect your assignments to be completed by the end of the week, whether you're going to the IMI or not, and seeing how you will be home all day every day it shouldn't be a problem.'

Susan swung her gaze pointedly at Lucas, her lips pursing momentarily before she continued. 'Lucas we are also going to leave you the keys to the Forester in case there is an emergency. We'll be travelling with Malcolm while we are away. This isn't an excuse for you to go practicing your driving skills. It's only to be used in an emergency. Any questions?'

Lucas and I both shook our heads.

George gave us both a pat on the shoulder and started to lug the weapons and the overnight bags outside to Malcolm's white Pajero, parked in the driveway. Susan embraced both of us together, patted our cheeks, kissed the top of our heads, flashed me a warning look that said *Elena, do as your told*, and then promptly left the house.

We both watched from the living room window as Malcolm and our parents backed down the driveway and then disappeared down the street. 'Well,' Lucas said slyly, 'I don't know about you, but I'm thinking I might have been suffering some temporary deafness, because I didn't hear one single thing that mum just said.'

I nodded and grinned. 'I think she said, "Blah, blah, blah Elena and Lucas can do whatever they want".'

'Yeah,' Lucas said, grinning in return, 'that sounds about right.'

We glanced out the window again when a shiny black and chrome car pulled up into the drive way. Surprisingly, it was the latest model Audi TT, with twin exhausts that thrummed lightly under the power of its three-point-two litre engine. That baby could go from zero to one hundred in under five seconds.

'That's a pretty car,' Lucas said, staring out the window in interest.

'A pretty car?' I answered, glancing at him in disbelief. 'That pretty car is the latest Audi TT. Looks to have the sports package upgrade too. It retails for almost ninety grand, Lucas.'

His eyes looked like they were about to pop right out of his head. 'How do you even *know* that?'

I gazed at the car adoringly. 'Look at it. It's a masterpiece of engineering, how could you not know that?' I nudged him with my elbow. 'Besides, what is it you think I do with all those copies of 'Wheels' magazine?'

Lucas shrugged. 'I don't know. Don't you just look at the pictures like I do with my magazines?'

I rolled my eyes. 'You read Penthouse and Playboy. How is that even remotely close to being the same thing?'

'Who do you think is in the car?' he said, glancing back out the window again, changing the subject.

'I don't know, and I don't want to find out without some kind of protection.' I ran into the kitchen and grabbed a knife from the top drawer. When I reappeared next to Lucas, he looked down and frowned. 'A butter knife? Are you serious?'

'Shut up. It's your fault Susan locked away all the good knives.'

'Oh my God, I scratch the benchtop once and—'

'Shut up Lucas.'

The front door of the Audi opened and out popped a long jean clad leg and then another. The driver ducked his head through the opening, shiny dark hair attached to a pale face wearing dark sunglasses.

I froze, dropping my knife in the process. 'He looks amazing, doesn't he?' I murmured, staring out as William shut the car door and straightened his T-shirt. Supermodels everywhere were cowering in self loathing and racking up another three million issues to be insecure about just looking at him.

Lucas turned and looked at me. I was still wearing old track suit pants and a Mickey Mouse singlet that was crumpled from sleep. My hair was in a tumultuous mess around my face and I still had sleep caked into the corner of my eyes.

'Compared to you, he's the Messiah,' Lucas muttered as he pulled on a piece of my dishevelled hair.

'What should I do?' I asked frantically as William approached the front door hastily, sticking to the shade and avoiding the sun.

'I'd say get a paper bag, but I guess a shower and brushing your teeth might help.'

'Right.' I spun on my heels and dashed upstairs to the bathroom.

'Umm, what do I do?' Lucas called up to me.

'Just talk to him and keep him busy while I make myself presentable.'

'I don't have a spare four hours.'

'Lucas!' I yelled down to him. 'Please!'

'Okay, okay, I'll show him the album with all your naked baby photos in it. That way next time he thinks about rubbing up against my sister, he'll develop his very own set of mental issues.'

'Lucas!'

'Okay, I'll be good.'

I slammed the bathroom door shut and whizzed in and out of the shower so fast that it might have had a revolving door on it. I ran a brush through my hair and gave it a quick blow dry to help it settle. I also rubbed a bit of moisturiser over my skin, brushed my teeth and added some lip gloss.

Okay, not too bad for ten minutes. I wrapped a towel around myself and studied my reflection in the mirror.

A minute later I was dashing across the hallway to the bedroom, stopping briefly on the way to make sure Lucas was behaving himself. I stumbled into my room, shut the door and dug out some suitable apparel to wear today. I chose the same denim shorts I had been wearing last night, as well as a little red singlet with a matching red cardigan in case it got a little cooler. I slipped on a few bangles, hooked some earrings into my ears, and rifled through my dresser until I found a pair of sandals. I did another quick study of myself in the mirror and decided that I was more than presentable now.

I grabbed my shoulder bag and knife, just in case, slipping it into the bag and heading down the stairs. When I got into the living room, Lucas and William were sitting awkwardly across from one another, neither one talking. Lucas was picking at the pilling on the edge of his armchair while his leg bounced emphatically against the floor, all nerves.

William was sitting relative still and glancing absently down at his hands in his lap. Both of them were more than a little relieved to see me when I finally entered the room, the awkward moment finally over.

William abruptly stood and crossed the room. He took my backpack from my shoulder in a gesture that was now surely lost on our current generation of men. 'You look beautiful,' he said as his eyes roamed suggestively over my figure, then settling onto my mouth.

Lucas snorted softly. 'You should have seen her ten minutes ago,' he muttered under his breath.

I felt something go flip-flop inside my stomach in response to his heated gaze and before I knew it I was grinning like the Cheshire Cat and batting my eyelids like Betty Boop.

Lucas studied the exchange between us like a hawk. He glanced from me to William and then back to me again before snorting in disgust. 'You know Elena used to pick her nose, right?'

I turned and looked at him in horror, my lips curling up into an automatic snarl as he looked triumphantly at William.

What was he trying to do to me? Ruin my chances at any happiness?

'Did you know that Lucas still does?' I retorted angrily.

'Only when I'm hungry.'

I gagged. 'You're disgusting.'

'Am I missing something?' William asked calmly, glancing between us.

I looked back at William and ignored my brother. 'Lucas is just pissed because we didn't take him with us last night.'

William took another step forward and wrapped an arm around my waist, pulling me in close to him. He smelled heavenly and it took everything in me to keep my knees locked into an upright position. 'There are some moments in life that aren't meant to be shared with siblings,' he said suggestively, as he placed a kiss lightly on the side of my cheek and ran his fingertips up and down my spine.

Oh, this guy is good. A little more of this and I'll be putty in his hands.

Lucas grunted. 'Did you know that when she eats onions she farts in her sleep?'

My head whipped to the side to stare irritably at my brother. 'Can I speak to you for a moment?' I said, lugging Lucas from his sitting position and dragging him off to the kitchen for some privacy. 'What are you doing?' I hissed. 'You're totally embarrassing me! Why are you saying this stuff?'

'What?' he said, raising his hands defensively and trying to look as innocent as possible. 'You do fart after you eat onions.'

'No, I don't!' I squealed. 'That's *you* who does that, not me!'

He looked up and tapped his chin in contemplation. 'Oh yeah, I guess it is.'

'Lucas, why are you being such a prat all of a sudden? I thought you wanted us to get to know the Vampires?'

He had the good grace to look ashamed. 'I do. It's just—you're my little sister. For sixteen years you've all but ignored boys, even that guy Stephen that you dated. He spent more time on the other side of the front door than he did inside this house, and now—well, now you look … different. I don't know how I'm supposed to act. I just know that it's always just been you and me. I don't want you to forget about me now that you have a boyfriend.'

I laughed and shook my head. 'He's not my boyfriend.'

'Then what would you call it then?'

'I'm going to call it *having a good time.*'

'And that's it?'

I shrugged. 'For now.' I grabbed him by the shoulders and smoothed his hair back. 'You're still my number one, okay? You always have been and you always will be. No guy, no matter how sublimely good-looking he is, is ever going to change that.'

'Promise?'

'Only if you stop telling William I fart in my sleep and pick my nose.'

He looked at my outstretched hand and shook it. 'It's a deal. But just so you know, you're no angel. Give you a full litre of any fizzy drink and you can burp the entire score from the sound of music in under five minutes flat.'

I smiled. 'I know, and that takes some serious skill on my part, but do you think for the sake of my blossoming attempt at a love life that we could keep that little gem just between you and me?'

We shook on it again and headed back into the living room. William was standing exactly where we had left him, his arms folded across his chest, and a small smile playing at the corner of his lips. I had no doubt that he had heard everything.

'So, did you come to break us out?' I asked, trying to change the subject.

He smiled and licked his lips. 'I overheard your parents talking last night about leaving for Townsville this morning. I thought while they are running around chasing down false leads I might come back for you and see if you would like to spend a little time in my world today.'

'Hang about,' Lucas said, holding up a hand. 'Are you saying that all of The Protectors are heading in the wrong direction?'

William nodded. 'Thomas and I cleared both Townsville and Mackay earlier on this morning. The scent trails lead us back here, to Cairns.'

'Well if you know that, then why aren't you out hunting them?'

'It's daylight in case you hadn't noticed, Lucas,' he said politely.

I shot Lucas a look to silence him. 'Where were you planning on taking us?'

'Just to the place where we are staying at the moment.'

'Where is it?'

'A few kilometres outside of Port Douglas. I thought we could spend the daylight hours talking and getting to know one another better before Thomas and I go hunting again at sunset.'

'What about Marianne?' Lucas enquired.

'She doesn't like to hunt,' William answered scathingly. 'I'm not even sure why I keep her around.'

'That's not very friendly.' Lucas countered.

William gave Lucas a wry look. 'You don't know her like I do.'

As we sped down the highway in the luxury Audi, which we were told William had merely 'borrowed' from the dealership, we discussed what the alpha's reason for staying in Cairns might have been. Since there were about a million different reasons, we didn't manage to stay on topic for long, particularly not when Lucas was pestering William endlessly about information on vampires. By the time we had discovered that coffins were optional, garlic just smells bad, and bats were filled with parasites, we were only five minutes from our destination.

William drove the car the same way that he ran—too fast. If I thought Kayla had blitzed the speed limits then I was sorely mistaken, because William blew the signs over as he roared past. Don't get me wrong—I liked to drive fast too, but I also liked to be able to see where I was going. A trip that generally took almost an hour from our place was completed in just over twenty minutes. Apparently it usually only took him fifteen, but we had to stop twice for Lucas to throw up.

When we arrived, I pressed my face up against the tinted window to peer out and drink in the sight before me. I'd seen places like this on the television or in magazines, but I never imagined vampires having so much … style.

I unbuckled my seatbelt and pushed open the car door the moment the Audi halted in the driveway.

I looked up at the modern glass and concrete structure in front of me and echoed Lucas's long wolf-whistle of both surprise and appreciation. The house itself was three stories high and cut into the edge of a cliff face. It was surrounded by trees on nearly all sides except for the rear, which probably overlooked the ocean. The driveway was covered in loose gravel that wound down the hill, through the trees, and intersected somewhere back with the road.

The building itself was painted stark white and seemed to glitter brilliantly in the morning sun. Through the huge glass panes we could see hardly any internal walls—you could almost see from one side of the house to the other. They also offered uninterrupted views of the ocean and sur-rounding forest.

'Wow.' Was all I managed to get out, as William closed the front car door behind him and loped under the cover of the front entry to avoid the sun's rays on his milky white skin.

'Looks like your boyfriend is rich, Elena,' Lucas said, nudging my arm. 'Do you reckon he could get me a Hummer?'

I glared at him. 'Behave yourself.'

Lucas rolled his eyes at me and then headed for the front porch where William was waiting patiently for both of us.

I followed behind as they entered the house, and all I could do was glance around in amazement. The few walls that were not made of glass were painted white and adorned with some very colourful and abstract paintings. The floor was white polished concrete with flecks of gold and silver that became quite luminous in the sun that filtered in through one of the many glass windows. All the furniture was very modern and tastefully presented, with only a few splashings of colour present, mostly on rugs and throw cushions. Everything else was neutral in colour.

William led us into the living room area, which was probably the size of our entire house. The views from this room alone were absolutely breathtaking. The crystal blue water of the ocean stretched out in front of us for what seemed like an eternity, the white sand of the beach below wrapping itself like a fitted sheet around the beautiful jagged coast line.

'What do you think?' he asked us.

'It's absolutely amazing,' I replied, completely awed.

'S'okay,' Lucas said, trying to sound nonchalant. 'How do you afford digs like this anyway?'

'Lucas!' I hissed.

William chuckled and raised his hands to calm me down. 'It's okay. If I'm honest, I don't. I've never really needed money. I merely convinced the owners of this property that they needed an extended vacation in Paris.' He smiled. 'Sometimes being a vampire has its perks.'

'You compelled them into giving you their home?' I asked, horrified.

He shrugged. 'Yes. It's only temporary. They can have it back when we are ready to move on again.' He frowned at the look on my face. 'Just like the car, Elena, everything is only borrowed. They will get their property back once I'm finished with it.'

I stared at him, unblinking. 'Should I ask what you do when you actually need money?'

'Let me guess,' Lucas said, laughing and interrupting, 'ask and you shall receive?'

William grinned at him. 'And who said that banks were all so tight-fisted?'

I shook my head at the both of them.

'Ahem.'

Both Lucas and I spun around to see Thomas and Marianne standing at the entrance to the living room, seemingly reluctant to approach any further, and to be honest, that was fine by me. Marianne looked less than thrilled that we were standing in her home, however temporary the arrangement might have been.

'Thomas, Marianne,' William said, more formally than I would have thought necessary, 'you remember Elena and Lucas, don't you?' He gestured for them to come closer.

Thomas led the way first and extended his arm out in front of him. He enthusiastically shook Lucas's hand and then my own. His smile was warm and inviting and I felt instantly calmed by his presence. I'd already decided that I didn't like his sister, but he seemed nicer.

Marianne hung back behind Thomas and studied something on her fingernails, completely ignoring us.

Fine by me, Blondie.

'It's good to see you both again,' Thomas said, a little stiffly. 'It's a nice change to be able to talk with people who aren't vampires or obsessed with killing us.'

Lucas coughed and I laughed nervously. That wasn't exactly true.

'William hasn't stopped talking about you, Elena.'

'Really?' I said, instantly smiling and looking in William's direction. He lightly punched his friend on the shoulder and thanked him for ruining his ambiguity.

Thomas nodded, but his face tensed. 'Yes, it appears that he's stepped into something with you that can't be unaltered.'

My smile wavered, as I caught onto the undercurrents of words I didn't specifically think were meant for me.

'Thomas, do you think you could shut up for a bit,' William said, glancing back at me with a worried expression on his face.

'Ugh!' Lucas interrupted with a groan. 'Could you not encourage the lovefest? I only ate breakfast an hour ago and I already lost most of that on the way up here.'

'Is that what that smell is?' Marianne said dryly, sniffing delicately at the air.

Lucas grinned and took a few steps closer to Marianne. He began wiggling his eyebrows at her suggestively. 'Feisty. I like that in a woman.'

She groaned and went back to studying her fingernails.

'That's okay,' Lucas said, smiling at her and dropping onto the sofa like he owned the place. 'Playing hard to get. That's hot too. It all works in your favour, Blondie.'

'Can I go back upstairs now?' she whined, looking at her brother. 'It's starting to get a little crowded down here.'

Thomas nodded. She spun on her heels and quickly disappeared back up the stairs, a door slamming shut behind her.

'I think she likes me,' Lucas said, tilting back on the sofa and lazily putting his hands behind his head.

Thomas glanced warily at William, some sort of unspoken message passing between them, before his features softened. He turned and clapped Lucas endearingly on the shoulder, and then sunk down into the seat beside him like they'd been friends forever. 'I wouldn't bet on it, Lucas.'

'Elena?' William said. 'Is something wrong?' He glanced between me and Thomas.

I shook my head. 'No, I'm fine.'

Just because we're kissing each other now doesn't mean I have to tell you everything I'm thinking.

William took my hand in his. 'Would either of you mind if I take Elena away for some private time?'

Thomas remained mute, and Lucas looked to me edgily.

'*Private time?*' Lucas said, glancing down at our entwined fingers.

'It's okay, Lucas,' William cooed. 'Thomas will not bite you while we are gone if that is what is bothering you.'

Thomas turned and winked at Lucas, which only seemed to make him scoot further into the corner of the sofa. He shook his head and pointed to our linked hands. 'I'm more concerned about where that is heading, and just exactly what 'private time' means to a vampire who wants to date my sister.'

'Lucas,' I hissed, 'you promised you wouldn't do this to me.'

He waved his hand at me and shot William a look. 'Fine,' he breathed. 'But if he tries to get too fresh with you just yell.'

I pinched the bridge of my nose in embarrassment.

'And on that note,' William said, spinning us around on the spot, 'I think we'll be going.'

William led me back through the living room and up a set of steel stairs just off the entry way. We climbed it slowly, as I surveyed every painting, sculpture and photograph that belonged to the banished couple. As we ascended, I could still see Lucas craning his neck to get a better look at us. It was a good thing that the stairs disappeared around a corner otherwise he could hurt himself.

On the first floor, William explained, there were two bedrooms, one of which Marianne was in, and the other being Thomas's. We didn't go into either, but he showed me through the library that was also located on this level. The mentioning of books piqued my curiosity.

The library had a sea view too, but the other three walls were lined with bookshelves overflowing with novels and encyclopaedias.

I walked over and studied the titles, noticing that there were a lot of books on geography, history, as well as more classic novels by people like H.G. Wells, Jane Austin, and Charles Dickens. Some were first editions, probably worth more than the entire house.

Looking at them, I asked, 'Do you like to read?'

'Very much,' he answered. 'As you can imagine I have a lot of time on my hands, though not truly enough to hunt through this library since we arrived.' He smiled. 'My attention has been diverted elsewhere of late.'

'Me too.' I said, feeling myself going slightly red in the face and turning away from him. 'I mean about the liking to read thing.'

'What genre?'

'Mostly fantasy or horror. I also like to leaf through car and motorbike magazines.'

He cocked an eyebrow. 'Car and motorbike magazines?'

I nodded. 'I'm saving up for a motorbike or a Bugatti Veyron, whichever one I can afford first.'

'What's a Bugatti Veyron?'

I felt like slapping him in the forehead. Wasn't he a guy? Weren't all guys supposed to be into cars? 'It's the fastest roadster in the world. It has a one thousand horsepower engine and can top speeds of four hundred kilometres per hour.' I grinned. 'You'd love it. But it's about one point seven million dollars to buy, so I think I'll be getting a motorbike first.'

'A motorbike is a little dangerous don't you think?'

I shook my head. 'Not when you can't get permanently hurt. I've got my permit and I've had more than a couple of lessons, but I really need some more practice before I go and buy one. I also need some more money too, but that's only a small oversight.'

I placed the much loved books back onto the shelf in front of me and wondered again for the millionth time what I'd be like when I was a vampire-slash-werewolf (possibly a vampwolf). It would be wonderful not to age, not to observe time the way that everyone else does—being able to do what you want when you want must be very thrilling in so many ways.

William ushered me out of the room, leading me back to the staircase and heading up to the top floor. I moved slowly, surveying all the artwork as well as the beautiful view of the surrounding forest. At the top of the stairs was a small landing of only about a metre square, with a door and little of anything else.

William turned the handle and swung the door inwards letting me enter the room first.

The area that stretched out beyond was so large that my eyes couldn't drink in the entire setting in one quick sweep over. The whole room looked very much like a conservatory. Half of the roof was encased in thick clear glass which sloped gently down to the glass walls that faced the ocean on either side. You could see the tree leaves brushing gently against the panes.

Kind of dangerous considering they don't like the sunlight.

The only opaque walls in this whole room were over on the west wall. In this direction lay a generous ensuite and walk-in robe.

I checked out the bathroom first. It was bigger than my whole bedroom. There was a double-headed shower, spa bath, toilet, and double basins, all perched on a marble vanity that spread over the length of one mirrored wall. I noted a single towel hanging on the rack that smelled of damp, soap and William's own personal scent. It was all I could do not to race over there and bury my head in the cotton threading.

Shaking off that thought, I wandered into the walk-in robe. I imagined that most of the clothes belonged to the owners, but there was a small section in the corner that I could see had been cleared to house William's personal belongings. I casually sifted through some of them, forgetting general etiquette as I pawed at his clothes, inhaling his intoxicating scent. Once again, I could feel my head starting to fog over.

I'd better get out of here before my brain turns to mush.

I left the wardrobe and wandered back into the bedroom. I finally noticed that smack-bang in the centre of the room was a massive four-poster king-size bed, decked out in white satin and silk, with a beautiful sheer white canopy strung around each post, cascading gracefully to the floor. The front of the canopy was tied back to allow for a view through the glass windows. I could only imagine how beautiful this room would be after sunset. Being able to see all the stars above you and hear the water lapping against the shore as you slept sure sounded heavenly.

William stepped up behind me and wrapped his hands around my waist. I didn't refute him. He brushed his nose across my cheek and gently nibbled on the edge of my ear-lobe.

'What are you doing?' I said, spinning around in his grasp and backing away.

His eyes were sparkling with an emotion I didn't quite recognise. 'I haven't been able to stop thinking about you,' he murmured as he again reached out for me.

So this was his version of 'private time'.

I held up a hand. 'Let's just take this slow, okay. I'm not sure what I'm doing and I'm especially not sure if I want to get too involved with someone … someone who is eventually going to leave.'

He frowned. 'I'm not leaving.'

I put my hands on my hips. 'You said downstairs that the owners will have their house back when you're ready to move on.'

He smiled and made a play for me again, circling his arms tightly around my waist so that I couldn't break free. 'Yes, when *I'm* ready to move on and that isn't going to be for a very long time.'

'How long?' I said, my hands flattening out against his chest.

'As long as you want me around.'

I smiled. 'I think I like that, me having all the power, I mean.'

He chuckled. 'I thought you might. Can I kiss you now?'

He leaned down and nuzzled at my neck with his lips. I gripped his head and pulled his face back up to look at me, his eyes already beginning to turn. 'Why do you do this to yourself? It can't be easy being with someone you'd rather bite than kiss.'

He rolled his head back and then sighed, his grip loosening. 'It's not, but my desires as a man are weighing far heavier on me than the urges of my thirst, and right now, the part of me who's a man just wants to be kissed.'

'I don't know, William, I think we shou—'

He silenced me with his mouth. It came down hard against mine; pushing my head back until his hand reached up and gripped the back of my neck, holding it in place. He wound his fingers through my hair. He pulled me harder against his taught body. My mouth parted slowly as I let him come into me, his tongue probing the inner warmth there, sending me into a fit of rapture. The sweetness of his breath blew through me, filling my lungs with intolerable fire.

I gasped for breath as his lips left mine, as they kissed their way down my chin and to the hollow in my neck, his tongue trailing circles on my skin. My body writhed against him, trying to pull closer to him in any way possible—we were already pressed together more tightly than should be possible.

His mouth now moved slowly down to the top of my red cardigan and singlet, parting it gently to allow his lips to graze the skin of my décolletage and shoulders. I briefly wondered if my flesh had suddenly caught fire. Everywhere he touched was burning, and my body longed for him in a way that I had never once felt before, not even in my wildest dreams. Heat built within my depths, those depths that the inexperience of my virtue and youth did little to help me interpret. All I knew with every screaming nerve ending in my body was that I wanted him. I wanted him the way a woman truly wanted a man.

I blushed at the thought, my entire body burning all over with the rush of blood that was thrumming through my veins.

He leapt off of me in an instant, landing hard against the glass panes of his bedroom window. The glass clanged thunderously in its aluminium framing, the weight of his body shuddering against its foundations. His hands and feet were splayed out behind him, holding him against the glass a couple of metres off the ground just as he had done only the night before. His eyes were back to their menacing black depths, those depths that spoke of his Vampiric nature. His canines were fully extended, his fingernails long black talons. Again I could see almost every vein running through his arms, legs, face and neck. His breathing was laboured and forced.

'William?' I said gently.

'Don't come near me,' he gasped.

I stopped moving and hastily retreated back towards the bedroom door, just in case. 'I told you this would happen,' I whispered.

He shook his head, his chest still heaving in and out. 'I'm sorry, I'm getting better, it's just that you blushed, and my mouth was already right there, right on top of your artery and …' He trailed off.

'I'm sorry,' I murmured, 'I couldn't help it.'

'Don't apologise!' he yelled.

I took another step backwards, surprised.

'Don't apologise,' he repeated, more calmly this time. 'It's not your fault. I'm tempting fate just being with you, but that's something I simply cannot help either. I have no intention of letting my thirst dictate what I can and can't have, and trust me, Elena, I want you.'

I grimaced. 'Maybe we should just cool it. I mean I like kissing you but—'

He looked over at me, his skin returning slowly to normal, his long dark claws retracting back into his fingers. He jumped down from the window and landed on the floor with a quiet *thud*. 'No,' he answered aggressively. 'I won't give you up, not now that I've found you. I will learn to control myself. I have not tasted human blood for over four hundred years and I aim to keep that promise to myself, even if it kills me.'

I looked at him hesitantly, my fingers brushing the handle of the door. 'I think it would be okay if you did.'

His eyes snapped to me and his lips pulled into an angry snarl. 'What did you just say?'

I faltered. 'I just mean, if you did bite me, it couldn't be any worse than what that vânător did to me. I'd heal. So if it does accidentally happen—'

'Stop!' he commanded, taking several fast paces across the room and grabbing both of my hands in his angrily. 'Don't you ever offer yourself to me again, do you understand me?'

I stared back at him in confusion. 'Why not?'

He dropped my hands and turned his back to me. 'Because I wouldn't be able to stop. Even briefly, I'd drain you dry. I'm still too young to even think of it.'

I touched a hand to his shoulder. 'You haven't told me why you swore an oath to only drink animal blood? You could live on Synth blood without hurting humans—why don't you do that?'

He didn't answer me for the longest time, his shoulders tightening. He turned around slowly, his eyes shifting back to their green brilliance, but still overflowing with self-loathing.

'William, tell me. What made you take that oath?'

He sighed and looked away, his eyes briefly closing and opening again. 'I killed my own mother.'

I wanted to say something but couldn't think of a reply. So instead I simply said, 'How did it happen?'

He was hesitant to try but eventually continued. 'She was there the night of my turning. My father hadn't arrived in time enough to nurse me through the change.'

He shook his head, trying to block out his memory of the past. 'He was supposed to have come to collect me the day before, but he was busy with important matters. He left me in the care of my mother, unbeknownst to her of what was happening to me.' He stopped and took a breath. 'When I awoke, she was the first thing I saw. I was thirstier than I'd ever been in my entire life. My throat felt like it was on fire, and all I could see was her and the warm blood that pulsed just beneath the surface of her skin. I tried to stop myself but I couldn't. I drank her, every last drop, killing her in the process.'

He stopped and ran a hand through his hair. 'Even when I was finished and became aware of what I had done, all I could think about was where I could get more blood. It wasn't until my thirst was completely satiated that I could take stock of what I had done and finally grieve over her death.'

'What about your father?' I said. 'Did he apologise for his absence?'

He spun around and looked at me, his eyes wild with fury. 'As far as I'm concerned I no longer have a father.'

I decided to pursue the matter no further. 'Would kissing me again make you feel any better?' I said cheekily, trying to lighten his mood.

His eyes softened and the corner of his lips quirked. 'Yes, I think it would.'

CHAPTER SIXTEEN: MISSING

You'd think leaving Lucas alone with a vampire would have curled his hair, made him roll into the foetal position and even make him mess his underpants, but it didn't. He appeared at ease with his present company. Lucas was obviously a little ballsier than I gave him credit for.

Both Thomas and Lucas were reclining comfortably on the same sofa that we had left them on, watching the cartoon network on the humongous wall-mounted LCD screen. They looked like two ordinary guys participating in a ritualistic bonding exercise.

Thomas had obviously discovered that the best way to Lucas's heart was through SpongeBob Square Pants, and apparently the best way to Thomas's heart was through a pack of AB Negative.

Lucas cradled a can of soda in his hand.

Thomas sat only about a foot away from him, much closer than I would have thought tolerable for either of them—Thomas because it would be like making friends with the cow before you ate the steak, and Lucas because he was suddenly no longer the top of the food chain in the room.

My surprise waned when I noticed that Thomas was sucking on one of those bendy straws jabbed into the top of a tetra pack of Synth blood. They were both oblivious to the giant elephant in the room, since Thomas was a thirsty vampire and Lucas was a human Protector.

The scent of the synthetic blood wafted across the air, as clear as freshly baking chocolate chip cookies. It wasn't as sweet or enticing as the smell of fresh blood, but it was still fairly appetising, regardless, and I licked my lips absently at the memory of the taste.

They both rolled their heads over to our side of the sofa as we entered the room. They performed the movement in perfect, almost rehearsed synchronicity. They were eerily similar in ways I wasn't quite ready to explore just yet. The world wasn't big enough for more than one Lucas.

'Wow, that was some *private time*,' Lucas said sarcastically, while nudging Thomas suggestively in the ribs and wiggling his eyebrows. Subtlety was apparently lost on Lucas.

'I showed Elena the house,' William replied evenly.

Lucas snorted and laughed again. Thomas looked a little uncomfortable about the topic. 'Did any of this *seeing* actually involve checking out the house—or just some of its contents?' Lucas queried.

Oh, he thinks he's a comedian.

'Trust me,' Thomas muttered, 'It *should* have just been a tour.' He turned around and looked pointedly at William.

William left my side, walked purposefully around the side of the sofa and punched Thomas hard in the arm.

Lucas immediately scooted over to the far corner of the sofa, pretending he had nothing to do with anything. Obviously Lucas's newly injected bravado only extended as far as Thomas.

'Ow!' Thomas muttered, rubbing at his upper arm and frowning up at William. 'I was only saying. If you and Elena want to spend all day making out, then fine. What can I do about it anyway?' He leaned forward and grabbed at the remote. 'There's an X-men marathon coming up next,' he said, looking at William again. 'I suppose Lucas and I can bide our time while you continue to shit on fate.'

'So you were listening in too?' William said more coolly than before.

Thomas looked at him hesitantly and then, suddenly, his face hardened. 'Only until the moaning and panting started and then we switched on the cartoons to drown out the noise.'

William flashed his canines in fury and then punched him hard again, deadening his other arm as well.

In the meantime, I went to my happy place and tried to pretend that the entire household had not just heard every private moment that had just passed between William and I back upstairs.

Lucas made an odd sort of gurgling sound in his throat as the sound of Thomas's bones crunching crossed Lucas's threshold of possible bystander immunity. He took one look at William's malevolent expression before leaping over the arm of the chair and coming to stand next to me. If he thought he was any safer standing next to me then he had another thing coming. 'You're a total pussy, Lucas,' I whispered. 'No one is going to hurt you.'

Except maybe me.

He sniffed and crossed his arms in front of his chest. 'I don't want to tempt fate by standing in the path of a pissed off steamroller with teeth.'

'Thomas will be fine. William's just letting off some steam,' I laughed nervously. 'I think.'

'Are you kidding me?' he hissed and discreetly pointed at William. 'The guy's got crazy eyes!'

I shook my head and gave him a playful shove, which

with my new strength meant an impact equivalent to a wrecking ball ploughing into the side of a building.

Lucas let out a gasp of disbelief as he went sprawling hard into the side of the sofa table, effectively sending it sliding about halfway across the room. A vase of flowers that was sitting proud on the top of the wooden surface, tilted, fell and smashed onto the floor below. Lucas landed with a heavy *thump* on his stomach, his hands splayed out in front of him.

Thomas and William immediately looked up from their confrontation to see what all the fuss was about. Thomas showed no mercy, bursting into immediate laughter that wracked his entire frame from head to toe. Given his stiff posture and awkwardness since we had walked through the front door, I'd never expected his reaction, especially from Lucas's wounded pride.

'Shit, Elena!' Lucas choked back as he tried to push himself back to his knees. 'Who needs to worry about the Vampires when your own sister treats you like a goddamn punching bag?'

I rushed forward to help him the second my brain caught up with events. 'Sorry, Lucas' I stammered as I helped him climb back to his feet again. 'I'm still getting used to being stronger than before.'

'Do you think for once you could try to be a quicker learner?' he said, dusting off his hands on the front of his jeans. 'If you learning how to control your strength is any-thing like you deciphering algebra, I'm a frigging dead man.'

I turned and frowned as Thomas roared with laughter again, falling back into the folds of the couch and covering his mouth with his hand.

Lucas shot him a look of displeasure. 'Don't laugh at me, Thomas, or I'll stake you in your sleep.'

Thomas laughed again, but quietened down considerably. 'Stake away, my friend, it won't kill me.'

Lucas snorted and cracked his fingers. 'Now that depends entirely on where I stake you, doesn't it?'

Thomas's good humour subsided. 'Where did you have in mind?'

Lucas leant forward slightly and began the same eyebrow wiggle from only a few moments before. Once again the translation was clear: grow brass balls or wear a steel cup to bed.

Humour returned to William's face as he glanced at his friend, who had turned even whiter than his already light pallor would allow. Laughter came easily to all of us when Thomas cupped his nether regions with both hands and stared at us, wide-eyed. Strangely, he smiled warmly at me before looking to William. 'I'll be quiet now.'

Lucas looked at me triumphantly and grinned, jerking his thumb in Thomas's direction. 'Now who's the pussy?'

After the whole arm punching incident and threats of disturbing the crown jewels, the four of us sat in the lounge room for the rest of the morning and most of the afternoon discussing anything and everything we could think of.

One of those things was Marianne.

From what I gathered from William and Thomas, Marianne wasn't a popular addition to the household. Apparently she was more annoying than a yapping chihuahua in your handbag, and that was on a good day. The only reason she was still around was because she was Thomas's twin sister, and from what I had deduced from the conversation, also had a major crush on William.

Looks like I had some competition in the form of a dead girl to look forward to.

That should be fun.

Thomas managed to loosen up a little bit once he got to know me a little better and Lucas put away the proverbial stake and started talking between them, conversations involving too many words like *animation* and *video games*, none of which were of any particular interest to me. In the meantime, William and I discussed the more interesting details of his Vampiric nature and the maturing process that I had to look forward to. Plus, we also touched lightly on his time in the Roman Guard.

Very lightly.

He cleverly skirted over most of my questions by distracting me with the seductive quality of his eyes, the licking of his lips, the glamour of his scent and featherlight caresses of my face and hands. I couldn't exactly understand why he was so reluctant to address this time in his life, or why he put so much effort into avoiding my questions, but I concluded it had something to do with his father.

By the end of our long conversation, all I could get out of him was that he was with the Roman Guard for just over a century and there'd been a falling out that involved him forming his own coven and moving as far away as possible.

How I'd managed to sit still for the majority of the conversation and be controlled, without ripping my knickers off, throwing them over my head and swinging my bra around my fingers in a *come and get me* gesture, I had no idea.

The hours passed by quickly between William and I, and soon the sun began to trace a path across the sky that led behind the mountainous ranges outside and disappeared from sight. It had mostly been a good day, even if Marianne remained surly and unsociable. Plus, we'd broken a vase that had probably belonged to Picasso at some stage. But despite those minor setbacks, it had been fun, and like all good things, they had to come to an end.

The Vampires had plans of hunting that evening, a venture that we all hoped resulted in a plausible trail to follow. Neither Lucas nor I were invited to participate in the hunt and we didn't ask either. We were already breaking so many of Susan and George's rules just by sitting in this house that we didn't want to push our luck completely.

William dropped us home a little after seven o'clock. Lucas made a quick exit from the car to puke up again (William's driving was still way too fast), while I lingered in the front seat with William, taking advantage of the relatively small cabin space and the proximity of his lips.

I came up for air shortly after, largely because Lucas's retching wasn't exactly conducive to romance, and I'd just heard the sound of the telephone ringing from inside the house.

Lucas and I shot each other a fresh look of panic.

I smiled quickly back at William before slamming the car door behind me and dashing for the house, right behind Lucas, fumbling through my bag to find the house keys. As I managed to unlock the front door, Lucas shoved past me and practically sprinted across the living room to answer the phone. 'Hello?' he puffed into the receiver. 'Oh, hey mum,' he said slowly looking at me with exasperation. 'What took me so long?' He glanced at me again and grimaced. 'I was upstairs in my room listening to music and I didn't hear the phone.' He paused. 'Yeah, Elena's here. Did you want to talk to her?'

I waved the phone away and slowly pacing back to the bureau to throw down my keys.

'No sorry, we didn't hear that phone call earlier either. We've both been in our rooms studying all day.'

I slapped my forehead and he shrugged. At least if he was going to tell a lie he should have said something a little bit more believable. If she believed that then she was even stupider than I thought.

God, he was a dumbass sometimes.

'No, we aren't studying anymore. Now we are listening to music.' He paused. 'Yes, we were listening to it together. Why?' He frowned. 'I know that I like trance music and she hates it … look, mum, are you getting to a point anytime soon?'

I rolled my eyes and tilted my head backwards in defeat. We had to be in some kind of trouble.

Lucas tapped me on the shoulder and shoved the phone into my hand, wandering off into the kitchen, leaving me to glare after his retreating figure.

I put the phone up to my ear and cringed. 'Hello?'

'Elena,' Susan sighed. 'You *are* there.'

'Where else would I be?'

Okay, rhetorical question.

Lucas's laughter sounded from the kitchen. I covered the mouthpiece with my hand and motioned for him to shut up. He continued sniggering anyway.

'Lucas sounded like he was lying to me, and badly,' Susan continued. 'I thought you might have snuck out of the house again. He said you were listening to music together?'

'Ah-huh. He was showing me this new band called Pussy Boy Punching Bag.'

I saw Lucas flip me off from over the kitchen counter as he unloaded the dishwasher. I poked my tongue out at him while trying to maintain a relatively straight face.

'Sounds delightful,' she said, sounding unimpressed and

carrying on, not waiting for an answer. 'Well your father, Malcolm, and I are in Townsville now. We've been settling into the hotel for the afternoon and we're just about to go out hunting now, so we'll call you again tomorrow.'

'Any time in particular?'

There was silence on the other end of the line. I cringed.

Idiot.

'Why?'

'I want to sleep in until at least lunchtime tomorrow and I don't want to be woken up by the telephone.'

If she buys that load of crap, then I'm packing up to go and sell ice to the Eskimos.

'Okay. Well, we're probably going to sleep through the day anyway, so I'll call you both sometime around dusk.'

Well, I'll be damned. Looks like I'm moving to Alaska.

'Okay, good luck!' I hung up the phone before I could say anything else stupid.

Lucas was putting what was left of the clean dishes away in cupboards, as well as restacking the next load into the now empty dishwasher. 'What happened?' he asked, hanging the tea towel back over the oven handle, and then turning around to close the dishwasher door.

I shrugged. 'She bought it. They aren't going to ring us until after dusk from now on. Sounds like they're going to hunt all through the night and sleep during the day.'

'At least we know they are going to be safe. If there aren't any vânâtors down the coast like William says, then we don't need to worry about something going wrong.'

I leaned back against the refrigerator and sighed. 'I guess that's one thing. That doesn't stop us from being in danger, though, does it?'

'Why is that?'

'Because the alpha knows my scent. If he liked what he tasted last weekend then he won't hesitate in coming back for seconds.'

He patted my shoulder. 'Don't get too ahead of yourself. We still have the Vamps on our side.' He grinned and then pretended to gag by sticking his fingers in his mouth. 'All thanks to you getting hot and heavy with one of them.'

I grimaced. 'That doesn't mean we should drop our guard, Lucas. We should be even more vigilant now than ever before. It's just you and me in the house and we're all alone.'

He looked around nervously and then glanced out the kitchen window and into the darkened garden. He swallowed. 'Do you want to get out of here?'

I grinned. 'You're not afraid of the dark, are you, Lucas?'

'No. I'm afraid of what *hides* in the dark. Let's just take the car, go into town where there are lots of people and plenty of lights and have dinner somewhere. Mum left us some money in the tin for emergencies. I'd say this is an emergency, so we should spend it.'

I cocked an eyebrow. 'I thought we were only supposed to use the car in case of a real emergency?'

He nodded. 'This is a real emergency. I'm starving.'

I laughed. 'And shit-scared.'

'Yeah, that too.'

With Lucas behind the wheel of the car it took over half an hour to get into the city—it should have only been about fifteen minutes there direct from our house. I was flabbergasted that he still insisted on driving ten kilometres under the speed limit, persistently stopping at every set of traffic lights, whether they were red or not.

Don't even get me started on the roundabouts.

When we finally reached the restaurant we had circled the block at least four times looking for a decent car park. Lucas then attempted the impossible.

Reverse parallel parking.

After we had zigzagged in and out of the car park five times without success, I started to imagine that Lucas was Austin Powers, our car his yellow golf buggy, reversing backwards and forwards in a thousand point turn, and never getting anywhere. I would have laughed if I wasn't so pissed off—that was my favourite part in the whole movie.

Lucas reversed again at least twenty five times before my patience ran out and I screamed at him to stop the car and get out before I killed him. For the past ten minutes, we had been the hot topic of conversation for every outdoor patron sitting in the restaurants that lined the esplanade. There were quite a few spectators by now, not to mention the ridiculously long line of one way traffic stuck behind us.

The gathering crowds and restaurant patrons cheered loudly as I threw open my car door, marched around to the driver's side, and pulled him out by the scruff of his neck despite his spirited protests. I banished him to the backseat with a furious point of my finger and loped back into the driver seat.

I spun the steering wheel in my hand, brought the car parallel and then reversed the car backwards into the parking spot the very first time, without any trouble. The line of cars that had been waiting not so patiently for the last ten minutes began to glide past. Most honked their horns in irritation and flashed us middle fingers as they passed.

Lucas cowered in the backseat, his arms folded across his chest in defiance and a heavy scowl implanted on his face.

I switched off the car and spun around in the seat. 'I swear to god, Lucas, you can't drive for shit!' I yelled.

He kicked the back of my chair in protest. 'The carpark's too small.'

'I suppose you think the car is too big then too?'

'Well that's a given, isn't it,' he said snidely. And he was supposed to be my *older* brother.

I rolled my eyes and pulled the keys out of the ignition. There was no way I was letting him drive home after that stunt. Drunks had better driving skills than he did. 'Come on, let's go and get some dinner.'

'No way,' he responded forcefully. 'There's an angry mob out there right now and a whole bunch of spectators that are just hanging out to laugh at me some more.'

'Can you blame them?'

He grunted. 'I drive just fine.'

'Yeah,' I said slowly and sarcastically, 'if it's in a straight line that doesn't have posted speed limits, roundabouts, traffic lights, parking spaces or any other vehicles.'

'Do you feel better now?' he said moodily, kicking at the back of my seat again.

'I'll feel better when they audit the department of transport for handing out licences like they're food stamps.'

He harrumphed.

I opened the car door, stepped out into the street and bowed down to another roar of applause from across the road. There weren't as many people as before, now that the spectacle had passed, but the ones that had lingered saw fit to show their appreciation. After the applause died down and interest in us waned, they all dispersed and refocused their attention back on their meals.

I looked back at Lucas who was now lying across the backseat, with his head in his hands. I couldn't help but laugh *and* feel sorry for him all at the same time. *Poor fella.* I supposed it wasn't really his fault. There were bad genes running in his family—just look at Susan's cooking.

I opened the back door and tugged at his ankle. 'Come on, there's a bowl of pasta at the Italian buffet that's calling out my name, and it would be rude to ignore it.'

'I'm not hungry anymore.'

'Sure you are. Now pull your head out of your ass and get out of the car.' I tugged a little harder, effectively pulling him halfway out the car door. He mumbled something unintelligible and then climbed out. Before he had a chance to change his mind, I grabbed his hand and yanked him across the street, darting through a line of traffic and bounding up the footpath in front of one of the restaurants whose patrons we'd recently provided amusement for.

'Nice parking!' someone yelled out to Lucas over the roar of the restaurant noises.

'Yeah,' another gruff voice sounded, followed by a roar of laughter, 'where's your seeing-eye dog?'

'Yeah, just say that to my face!' Lucas yelled out, practically puffing up his chest in anger.

The patrons fell quiet, sensing an imminent confrontation. A bald-headed man that was almost seven feet tall, covered in tattoos, wearing bike leathers, and built like a brick shit-house stood up at a table close by. He placed his thick, corded arms onto his hips and kicked the chair that he was sitting on out behind him.

Lucas took one look at him and swallowed uneasily. His entire face went white. 'H-hey man,' Lucas said, stuttering slightly, and holding his hands up in defence. 'We're cool.'

The bald man eyed him for a short moment, studying

his weedy frame and obviously deciding that Lucas wasn't worth the expended effort. He sat back down at the table with his dinner companions.

'Yeah, you better sit down,' Lucas half-heartedly called out across the room.

I shot Lucas a look of utter disbelief as the bald guy rose back to his feet again and Lucas grabbed my hand and yanked me quickly through the crowd of tourists. He pulled me all the way down the strip and into the food court, peering back around the corner just to make sure the bald guy hadn't followed us. I was pretty sure I had laughed the whole way there.

He grinned. 'That was close.'

I slapped his shoulder very gently. 'You're nuts. That guy could have crushed you like a bug.'

He rubbed at the spot where I had hit him, but didn't seem too concerned. 'What? That guy was an ass. Besides, I've got you with me if I get into too much trouble and if I get really desperate, I could always show him what it really means to need a seeing-eye dog.'

I laughed. 'You're not allowed to use magic in public.'

'For him, I'd make an exception.'

I stopped laughing when I noticed the sign plastered over the glass shop window behind Lucas.

'What?' he said, flicking his hair around. 'Do I have dandruff?'

'Yes, but no. Turn around, Lucas.'

He spun on the spot and almost slammed his head into the glass panel behind him.

I shook my head at him and refocused on the poster. At least he had a firsthand view of the sign with his nose practically on top of it. On the top of the page and roughly covering three-quarters of the viewable area was a large colour photograph of a girl with short cropped auburn hair, lovely pale skin, vibrant green eyes and pink pouty lips.

It was a close-up shot that was obviously taken by an amateur, but the image was obviously snapped during a very happy moment in this girl's life. Her smile belied any danger on the horizon for her, yet the presence of the poster alone proved that someone as happy and as beautiful as her was never safe from the things that went bump in the night. Underneath the photograph there was a short captioning.

MISSING
HAVE YOU SEEN THIS GIRL?

Elizabeth Mary Stuart, aged seventeen, was last seen leaving her home in Bentley Park on Sunday morning, September 2nd at around 11.30 am. Her intended destination is as yet unknown and we appeal to the public for any information regarding her whereabouts on the day of her abduction or any other information that may pertain to her disappearance.

She was driving a pale-blue Daihatsu charade with license plate number PXQ 294, which the police are also yet to locate. She was last seen wearing a short pale green sundress and gold sandals. If you have any information that may lead to finding Elizabeth, please call the police on the below number.

Lucas and I stared at the poster for a long time. It was no coincidence this girl had gone missing. 'It's definitely here,' Lucas murmured. 'The alpha is in Cairns.'

I nodded in agreement. 'William was right. You know what this means don't you?'

He shook his head. I pointed to the photo of Elizabeth to

reiterate my point. 'It means she is either dead or has been recently impregnated with werewolf spawn.'

'Ah, shit.'

'Exactly.'

'What should we do?'

I shrugged. 'What can we do? The only skills that you and I have are only good during battle. Neither of us can track and hunt a vânător without help.'

He touched a finger to my nose. 'What about your honker?'

I shook my head. 'I can only scent blood, not werewolves. I'm virtually useless. We're going to have to just stay out of trouble and just leave it to the experts.'

Lucas stared at me, dumbfounded.

I nodded and held my hands up in front of me. 'I know, I know. Elena Manory just chose the path of common sense over danger, intrigue, and mystery. I get it. I just said something completely out of character, no need to rub it in.'

Lucas's lips moved but nothing came out.

I rolled my eyes. 'Come on, let's get some food into me before I decide to save the whales and rescue orphans as well.'

Lucas snorted. He knew me too well.

CHAPTER SEVENTEEN: TAKEN

I stared, mesmerised at the boiling saucepan of water I'd placed on the stove top nearly ten minutes ago. It was frothing and bubbling away manically, waiting for me to stir the rice that I had thrown in only moments before—except I didn't. There were things moving across the surface of the water. I could see a veritable family of tiny bodies wiggling across the water's milky white surface.

I grabbed a spoon from the top draw and scooped across the top of the water to collect some of the frothy scum that had begun to settle around the edges. I brought the spoon up close to my face to investigate. There were definitely some suspect insects that should not have been in our dinner.

Ugh, gross.

I threw the spoon into the kitchen sink and picked up the packet of rice that was still sitting on the bench top, studying it.

Weevils, just lovely. Now what am I going to cook?

I tossed the rest of the packet into the rubbish bin in disgust and switched off the stove. I grabbed the saucepan of contaminated rice and promptly began washing it down the sink. There was no way we could pick our way around those bugs and there was no way that I was going to. We'd just have to come up with something else for dinner.

Okay, I'd just have to come up with something else.

'What are you doing?' Lucas groaned as he rounded the corner. He'd been moaning about how hungry he was for the last half hour. God forbid that he would make an effort to cook the dinner for himself.

I showed him the little dead bugs that were still entrenched in our now gluggy rice.

'Gross,' he said, 'I'm ordering pizza.'

I nodded. 'Sounds like a plan.'

While he went to order us our dinner, I emptied the rest of the contents down the sink and rinsed the saucepan, before shoving it into the dishwasher. While I was at it, I threw in a detergent block, shut the door and turned it on. The machine purred to life with a slight whirring and splashing sound.

I wiped down the remaining benches and cleaned up. At least I had tried to cook something for us for dinner last night. It wasn't fancy, just some steak and vegetables, but at this rate we were going to burn through that emergency money before we knew it. As it was there was only about fifty dollars left. Our Italian buffet the other night had cost a little more than either of us imagined. At least I had made an effort to cook tonight. It wasn't my fault that the pantry was so full of food that none of us ever ate and had now become a refuge to bugs.

I rinsed out the cloth and hung it over the kitchen tap to dry. I stared out into the darkness of the empty garden and beyond. It was pretty scary at night, particularly when the wind pushed the jacaranda trees' gnarled and tangled branches weaving around into the night air like giant octopus tentacles. The sunflowers below looked like faces staring back at me. The overgrown grass and weeds didn't help either.

Anything could be hiding out there amongst the mess and we wouldn't know, given that everything was almost waist high. Our garden was a jungle, the perfect place for an unwanted visitor to hide.

We'd spent all of yesterday holed up in the house considering our options and trying to formulate some sort of plan on how we could assist either The Protectors or the Vampires.

We hadn't gotten far.

The best we could come up with so far was alerting William to the fact that another victim had been claimed. Thankfully, William and Thomas were now on the trail. I'd told them all about the poster we'd seen and they'd gone to the police station yesterday to glamour some information. They'd already been to her home, gathered her scent and continued trying to cross reference trails last night. I hadn't heard from them yet so I had no clue as to how the hunt was going.

As expected, according to Susan, The Protectors were coming up empty handed every night, despite their hunting and laying of traps. Lucas and I wanted to tell them that they were searching in the wrong area, but then that would mean I'd have to admit that I was fraternising with vampires—there was no way I was about to do that.

'Pizza's ordered,' Lucas said, interrupting my thoughts. 'It should be here soon. They think about half an hour, tops.'

'Okay,' I answered absently, as I glanced out the kitchen window again and noted the easily recognisable shadow that quickly climbed through my bedroom window. I hid my smile, before turning on my heels and heading upstairs.

'Where are you going?'

'Just to my bedroom for a little while. There's a copy of Wheel's magazine with my name on it.'

'Well, I'm just going down to the shops to grab some drinks to have with dinner. Do you want anything?'

'Chocolate,' I yelled down the stairs.

'Okay, see you when I get back. I might be a while so don't worry.'

Slightly alarmed, I paced a few steps backwards down the stairs and poked my head around the corner to look at him. 'Why?'

He pulled a ten dollar note from the tin above the microwave and shoved it into his pocket. 'I'm going to walk.'

I frowned. 'You're not taking the car? It's dark outside, Lucas.'

He nodded. 'It's fine, I want to. I need some fresh air after being stuck in the house all day again.'

'Lucas, I really don't know if that's a good idea.'

He smiled. 'I'll be fine.' He held his hand up in front of him to show me the blue light that pulsed across his fingertips and then lifted his shirt to show me the silver dagger tucked into the side of his jeans. 'If I get into trouble, I'll sort it out. You're not the only one capable of killing wolves, you know.'

I glanced up the stairs and then back at Lucas again. 'Okay, but be careful and take your phone with you, just in case.'

'Yes, mum.'

'Ugh! Don't call me that,' I said, shaking my head and taking off up the stairs again.

Putting thoughts of Lucas traipsing through the dark on his own out of my head, I raced down the hallway, pushed open my bedroom door and peered into the darkness beyond. The door slammed shut behind me and I was pushed roughly against the back of the door, soft, cool lips coming down hard on top of mine and claiming them with a fevered urgency. I didn't resist.

'What took you so long?' William whispered up against my lips a moment later.

'My legs don't move as quickly as yours, remember?'

He groaned and kissed me again, my heart doing a giddy little flip-flop inside my chest. 'I've been thinking about you all day,' he murmured.

'You have?'

He nodded.

'Good things, I hope?'

His answering kiss told me exactly what thoughts he'd been having and I was more than willing for him to show me just how good they were. I could argue plenty of points why William and I shouldn't be going down this path together, but when his mouth moved against my own with such expertise, it was pretty impossible to find a plausible excuse. The two of us seemed to fit together so perfectly. Although, there was always a niggling doubt in the back of my mind, a small piece of myself that sometimes didn't feel like his were the right lips to be kissing. A very small piece, though.

I pushed my hands against his chest as I felt my composure start to ebb away. His body was altogether too enticing to ignore and I had too many questions about the hunt to ask. Our burning desire would have to wait. 'William, stop now,' I breathed as I pushed against his chest.

'Why?' he murmured, as another wave of compulsion hit me and he brushed another tantalising kiss across my lips.

I searched my mind for the answer. It was empty. 'Umm … I forgot.'

He claimed my lips again with his and pressed himself against me in a way that made me want to melt away.

Then he pulled away, both our breathing heavy and slightly laboured. I couldn't see his eyes properly in the dark, but I knew what they'd look like. I knew that we were dancing across his threshold of sanity—it was time to end the intimacy before we crossed a very dangerous line.

'I've been wanting to do that all day,' he said, after a few short seconds of simply standing still and trying to compose himself.

I ducked under his arm and placed some distance between us by pacing over towards the window, a smile on my face. 'It's nice to know that I'm wanted.'

He crossed the room in an instant, taking me by surprise as he wrapped his arms around my waist and pulled me back in close. 'Oh, I definitely want you.'

I laughed. 'I wasn't talking about for dinner.'

He smiled and brushed a light kiss across my lips. 'Neither was I.'

I struggled in his embrace, but managed to push him away with a few little twists and turns of my upper body. 'Stop trying to woo me and tell me what's going on with the hunt,' I said, finally remembering.

His arms dropped down to his sides and he took a step back and leant up against the window frame, his eyes watching me with keen interest. 'You don't like it when things get too personal do you?' he said.

Where did that come from?

I crossed my arms and sat down on the end of the bed. 'Neither do you. You've barely answered one of my questions about your past.'

'Four hundred and forty odd years of life can take an awfully long time to explain, and sometimes there are things that are always better left unsaid.'

'I disagree.'

'Well if you believe in full disclosure then you'll understand why I have to tell you that I'm in love with you.'

What the hell?

I sniffed and looked past him out the window. 'Okay, *that* you could have kept to yourself.'

'I disagree.'

'Well you would, wouldn't you?'

Jesus Christ! He was in love with me.

Don't panic. Just keep changing the subject.

He chuckled. 'Why are you so afraid to feel something for me, Elena?'

I looked back at him. 'Why are you so afraid to talk about your past?'

'Touché. Perhaps this is something we both need to work on.'

'You first.'

He laughed again, stepping forward and trying to pull me into his arms. I scooted over to the other side of the bed.

'Well,' he said lightly, 'I can see that you're making a stand here. How about we compromise? You admit that you love me too, and I'll tell you some more about my time in the Roman Guard.'

I shook my head. 'No way. I have a better deal. You tell me everything, the same way that I spilled my guts to you on the tower, and then we'll see about the possibility of, well, you know ...'

He raised an eyebrow as high as it could go, his lips twitching slightly at the corners. 'You're going to hold out on me until I tell you what you want to hear?'

I nodded.

He laughed quietly to himself and shook his head as if remembering the punchline to an extremely amusing joke. 'It's good to see that some things never change no matter how many centuries have passed.'

'What's that supposed to mean?' I said, frowning at him again.

'It means that whether human or vampire, women continue to use sex as a bargaining chip to get exactly what they want, and it appears that you, my love, are no different.'

I straightened up off the bed and looked at him square in the eye, brushing aside the comment as a slip of the tongue. 'Does it usually work?'

He grinned. 'Always.'

'Well then I guess you better start talking or your lips are going to get very lonely.'

He took a step towards me, the pungent smell of his essence suddenly invading my nostrils again. 'And you? What about your lips?' he said seductively, his eyes trailing a heated gaze across my mouth.

I wish he wouldn't do that.

I grimaced. 'Don't you worry yourself about my lips, William. They'll do just fine without you.'

'You drive a hard bargain, Elena Manory.'

'So start talking.'

'I can't,' he said, shaking his head again, 'it takes too long to tell you everything and I only stopped by to tell you that we dug up a few new scents today. Thomas and I are going to split up tonight so that we can try and see where they lead.'

Convenient.

'What about Elizabeth's scent? Did you make any progress there?'

He nodded. 'Yes and no. We trailed her as far as the city and then out towards the northern beaches, but then her scent just disappeared.'

'What does that mean?'

'It means the Vânător probably jumped.'

I looked at him confused. 'Jumped?'

He nodded again. 'Sometimes both vampires and vânǎtors jump as a method of confusing scent trails or getting somewhere fast. We basically become airbourne, and can jump over great distances. With Elizabeth's scent it was clear that she was with a vânǎtor at the time, because both of their trails just disappeared in an instant.'

'You said that you found some new trails today?' I asked.

'Yes, we did. Unfortunately the news isn't good.'

I frowned. 'What's happened?'

His face was grim. 'I hope you don't mind that I didn't consult you first, but I've already contacted your parents and told them what's going on. I've asked them to get everyone back to Cairns as soon as possible. There isn't just an alpha here anymore. Thomas and I picked up two extra scents today. The alpha has already started forming a new pack.'

I cupped a hand to my mouth in shock. 'Did they believe you? Are they coming back?'

He shrugged. 'I hope so. I spoke to Susan. She's a little more agreeable.'

I gulped. 'Did you mention anything about us?'

He frowned. 'Should I have?'

I let out a small sigh of relief. 'No. I would prefer if our little, whatever this is, stays just between us.'

'This *thing* between us Elena is called *love*,' he said unapologetically.

I groaned. 'Stop that, will you? My head doesn't have room for nonsense right now.'

'Who said anything about nonsense?'

'Don't you have some werewolves to catch?' I muttered.

He grinned again, swooping down and brushing a quick kiss across my forehead before jumping up onto the window sill, about to leave. 'I'll see you tomorrow,' he said, letting every word roll off his tongue as a sensual promise.

'Bring the story of your past with you when you come.'

He smiled suggestively and then winked. 'Good night, Elena ... my love.'

'Ugh! Get out of here before I push you off the window sill myself.'

His laughter trickled down into the garden and disappeared as quickly as his physical presence allowed.

I closed the window behind him and locked the latch, just in case. With a new pack roaming around Cairns, I didn't want to leave a big welcome mat under my window by giving them easy access. Mind you, if a vânător wanted to get into our house, there was very little that Lucas and I could do about it anyway. The locks on our doors would be no match for the realm of the supernatural.

I shut the bedroom door behind me and wandered back down the stairs. Lucas had only been gone for about fifteen minutes. Besides, he was right. He was just as capable of taking a vânător down as I was. He'd even been training a year longer than I had, so if it came down to it, he should be able to take care of himself.

I settled into my favourite chair in the living room and flipped on the TV. I flicked through all of the stations a couple of times—there was absolutely nothing on. I didn't know what I wanted to watch anyway. All I could think about was William being in love with me. What a ridiculous notion. We'd only known each other for just over a fortnight.

It was ridiculous. Wasn't it?

Why did he have to go and do that anyway? What was wrong with things just staying casual? Why did he have to go and get all heavy with the love stuff? Don't get me wrong. I liked William, liked him a lot. But I wasn't ready to commit myself to him in a sexual way. I'd just wind up getting my heart broken in return.

I decided to ease my mind by burying myself in a mind-numbing movie that involved plenty of action and little of anything else. Perfect for drowning out notions of love and matters of the heart—those were best left reserved for Jane Austin novels and sentimental idiots who believed that love conquered all.

I ended up scanning through the DVDs we owned and selecting one of the action flicks. Plenty of fast cars and things getting blown up should pass the time and keep me occupied before the pizza arrived.

I settled back into my chair again, fast-forwarded through the opening credits and dove straight into the first lot of action sequences from *Commando*. I had heavy expectations that thoughts of love and happily ever after were about to be annihilated from my mind by Arnie's big machine gun. I watched the movie, absorbed, for about twenty minutes, only to glance up at the wall clock and wonder how much longer dinner and Lucas would be. It was only Thursday. There should have been no reason pizza was taking so long. But Lucas did walk about as fast as he drove. I wasn't expecting him home for at least another fifteen minutes.

A hollow knocking sound came from the front door.

Must be the pizza.

'Just a minute,' I yelled as I switched off the movie, got up from my chair and headed for the front door.

I peered through the peephole first to verify it was the pizza delivery guy standing on the front porch. It was, but he was shrouded in darkness. The sensor light must have broken.

'Pizza delivery,' the muffled voice sounded from the other side of the door.

I took another cursory glance through the peephole, just to be safe, and then unlocked the latch, pulled back the chain and opened the door. The scent of blood immediately assaulted my nostrils and sent me reeling backwards.

On the other side of the door was a man in his late twenties. He had shoulder-length brown hair covered by the standard blue and red baseball cap that came with his uniform, and a blue shirt that was covered in a mass of wet red stains, not pasta sauce but stains that I knew to be fresh blood. Even the smell of pizza and garlic bread could not dull the smell.

This man was in no way shape or form human.

'Wait here,' I said shakily, 'I'm just going to grab your money.' I started to close the door on him, but he was fast. He wedged his foot in the door so I could not close it any further. As he proceeded to smash his way through the door, the wood exploding into splintered debris, I cursed myself silently for not having my knife on me. But there wasn't too much I could do about that now.

With the front door now strewn across the living room floor and my pizza and garlic bread now lying face down on the porch outside, I backed up quickly, towards the stairs. My plan was simple—get the knife from the bag in my bed-room, stab this damned werewolf wherever I could, and then get the hell out of here so I could find Lucas.

'Where do you think you're going?' he said, tilting his head to the side as he watched me back step up the first stair.

'I'd leave if I was you,' I said, more confident than before. 'This home is owned by The Protectors and one of them is due back at any moment.'

Well, that was semi-true.

He crept forward again. 'I'm not afraid of you, little girl.'

I frowned. 'You should be. Have you seen what I did to your alpha's shoulder?'

He growled and I took another few steps up the stairs. In my head I'd calculated that it was a short run through the hallway to my bedroom. I hoped I could make it.

Without waiting a second longer, I spun on my heels, leapt up the stairs three at a time and sprinted down the hallway to my bedroom. He was fast. He caught up to me before I had even reached the door, grabbing at the top of my jeans and dragging me down to the ground. The air rushed out of my lungs as the hardwood floor hit my chest and stomach, forcing my breath from me.

I struggled to my knees, sucking in air as the pizza man grabbed at my legs with strong, able hands and yanked me back under him, his putrid breath, so close to my face now. He grappled me around my waist, trying to shake me around like a ragdoll. Before he could spin me around completely, I bought my elbow up hard underneath his chin, connecting with a mighty *thump* and sending his head and upper body whipping backwards.

I scrambled back to my feet and tried to scoot past him to the bedroom. No good. He had his hand on my ankle in an instant and I was back where I started, lying on the hardwood floor next to him. I tried to roll away and get up, but he punched me hard in the face, breaking my nose and sending a fresh tidal of blood running down my face and neck. While I cried out in pain, the Vânător abruptly stopped and sniffed at the air, his eyes transforming from human to black, demonic slits of fury and hunger.

I struggled, kicking out with my feet, but he managed to pin me underneath him again with his legs. He held my hands tightly above my head, but he wasn't much stronger than I was, and I knew if I persisted eventually I would break free of his grasp and finish what he had started. By breaking *his* nose.

Bastard.

I already felt my nose beginning to heal. There was a slight cracking sound as cartilage and bone re-set, and the blood beginning its slow progress back inside. But the Vânător wasted no time—he was too consumed with thirst.

He leaned down towards me, and with his tongue, began to sweep a wet path along the flesh of my neck all the way up my face and back to my nose. I convulsed in disgust underneath him, suddenly aware his skin had taken on a greyish tinge, the surface sprouting soft, hairy down. His claws extended. I could hear them scratching against the hardwood floor next to my ears.

He leaned forward again, this time throwing his head back slightly to reveal a set of teeth that were pointed and sharp and stained heavily in yellow. I couldn't afford for him to bite me. It would drain me of too much energy and I needed to get out of this unscathed. 'Get away from me!' I screamed, pulling my knee up underneath me with as much brute force as I could muster. I connected with his groin with relative ease, sailing up between his parted legs to wallop him where it hurt.

He let out something that resembled a cross between a howl and a grunt and I managed to break free again.

This time I didn't waste time trying to get to my bedroom—his body blocked the passageway. Instead, I took off back down the stairs, trusting that my legs would get me there safely without buckling. There were plenty of knives in the kitchen and with the front door now very open I'd have an easy escape if things got too rough.

Where the hell is Lucas?

I rounded the corner at the bottom of the stairs, my shoes skidding on the floor as I flung myself through the opening, gripping the wall to steady myself. I booked it into the kitchen, and quickly searched through the second drawer, trying to find any of the sharper knives. I almost kicked the dishwasher in when I remembered they were all there getting cleaned. It didn't matter now anyway. This wolf was determined ... and fast.

He reached me a second later, pushing me backwards into the bench top, my lower spine groaning in protest. I could only rely on my hands now and I knew enough about hand-to-hand combat, thanks to Peter's training, that I could take this wolf down if I just concentrated hard enough.

Before I had a second to think, he grabbed me fiercely by the neck and hoisted me off the ground, my feet kicking wildly in the air. I struggled, his grip on my throat was tight, but not enough to kill me. If he wasn't going to kill me, the alpha obviously wanted to keep me alive, either to feed from me again or mate with me. Either prospect was unappealing.

I took a second and tried to calm myself. I balled my hands into fits and swung at the Vânător's face as hard as I could in a one, two, three punch combination. I started from the left, then the right, finishing with one massive hit under the chin.

I watched as my first hit connected with his face, breaking his nose, the second practically exploding into his cheekbone. The third snapped his head backwards, knocking a few teeth out of his jaw. Blood started to spill down his decimated nose and pool around his mouth, dripping onto the floor.

He staggered backwards in surprise, releasing his grip on me so that I fell back clumsily onto the floor, gripping at the edge of the counter for support and rubbing at my sore gravelly throat.

He roared out in pain, the sound erupting from the pit of his stomach soon turning into a mighty howl that spat blood in every direction. His whole body began to quiver in front of me as his skin started to tear open, and thicker tufts of grey matted fur began to poke their way through.

His arms and legs began to grow, the bones shifting within them to allow for the transformation. His fingers and toes pushed through the end of his sneakers, disintegrated them with long black claws. The T-shirt he was wearing began to rip away from his body as he grew larger, the confines of the cotton no longer able to contain his growing form. I could hear and see the bones of his rib cage snapping and contorting painfully in his chest as the beast within released itself from the last of the flesh containing him.

Run, Elena!

This time I listened to the voice. I was not certain it wasn't mine, but I followed the advice anyway. I swallowed hard and ran as fast as I could, ducking my way around him while his head was being warped by the beast inside of him. I had never seen anything like it, but I had no time to stop and observe. I needed to get out of there as fast as I could.

I ran through into the living room and past the bureau, backtracking momentarily to grab the car keys. The sound of ripping flesh and grunting was still coming from the kitchen. I shot through the front door in an instant, the darkness outside enveloping me completely.

Why hadn't the sensor light come on?

I got my answer right away when my sneakers crushed the remainder of the light bulb. I didn't have time to deliberate.

I ran for the Forester and fumbled around with the car

keys until I found the right one, and shakily tried to push it into the lock. The darkness around me made it extremely difficult to see what I was doing, but on the second attempt I managed to get it in the keyhole. I quickly opened the door and got in. I was still inserting the keys into the ignition when the giant wolf appeared at the front door.

Shit!

He howled loudly before running full pelt at the car, slamming its body into my door, denting it heavily and pushing it into the cabin, the window fracturing and shattering into my lap.

I twisted the keys in the ignition, praying for the car to start as the beast rammed itself against the car for the second time. The sheer force of the impact lifted the entire driver's side of the vehicle off the ground, only to crash heavily back onto the concrete driveway again, the rest of the windows shattering with the impact.

Where are all the neighbours? Usually Bob would have ducked his head over the fence by now. Can't anybody hear this?

His howling pierced the night sky. I clasped my hands over my ears and tried to protect my face as the wolf sliced its talons through the car door, ripping it right off the hinges. He threw it high into the sky and it landed with a heavy crash on the timber fence, the posts splintering and tumbling to the ground like toothpicks.

I scrambled as quickly as I could over to the passenger seat, but the Vânător had taken hold of my ankle, his sharp claws pulling me roughly back the way I had come. My hands dragged through the shattered glass on the seat, spilling my blood all over the upholstery, as I looked for something to hold onto.

My bloodied fingers gripped onto the edge of what was

left of the car door and hung on as long as I could. The wolf dislocated my shoulder as he pulled me out from inside of the cabin with enough force to fracture. I yelled out in pain and swore, letting go and grabbing at my injured shoulder. My body crashed heavily against the concrete driveway, the stone scraping the front of my knees as he continued to haul me as far away from the car as possible.

The wolf seized the opportunity to grab at me again, clawing at the skin of my lower legs, tearing away at my flesh. It bloody hurt, but I felt my body courageously trying to fix itself. My shoulder was already popping back into place and the skin of my legs was healing over again.

He grabbed at my legs again before I had a chance, digging his claws into the flesh below my knees and dragging me underneath him. I would have given anything to have my knife on me right now. His snout was matted with blood and sitting at a relatively odd angle thanks to me breaking his nose while in human form, and there were definitely some teeth missing—it didn't appear to be slowing him down.

I began punching and kicking again, using any part of my body to land blows to the softer skin of his abdomen, stomach, and even his face and neck. He had figured me out by now. He knew that I could heal myself, he knew that my blood contained traces of both races, and knew what drinking it would do to me.

He sunk his sharp teeth into the flesh of my neck and began to drink the vital liquid that spilt forth from my now open veins.

I writhed underneath him, gripping at his snout and trying to wretch it open again, but with every mouthful of blood that he took, my strength waned. I could feel my grip on him slipping, my legs suddenly feeling very heavy as I struggled.

Where are you, Lucas? Are you okay? Did he get to you first?

Please, let him be okay.

I slapped at his snout, effectively with the strength of a guinea pig, and made one last attempt to roll away. I failed. The Vânător was draining me of every last ounce of strength that I could muster, and even breathing felt difficult. My head clouded over, the blood loss too much for my system, and this time I didn't have the same tasty offering in return. I was alone and lost in the dark and there was no one here to help me, not even myself.

My hands fell back down to my sides and my head lolled to the side. I wanted to fight, I wanted to kill, but I couldn't.

Darkness folded me in its grasp, my eyes closing under the weight of my weariness. I felt light as a feather, weightless. There was wind here too in the afterlife, plenty of it. It rushed past my body, blowing backwards, a strange sensation in hindsight as my face was the last extremity to feel it. Maybe I really was dead this time?

I kept my eyes squeezed shut and let the darkness swamp me completely, blotting out the feel of the wind, the coldness of my skin, the weariness of my muscles and my thoughts. It was peaceful here, and I surrendered to it, letting go of trepidation and allowing the unknown to encompass my being.

I simply let go.

CHAPTER EIGHTEEN: HOSTAGE

I cracked open one eye and then the other, seeing nothing but a blurry set of feet racing across the ground with such speed that everything beneath me was merely a smudge of colour and poorly detailed elements. My hands were also waving around above my head like I was preparing for a Mexican wave. Was I upside down? How had *that* happened? The most surprising and clearly devastating part of my awakening was that there was also a lily white backside bouncing around in front of my face.

I tilted my head so that I could look up behind me and confirm my suspicions. It was the Vânător back in his human form again, naked, and covered in blood—my blood, probably.

I shuddered. That meant that my face had been bouncing around against his naked rear end the entire time.

How delightful, a face full of ass.

I reached up and touched my neck. It was smooth and bite free. I couldn't say the same for my T-shirt. It was covered in holes, as well as a generous dousing of my blood. How long had I been knocked out for? Minutes? Seconds? Hours?

I ran through a couple of options in my head. I knew that it would be impossible to outrun this creature, so somehow breaking free and trying to make a run for it probably wasn't going to be an option. I was going to have to kill it and then make a run for it.

Or would it be better to see where it was that he was taking me. If William was tracking him he might be able to pick up a scent trail from my house to the werewolf's lair. No, I couldn't rely on that. What if the Vânător had jumped while I was passed out? If there was no trail left to follow I was stuck. My best chance of survival at this stage was to give as good as I could take and that was going to start right now.

I closed my eyes and tried not to cringe at what I was about to do.

I grabbed white butt cheek between my hands, feeling it tense slightly as he persisted on running.

I opened my mouth wide and then clammed down hard upon his flesh.

He screamed into the wind behind me, the howl ringing in my ears as warm, sweet blood poured into my mouth like liquid chocolate. I didn't get much of a chance to revel in the taste of his blood before he flung me from his shoulder and sent me sailing through the air. The world streaked past in a blur of darkness. We had already been moving so fast on foot that I shuddered to think just how hard and how fast he had thrown me.

I caught a glimpse of passing trees. The world was apparently starting to slow down now, my body decreasing in speed and—

Uuuhh.

Pain exploded all through me, like nothing I had ever felt before. Stars danced in front of my eyes and I bit my tongue in a sheer agony that tortured my entire being. My head lolled forward, my hands reaching up shakily to grip at the tree trunk that was protruding from the centre of my abdomen. The slick wetness of my blood dripped from the gaping wound in my chest and spilled down my pants and onto the ground below in a small, ever-expanding puddle.

My legs dangled freely in the air. There was no sense of leverage. All that was behind me and in front of me to grab onto was tree trunk and every single movement in any one direction was agonising.

I wanted to die. God, there couldn't be a pain any worse than this.

How the hell am I supposed to get out of this?

I groaned in pain again, wishing that my body wasn't fighting so hard to try and heal me. It was almost as painful as the trauma itself. My skin kept trying to grow along the branch in front of me, searching out the other points of contact in order to seal the wound. But it could not do its job while the foreign object was still embedded in my system. My own body was squeezing down on that tree branch to try and connect the pieces back together again, and in the meantime, I suffered.

Blood was smeared from the very tip of the branch all the way down to where my body hung from the tree limb. It wouldn't be long now until he found me again. The smell was incredible. William had been right, there was definitely something different about my blood. I'd never noticed it before. It was good, better than any blood that I had ever smelt yet.

Curiosity and just a touch of hunger had me bringing my blood-stained fingers up to my mouth just to see if my blood tasted as good as it smelt. Closing my eyes again so I could block out the image of what I was doing, I surrendered a bloodslicked finger to the inner sanctum of my mouth and sucked it clean. Flavour beyond my wildest expectations danced along my lips and sang songs of pleasure and sweet succulence across the surface of my tongue. All of the pain that I had been feeling only moments ago seemed to vanish into thin air as my mind surrounded itself with bursts of fevered energy. The taste surged throughout my system, begging me for more sweetness.

This is what William had been afraid of. Taking my blood and not being able to ever stop. I definitely could appreciate the fear of wanting something so badly that it was all your mind could concentrate on. Even I wanted to have some more, and it was *my blood.*

The rustling in the trees ahead made me snap back to reality—I was still in a whole world of hurt and the Vânător had found me.

His pale body stepped out from behind one of the trees. I looked away. The small amount of common courtesy I had learned over the years was telling me it was rude and inappropriate to stare at his groin. Obviously a wolf's shift didn't come with a fresh set of clothes.

He slunk forward through the long grass, coming to stop just to the side of me. His black eyes surveying the tree branch embedded in my abdomen. Gripping the branch just in front of me, with a quick flick of his wrists he snapped off the end of the trunk. The sudden fracture and shaking of the branch reverberated inside the wound, causing me to cringe and call him something that was not particularly ladylike.

He ignored my protests as he buried his face against the underside of my wound and drank down some more of my blood—blood that he simply could not resist. Before I went all weak and useless again, I lashed out, ignoring the pain lancing through my chest like red hot pokers, and kicked him as hard as I could in the groin.

That'll teach you for waving it around like a flag.

As he fell to the ground, howling like the giant dog that he was, I inadvertently managed to swing myself free of the branch. I landed on my knees in a pile of damp earth and blood, clasping my hand to my chest and trying not to cry or pass out, or both. I couldn't even begin to explain how much being impaled actually hurt. It was beyond anything I could ever imagine or had ever felt before. No wonder staking vampires was considered cruel. It must hurt like hell, but never actually killed them. Decapitation or direct lengthy exposure to sunlight was the only way to finish off the job properly.

I quickly sprung back to my feet while my attacker was still incapacitated, and clutched at my chest again. Blood was still dribbling from the wound and my hands were covered in it. I resisted the urge to get lost in my own scent, and instead balled my hands into fists and held them calmly by my sides. I watched my attacker moaning in pain and cushioning his damaged package with his hands. I wanted to scream at him.

So, down or not, I began kicking that vânător again and again until he no longer moved. My chest ached from the effort, but I could not allow this creature to get back up. Besides, that would bloody teach him for impaling me onto a tree trunk.

I looked down at his crumpled and bloodied body and felt for a pulse. There was one, but it was extremely weak. If he survived the bashing, there was a good chance that he would never walk again. The best thing I could do for him now was put him out of his misery.

I took a deep breath and tried to ignore my conscience. I'd never actually killed anything before with my bare hands. The knife was one thing. It was an extension from my body, a weapon or a tool of destruction that carved a path of death without true input from me. The blade was what tore through flesh and extinguished life. The hand that wielded it was merely the compass. But using my hands, to feel the consequences of my decision to kill beneath my grip, was going to be an experience that I would not relish.

Kill or be killed, Elena.

So why was I hesitant?

Pushing aside my doubts, I crouched down behind the beast and placed a hand on either side of his head. I closed my eyes momentarily when I heard him whimper, and before another sound could ever escape his lips—I snapped his neck with an audible crunch.

I rose back to my feet and wiped a hand across my eyes, wondering if I would ever forget today, the day I'd killed a human-looking creature with my bare hands.

I turned away, instead trying to figure out exactly where I was. Not an easy task when all that was surrounding was green, green, and more green. I was in the rainforest, somewhere. That much was obvious. But it was night-time, and very difficult to discern any real direction. I'd never paid attention during Malcolm's lesson on using the stars to find north, south, and whatever. Pretty stupid in hindsight, but then again, I never thought I'd be stranded in the middle of the bush either. I couldn't even smell anything that resembled civilisation, just the aroma of damp earth, rotting timber, and dried leaves.

An intensely loud howling thundered through the night air somewhere in the clearing behind me, spinning me around on the spot. I surveyed the darkened tree line and bolted in the opposite direction. North or south, I didn't really give a crap, there was already another vânător close by, and with no weapon to call my own, being as weakened as I was, the best I could hope for was putting as much distance as possible between *this* dead body and the live one somewhere out there.

I ran as fast as my human legs could carry me. Stamina at least was not going to be a problem—my body constantly maintained its healing responsibilities, inflating my lungs with air and continuing my heart beat at an even keel. Marathon runners everywhere would be jealous if they knew my capabilities.

I ran through the trees and jumped over the undergrowth as I sped through the forest without a clue as to where I was heading. Not that it really mattered. The problem was, I knew that no matter how far I ran, he was going to find me. It was only a matter of time. I was leaving an invisible scent trail with every footstep that touched the forest floor.

I pushed myself ahead faster as another howl ripped through the trees behind me, closer than it had been before. I was definitely being hunted again. Vines were scratching at my arms and legs as I passed, and a couple of grasping tree roots caught at my sneakers, sending me sprawling to the ground each time. But when I pulled myself to my feet, not bothering with a dust off or an inventory check of damaged body parts, I took off again as fast as my legs could carry me into the darkness.

It wasn't long before I heard the howl of the Vânător rip through the night air again close by, piercing the relative silence around me. This only made me run harder and faster, trying to put as much distance between us as humanly possible. I listened carefully as I ran, trying to hear the sound of footfalls or the rustling of undergrowth behind me, but there was nothing but the sound of my own breathing and the heavy destruction of wooded debris under my feet.

Silence has to be a good thing. Right?

Then a sudden force on my back hitting me like a ton of

bricks, sent me plummeting down to the dampened earth at my feet with crushing force. Dried leaves blew up around me as my face landed against the dirt, forcing mud and god only knew what else into my mouth and nose.

I spat as I struggled to get up, the wolf laying heavily across my back. Something wet and warm fell from above and landed onto the side of my cheek, drool rolling steadily down the side of my mouth. I nearly vomited right then and there from unabated foulness invading my nostrils. I used my shoulder to wipe it away as, my hands were pinned underneath me at an awkward angle. The last thing I wanted was that crap getting into my mouth. I'd rather eat the dirt.

The Vânător tilted back his muzzle and howled deeply and loudly into the air above, piercing my ears. Nesting birds in the trees above squawked loudly and flew from their nests in terror, dispersing into the darkness above without hesitation. I could feel the anger rolling off this werewolf in waves. He was not happy about me killing his pack member.

I tried rolling to the side, trying to free my hands from under me. All I got for my efforts was a feral snarl and a few snaps of his snout right next to my ear.

I got the message.

Stay put, or lose an appendage.

He sniffed at the side of my face, his cold, wet nose brushing against the flesh of my cheek, his whiskers tickling the corners of my nostrils. I didn't move. I barely even breathed.

He stepped to the side of me slowly, removing his crushing weight from my frame. A long, warning growl sounded in the back of his throat as he watched me roll onto my side and then climb back to my feet hesitantly.

What was his game?

I took a step forward and he growled again, his muzzle drawing back to reveal a complete set of yellowed fangs just dying to tear the flesh from my body. 'What do you want from me?' I choked out.

He garbled a strange sort of sound in the back of his throat and flicked his head behind him.

'You want me to follow you?' I asked, staring into the dense foliage ahead and noting nothing of significance.

The wolf bobbed his head up and down before padding around behind me and pushing his snout into my back to make me move.

I resisted. 'I'm not going anywhere until you tell me why you've taken me and where we're going.' I already had a pretty darn good idea what the answer was, but still, I wasn't about to make this easy for him and stalling seemed like a pretty good idea until I came up with a better plan.

He opened his snout, barked at me angrily and then snapped it shut again, shoving me hard in the back and sending me stumbling forward into the underbrush.

'Push me all you want, vânător, but I'm not going with you,' I said, climbing back to my feet and staring down the big grey wolf standing behind me.

He tilted his head to the side, his black eyes narrowing, assessing me. He pushed back on his front paws and rose to his full height, looking down on me. Without hesitating he lashed out with his long dark claws and swatted me hard in the side of the face. I didn't even see it coming. The force of his blow sent my body flying through the air again and straight into the side of a toughened tree trunk.

What was with me and hitting the damn trees?

My head swam with pain and barely contained consciousness as the tree cracked under the severe impact of my body as I slammed into it. My back, shoulders, and head all suffered from the impact, effectively breaking a couple of key vertebra in my spine. And despite my healing capabilities, my legs were completely inoperable. I just prayed that it was temporary, else I was going to need some serious therapy after all of this was over and done with.

I fell to the ground in a heap, my eyes opening and closing as the blackness of my mind started to close in on me. The head trauma was obviously worse than I thought. At least there was no pain anymore.

The last thing I saw before I closed my eyes for the final time was the werewolf. He was stalking towards me again on all fours, his razor sharp teeth exposed and his black claws drawn and ready to take my life.

The smell of damp earth and rotting flesh was assaulting my senses long before total consciousness returned. It weaved its way through my air passages, clogging my lungs with mustiness and washed my unconscious self with dread. I was definitely not in the forest anymore.

My eyelids fluttered and faltered slightly, before I slowly began to open my eyes.

I sat up slowly at first, waiting to see if my luck had run dry and if my healing abilities were not strong enough to fix the severe damage that had been inflicted upon me. Fortunately, my spinal break had obviously only been short-lived as I could now move my limbs again.

I was still definitely looking a little worse for wear. My hair was a total disaster. I didn't need a mirror to know this to be true. The ringlets had taken hold and claimed the rest of my hair, turning it into a prisoner of war, my usually straight hairdo changing to a wretched curly mess. My fingernails were covered in dirt and caked with blood and, from the state of my skin, I looked like I hadn't been bathed in weeks. I didn't smell too great either. My clothes were another story entirely. My jeans were completely shredded from the knees down, my sneakers covered in mud and more blood. The T-shirt that I was wearing had more holes in it than a sieve, and was covered thickly in a sticky mess of blood and dirt.

I reached around and felt the back of my head, remembering I'd had hit the tree hard enough to crack my skull, but all that I found there was mud and some dried up blood.

I pushed off the dirty little cot that I had been lying on and looked around me for the first time since opening my eyes. Judging by all the steel and lack of windows, I gathered that I was being held in some kind of cell. It was only about two and half metres long and wide, with a small metal door. The door had a tiny barred window set into it. The walls themselves appeared to be constructed from the same steel that the door was made from. The floor was simply mud and dirt.

Great. If things did happen to get really hairy, I could always dig my way out of here.

In the corner of the room was a dirty bucket, which I presumed was my bathroom. Next to that were some cardboard boxes which were filled with tins of long-life foods.

Perhaps I had been wrong about this being a cell. Maybe it was intended as a fallout shelter at some stage. Why else would there be tins of ten year old food collected in such vast quantities?

I closed the cardboard boxes and walked over to the door and peered out through the tiny window. All I could see in the dim light was a short, rusted steel passage that sloped off to the left. Directly in front of my door there was a simple globe left hanging over a metal hook in the wall. It was the only source of light for both the passage and my cell, and its lack of illumination and warmth left the whole place feeling exactly how I felt, cold and alone.

I heard a door open from somewhere nearby and more light spilled into the cell and across the passage walls. There was the sound of footsteps pounding against something hard.

Timber, maybe?

I could see shadows dancing along the passage wall in front of me and shortly after the unmistakable sound of footsteps on the squelching dirt.

Crap, someone's coming.

I ran back over to the cot and lay back down carefully, so that the springs didn't groan too much in protest. I figured the best way of getting some information was to play dead. Vânători weren't exactly known for their intellect. But then again, what did it say about me if I allowed myself to be captured?

I closed my eyes again, pretending that I was still passed out, and focused on using my other senses instead. If I was going to try and escape, I had to get a better idea of the layout of the area. Beyond the reaches of this room was a mystery, and if I did try to make a run for it, how far would I get with a vânător still on my tail?

A lock turned in the cell door. It groaned noisily as someone opened it and stepped inside. I dared not open my eyes to see who, playing dead. I could hear two, possibly three, sets of footsteps entering the cell. It was hard to tell with all the mud lying around the place.

One of them stepped over, poked gently at my legs to see if I was awake. I kept up the pretence and didn't move, waiting to see what they would do next.

'She's still out,' I heard a man say.

'You sure?'

Someone poked me again, harder this time. 'Yeah, she's out cold. I threw her pretty hard up against that tree. If she was a normal human she'd be dead right now.'

'You don't think she's human?'

'No. She killed Patrick and you've seen what she did to John.'

'Why didn't John mention her to us?'

There was no answer. 'So what are we going to do with her?' the first man said.

'We stick to the plan.'

'She wasn't part of the original plan.'

'Well she is now, and John wants to have her, so we have no choice but to follow orders. He's our alpha.'

Okay, so the head dog had a name—John. How generic.

'But—'

'Adam! We have to follow orders. We're still too young to make our own decisions yet.'

'Okay', the one called Adam answered, a little reluctantly.

'Did you leave a trail that they could follow?'

'I'm not entirely sure what Patrick did before I found her. I'm assuming he followed the plan.'

What plan?

'Come on,' the second voice said after a few moments. 'There's nothing more we can do right now. John should be back soon, and it's almost dawn. Let's go and get some sleep. We'll come back and question her at dusk—she'll be well and truly awake by then if she heals like you keep saying she does.'

'Oh she heals alright, and she's strong too.'

'Whatever. Let's go.'

They promptly left the cell after that, locking the metal door behind them again, the clinking of keys and the turning of metal pieces within the lock audible.

I opened my eyes and bounded up off the cot when I heard the last of their retreating footsteps. The cell had grown darker at their departure, as the light that had streamed down from the room beyond was now extinguished. Once again, all that remained was a single solitary bulb to light the entire metal dungeon.

I walked back over to the cell door and tried pulling at the handle, seeing if with all my strength I might be able to budge it. The handle creaked in protest, but even with my generous strength I wasn't able to move it. I needed those keys.

I tried threading my arm through the little window to see if I could reach the latch from the outside, but it was no use, it was too small. There was no way out of this cell unless someone decided to let me out or I simply got lucky. One thing was certain—I wasn't entertaining company for at least another twelve hours.

If what those two vânători were saying was correct, then I had been knocked out since about nine o'clock last night. If dawn was approaching, I'd already been missing for half a day. Susan and George would well and truly have come home by now and discovered what had happened. Hopefully they found Lucas unharmed and had already started looking for me.

I wonder if they told William I was missing?

'Hello?' I heard a frail voice call out to me from somewhere in the tunnel.

I pressed my face against the little window and tried to peer out into the passage. 'Hello? Who's there?' I whispered. I could hear the start of uncontrollable sobbing echoing down the passage. Obviously this little fallout shelter was a bit bigger than I first thought. 'Are you okay? Who are you?' I asked again, trying not to be too loud.

'My name's Elizabeth,' she said, still sobbing.

Elizabeth?

I pressed my face back against the small opening again. 'Elizabeth Stuart?'

'Yes,' she sobbed. 'How do you know my name?'

'I saw a poster recently, saying you'd gone missing.'

Her crying came down from the far end of the passage again and filled my ears with dread. I wasn't too good with people crying. I never really knew what to say.

She started sobbing again, followed by a small moan of pain or discomfort.

'Are you okay?' I asked again, shaking my head, knowing it was a stupid question. Of course she wasn't okay. She was stuck down here with me in a muddy cage with no chance of escape.

'I don't think so,' she said, more quietly this time.

'What's wrong? Have they hurt you?'

She sobbed loudly at the question, as if *I* was threatening her now, huge racking sobs that seemed to bellow down the passage and echo off the walls.

'Shhh, Elizabeth,' I said, trying to comfort her, 'you have to keep your voice down or they will come back.' It probably wasn't true given that it was now daylight outside, but I was willing to say anything to get her to stop.

'It doesn't matter if they do come back now, it's too late anyway,' she said, her voice barely above a whisper. 'They've already got what they wanted from me. It can't get any worse if they do it again.'

I swallowed hard, knowing exactly what she was referring to. I felt sick to my stomach just thinking about it. 'How long ago did they come for you?' I asked quietly.

There was a short pause. 'I don't really know. I can't see daylight so I don't know how long I've been here.'

'Was it before or after they brought me in here?'

'A few hours before.'

I swallowed and closed my eyes, not wanting to know the answer. 'How fast is your stomach growing?'

She sobbed again. 'Who are you? How did you even know what they did to me? Why am I even here?'

I rested my forehead against the cool metal of the door, trying to block out her sobs. There was absolutely nothing I could do to help her now—it was too late. Even if The Protectors and William got here soon, there would be no way to reverse what been done to her. 'I'm so sorry that this has happened to you, Elizabeth, but I don't think that an explanation is going to make you feel any better.'

'What is your name?'

'Elena.'

'Elena, am I going to die?'

I wanted to lean out the window and tell her that, yes, everything was going to be okay, but I knew better than to give her false hope. She deserved to be told the truth.

'Yes, Elizabeth, I think that you might,' I said, taking no pleasure in my honesty.

The passage was silent around me again. There was no sounds from the direction of her cell, just the sudden realisation that any hope that she had had just been squashed by what I had said.

I'm so very sorry …

I closed my eyes, unable to bear the thought of it. I had seen and done more things than a sixteen year old girl of my age should ever have to, but listening to that girl's pain as she suffered through the next twenty four hours of an accelerated pregnancy was going to be an absolute nightmare, for both of us. Where was the justice in this world when people my age were killing creatures with their bare hands and innocent women were raped by hideous beasts?

I slumped against the door and slid all the way down to the floor until I was on the ground, with my back against the cool metal.

I started to think through everything that the Vânǎtors had talked about, trying to distract myself. For all I knew, there was no way out. William had been hunting this particular alpha and his old pack throughout England for the past few years. If it took him that long to locate the den there, then how long would it take him to sniff out the new den here? The Protectors weren't going to be any good, at least not until they located the alpha. The only chance I had of survival was escape, or retaliation.

I pulled myself up from the floor by the door and dropped down onto the cot noisily, spreading my arms over my head and stretching my legs out in front of me. Crazy as it might sound, I chose to sleep through the rest of the day. It was the best way of blocking out Elizabeth's moaning as best I could, and I'd be no use if I couldn't recuperate my strength for the evening. The Vânǎtors were going to come for me after sunset, and I needed to get physically and mentally prepared.

Sleep was my only option.

CHAPTER NINETEEN: INTERROGATION

I bolted upwards in fright, clutching a hand to my chest as Elizabeth's tormented and rather loud scream woke me from my slumber. I sucked down a huge gulp of air to try and calm my racing heart, rolling awkwardly off the side of the cot and scrambling over to the window in the door. 'Elizabeth, are you okay?' I asked groggily.

'No!' she screamed, before she started panting. 'I think it just broke one of my ribs.'

'Try and stay calm, okay? Just take shallow breaths.'

'Just get me out of here!' she screamed again. 'What have I done to deserve this?'

I cringed. *Nothing.*

The door to the outer passage slammed open, light spilling out and illuminating the corridor. 'Shut up!' The one called Adam yelled at her as they entered the passage again.

'It hurts!' she cried. 'Please, let me out of here. I won't tell anybody what's happened. Please, I beg you, just let me go.'

'I said shut up!' Adam rasped as he hit something hard against the metal of her door. The reverberation was particularly noisy in the small area, with nothing but the ground to help absorb the fierce sound.

'Leave her be,' the other one said, cutting through the

clang of metal on metal. 'It isn't going to work anyway, you know that. Let's just get the half breed and take her upstairs to see John. He's hungry.'

Is anyone ever going to look at me just like an ordinary girl instead of an entree?

I scrambled away from the back of the door and over into the corner behind the cot. They were making their way up the corridor towards me. There was the familiar sound of keys jangling just outside the cell door which swung open, groaning in protest. Two *very* naked vânători in human form stepped into my cell and I was pretty sure I hadn't seen these two before.

God, haven't these creatures heard of clothes?

One of them was in his mid-thirties, with short blonde hair and brown eyes. The other one looked like a child, no more than fourteen or fifteen years old with short, curly brown hair and a smattering of freckles across his nose. 'Careful, she's strong,' the older male said to the little boy.

I recognised the voice. It belonged to the one called Adam. The one that had found me out in the woods and brought me back here.

Wherever here is.

Both of them approached me slowly, cautiously coming around either side of me, their hands stretched out in front of them and ready to grab me should I consider running. If I hadn't known what they were capable of then, I truly would have considered it.

I kept looking from one to the other. I knew that the young one was a werewolf, but I still couldn't shake how badly the idea of hurting him bothered me. I knew that I was being ridiculous, and that this was only his human form until he found his next meal, but, still, a child? I couldn't beat up a kid.

I focused on Adam instead. After all, he'd been the one to throw me against a tree and break my spine. He deserved a little reprisal.

They both stepped towards me at the same time. I instinctively lashed out, hitting Adam square in the face with a solid punch to his lower jaw. My hand objected to the sharp pain shooting through my knuckles and wrist, but as he reeled backwards and yelped, it seemed totally worth it.

The younger one came forward a second later, trying to land a punch to my face. I ducked quickly to the right, using the cot as a barrier between us. He missed, but it didn't stop them both from trying to come at me again.

I scuttled backwards further into the corner, trying to put as much distance between us as possible. It was futile.

They grabbed me roughly by the shoulders and arms, spinning me around on the spot, and shoving me face first into the wall, tying my hands together with rope. 'I told you she was strong,' Adam said as he flicked me on the ear.

'Looks like she healed quite nicely, though,' the young one said. 'John will be quite pleased.'

They both forcibly walked me out of the damp cell, down the short passage and up a set of rickety homemade stairs that led to a badly painted red timber door. I counted exactly twenty seven steps to the bottom of the stairs, and then another seven steps leading up to the red door.

I squinted briefly in the light now surrounding me. While my eyes struggled to acclimatise to the light, they threw me roughly down onto an old armchair and started to tie me up with extremely thick rope. I assumed they were concerned about me escaping and looked like they weren't taking any chances, either way.

Smart.

I thrashed around a couple of times, trying to escape

from their grasp, but all I got for my efforts was a gut-wrenching punch to the stomach. They secured the rest of the ropes with little resistance.

'And there's more where that came from,' Adam said, rubbing at the purple bruise that was already starting to well up on his jaw. 'If you move again, I won't just hit you, I'll make it count.'

'And I'll make sure that next time I hit you, you won't get up again,' I spat out.

Adam growled. At least I knew I had hurt him.

Good.

The young one came and sat down in front of me, on a dirty white ottoman that was ripped at the corners. Adam leant up against the wall, still rubbing at his chin. I smiled.

'What's she smiling about?' Adam ventured, taking an angry step forward.

I let them bicker about whether or not I should be smiling while I discreetly surveyed the area.

I was in a house. That much was obvious now. The lower level I had just come from was either a basement or the makings of a fallout shelter, as I had first suspected. Judging by the state of the house around me and the unfinished nature of my cell, stairs and passage, the owners had vacated a long time ago. The furniture around me was old, musty and caked with dust. An ugly blue brocade sofa sat to the left of me, and was pushed up against old lace curtains that hung in tattered shreds from the small square window in the wall. In front of that was an antique-looking nineteen sixties era coffee table with uneven legs and scratches all through the surface.

The walls, which I suspected were originally painted off-white, were now heavily covered in mould stains. The floor on this level, which I assumed was ground level, was constructed from roughly lain timber floor boards that butted against each other unevenly. Some corners were bent and had popped under the strain from years of being subjected to moisture and mildew. They were swollen so badly that, in some places, the boards were missing from the floor entirely.

But none of this was that important to me. What was most crucial, and what made me smile even wider than before, was that I could see the front door through the darkness of the other room.

'She's smiling again,' Adam said and pointed at me.

'So I see. Is something funny?' the young one asked me.

'Not especially.'

'Then *why* are you smiling like that?'

'Why do you care?' I said, turning my attention back to the young one standing in front of me.

He frowned slightly and leaned forwards, his breath stinking. 'We'd like to ask you some questions.'

'I'm sure you would, but that doesn't mean that I'm going to answer any of them.'

He sneered. 'Are you sure about that?'

I looked upwards as if genuinely searching out an answer. 'Um, yep, pretty sure.'

'And there's nothing I can do to change your mind?'

'A Tic Tac might help.'

He looked confused at that, so I helped him out. 'Your breath stinks.'

He growled loudly and leaned forward on the ottoman so that his face was within inches of mine.

Now he's just being mean.

He eyed me momentarily, his glare icy. His fingers crept up the sides of my legs to rest on the top of my knees. He grabbed the ripped fabric of my jeans and tore them off so that everything from my thighs down was completely exposed.

I looked up at him, trying to hide my alarm.

Is this going where I think it might be going?

He gave me another vicious sneer, the corners of his lips curling into an evil kind of grin. He raised both hands in front of him and then slammed his fists down hard onto the top of my kneecaps. White hot pain lanced through my legs, as my eyes widened and my mouth involuntarily emitted an agonising scream.

'Well, wasn't that fun?' the young one said impertinently, listening to me scream with barely concealed glee. 'I could do that all night. I suppose I might if you decide to be disagreeable again and not answer my questions.'

I panted slightly from the pain. My body was already healing, but I was resolved to not make this easy for them. They could shatter my bones as often as they wanted to, but I would never reveal the secrets of the Vampires or The Protectors.

He raised an eyebrow at me and, when I didn't answer him, he put his hand on my knee again, waiting for me to defy him.

I looked down at the hand that circled my kneecap. My knee was still trying to piece itself back together, and he kept digging his fingers in between the broken bones to prevent reconstruction. He stroked my nerves, and the pain was mind-numbingly awful.

'Let's start with an easy question, shall we? How is it that you have both Vampire and Vânător in your blood?' He gave me a minute, but when I didn't answer him his fists came down hard again on my knee cap, causing my head to swim, forcing a fierce scream out of me out in protest.

'Do you want me to do that again?'

I shook my head at him, trying to swallow the lump of rising bile in my throat. My head felt dizzy from the pain.

'Then answer the question.'

I looked up at him in angry defiance, my brow perspiring and my eyes narrowing.

'Well it goes like this,' I said, talking very slowly as if I was explaining to a three year old. 'When a mummy and a daddy love each other very very much—'

He stopped me there by slapping me hard across the face and baring his teeth at me. 'Do not test me, girl!'

I laughed. 'Who are you calling, girl? You're barely pubescent.'

He slapped me again, pain searing through the side of my face.

'Look,' I shouted, 'why don't you just tell me why I'm here? I'm never going to give you information so you might as well just get on with whatever your master plan is and stop slapping me like a little girl.'

'Greg,' Adam said, right before he hit me again, 'why don't you just go and get John?'

Greg gave Adam an angry look. 'John told me to question her, so shut up and let me question her!'

'But it's not working.'

'Don't make me hurt you, Adam. I'm older and stronger, despite what she might think of my *current* physical appearance.'

I looked from one to other and then smiled again. God only knew where I was digging *that* bravado from.

'What?' Greg yelled at me. 'Why must you keep smiling? Do you not realise how much shit you're in?'

I attempted a shrug which was rather difficult considering I was bound with rope. 'Hey, if you two want fight to death over who's questioning me, then don't let me stop you. I won't have a chance to be too concerned by how much shit I'm in once one of you is dead. Besides, it just means one less of you I have to kill later on.' I wiggled my fingers. 'So please, continue.'

Warm, rich laughter sounded from the other room. 'She does have some spunk, doesn't she?' a new, deeper voice said before its owner entered the room.

Greg bounded off the ottoman in an instant. He bowed his head as he walked backwards to stand next to Adam by the archway, kowtowing.

He must be the Alpha.

A tall, blond haired man in his late twenties, with more pectorals than body parts, entered the room. He had piecing green eyes and was sporting an angry red wound on his shoulder that had been roughly sewn together, as well as some stitches across the top of his nose.

I looked him over, from head to toe, sucking in a deep breath of the powerful scent surrounding him. Virility rolled off of him in waves.

He too was obviously offended by the notion of wearing clothes, but with him, I could totally understand why. The current body that he was hitching a ride in was absolutely magnificent. But aside from his strapping good looks, he exuded an air of confidence that left little doubt that he was the one who was running the show.

He strode across the room with calm purpose, stopping only briefly to touch each of the other two on the shoulder, in reassurance, before continuing on.

He stopped in front of me, my innocent eyes all but deflowered by the large amount of naked flesh I had gawked at in the last twenty four hours.

I looked away, out the window. I'd seen enough franks and beans to last me a lifetime.

'Is something the matter?' John drawled as he sat down on the ottoman in front of my chair.

I turned back to look at him, my face impassive. 'What do you all have against wearing clothes?'

He looked at me for a moment and then glanced down at his naked form, before lifting his amused gaze to meet mine. 'To us this *is* like wearing clothes. You have to remember that we're wolves, not humans.' He touched his chest and pinched at the flesh with his fingers. 'This skin that we wear is the mask. Who we really are and our true form is the wolf inside. So if our human skin offends you I apologise, but it certainly is easier to communicate when we have human tongues, human minds, and their language to control.'

I snorted. 'Of all the things you *could* apologise for, you choose to apologise because you're skin *offends* me? Don't apologise to me because you can't be bothered with a pair of underpants, apologise for beating the crap out of me, impregnating all those innocent, young women, and for plaguing the earth with your sick desire to drink and eat everyone that you see.'

John shook his head. 'That's really rather harsh given that you, too, are a part of us. We're in your blood.'

'I'm nothing like you,' I spat out.

He arched an eyebrow and leaned in closer. 'Was it not you who killed three of my packmates? And weren't you the one who injured me, drank my blood? You even looked like you enjoyed it. Now correct me if I'm wrong, but I do believe you've just accused me of doing those very same things—yet I'm the one who is sick and underhanded? At least I don't pretend to be anything other than what I am.'

'It's not even close to being the same thing. I'm not one of you. I don't kill innocent people and I reiterate the word *people …*'

He chuckled. 'See this is where you and I differ. I do not kill people because I want to. I kill people because I have to. I was born a hunter and a natural killer, but the Vampires have ingrained me with a natural want to feed, to feed constantly off the blood of humans and vampires alike. Why do you judge me so harshly for something that is beyond my control?'

'I judge you because you must know the difference between right and wrong. You could choose to feed from synthetic blood and co-exist peacefully as the Vampires try to do, but you don't. You hunt humans who, in comparison to you, are weak and vulnerable.'

'Synth blood—yeah, right,' Adam said, chuckling and elbowing Greg in the ribs.

John turned and looked at him sternly.

He went instantly quiet, his head bowing down in front of him again.

John turned back to me again, his green eyes sizing me up. 'Why should we have to conform to human ethics? We are the stronger race. It doesn't make sense that we curtail our behaviour to suit the requirement of your Protectors and the other humans.'

'Ugh,' I muttered. 'With an attitude like that, you'll always just be animals. No wonder everyone hunts you.'

'You'll soon be the hunted too, Elena.'

I wriggled around in my confines and narrowed my eyes at him. 'How do you know my name?'

He chuckled lightly and slapped a hand against my thigh, squeezing it tight. 'I know a lot of things about you, Elena. For one, I know that you have been raised by the magical folk and are quite proficient at defending yourself. You've shown that with the death of three of my pack mates.' He took a deep breath and frowned. 'I know that you are currently growing, shall we say, more intimate with a vampire—one that has been a thorn in my side for years. I can still smell him on your breath. And I also know that you are a *born* vampire, but a vampire that also happens to be carrying the blood of the wolf. Now how do you suppose that happened?'

'It's like I told your buddy over there, when a mummy and a daddy love each other very—'

His laughter cut me short. 'A comedian too, I suppose,' he said, smiling again too widely. 'I'm aware that you also heal like the Vampires? That certainly would have been a favourable gift to have received from our makers, rather than shifting. Do you know how difficult it is to survive three hundred years without dying?'

'I don't really care,' I answered in an offhand manner, staring out the window again and trying to make sense of the trees that I could see outside. Were we still in the forest somewhere or just on a really big property where no one could hear the screams?

He laughed again, leaning forward further on the ottoman and redirecting my face towards his with his fingers. His eyes were now level with my own. 'You will care when I bleed you dry, again and again, until I get the answers that I need. And, believe me, I will enjoy it, because your blood,' he said, pausing and licking his lips, 'is delicious.'

'And if you had your answers? What would you do with them anyway?' I said as I glared at him.

He let go of my chin and leaned back on the ottoman. 'The answer to our victory is in your blood, Elena. If we could somehow harness or transfer your immunity to ourselves, so that we could self-heal, then nobody would be able to stop us. Not even your pesky boyfriend.'

That's what I thought.

William was right. All the Vânǎtors longed for was power and domination. 'I won't help you do that,' I whispered.

'You'll be surprised what you're capable of when other people's lives are in your hands, Elena. Take that vampire that you love so much—he's been hunting me and decimating members of my packs for years. I have escaped his deadly intentions more times than I can count. It wasn't until I fought him in Mackay that I realised his mind was distracted now, by something other than the hunt. Well I've decided that I'm going to kill two birds with one stone. I'll use you as the bait, lure him to me for a final show down, and then once he's out of the way I can get back to the business of recreating my pack, and unlocking the secrets of your blood.' He ran a finger down the side of my neck and licked his lips. 'And that shall be my favourite part.'

He leaned in close to me again and brushed his nose along the side of my jugular, taking deep, lingering breaths. For a brief instant his tongue flicked out and caressed the flesh of my neck, something deep within me responding. Horrifyingly, I could feel heat rising within me, my blood boiling slightly under his touch and the scent of his skin so close to mine making my skin prickle with anticipation.

What the hell? Am I ... excited?

John leaned away from me, my whole body momentarily devastated by the break in contact. He had a satisfied smirk on his face, his eyes black as pitch and teeth were drawn and ready to take their fill. I should have been terrified, I should have been screaming my protests in every undesirable word I could think of, but for some strange reason all I wanted was for him to get close to me again.

He silently obliged by leaning forward again, but he did not go for my neck. Instead, he dipped his head down towards my thighs, his head tilting to the side and watching me as he sniffed lightly at the air. A smile spread across his face as he closed his eyes and inhaled deeply. Then he lifted his head back up to mine again and touched my slightly parted lips with his own.

I sat in stunned silence; having no clue as to why this would be pleasurable. I didn't move and I didn't respond, but I also couldn't pull away either.

What the hell is wrong with me?

His tongue danced lightly across my lips and then pulled away. Adam and Greg stepped forward and watched the proceedings, their growing interest extremely... evident.

'Well, that was an interesting little discovery,' John said, looking down at me with black emotionless eyes.

'What's happening, John?' Greg said as he looked back and forth, from me to John repeatedly.

'Elena is responding to her alpha.'

'You mean ...' Adam said in surprise and pointing directly at me.

John nodded. 'I can smell her heat.'

I wanted to roll over and die. What he was saying couldn't be true. How could I be attracted to an animal? It was just disgusting.

'You know, Elena,' John said, leaning forward and brushing a finger across my cheek. 'Our time together could definitely be more interesting if you just allow your wolf nature to bubble to the surface.'

I flinched away from him. 'I will never do anything for you,' I growled, though I could hear the doubt in my own words.

He chuckled lightly and scooted closer on the ottoman, so that his thighs were clamped tightly around mine. 'Your vânător blood says otherwise. I never imagined that us sharing blood with each other would give me possession over you. Don't get me wrong, you are strong. I can feel your resistance to me, but I can also smell your need to please your alpha.'

'Get away from me!' I hissed.

He shook his head. 'I don't think so—things just got a little more interesting. Besides, if I can't get from you what I want to know, then I can always use your body for other things. I do enjoy your blood, but as a self-healer you will be able to bear me pups, over and over again, a whole litter.'

'You can try, Vânător, but if you put that thing anywhere near me, I'll kill you.'

'Hmm, we'll see,' he said distractedly, as he pulled back his lips and lowered his sharp teeth down towards my neck.

Darkness was starting to become welcome relief. In the dark there was no noise, no people, and no fear of pain. It was a numbness that was comforting. It was just a dark empty space in my mind that my body automatically reached out to each and every time blood was taken from me, draining me of life and any will to live.

During that time, pain was always the first thing I felt—mind-numbing pain that soon stretched into an easy reluctance, and then, finally, into nothing at all except the knowledge that he was taking precious blood from my body again. Even my veins ached under the absence of warmth my lifeblood provided.

John was greedy and unrelenting. How many hours had I been strapped into that chair while he took my life from me I did not know. How hungry could one wolf be? Or was he sharing me with his pack mates now?

As I curled up in the middle of the darkness, I noted

that embers of light were starting to penetrate my vision. They were small at first, only dancing around the edges before turning into soft beams of light, and flashes of colour, and objects that I had no desire to see ever again. Voices were rampant now. There was so much sound in one tiny space. Talking, talking, talking and on top of that, a muffled screaming. Was it me? Was I screaming?

An eyelid fluttered open. I was still sitting in the living room, strapped to the leather chair with rope, thicker than my wrists, tied all around me. Where was everyone?

I closed my eyes again, wishing for darkness to engulf me. I heard another scream. My eyes flicked open again. It was Elizabeth. I could hear her clearly now, even from up here. She was screaming from pain and screaming for a help that wasn't coming.

I swallowed. My throat felt raw and dry. How long had it been since I'd eaten or drunk anything? A day? Two days?

'John, she's awake,' a new voice said, coming forward and tapping me on the side of the face.

I scowled at the stranger. 'Don't touch me.'

'And she's feeling much better.'

John stepped around the corner, his body tall, lean, muscular, and practically glowing with a renewed sense of vitality. 'Good, thank you, Greg.' He paused. 'Get her cleaned up and then bring her back in here. I have more questions for her. I think she won't have any trouble answering today.'

How long had I been knocked out for?

I looked out the window and saw that it was still dark outside. It could have only have been for a few hours tops. They would have locked me back up again if daylight approached, and my body healed far too quickly for me to have passed the day away without knowing about it.

'Clean her up?' Adam asked, a puzzled expression on his face. He glanced between John and the new stranger that I didn't recognise.

I looked curiously at the one that John now referred to as Greg. His was a different human form all together. This one was of an older man, mid-forties to early fifties, with greying hair and steel grey eyes. Obviously Greg had been let off guard duty to go and feed, hence the new skin suit.

'Yes, clean her up,' John answered. 'She smells like shit.'

'Is it terribly unappealing to you?' I snapped at him.

'Yes, very.'

'Well then leave me where I am so I can fester.'

John laughed. 'She's going to make a fabulous addition to our pack when she finally accepts she is one of us.'

'Dare to dream,' I said, rolling my eyes and looking away from him.

Greg moved behind me and started loosening the ropes. I immediately started shifting around, looking for an angle of escape.

'Elena!' John asserted using a hard-edged double-timbre voice that I hadn't heard before. 'You will behave. You will not try to escape, and you will do exactly as I ask of you at all times.'

His voice rolled over me with a wave of authority that was not to be denied, and much to my surprise, I immediately became still in the chair.

What the hell? Get Up! I screamed silently at myself.

I stared down at the ropes loosening around me, wanting very much to run away, but my body completely ignoring the insistence of my mind. 'What did you just do to me?'

'I gave you an order.'

'How?'

He smiled wistfully. 'You are part-werewolf, Elena, and that means total submission to the wishes of your alpha.'

'You mean nothing to me,' I spat.

'Your body begs to differ.'

The ropes loosened completely and fell to the floor. I remained sitting still even though I was screaming at myself.

Run, run as fast as you can, run as far away as your legs can carry you!

I glared furiously back at John, my nostrils flaring as he smiled back at me. 'Now get up and follow Greg and Adam into the bathroom,' he asserted again, power rippling in his voice. 'And clean yourself up. I no longer want to smell the Vampire on your skin. I wish to make you mine.'

My legs pushed me off the chair involuntarily, and I dutifully followed behind Greg and Adam as if held on an invisible leash. 'I'll never be yours,' I said in his ear, as I obediently followed him past the front door and down a tattered hallway that led to the bathroom. All I heard in reply was the assured authority of his position over mine, and the delicate sound of his sanctimonious laughter behind me.

Cockroaches ran over every corner of the room and scurried behind cupboard doors and between the floorboards, all haste, and trying to get away from us as we entered the bathroom. Every tile in the room was covered in scum and mould. I felt as if I would get seriously ill just by breathing the air in this space. On the upside, there was a small window in this room that was left open and I could see outside. But from this particular viewpoint, all that could be viewed in the darkness was a section of overgrown lawn leading over towards a dense tree line.

There were no gardens that I could see around the

house, only grass and the trees that wrapped around the perimeter.

The house appeared to be on a piece of land, surrounded by rainforest, possibly the same forest I was running through earlier. But if not, this dirty, insect-infested hovel that they were keeping me in had to be near civilisation. There had to be a driveway or path or any discernible track that would lead somewhere back to other people.

I thought about screaming at the top of my lungs, but would anyone hear me? If I did manage to get out of this hellhole, then where would I run too? Would I end up in exactly the same predicament as earlier, running through the scrub until the Vânătors found me?

Adam pushed me roughly into the shower cubicle and turned the faucet on, holding my head under the shower-head. The water that spurted from the rusty nozzle was brown and smelly, and I closed my eyes and mouth, hoping that the contaminated liquid wouldn't get inside of me.

Ugh, it's so cold.

With the alpha's command still running through my system, still yet to be fulfilled, I reached out and plucked the bar of soap from the holder on the wall and started to wash myself, shuddering at the thought of who might have used it in the past.

I soaped down my shredded T-shirt and my half-jeans, as well as my hair, face, and anywhere else that was covered in dirt and blood. My clothes stayed stained, but at least they were rinsing clean underneath the water, the mess running clear of me, onto the tiles at my feet. I scrubbed at my skin until it felt slightly raw, trying to wash away the scent of William on my skin, as John had commanded. I'd have given anything to smell his aroma of sandalwood and spice right now. I'd even take Thomas's scent of lemon myrtle if it meant that I was being rescued.

Adam turned the water off and yanked me out of the shower by my wet hair, Greg assisting him.

'Hey!' I yelled at them and slapped them both in the side of the head. 'Don't you frigging manhandle me!'

Greg tried to get in a punch, but I ducked. Unfortunately, Adam's fist fell right on target and cuffed me hard in the side of the ear. I hit the shower screen with a *thump.*

'Elena! Behave!' John's alpha tones bellowed from down the hallway.

Greg and Adam both laughed as they threw a somewhat clean looking towel at me. 'Yeah, behave,' Greg said. 'Or we might just have to show you exactly what happens to those who don't do as they are told.'

I snorted. 'I'm shaking in my boots.'

'You should be,' Adam answered.

I laughed and lowered my voice to a whisper. 'Do you want me to give you a play by play of what I've already done to three of your pack mates?' They didn't answer. 'Yeah, that's what I thought. So shut your mouths before I show you what happens when you really piss me off.'

While keeping one eye on the angry wolves in front of me, I mopped up my face and hair, then towelling down my wet T-shirt and pants until they were just merely damp. It would take a lot more than a towel off to dry what remained of my jeans.

Greg yanked the towel off me once they were through scrutinising me, and Adam pulled me back towards the chair in the tattered living room again, tying me up again before the command of the alpha began to wear off. I could already feel the tingling sensation of his authority dissipating.

'There, now, does that feel better?' John asked me as he slowly sat down in front of me again.

'It doesn't matter if you feed me and give me a bath. I'm still not going to give you any information. I'm not a frigging dog! You might as well put me back down in the cell and lock me up for good because I ain't talking.'

He nodded thoughtfully. 'Yes, we can see that injuring you only has a momentary effect. You have been quite strong to withstand what must be a lot of pain, but I have thought of something that you won't be able to resist. It is a little brutal, I must admit, and not what I would like to resort to, but you have left me with no other choice.' He motioned to Greg with his fingers and then whispered something quietly into his ear.

What were they up to now?

He disappeared into the other room and then came back a few minutes later with a girl about my age who was crying, and flailing pathetically against Greg's strong grip. She looked at me in horror, probably wondering what fate would befall her as she saw me strapped to the chair, surrounded by two strange and naked men. I had a feeling I knew where this was going now and I was worried that I wouldn't be strong enough to see it.

She kicked about wildly, but he easily restrained her with one of his arms, using his other hand to keep her from screaming.

'So, what's it going to be, Elena? Do you think that this poor girl's life might be worth answering a few questions for us?'

I looked from John to the terrified girl in front of me, her eyes pleading with me to do whatever I had to do to ensure her safety.

'How did you become the way you are?' he asked me, almost gently.

I looked at the girl again, not exactly sure how to proceed.

Were they bluffing?

I waited. I didn't want to answer. For that matter, I didn't want to answer any of their questions. Was the fate of one girl's life worth revealing a secret that could lead to the deaths of hundreds, possibly thousands of innocents?

The girl looked at me, pleading with her eyes for me to answer the question, but I held my ground. Though my stomach churned violently, and my knuckles ached and cracked from how tightly I held my curled fists, I had to think clearly.

John shook his head and waved his hand at Greg to continue. Greg slowly opened his mouth wide, allowing enough room for his fangs to grow to their full length. His eyes darkened and his skin turned a funny shade of grey as he lowered his mouth down to savage the girl's neck.

I closed my eyes. I did not want to see what fate I had condemned her to.

'Elena, open your eyes and watch,' John asserted, his alpha tone thrumming inside my mind.

My eyes flew open against their will and settled on the girl. She was thrashing about wildly beneath him, trails of blood oozing down her neck to spill onto the flimsy material of her tank top.

'Stop!' I yelled, unable to look away. 'This is the reason why you're being hunted in the first place, you cruel bastards. Can't you see that?'

John motioned for Greg to stop and Greg reluctantly pulled away, blood smearing his mouth and chin. He promptly wiped it away with the back of his hand. The girl was hanging limply from his arm, still alive, but a little dazed and confused.

I had a feeling that they would probably kill her anyway. Their cruel nature insisted that this girl was no more than a means to an end, and I didn't particularly want her death on my conscience. It was bad enough that I couldn't help Elizabeth, let alone this innocent. But I kept trying to tell myself that the sacrifice of one would be the saving grace of many, or I would never be able to look at myself in the mirror ever again.

'Are you ready to speak?' John asked me

I shook my head and looked up at the girl. 'I'm so sorry.'

John leaned in close to me again, his lips only an inch from my own, his breath pouring into my mouth, making me slightly giddy. 'You're more like us than you realise, Elena,' he murmured against my lips. 'You are willing to do what it takes to protect those around you, those that you love, even if it means sacrificing the life of an innocent.'

'I'm not protecting my loved ones. I'm protecting the entire human populace from ever being plagued by you.'

'Now, now, calm down, Elena. You wouldn't want Greg to do something he might regret.' He pointed to the girl now struggling again in Greg's arms, blood still slowly seeping down her throat.

Greg slid his head down to her bloodied neck and licked up the arterial spray on her skin, lapping at it until all I could see were the seeping puncture marks.

'Please let me go,' she moaned against his face, her soft cries barely audible.

Greg placed a finger on her lips and then flashed his set of sharp fangs again to remind her who she was dealing with.

She tried to writhe backwards in his grasp, trying to get her body as far away from his teeth as possible, but his grip was sure and strong. Even I could smell the fear that was clearly evident in her watering eyes as she submitted to his demands.

I looked back to John, swallowing my guilt.

'What's it to be?' he said, touching a finger to my lips again, his alpha scent washing over me completely, a stark mixture of raw earth and sweat.

I shuddered under his touch and closed my eyes to fight back the heated response that was building up inside of me again. 'You have my answer.'

He dropped his finger from my trembling lips and then leaned forward, grabbing my head in both of his hands and lowering his mouth to mine without hesitation.

I gasped as he captured my lips with his, covering me with the pure heat and taste of male virility. His movements were assured and demanding as he took from me without remorse or doubt. I wanted to scream and shout, and scream some more, but my body was riding another tangent, something that my mind was no longer a part of. My mind rebelled but it was still enjoying his touch, despite how much it sickened me inside.

He pulled away a moment later, releasing my face and staring at me with hungry black eyes. He turned to Greg in the next instant and snapped his fingers, pointing at the girl who was still moaning gently.

Greg smiled menacingly and then tilted the girl's neck back as far as it would go, then sinking his teeth into her flesh again. He suckled at her greedily, her arms and legs swatting uselessly at him as he held her steady and took his fill. Soon, her struggles became too weak and her legs collapsed underneath her, her eyes rolling back in their sockets. Her body was lifeless within minutes. All I could do was watch helplessly as Greg drank down the last of her essence, the very thing that kept her heart beating and her body warm. After that, he callously dropped her body onto the floor in a heap, like a crushed coke can. He licked the blood off his lips in slow, suggestive motions.

I turned away from him and stared down at the crumpled body lying at my feet, her lifeless eyes looking up at me accusingly.

'I think we are done here for now,' John said, touching a hand to my cheek again and motioning for both men to clean up.

Greg and Adam began to untie me, and I watched as John got up from the ottoman and exited the room without a backward glance.

CHAPTER TWENTY: LIFE

dam and Greg escorted me back to my cell, locking me back in the confined space and yelling for Elizabeth to 'shut up' for the umpteenth time. They disappeared back up the stairway again and slammed the red door shut behind them, once again shrouding the basement in near darkness.

I pressed my face up against the barred window of my cell door and listened to the now silent passage for signs of Elizabeth. There was nothing. 'Elizabeth. How are you doing?' I asked, my voice echoing around the silence.

There was a small, choked reply. 'I'm alright at the moment. The baby isn't moving right now.'

'How big are you?'

'My belly's the size of a watermelon, maybe bigger. I can't see my feet anymore. The skin is all red and stretched.'

'Have they been feeding you?'

'Only every other day. I'm starving.'

Yeah, me too.

'Do you have any of that canned food in your cell?' I asked, looking back at the cardboard boxes piled high in the corner.

'Yeah, but I can't get into the cans. I've tried.'

'Is there anything else in there except for tins?'

'Not in my cell.'

I left the window and hurried over into the corner to

grab one of the long life tins of baked beans. I was starving. I wanted to help Elizabeth by getting her some food, but there was no way I could help from here.

I held the tin in my hands and squeezed hard until the lid popped off under the pressure. Baked beans spilled over the edge, splattering the wall and covering my hand in red sauce, but I didn't care. I was pretty sure that it was almost Saturday morning and I hadn't eaten anything since Thursday lunchtime.

I licked the sauce from my fingers and then lifted the can to my lips, where I greedily swallowed down giant mouthfuls of beans. I barely even chewed. When I'd finished the first can, I cracked open a second, indebted to my powers of strength more than ever before.

Hunger could do strange things to a person.

'Elena?'

I looked reluctantly at the window and then back at the can in my hands before swallowing the last of it. 'Yes?'

'I heard you screaming a few hours ago,' she said quietly. 'Did they do it to you too?' Her voice tinged with sadness.

'No. They are keeping me here for information and to use as bait.'

'Bait?'

'Yeah, they want a friend of mine.'

'I'm sorry, Elena.'

'Don't be. When he finds me he's going to be pretty pissed. He'll be the one person who can get us both out of here.'

'Is he a cop or something?'

'Yeah,' I said, smiling to myself for the first time in days. 'Something like that.'

'I hope so. I don't know how much longer I can take the pain. My skin feels like it's going to split open any moment and this thing inside of me keeps hammering at my organs with its feet.'

Just as she finished her sentence, she let out a roaring scream of pain.

'What happened?' I yelled, but she continued to scream, unable to answer.

It's happening.

I started to slam my body against the door, trying to break it down so that I could get to her.

I ran from one end of the cell to the other, repeatedly ramming my body against the door, trying to make it budge. I put a few massive dents in it, but didn't have an effect on its hinges. It was not going to open for me anytime soon.

I heard the red door open and someone run down the stairs, into the muddy basement.

'It's happening,' I heard Adam yell out. 'She's having the pup!'

A few seconds later, another set of footsteps came running down the old rickety staircase and into the basement.

I pressed my face up against the little window of the door, trying to hear what was going on.

'It's working. It's actually working,' I heard Adam shout gleefully.

'Have patience, Adam. We don't know for sure yet,' Greg answered.

Elizabeth screamed again, long and hard, and it rang in my ears like a siren.

'Should we get John?' Adam asked, sounding alarmed.

'No, he's busy on the telephone with one of the other pack alphas. He doesn't think this is going to work either.'

He's talking to the other alphas?

It must be about me.

Well, shit.

'Yeah, but look at her. She's about to burst. It has to work this time.'

'That doesn't mean anything. Do you think you're the first one to try? John and the others are the only ones capable—you know that.'

I couldn't drag my ears away from the door. If this pregnancy was not going according to plan, that gave me a little bit of hope for her yet.

Elizabeth screamed out again and again. My eyes teared up in sympathy for her.

'It's coming,' I could hear Greg say now, sounding a little more excited. 'Look, it's coming through her stomach.'

I couldn't see what was going on, but Elizabeth screamed one final time. All I could hear afterwards was a tormented, lacklustre moaning. She sounded like she barely had the energy to breathe.

Then everything from the other cell went quiet. I did too, listening for anything that would tell me if Elizabeth was still alive. The one thing that I did instantly become aware of was blood—thick, red, warm and intensely satisfying blood. The sweet, salty undertones drifted down the passageway, filling me with uncertainty. If I could smell blood then Elizabeth was not in good shape.

'It didn't work,' I could hear Adam say dully.

'I told you it wouldn't,' Greg answered.

'I had to try.'

'You shouldn't have, anyway. Now we have to get rid of another body.'

'She's not dead yet.'

'She will be soon.'

My heart convulsed in my chest. I had known that it would end this way, but my own words of encouragement had instilled a new sense of hope in me that William would come in time, that everything would be alright. It was silly to have hoped I could save Elizabeth. I had known death to be her eventual companion. Perhaps I had wanted to believe that if she could be saved, then I could too.

I still wasn't sure what was in store for me, although I doubted it was amnesty. John wanted me not only for breakfast, lunch and dinner, but as a bed companion as well. When he tired of that, I was sure to be as disposable as poor Elizabeth.

Well, he could stick that idea where the sun don't shine.

Hang on a second. Let's be cold and clinical here, Elena. Why didn't the birthing work? There has to be a reason.

It was common knowledge that a vânător mating with a human produced more vânător offspring, so why hadn't the union between Elizabeth and Adam had the same result? Adam was a pup and as far as I could tell, first generation offspring, directly from John himself. Now if Adam, a first generation wolf, couldn't successfully reproduce with humans could I safely assume that only alphas have the capability to extend the packs? Could this be their main purpose?

Bloody hell. Could it be that simple—Kill the alphas, kill them all?

'Don't do this again. You have to learn to control yourself, Adam,' Greg's voice said, cutting into my thoughts.

'I will, I know better now. I just thought that maybe things might have changed and being born of an alpha that I might have been able to—'

'Adam, shut your mouth! We are all born of alphas. Do you not think before you speak? You know who is listening.'

Bingo. These two drongos are complete idiots.

'I'm sorry, I didn't think.'

'No, you didn't. We have to be smarter than that if we're going to survive the Vampires and the magic ones.'

'I won't do it again.'

'Good.'

'What do you want me to do with the bodies?'

'Burn them. We don't have time to eat them before the vampires arrive.'

I think I'm going to be sick.

Hang on—did he just say when *the vampires arrive?*

'What about her?' Adam asked.

I had no clue if he was referring to me or to Elizabeth.

'You know what to do,' Greg answered.

'Should I do that now or sort the bodies out first?'

'The bodies.'

'Are you going up to get ready?'

'Yes, I'll see you in a few.'

The conversation ended and I heard a set of footsteps retreat back up the stairs and then a door closing. I assumed that this was Greg retreating and leaving Adam behind to clean up. Maybe this would be when I could take my chance to escape considering Adam didn't appear to be all that bright.

Greg had said that the vampires were on their way. I could only assume William was among them.

Hope spurred me on, as I backed up against the wall next to the door and ducked down so that I wouldn't be seen through the little window. 'Hey, Adam,' I called. 'Did you know that John and Greg think that having you in the pack is a big mistake?'

I heard the shifting of feet in the mud as he approached. 'What are you talking about?'

'They think that you're stupid and incompetent, particularly in light of what just happened.'

He smashed something hard and metallic against my cell door. 'Shut up. You don't know what you're talking about.'

'Oh, I do. John told me when he kissed me. He whispered it in my ear. He wants to start a new pack, just me, him and Greg.'

He hit the door again. 'I don't believe you.'

I laughed bitterly. 'Do you doubt how much John wants me? Why does he always ask Greg to do his bidding? What has he asked of you lately? Nothing. He cares for you so little now that he even lets Greg tell you what to do. You mean nothing to them, Adam, absolutely nothing.'

'Shut up!' he roared, dropping the piece of metal onto the muddy dirt outside my cell. He unlocked my door and rushed into the cell, presumably to grab me.

There was zero hesitation. I took my chance and rushed him, placing my hands on either side of his head and twisting with a fast motion of my wrists. His neck jerked around with an audible crunch, before falling to the ground in a pile of flesh and bones.

I felt his neck for a pulse and found nothing.

One down, two more to go.

I grabbed the cell keys from his still fingers and then ran down the short passage to Elizabeth's cell.

Oh no!

I clasped my hand to my mouth in an effort not to throw up. Looking through the small window in her cell door, I could see she was lying on the cot in her cell, her stomach torn open. A small, dog-like creature lay dead, draped over the top of her thighs.

I fumbled with my keys until I managed to get them into the lock, and opened the door. I ran to her side and felt for a pulse—there was one, but it was weak. Her skin felt cold and clammy to the touch, but at least she was still alive. I wasn't sure for how much longer. The wound on her stomach was oozing blood and her breathing was shallow.

I tore both of the sleeves off my shirt, as they were still pretty clean, and pressed them firmly onto her torn stomach. It wasn't as bad as I thought it could have been. The opening was only about fifteen centimetres long—just large enough for the wolf spawn to slip through. I had been imagining torn and ripped flesh, blood everywhere, her insides all over the floor. I was thankful for the small mercy, praying that I could at least keep her alive long enough for more competent help to arrive.

Her head lolled to the side, her eyes fluttering as she attempted to open them, her breath coming in sharp gasps as she slowly regained consciousness.

'Elizabeth!' I said, feeling a fresh wave of relief. 'Breathe, that's it, nice and deep, just long, deep breaths. You're going to be okay.'

She coughed and winced, the jerking movements making blood well up from inside her wound. Her skin was so pale, so pale she looked sick. Her face was that of a shadow of the girl I remembered from the photograph, sweat and blood mingling with the dull strands of her tangled hair.

'It's okay,' I repeated, more for my benefit than hers. 'I'll get you out of here.'

I tightly compressed the wound on her stomach, trying to stem the flow of blood. It seemed to be working, but I knew I was fighting a losing battle.

I pushed the dead creature off her and onto the floor, away from her. I did not want her to see what had happened. I imagined that it would be too much for her to take in.

'You saved me,' she choked out.

'Shhh, don't talk. You need to save your energy.'

'The baby? What happened to the baby?'

'Shhh, you really need to keep your strength up. Here, you need to put pressure on this so you stop bleeding,' I said, putting her tiny hand over her wound. 'I have to try and get out of here so I can get you some help.'

'You're leaving me?' she said, sounding panicked.

'I have to. I need to get us both some help and you need urgent medical assistance.'

'What if they come back?'

'I don't think they will. It's me that they want.'

'What about my baby?'

I stood up and looked around, discreetly picking up the wolf pup's corpse as I walked out of the cell. I tossed it into the corner of the darkened passage. 'It's just us now, Elizabeth.'

She didn't answer.

I came back inside, avoiding her face as I rifled through the cardboard boxes in the corner of her room. I pulled out a tin of peaches. I figured the sweetness would be good for her blood sugar levels.

I busted the can open and went back to the cot to help her drink some of the liquid. She sucked it down greedily, letting the sweet juices dribble down her chin and pool around her neck in a sticky mess.

I fed her a few of the peaches. In her eagerness, she accidentally bit my fingers a couple of times but at least she didn't draw blood. There was already far too much of that lingering around and messing with my sanity.

'Is that a bit better?' I asked, as she drank down the last bit of juice.

She smiled hesitantly, her eyes still dim and tired. 'Who are you?'

I smiled wryly in return. 'Believe me, you don't want to know.'

I picked the keys up off the floor and showed them to Elizabeth. 'I'm going to lock you back in the cell now and toss you in the keys. No one will be able to get to you unless you give them the keys, okay?'

She nodded. 'What are you planning to do?'

I stood up and wandered over to the door. 'Kick some serious ass.'

I hoped that I was doing the right thing, leaving her alone in the cell. I knew that the Vânătors would have just as much trouble getting in as I had trying to get out, so at least she would be safe until I could get her some help.

I walked quickly through the squelching mud and back to the stairs, climbing them one at a time, listening for any sounds of movement upstairs and trying not to make any noise. Once at the top I pressed my ear to the red door, but the room beyond was silent.

I clasped the brass knob and slowly began to turn it, swinging the door open and peering into the dimly-lit living room beyond. There was no one in the room when I entered. The small lamp was still on in the corner, but otherwise there were no other signs that anyone was around.

Where were they?

I listened to the sounds of the house, but heard nothing other than the creaking of the corrugated iron roof contracting slightly from a day in the sun.

I stepped quickly and quietly through the room, eyeing the patch of blood on the floor where the other girl had been left earlier. I assumed that she must have been disposed of by now. The Vânătors easy disregard for human life was what made them monsters in my eyes. It was the one part that I wished I could cleanse from myself as easily as the mud and blood that had washed down the shower drain earlier. But unfortunately that would never be possible.

I made my way as silently as possible to the next room, heading directly for the front door. I stopped and glanced briefly down the darkened hallway, checking for any signs of movement. It was completely dark except for the puddle of moonlight that was seeping through the open bathroom door where they had hosed me down earlier. Apart from that, the area was completely uninhabited.

The silence that engulfed me sent shivers skating down my spine and caused sweat to break out across my brow. I felt my nerves contracting my body, making my hands shake, and my bottom lip tremble.

I wasn't even sure what scared me the most—the fact that I had encountered no one so far, or the fact that leaving the house could put me in even more danger than if I stayed? If John and Greg were not here, then they had to be outside. Whether near or far, I had no doubt that they could track me down once they realised I was loose.

I swallowed my rising fear and opened the front door, the hinges creaking noisily in protest. I ducked my head outside and glanced around warily, but I could see nothing other than the darkened tree line. The moon was out tonight but presently was hidden behind a thick cloud bank, leaving the front of the house in complete darkness.

I said a silent prayer and closed the front door behind me, pushing it gently back into the timber jamb, quietly. It would be immediately obvious to the Vânătors that something was amiss if the front door was left swinging open.

Then I looked down at Elizabeth's fresh blood on my hands and knew that leaving evidence was probably the least of my concerns. They could probably smell me from a mile away anyway, but I at least had to try. I had gotten this far by myself and all I had to do now was finish it.

Okay, deep breath … now run!

I dashed out into the night, towards the tree line, running as fast as my legs would carry me across the grass.

'Please help me.'

Who was that?

I stopped in my tracks as a small moan captured my attention. I was sure it was coming from the house.

I circled back slowly, listening, when I saw where the helpless plea had been coming from. The girl from the living room was sitting propped up against the side of the house. A few bushes had been hiding her from view.

I couldn't believe that she was still alive. I was sure that I had seen her eyes go lifeless and empty. Obviously, I was wrong.

I ran over to her and bent down to get a better look. She wasn't in great shape—very pale, with hair matted around her face both by perspiration and the blood that was still slowly seeping from the teeth punctures in her neck. She was dressed in a short tartan skirt and a skimpy black boob tube—she looked like she had been out at a party. There wasn't enough fabric on either item of clothing to help stem the flow of her blood.

'Are you okay?' I whispered, taking in a deep breath and frowning. I didn't remember her blood smelling like that earlier. Before her blood had smelt pleasantly sweet, with a slightly metallic undertone, delicious enough to make my mouth water at the prospect of tasting it. Now it was sweeter, almost cloying. I shook my head.

'I think so,' she groaned.

'Do you think you can stand?'

'I'll try.'

I helped her get to her feet. She swayed briefly on her unsteady legs and fell right into my arms. I propped her up again, and she steadied herself, rubbing her fingers over her neck where she had been bitten. She winced at the pain and then rubbed her fingers together to look at the colour of the blood on them. 'He bit me,' she said, sounding bewildered. 'He actually bit me, like some kind of fricken' vampire from the movies.'

I caught a whiff of her blood again. There was definitely something different about it.

'Do you think you can walk?' I asked again in hushed tones, pushing aside my doubts. The girl had been drained of blood; perhaps a person's blood just smelt different when it was trying to recuperate supplies, so to speak.

She took a couple of tentative steps forward and then smiled at me. 'Yeah, I'll manage.'

'Okay, good, because we need to get out of here and fast.'

'My name's Kate.'

'Elena.'

'I know.'

'How do you know my name?'

'That's what those psycho's kept calling you, isn't it?'

I smiled at her. My time as a captive was really making me paranoid.

I ripped another piece of my shirt off the bottom, leaving most of my stomach exposed. It was barely worth wearing the T-shirt anymore, but what was left helped to keep me marginally warm. I had one part of a sleeve left and enough fabric to cover most of my chest area and back, but I was already shivering. I wished I was at home in my warm bed, snuggled under the covers and pretending this was all just a horrible dream. But it wasn't. Reality assured me, the cold night air wrapping me up in its icy tendrils and testing the strength of my resolve.

'What are you doing?'

'Here, put this against the wound, it should help stop the bleeding. I know it's not the cleanest, but there's no blood or dirt on this part.'

'Thanks.'

I draped one of her arms over my shoulders and walked her as quickly as I could to the tree line again. Just ahead was a dense thicket of melaleuca trees, tall and ominous against the darkness. In between were ferns, and wild orchids, and would provide convenient hiding places for predators in the night.

Which way should we go?

I peered into the undergrowth, scanning the moss-strewn forest floor, trying to locate a path so that we weren't just wandering around aimlessly in the scrub. Since we'd just come from a house, there had to be a discernible path somewhere amongst the surrounding scrub.

I found two possibilities almost straight away, a couple of metres apart. One was a smaller path, and the other was much bigger, almost as if at one time or another it could have been a driveway, but now it was all grown over. Cycads and long grass seemed to have made a home in the left over gravel, and the few kopper's logs that had marked the edges were now silvering with age, cracked and overgrown with moss.

My instincts told me to take the driveway. After all, eventually it was bound to lead to a road. But, in contrast, the smaller path looked to be well worn, or at least more defined.

So which way? Should I head for the road or the possible safety of a neighbour?

Supposing the neighbours are even still alive?
The road.

I lugged Kate over to the driveway path and started to brush away some of the overgrown weeds and underbrush. There were scattered leaves and branches from the larger trees above that were also blocking the path. Kate tugged on my arm with a ferocity I wouldn't have expected from someone with severe blood loss.

When I turned to her the horrified look on her face made me backtrack to her side. Fear and a rush of adrenaline could give people all sorts of capabilities when they least expected it. 'What's wrong? We have to keep moving or they'll find us,' I said, starting to pull her forwards again.

They'll probably find us anyway. That blood on her is like a god damn homing beacon.

She held her ground. 'No, Elena. I saw them. They both went this way after they left me by the side of the house. I think they thought I was dead. But I definitely saw them go this way which means they will probably come back this way too.'

I looked down the overgrown driveway and back at her scared face. My instincts still told me to take the driveway. It seemed like the most logical choice for escape, despite her words. 'Are you sure?' I said. 'It's just that this path is probably the more likely of the two to get us out of here.'

'I definitely saw both of them go this way. Please, Elena, I don't want to see them ever again. Please can we go the other way instead? It must lead somewhere, maybe to another house or a neighbour or something. Please.'

'Would it be better if you stay here somewhere and hide? I'll keep going and see if I can bring back some help, and then you won't have to face them again.'

She looked at me, horrified. 'No! You can't leave me

alone. We have to take the other path.' She paused, her eyes dead. 'You owe me, Elena. You let them try to kill me, and you did nothing.'

I couldn't argue with her—the guilt of her words was too strong. She seemed so certain.

'Okay, I hope you're right, Kate.'

Or we're both dead.

'I'm positive, they went that way,' she said, pointing at the overgrown driveway again.

I wrapped her arm around my shoulders and led her back to the other path, which was a little better worn than the driveway. Someone had definitely been using this track in the last couple of years, so it had to lead somewhere.

We hurried, both of us trudging through the damp earth, walking as quickly as we dared while Kate was so injured. 'Do you want me to carry you?' I asked, after five minutes of not progressing very far.

'I'm too heavy for you. You're at least ten or fifteen kilos lighter than me.'

'It's okay, that won't matter to me, just jump up onto my back.'

She took a step back from me. 'No, it's okay, I think I can walk fine on my own now.'

I frowned and narrowed my eyes at her. 'Are you sure? Because we need to move a lot faster if we are going to get away from them.'

'No, I'm fine.'

I looked at her face. The puncture holes on her neck seemed to be clotted now. The colour had returned to her face and from what I could see, she appeared relatively fit. Technically that should not be possible.

Do I even have time for this? Get moving before they find you both!

I shrugged my shoulders and kept walking. If she fell over or started to slow me down, then I would fling her onto my back whether she liked it or not.

We walked more quickly now, on the verge of a jog, pushing our way through some of the overgrown scrub. I turned and looked at Kate occasionally to see if she was still keeping pace. She stayed right on my heels, following my lead, and hedging her way through the forest ferns and shrubbery.

Stopping briefly, I listened to the sounds of the forest, keeping alert for any sign that we were being followed. I heard nothing.

We walked for another ten minutes or so until I brushed through a final clump of ferns and into a clearing. The moon had come out from behind the clouds now and was illuminating the scene before me. The clearing we were in was almost the size of a football field, with nothing but soft grass growing in its centre, fenced round with rainforest trees and palms.

I scanned the tree line. I couldn't smell anything on the wind, except Elizabeth's blood on my hands and the now dried blood on Kate's neck. 'Kate, just rest here for a minute. I need to find a path out of this clearing.'

'You'll come back for me right?'

'Of course I will, just sit tight. I'll be right back.'

Please let me find a path.

I took off at a quick jog around the outskirts of the clearing, staying close to the edges.

I could see no definitive paths, and I knew that if we pressed on we would probably just wind up lost and in even more trouble than we were in now. I was right. Vânători or not, we should have taken the driveway path. This place felt wrong.

In five minutes I'd reached Kate again, sitting on a mossy rock waiting for me expectantly. 'We've come the wrong way,' I said, already knowing the truth of my statement. 'We need to head back.'

She got up from the rock, smoothed her skirt down around her legs and looked around her. She scanned the tree line as I had done, looked off across the far side of the field and stared absently into the darkness. The moonlight softly illuminated the determined set of her jaw, and the sudden hungry look in her eyes. 'No, we are in the right place,' she said calmly, walking towards the centre of the clearing.

'Kate! What are you doing? Don't walk out into the open they could see you!' I hissed, trying not to raise my voice too loudly.

'Elena, it's okay, we came the right way.'

'Do you see a path?' I asked, trailing behind her, thinking that maybe she had seen something that I had not.

'No.'

'Then what are we doing out here?'

'Waiting.'

I stopped, my eyes narrowing as I watched, her back to me as she continued to walk boldly into the centre of the clearing. There was no longer any fear radiating from her, it was replaced by a strange confidence. I quickly reassessed a few details of the last minutes that I had stupidly ignored.

'Kate, what are we waiting for?' I asked, frightened and already suspecting the answer.

She stopped about twenty metres in front of me and turned around, smiling a sickly twisted smile that made my insides quiver. She raised her left hand and pointed, turning back to watch the rapid approach of five dark and deadly creatures.

I should have taken the damn driveway.

CHAPTER TWENTY-ONE: ATTACK

I followed Kate's gaze, my heart sinking deep in my chest at the realisation that I should never have ignored my intuition. If I lived past this, I never would again. But, worse still, I should have known that escape would never have been that simple.

I watched as five grey werewolves, walking side by side, emerged from the trees and walked into the clearing. Under the stark blanket of moonlight, their enormous white fangs were exposed, razor sharp and ready for combat.

A wolf, much larger than the others, took the lead. His black eyes were empty, the soulless depths piercing through me, filling me. There was no mistaking his wolf-form. He had fed from me mercilessly and I had fed from him in return, and now the connection between us was irreversible.

He was my Alpha.

I found myself stepping backwards, but I was unable to turn and run like my head was commanding. All I could do was stare at the approaching wolves. I was completely mesmerised by John's size and power; his total domination over the other wolves, his supremacy, rolled from his frame in continuous waves. Even the forest itself was silenced by his presence. There was a look about him that could not be denied.

I briefly looked back at Kate. Her mouth was still slightly

upturned in that ghastly smile of self-satisfaction. I felt sick to my stomach. I had been led astray so easily! Even my nose had told me that her blood smelt all wrong, so why couldn't I have trusted myself not to walk willingly into a trap?

This Kate was not the poor girl I'd witnessed dying in the living room. I had seen the light leave her body and her life extinguished, yet I had still refused to see the truth.

I shook my head. It was too late now.

Kate turned around to look at me, her smile brightening as she shimmered, her body morphing into another human form.

Her limbs expanded and lengthened, her hair changing colour and length as her skin changed pallor. The once soft femininity of her curves filled out and hardened into Greg in human form.

William had warned me that they could morph into anyone they had ever tasted, but I had disregarded that information as easily as I had disregarded my intuition. How foolish that had made me look now.

'Thanks for the escort,' Greg said snidely, taking a few steps towards me. Matching his stride, I stepped backwards.

'Where are you going?' he said, laughing. 'There's nowhere for you to run to.'

I knew that he was right, but my legs continued backwards regardless. I had done this dance before and knew that the backwards shuffle was no more an answer than running away was. But still, I couldn't resist the urge.

I briefly shifted my attention from Greg. The other wolves began to sniff at the air with barely concealed interest, their giant snouts raised upwards, muzzles pulled back to reveal rows of sharp, pointed teeth. They snapped at the scent as if trying to taste it with their tongues.

I too focused my senses, wondering, but daring not to hope that maybe William might have found me.

I drew in a breath, drawing the cool night air deeply down into my lungs and inhaling any scents that might be mingling with the prevailing winds. I smelt something but I wasn't sure what. There was spice, for certain, and a slight citrus tang but that did not mean it was the smell of my salvation. I had to rely on myself to get out of this.

I started briefly when all five wolves whipped their heads back into the air and howled simultaneously.

Something or someone is definitely coming.

As I continued my backpedalling, I watched as Greg turned his full attention back to his pack, sniffing at the air in excitement, seemingly forgetting about me. I took my chance and spun on my heels, and ran back down the path. I knew deep down that the action was futile.

An angry snarl came from behind me, but I kept on running regardless. I could kill one, maybe two if I was lucky, but I was no match for six.

I gasped as John leapt in front of me, his paws thudding against the hardened earth, his claws scrunching against dried twigs and leaves as he lowered himself into a predatory crouch. I started a brand new backwards dance, my pounding heart keeping rhythmic time with my moving feet, and the short, sharp gasps of breathing.

He growled loudly and I froze, knowing that if I moved another inch it was likely I'd have my head torn off. As I slowed, I watched the wolf in front of me shape-shift back into his chosen human form.

It was different to watching them change into wolves or other humans. When the so-called 'pizza boy' had attacked me and transformed at my house, his body and skin had ripped apart allowing for the creature inside of him to be released. But John transforming back into human looked a lot gentler.

The hair of the wolf simply fell off John's body, his limbs beginning to shrink and change slowly back into arms and legs. Then his spine straightened and he stood, his skin changing from the greyish hue of the wolf into the more subtle pink of human flesh. His muscles shaped themselves into sinuous curves of strength and virility, over his torso, thighs, and upper arms. John's skin stretched and moved to create a perfect covering for each portion of his lean, hard body.

I licked my lips.

His obsidian-coloured eyes changed from the soulless depths of midnight to brown, and then finally settled on mint green. The fangs lining his muzzle shrunk and retreated into his jaw, human teeth now hidden by soft, sensuous lips.

He straightened up, hitching his shoulders towards his ears, slowly rolling them back until his spine cracked. He flexed his neck from side to side, cracking it sharply. Then his eyes settled upon me.

I shivered slightly as I felt his alpha-scent roll over me, as he beckoned me with his hand for me to come to him.

No frigging way.

'Elena, are you going to make this hard or easy?'

'Which one would piss you off more?'

He shook his head and reluctantly smiled, reaching out to touch my face. I shrunk away from him. 'I do love your spirit, Elena,' he continued, 'but now is not the time to irritate me.'

'Shall we continue in let's say ... five minutes then?' I said sarcastically.

He closed the distance between us in an instant and

pulled me tightly against his hard, naked body. 'You will watch your tongue, Elena,' he whispered into my ear, 'or I'll bite it off.'

I swallowed, saying nothing.

'Good girl,' John purred to me in his alpha tones, his hot breath on my cheek, his hands running down my back and cupping my bottom in heated possession. 'Now go and join the pack, and stand very still and do exactly as I tell you to do.' He released me and I turned around reluctantly, mechanically walking towards the five awaiting wolves even though my head was screaming a chorus of protests.

He slapped my behind as I walked—I wanted to turn around and throttle him, but I couldn't. The pull of his authority weighed down on me, as heavy as a tone of bricks. It was as if all free will had been taken from me and my body now operated robotically, functioning on autopilot.

I stopped a little way away from the other wolves, not wanting to get close to any of their razor-sharp fangs. Who were all of these wolves anyway? I knew which ones were John and Greg, and I had killed Adam, so who were the other four and where did they come from? William had said five had travelled from London. So, if my calculations are correct, Adam must have been spawned here. I'd killed two in Brisbane, and the vampires also claimed one themselves, which left two originals—John and Greg. So, including Adam, John had birthed a further five wolves since arriving on Australian shores.

I looked back at John. *This guy seriously needed to be neutered.*

The wolves tilted their snouts to the air and howled again.

'Calm yourselves, children,' John said, circling his arms

around my waist from behind and pulling me intimately against him.

I'm totally going to kill him when this alpha command wears off.

'They will be arriving soon. I can smell them in the air.'

'Who's arriving soon?' I said as he nuzzled his face in the side of my neck. God strike me down, but it felt good.

He licked at the flesh behind my ear and then chewed teasingly on my lobe, running his fingers across the bare flesh of my stomach. I tried to ignore the rising heat in my body, but it was difficult. 'John?' I persisted. 'Who is coming?'

'Hmm?' he murmured against my throat. His fingers brushed across the top of my pants and dipped ever so slightly underneath the rim of denim.

My knees buckled under his touch and he swept me closer to him, so tight that I could feel his need for me against my back.

'John!' I snapped, barely breathing. He may have control over my body, but he certainly held no sway over my mouth and mind.

Well, unless he tells me what to say.

'Your boyfriend draws near,' he replied, still distracted by my scent and body.

I wanted to tell him that William was *not* my boyfriend, merely a curiosity at this stage, but I couldn't figure out how that would actually help the situation, so I just went with it.

'Then I suggest you stop touching me before he rips your head off.'

He chuckled throatily in my ear. 'There are seven of us and only two of them. Your boyfriend will care very little for where my hands have been when he's being torn apart limb from limb.'

My heart sank. John could only smell William and Thomas. Did that mean that The Protectors weren't coming? Had something happened to Lucas?

Hang on–did he just say seven of them? John, Greg and the four others, that's six.

Ha! He doesn't realise that Adam isn't coming.

He dipped his head back to my neck again, his tongue teasing at my throbbing jugular.

'I hope you're not expecting Adam anytime soon,' I said, my knees still quaking from his touch.

John lifted his head from my neck. 'Why?'

'I think you'll find poor Adam is feeling a little bent out of shape.'

Well, more like broken, but you get the point.

He straightened up, his hands stiffening against the flat planes of my stomach. 'What are you talking about?'

I resisted the urge to laugh as the other wolves turned, looking at me expectantly. 'He's dead.'

A deep growl resonated in the back of his throat. 'You lie. I personally instructed Adam to open your cell door so that you would think you had escaped. He was to open the door and then let you leave.'

I frowned. 'Why would you tell him to do that?'

'You have killed three of my pack members and have even wounded *me*. Getting you to come here of your own free will was far simpler than getting Adam and Greg to drag you here kicking and screaming.'

My eyes narrowed as a thought began to occur to me. 'Why didn't you just order me to follow you here?'

He shook his head. 'I was busy. I didn't have time to babysit you.'

My eyes narrowed suspiciously. 'It would have taken a few seconds to implant the suggestion. Don't tell me you were too busy to make life easier on yourself?'

He didn't answer, but a small throaty growl told me I was pushing the subject, so of course, I pushed. 'Unless there's another reason? Something that might make you appear weak in the eyes of your pack mates?'

He growled again, spittle landing on the side of my cheek. I ignored the projectile, focusing instead on the errant thoughts coming together in my head. Logic dictated luring me here via his directive would have been easier, but he'd said it was an inconvenience to accompany me. Did that mean he needed to be in close proximity for the alpha command to stay effective? It would make sense since I was half vampire and even compulsion was not one hundred percent effective on me. If that were the case, it was good information to know and something I was going to keep to myself until I could test the theory.

I changed the subject, deciding to make him feel insecure about the impending fight rather than figuring out I was on to him.

'Guess it's just the six of you then,' I said, triumphant. 'Sucks to be you.'

'No, actually, it sucks to be you.' He lowered his mouth to my neck and bit down hard on my flesh.

I moaned in pain, in shock, as his teeth punctured my tender flesh, my lifeblood spilling down my neck and into his waiting mouth. He suckled my skin greedily, a fresh wave of commanding scent blanketing my skin, forcing me into easy submission.

Damn him!

I blinked slowly, trying to gain some clarity. I felt my strength waning. 'Do you really think that by repeatedly drinking my blood, and forcing me to bend to your will that I'll eventually cave and help you?'

He stopped and lifted his blood stained lips away from my neck. 'One way or another I will get answers, Elena. And if not, then I still get to enjoy tasting your warmth … in more ways than one.' To emphasise he pressed himself against me suggestively.

I ignored his sexual innuendo and went on. 'I know you're not just hoping to self-heal. I know you're trying to figure out how your first generation of offspring can copulate without sending out dud swimmers.'

He tightened his grip on my flesh. 'How do you know about that?'

What, were all vânătors idiots?

'Um, you locked me up with a pregnant girl. I'm not stupid, you know.'

He grunted but didn't say anything.

'So it *is* true?' I said in wonderment. 'Only the original vânătors can breed?' I started to smile. 'I can't believe you just confirmed the most vital piece of information to the survival of your species.' I laughed heartily.

'That's enough!' John roared as he turned me around, bringing his hand up and slapping me hard in the side of the face. The blow sent me sprawling onto the grass, the impact flinging me several metres from where I had been standing.

Pain lanced through my cheek like red hot fire branding my skin.

Yeah, because hitting me will make you less of a moron.

Whatever helps you sleep at night, Fido.

A few moments later the swelling in my face subsided completely and I rolled to my knees, and pushed myself back up off the ground, my hands shaking. He paced the ground in front of me, his hands now folded behind his back in thought. I had definitely rattled him.

'Greg, where's Adam? They'll be here soon and we need as many claws as we can get.'

Greg howled something to him, a couple of short barks and grunts that I wouldn't be able to understand unless I was Doctor Doolittle.

'Okay, so he shouldn't be far away then,' John answered, continuing to pace.

I groaned. 'I already told you he's not coming.' I dusted grass off of my knees and watched John's face carefully. 'I hope that the success of your plans didn't hinge on him being here.'

All the wolves were staring at me now, watching my every move.

'Do not worry, my children,' John said, more quietly now. 'Adam shall be with us shortly. The bitch is only trying to sow doubt in our minds and rob us of victory.'

The wolves' short howls of agreement rent the air. They turned and snarled at me. I couldn't help myself—I began to giggle. Abruptly, they quietened, watching me again with unadulterated ire.

John stepped closer to me and grabbed me roughly by the arm. He pulled me close, enveloping me with another fresh wave of his essence. Earth, sweat and raw masculinity invaded my nose, wrapping a rapidly tightening cord of power around my body. 'Where is he?' John growled at me, his hot breath blowing across my lips.

I frowned. 'How many times do I have to tell you before you listen? The guy is dead. *D.E.A.D, dead.*'

John didn't even have time to react, because the snarl that ripped from Greg's throat tore through the night air, just as I imagined his teeth were about to do to my throat.

He broke rank and charged at me, his teeth snapping, his powerful legs striding quickly towards where John and I stood.

John was still hanging onto my arm angrily, his fist balled tightly in my face in a gesture of what was to come. I waited for the fist to hit me and Greg to pounce. I had no ability to move on my own accord.

I watched helplessly as Greg leapt high into the air, his body gliding across the night wind as if he were no heavier than a kite in the sky on a hot summer's day. His razor sharp fangs were visible and ready to rend flesh.

'*Hevannatara!*' someone screamed from across the clearing, a blue bolt of light shooting through the black and blasting Greg straight in the side of his stomach. He froze, dropping to the ground like a lead balloon, his legs in midstride and his muzzle reared. His fangs were revealed, fangs which only moments before had been set to rip out my jugular.

John dropped his fist and spun around to stare at the cavalry arriving just across the clearing.

A giddy happiness spun through me, and as I tilted my head to the side to see George standing across the field, his hand held out in front of him, Susan and Lucas flanking him on either side, I couldn't help but feel relieved.

My family are here! And Lucas … thank God he's alive!

Jumping down from the tops of the trees and landing in front of them was William and Thomas. Their fangs were exposed, their skin translucent, and their long, dark talons unsheathed and ready for battle. As they landed, both settled into a lethal crouch and set their black luminous eyes on the wolves. I had never been so happy to see anyone in my entire life than I was right now.

John spun me around so that I was standing in front of him. He wrapped a possessive arm around my waist, pulling me up hard against his body. My hormones went wild, but my stomach turned in revulsion.

The wolves began to snarl and move forward through the grass, stalking towards my family and the vampires, one who crazily claimed that he loved me. Maybe I was the one that had it wrong? Maybe they all *did* love me and *I* was the idiot that kept shutting everyone out.

Puzzling.

I'd have to give that some more thought when I didn't have a naked werewolf wrapped around my bits.

'Kill them all,' John commanded. His wolves broke off from formation and padded across the field to engage my family.

As the wolves came on, they howled in unison.

Through the trees I could see the other Protectors making their way out onto the field. Malcolm, Peter, Martha, Sarah, Kim and Vincent were all there, including the two younger girls, Karina and Lisa. They all came and stood with my family, their hands held up in front of them in preparation.

Every single one of them narrowed their gazes at me, including William. He turned to look at me first, his black eyes zeroing in on mine. A horrifying snarl ripped up from the back of his throat as he looked at John holding me possessively against his body. His eyes noted the lack of rejection from me. It must have looked pretty bad. Either that or I looked damn awful dressed in my raggedy, bloodied up clothes and matted hair.

'Be careful, my children,' John said, pulling me backwards.

'They have brought the magical ones with them. The fight will not be as easy as we first thought.'

'You got that right,' I answered. 'You're in deep shit now.'

John growled in my ear and tightened his grip on me.

The Vânători started to spread out, stalking around the sides of The Protectors, circling them and readying themselves for attack. One of the wolves threw his head back and howled angrily at the moon, signalling the commencement of their attack.

They were incredibly fast, their bodies' blurred motion as they darted across the field towards my friends, changing direction constantly to evade the immanent attacks.

I saw several of the older Protectors—Malcolm, George and Peter—casting the Light of Mellar and throwing it at the Vânători. Coloured lights danced across the field and hit two Vânători square in the face. They stumbled around haphazardly, unable to see, blinded and temporarily neutralised. While the other Protectors turned their attentions to the other advancing werewolves, William and Thomas seized the opportunity for an easy kill.

They sprang lithely into the air, landing in front of the two stumbling wolves.

William lashed out and punched the first vânător hard in the mouth, sending the wolf flying backwards through the air and hitting the ground hard behind him. The impact sent chunks of earth high up into the air, and then raining to the ground in a torrential downpour of dirt, stones and leaves, that covered William's skin with flecks of moist soil.

Before the dust had even settled, William was launching himself through the air. He landed directly on top of the fallen vânător, his feet crushing the bones of the wolf's hind legs, preventing all movement but crawling on forepaws. The wolf whimpered loudly, his claws scratching helplessly at the dirt and grass.

William repositioned himself, fangs lengthening as he snapped the wolf's muzzle together using both hands, wrapping his fingers tightly around its length and temporarily silencing the howls of pain. He yanked the wolf's head to the side and hungrily sunk his fangs deep into the wolf's neck, tearing at the flesh and letting the blood flow thick and fast.

I licked my lips and watched eagerly as the Vânător thrashed wildly beneath William. He kept his teeth buried firmly in the fleshy folds of the wolf's neck, tearing and ripping until it no longer moved. When his head came back up again his mouth was covered in blood, some of the arterial spray spread in an arc across his cheek.

He spat some of the blood out onto the ground, almost as if it disgusted him, though I knew from the pulsing just under his semi-translucent skin that he had enjoyed it. The kill was part of his nature, and blood lust was more a part of him than his repugnance for the Vânători.

Thomas had taken a very different approach to the other blind wolf that was still staggering around the field, trying to use his sense of smell to locate his enemies. He was dancing around the wolf as if playing a very amusing game, taking swipes at the Vânător's throat with his clawed fingers and spilling blood out and onto the grass. The continued swipes were blanketing the clearing in arterial red. The wolf howled in pain as every hit raked through its flesh and it wasn't long before the wolf stumbled to the ground in defeat, howling to his alpha for help.

John prided himself on showing no mercy—so did Thomas.

He raised his clawed fingers into the air and then sliced down through the jugular with one, quick movement, ending the fight.

'*Hevannatara!*' I heard Lucas shout out across the clearing, hitting one of the other two wolves as they began to swiftly circle.

My heart began to beat faster, thumping in time to the dancing nerves that seemed to be the cause of nausea in my stomach. Lucas was a good Protector, but that didn't mean I'd ever get used to seeing him in danger.

Thankfully, the wolf froze the moment Lucas's spell hit, the blue flames still licking the tips of his fingers as he stood back to allow the final blow. Vincent darted forward, swinging a sword above his head and promptly slicing the Vânător's head from its body.

The wolf dropped to the ground in a heap—now just flesh, bones, blood and severed body parts. In an uncharacteristic display, the remaining vânător edged away from them slowly, the realisation dawning on him—he was severely outnumbered and my rescuers were more than eager for his death.

I watched now as William played with him, running quicker than thought backwards and forwards in front of him to stop the wolf from approaching my brother, who was lingering dangerously close to the Vânător. The other Protectors were seemingly unconcerned about whether or not William was caught in the crossfire. They began casting spells in retaliation, light flickering across the dark clearing. They all seemed to miss their mark, both William and the Vânător cunningly ducking and weaving between each spell. The magic that did come their way eventually fizzled into nothingness, leaving behind only the acrid smell of smoke.

The Vânător's black eyes were wary, taking in his foes and testing William's defences, but also keeping an eye on Thomas who was edging ever nearer. William was the bigger threat, however, as he was slowly weakening the wolf each time he passed, his talons slicing to the bone.

Greg was starting to move again. His paws began to twitch and he was opening and closing his mouth, but did not get up. I kept a close eye on him.

Thomas was now running circles around the other vânător, the one William was taking great pleasure in toying with. He occasionally ducked in to swipe at the beast, focusing most of his attentions on its rump and hind legs so he could force it to the ground.

Peter stepped forward, his scar illuminated in the soft glow of the moonlight as he held his hand out in front of him in readiness and concentration. Light rippled from his fingers and struck the last wolf, his cry of 'Hevannatara' still on the wind, and it was easy for both William and Thomas to dispatch their helpless foe.

Other than John, the only other vânător left in the clearing was Greg. He had climbed unsteadily back to a standing position. With a baleful glance, he howled at me before taking off on all fours directly towards Thomas and William. They looked up from their latest kill, Greg's fur, teeth, and powerful claws a blur that was already only meters away. But they were faster than the wolf, much faster than Greg had anticipated. Thomas and William had already advanced, their bodies leaping through the air and fronting the attack.

Greg skidded to a stop, quickly turning on the spot and bounding back towards me and John—but William and Thomas were already there. No matter which direction Greg tried to run in, William and Thomas intercepted him, pushing him back towards The Protectors who were standing ready.

'Allow me,' Susan said, casting the Light of Mellar and throwing it directly at Greg. The shimmering ball left her hands, trailing light across the clearing and streaking through the night before slamming into the side of Greg's head.

Both Thomas and William advanced on Greg, watching as he helplessly wandered from side to side, howling out for a help that was never going to come. John had made no move toward him, no doubt hanging onto me so he could use me as a bargaining chip. He wasn't going to risk his neck for Greg, especially now that he had failed John. The disdain he felt for Greg was clearly evident on his face, in the cruel twist of his lips.

Thomas leapt up onto the wolf's back and stomped heavily onto his spine. The wolf howled the most pitiful, pain-filled scream I had ever heard, and then fell to the ground, twitching and helpless.

William wasted no time, lowering his head and tearing at the flesh and fur at Greg's neck. He spat out the chunk of flesh, blood oozing down his chin before he went back for seconds, draining him so vigorously that soon Greg was limp and lifeless.

John had obviously seen enough. He pulled roughly at my arm, dragging me back towards the edge of the forest clearing and towards the path that led back up to the house. I stumbled repeatedly, tripping not just on the fallen twigs and uneven earth but on John's feet as he used me as a shield, dragging me backwards. I could sense his fear. His breath came quickly, the hot sweetness of it fanning across the side of my cheek and tickling my ears. I was tempted to smile, but I was nowhere near out of trouble yet. If John got too desperate, he might still kill me.

'Um, a little help, please?!' I yelled out as John pulled me, my legs obeying despite my head's desire.

John clamped a hand over my mouth and nose, silencing me and cutting off my oxygen.

My eyes went wide as I saw the two Protectors who were steadily approaching us. It was Kim and Sarah, the only people among the group that probably wouldn't care if I suffocated to death. I started to panic, my legs wildly trying to kick out at John, my nails scraping against the flesh of his fingers, digging in and drawing blood. But he resisted me and was strong.

He grunted as a few of my kicks landed blows against his shins, and hissed as my nails left bloody trails on his skin. I tried to concentrate on fighting him off, straining for oxygen, but the lightheadedness robbed me of sensible thought.

John continued to drag me, though the task was made difficult by my flailing limbs. My vision started to blur—everything was tinged with red. I saw William abruptly stand up from Greg's lifeless body, his eyes narrowing at the hand that threatened to kill me.

William pulled himself fully erect, the muscles of his arms corded and deadly as his hands balled into fists at his sides. His fists were so tight his nails drew blood from the palm of his hands.

William snarled, the sound tearing through the night air and making John twitch, his hand leaving my mouth long enough to grab both arms and drag me back faster.

I gasped, dragging in air as quickly as my lungs would allow, tripping over a small stone and falling back against John's chest. I coughed, my throat dry and air still evading me. When I looked back at the group, William was gone. He appeared only a second later, just in front of us, only a few meters away, halting our pointless backward dance. John's arm snaked its way around my waist and he pulled me in close. 'Be careful, Vampire. Do you really want to be the one to get Elena killed?'

William's chest heaved up and down as he stared at John's arm that was tangled intimately around the bare flesh of my waist. His face was covered in the blood of dead wolves and his eyes were as black as the night. His fangs were still dripping with Greg's blood, and the fierce expression on his face said he was more than willing to add John's blood to the mix. Every powerful muscle of his chest, stomach and arms were tensed, his veins pulsing dangerously against the surface of his skin. He was a masterpiece, a carving of the most magnificent marble statue that you could imagine. A rage burned in his eyes as he looked back at John with disdain. 'Let her go,' he said, his voice strong and demanding.

'No, I think not. Elena and I appear to have a lot in common and I plan on making her mine.'

William growled and took a step forward. 'You've seen what we did to the rest of your pack. The odds are not in your favour, vânător. I suggest you let her go immediately.'

John laughed. 'She is quite happy here with me. Aren't you, Elena? You want to stay here with me.' He paused. 'Say it, Elena. Say that you want to stay here with me.'

As he spoke the words in his alpha timbre and a fresh wave of his scent engulfed me, I was powerless to do anything except agree with him. 'Yes ... I want to stay here with you.' My teeth gritted together as I spoke, my whole body stiffening, wanting to repel against the words.

The Protectors approached us cautiously, but hanging back should William need assistance. There was a hiss from Lucas as he heard me utter the words, my eyes tearing over as every one of them looked at me with disbelief, and to some extent, contempt.

William focused his gaze on me, his dark eyes searching my face for the truth of my words. 'Is this true?' he whispered, the words catching painfully in his throat.

A single tear rolled down my cheek as I fought against every aspect of John's hold on me, my head aching from the strain of trying to resist.

John tightened his hold on me to get me to answer.

'Y-yes.'

An uproar of muttered disbelief and shock ran through The Protectors, and Sarah looked at me as if she had known all along that this was all I was ever going to amount to. Susan and George were both covering their mouths, incredulity etched on their features, while Lucas looked on angrily. Surely he was the one person who would see through the ruse? He knew me better than anyone. He would know that this was not something that I wanted.

Wouldn't he?

He stared at me for a long time, my eyes pleading with him to search his heart. 'She's lying,' Lucas said. 'I don't know what he's doing to her, but look at the fear in her eyes. Elena would never want this.'

Thank god!

John ran his hands possessively across my stomach and then spun me around to face him. William and everyone else watched on in horror. 'Are you sure about that?' John said. 'Elena, why don't you kiss me and show everyone just how much you want to stay with me?'

'I don't—'

He silenced me with his lips. They pressed down hard upon mine, so strong and so powerful that I almost believed that this was what I truly wanted. His breath was hot inside my mouth, his lips soft but demanding as they caressed my lips with heated need. I all but succumbed to him as he wound my arms around his neck and then pulled me close against him again.

He felt so good.

He tasted so good.

In the next instant we were being heaved apart by William with such force that I was sent flying backwards into the arms of my family. Lucas caught the brunt of my weight, both of us toppling over and onto the ground.

'Don't you ever touch her!' William roared as he punched John so hard he flew halfway across the field.

His body sailed through the air above us, shimmering and shaking as he attempted a shift in mid-flight, the grey hair of the beast ripping its way through his skin. He landed in full vânător form, snarling.

Lucas and I struggled back to our feet as The Protectors surged forward. Thomas and William were already at the centre of the clearing, circling John. 'Tell me that you didn't just enjoy that kiss?' Lucas said, dusting off his pants.

I ignored him, wrapping my arms around his neck and pulling him in close. I was so happy to see him alive and well.

He held me away from him and looked at me in disgust, his nose wrinkling. 'You stink.'

I laughed and hugged him again. 'I knew you'd come for me Lucas. I knew you wouldn't give up on me.'

He patted my back with one hand and held his nose dramatically with the other. 'Yeah, well, the house is really lonely without you. You'd be surprised how much I miss being called dumb ass.'

My responding smile dimmed and my heart began hammering as across the clearing I saw John leap to attack

William. They met head on, a blur of teeth and claws colliding, a thunderous *crack* echoing around the clearing. They fell to the ground growling and clawing at one another, each grappling for purchase on the other. My eyes strained to see the detail of the action through the darkness—I dared not move any closer.

I took a step backwards instead using Lucas as my shield. He felt safe, comforting.

'How did you find me, Lucas?' I asked.

'I didn't find you. I mean, I wanted to, but William was the one who spent the last two days hunting down their trails. He even figured out how many vânătors were going to be here—that's why we've gathered everyone, just in case they needed our help. It's William you should be thanking. He hasn't stopped looking for you since he found out you were missing. I think that guy has it for you pretty bad, Elena.'

'How did he find out? He was supposed to be hunting that night.'

Lucas shrugged. 'He must have come back for some early-evening delight or something, and saw the state of the car, the front of the house, and the fence you'd demolished. Somehow, he pieced it all together.'

I could remember the fight with Patrick vividly, and inside I shuddered.

I shook my head, hoping to dispel both the thoughts and images of the present. 'Do Susan and George know about me and William?'

He shook his head. 'I don't think so, but given how pissed he was about that lip-locking that you just gave the alpha, I think they might now have an inkling.'

I looked out over the field, noting that Thomas had now joined the fray. His talons slashed at John's hide, taking him down much the same way Thomas had dispatched the other vânătors, disabling the hind legs and rendering crawling as the only viable option. The Protectors merely watched, Susan and George standing towards the front, their gazes locked on the battle.

'I was hoping they wouldn't find out any time soon,' I murmured, watching Susan and George intently as they studied every move both the vampires and vânătors made.

Lucas laughed. 'Seriously? You're worried about them finding out about you and William when you just made out with a dog?' He chuckled at me. 'You're nuts.'

I grimaced. 'I couldn't help it you know.'

'Well, you looked like you were enjoying it. I doubt William's going to be real happy with you.'

I frowned. 'Look, I was being controlled by his alpha scent, his essence. I'm susceptible to it because I'm part Vânător. I'm not going to feel bad about something I have no control over.'

'That's right,' Lucas answered wryly. 'You have to keep your options open—there's always Alsatians, Labradors, dingoes and plenty other canines out there.'

'You're such a dumb ass.'

'Oh God, I missed you!' he said, laughing.

He turned around, grabbed at my wrist and started trying to tug me across the field. 'Come on, we don't want to miss the rest of the fight. The view back here is shit.'

My stomach rose, bile burning the back of my throat. For some reason, the thought of watching John's eventual end made me sick. I wanted him dead. There was no denying that, but a part of me knew that witnessing his death would change things. I could already smell his blood on the air—thick and syrupy, laced with the taste of defeat. That was enough for me.

'I can't,' I said, holding back.

'Why not?'

'Because the closer I am to John, the more likely he is to be able to control me. I don't want to hurt anyone. You go on ahead and finish up. I have something pretty important to sort out anyway.'

'Where are you going?'

I smiled. 'I have to go and get Elizabeth.'

CHAPTER TWENTY-TWO: RESCUE

ran down the path as fast as my legs could carry me. I could hear John's snarls and the snapping of his jaws receding behind me. Despite what John had done to me and how much I wanted him dead, I couldn't be present for it. We were intricately bound to one another both in pack and blood, and I felt that witnessing his death would cause me pain. I didn't like John and I wouldn't miss him, but he was still a part of me and no matter how fast I ran down that path, I shuddered at the thought of never feeling his touch again.

I pushed these thoughts aside as I heard a howl ripping through the night, John's final defiance, and then silence. I concentrated instead on the pounding of my footsteps upon the earth and the steady pace of my breathing. The fever that had almost gripped me before now clung to me tightly, coating my skin in fire and twisting my insides.

I kept on running.

I reached the house more quickly than I realised, and without hesitating, threw the front door open. I ran through the living room, bolted down the stairs and into the basement. 'Elizabeth, are you alright?' I yelled out as I jumped the last step.

I rounded the corner of the damp passage with haste, slipping on the mud and sliding awkwardly along the ground, arms flailing like a windmill. I managed to catch

Elizabeth's cell door handle, slamming against the steel surface before my rear end landed in the mud.

Hastily, I pulled myself upright, steadying my shaky legs and trying to push away the ominous feeling inside.

I pressed my face up against the bars of her window and peered inside. 'Elizabeth?'

My heart sank. There was no response and I now knew why. Elizabeth's eyes were open, fixed in the direction of the door where I now stood, glassy and lifeless. Her mouth was slightly ajar, but her breath no longer stirred the air. Her arms dangled off the sides of the cot, her fingers dipped in the mud on the floor.

She no longer moved, she no longer spoke, she no longer lived—Elizabeth was dead and I was too late.

I closed my eyes, taking a moment to swallow back the rising feeling of failure and to digest reality. Both Kate and Elizabeth had died since my capture. I had no idea how I was supposed to feel about that. Regret, anger, and sadness were all present, as well as a lingering certainty that a part of me had fundamentally been changed. I'd felt it the moment I had broke Patrick's neck in the forest. I'd felt it again when I'd decided Kate's life as an individual was not as valuable as the human race as a collective group. And now I could feel that change again, prickling across my skin in a cold sweat, as I had looked down at Elizabeth's lifeless body. My choices had led to this outcome.

I took a deep breath and re-opened my eyes, immediately turning away from Elizabeth's cell. I placed one foot in front of the other and walked away, not once turning around. I'd seen enough.

I carefully manoeuvred the slippery floor, rounded the corner of the passage for the final time and headed back up the stairs. The wooden floorboards creaked underfoot when I reached the living room, but there was no one left to fear.

I crossed the living room, passing the armchair with the thick corded ropes that had held me in place. When I got to the door, I hurriedly crossed the threshold. In front of me the rising sun was now poking its head above the mountains in the distance. Early morning light gently spilled like a blanket over the surrounding forest.

I took a minute to let the sunrise wash over me, the feeling of freedom filling the air with more potency and effectiveness than John's scent ever had. I could taste the approach of the fresh spring morning, and hear the birds waking up as they chirped from their nests above. As the wind billowed through the trees, dancing a tune of happiness, I felt a renewed lightness in my heart.

I headed back down the small path again, making my way as quickly as possible through the greenery and towards the safety of my family.

I could now smell smoke and the scent of burning flesh on the wind. I wrinkled my nose in distaste and quickened my pace. As I broke through trees and into the clearing again, I noticed small piles of ash scattered over the grass. The remains of the Vânätors had become sooty smudges across the landscape, their bodies disposed of by the emerging morning sunlight. A haze of smoke still drifted up from some of the still burning embers, mixing with the cool morning air and diluting the smell of death, but not entirely eradicating it.

Sarah, Kim, Martha and the two girls were carefully walking across the field, inch by inch, to ensure that no body parts had been missed. Some of the others were talking to William and Thomas by the tree line, and I could see Susan and Lucas waiting eagerly for my return.

William turned when he saw me cut through into the clearing, and our eyes locked for the briefest moment. Then he turned his attention back to George again, effectively shutting me out.

They shook hands, and then both he and Thomas disappeared into the forest without so much as a backwards glance. I told myself that he had to leave because of the rising sun, and that he was trying to stop *anyone* finding out about our relationship, hence the cavalier attitude. Yet as I stared at his retreating back, I felt nothing but cold, emotionless emptiness rolling off him. I had to wonder.

Why didn't he at least ask if I was okay?

I sniffed. I'd been kidding myself, that's why. The guy didn't love me. He was just doing his duty. Now that the job was over, he could return home to England and forget all about the pretty brunette who had momentarily stirred his heart strings.

It was a good thing I hadn't allowed myself the luxury of loving him. I'd be a mess right now if I thought about never looking into those eyes again, never touching my hand against his chest, curling my fingers through his hair or pressing my lips against his. If I had to think about how lonely I'd be without him I'd probably go mad with grief.

I straightened up. *So it's a good thing you don't love him then.*

But why does it hurt so much then?

'Elena!' Susan cried 'I'm so glad that you're okay.' She brushed her fingers through my knotted hair and patted the side of my face. I could sense hesitation in her touch.

A look passed between Lucas and I as I skittered my eyes over towards the trees where William and Thomas had just left. He took my meaning, nodded and mouthed 'I'll tell you later'.

'Where did you go?' Susan said, uselessly trying to straighten my messy hair again.

I waved her away. 'I went back to the house where they were keeping me.'

'Why?'

'I left Elizabeth Stuart there. She's the Cairns girl that was abducted.'

'Is she still alive?' Susan asked doubtfully.

I shook my head. 'No. She must have passed sometime during the fight.'

Some of The Protectors started wandering over to listen in.

'She birthed one of their pups just before everyone arrived. I tried to help her but ...' The words got stuck in my throat.

'It wasn't enough,' Susan finished.

Way to make me feel better.

'What about the pup?' Lucas interrupted. 'Was it part of the fight?'

I shook my head. 'No, it was stillborn. That's one of the things I really need to talk to you all about. I've found the key to defeating the Vânători, once and for all.'

There was an audible gasp and The Protectors looked at one another sceptically.

Peter stepped forward. 'For over three hundred years our ancestors and the Vampires have been fighting these beasts. If there was a way to kill them off completely don't you think we would have an answer by now?'

I wasn't in the mood for debating logistics. 'It's true, Peter. John more or less confirmed it for me.'

'Now's not the time,' Malcolm said, snapping his cell phone shut. 'Elena, you said the girl is in a house?'

I pointed to the path behind me. 'It's at the end of that

path. Follow it and you'll find the house. Elizabeth's in the basement.'

Malcolm nodded and then indicated for Vincent to follow.

'There's a vânător in the basement, too.'

'Alive or dead?'

'Dead.'

Malcolm patted my shoulder, and started for the path. 'Wait!' I said, stopping him. 'What are you going to do?'

Susan reached out and clasped my shoulders tightly. Vincent looked away, avoiding my eyes. 'We're going to burn the house down,' Malcolm explained. 'We can't leave any evidence of the supernatural. That includes the girl.'

I numbly nodded, understanding. I didn't like the idea of it, but I understood the reasoning.

Malcolm and Vincent left. Susan's grip on my shoulders relaxed.

'There's also the one that took me, too. I don't know where he is though. We were in the forest at the time.'

'He won't be a problem,' Peter answered. 'If you killed him, then either wild animals or the sun would have disintegrated his body by now.'

Sunlight completely filled the clearing now. The early morning sun's rays streamed through the trees, causing any stray drops of vânător blood and undiscovered body parts to erupt into flame, evaporating.

'We'd better get going,' Kim said, tugging on Sarah and Martha's sleeves.

'Yes,' Martha answered. 'There's nothing more we can do here.'

'Quite right,' Peter agreed. 'Perhaps we should all go.'

Malcolm and Vincent returned a few minutes later, puffing and panting as if they hadn't done any running in a long time. 'It's done.'

'You left no evidence?' George asked.

Vincent's pointed finger drew our attention to the cloud of black smoke rising above the canopy of trees in the distance. Acrid smells of charred flesh were still present in the clearing, but the crackle of burning timber and the sound of breaking glass clearly indicated the job was done. 'The house is ablaze. I have little doubt that any evidence will remain,' Malcolm said.

Lucas's eyes narrowed. 'That's a lot of smoke. Are you sure you didn't start a bushfire?'

'It's a risk we had to take,' Vincent answered.

'Then we should definitely be leaving,' George said. 'As Martha mentioned, there is nothing more we can do.'

The Protectors shared a look and started to head off.

Lucas lingered, his eyes locked on the spiralling smoke in the distance. 'How bad was it?' he said, finally turning and looking me in the eyes now that the others were gone.

'I'm okay.'

He gave me a knowing look, his lips pressed together in a hard line. 'You're lying.'

I sniffed, a small grimace forming on my features. No one knew me like Lucas. 'I can't talk about it just yet. I need to digest everything and figure out how I feel before I spill.'

He nodded sombrely.

'After I've had a shower, maybe got some edible food in me and started feeling normal again, maybe everything will be okay.' Lucas didn't look convinced, and sadly, neither was I.

'Come on,' Lucas said, taking my hand. 'We have to go.'

I turned my head and followed behind Lucas. He held my

hand tight, leading me through the underbrush and back to the path The Protectors had followed on their way in.

Fifteen minutes later we arrived back at another small clearing. There were tyre tracks embedded in the soft dirt and a disruption to the long grass to the left of the clearing where cars had obviously come and gone. There was nothing here now though. Well, nothing that I could actually see.

Sarah, Kim, and some of the others got into one of the invisible cars and disappeared underneath their magic—the rest of us piled into Malcolm's Pajero.

No one said anything to me during the trip back home, not even Lucas. In fact, there was zero discussion. Everyone was lost in their own thoughts, including me. I centred my thoughts around William, mostly because I needed distracting from the disturbing mental images that were stuck in my mind. But most of all, I craved answers, like why had William been so cold and distant towards me?

I shook my head and crossed my arms in front of my chest to stop from fidgeting. Why should I care anyway? If he didn't want to be around me anymore, then so what? I could move on. He wasn't the only vampire on the planet.

You're only lying to yourself, you know.

Didn't I tell you to shut up earlier?

You can't tell yourself to shut up either, it's illogical. You just have to admit that you like him.

No, I don't.

Well then why do you care if he leaves or not? If you're so unconcerned then why does your heart ache inside your chest?

I'm not listening anymore. You don't know what you're talking about.

Ah-hah, sure. Are you really going to keep this tough girl facade up forever?

A short time later Malcolm's car pulled up in our driveway. I clawed at the door handle, practically falling out as the door swung open, desperate to be home and surrounded by familiarity. The silence in the car had slowly eaten at me. I'd tried thinking only of William, his absence, and the reasons behind it, but my capture still ran rampant through my thoughts. It wasn't so much the violence that bothered me, as it kept on looping through my head, but my reactions to the violence and the sense of loss I felt.

Normal people would have been curled up in a corner, crying or numb from shock. I didn't know what I was. I just knew that images of heated kisses between John and myself should not have kept playing through my mind. I should've hated him, but I couldn't.

'Talk to me,' Lucas murmured, smoothing a hand across my back. Susan and George were handing out official thanks to the rest of The Protectors, seemingly oblivious to my depressed state.

I grabbed him by the wrist and dragged him towards the house. 'Distract me. Tell me everything that happened after I left.'

He tripped over his own feet, quickly correcting the clumsy move as I shoved him towards the front door—newly installed in my absence. I noted the front fence was still a shambles and glass littered the driveway where the Forester had been parked, but otherwise the place looked the same.

Once Lucas's key had twisted free of the front door, I pushed him inside, hustling him towards the stairs and up to the relative privacy of our bedrooms.

'Geez, E! Could you give me a sec to get inside?'

I shook my head, grabbed his flailing arms and pulled him towards the stairs. I made him run until we were inside my bedroom, door closed. 'You have to tell me everything, Lucas,' I said, releasing him so I could pace the floor. 'Tell me what William said so I know where I stand. Tell me *anything* so I don't think of … of him.'

'Well, this is new,' Lucas joked. He pressed a hand against my forehead. I slapped it away, unable to be amused. 'Since when have you ever cared if a guy liked you or not?'

'I don't care.'

'So why ask?'

'Because I don't want to keep thinking about John's hands on me,' I muttered, finally stopping the frenetic pacing and dropping down onto the edge of the mattress.

Lucas joined me, casually slinging an arm around my shoulder. 'William is coming by to meet you later tonight.'

'He said that?' I replied, my voice sounding strained even to me. 'He's not pissed off about me kissing John?'

Lucas laughed. 'I know, the guy's totally bonkers, right? I would have dumped your ass if you were my girl-friend.'

I frowned. 'He's not my boyfriend, he's—'

'I know,' he said, shaking his head in exasperation and rolling his eyes. 'You don't have to try and squeeze *senti-mental* out of that emotionless body of yours. It would be more likely for me to suck steak through a straw than get you to admit that he was your boyfriend and that you loved him back.'

I shrugged. 'It's not that simple.'

'Sure it is. You just make everything seem more compli-cated than it really is.'

'… You're right.'

He raised an eyebrow in disbelief. 'I am?'

'Yep, sucking steak through a straw is hard.'

He rolled his eyes again. 'I can't believe I'm going to say

this, but it might change your perspective on a few things and hopefully warm the icy cockles of your heart.'

'What will?'

'The message that William asked me to give to you.'

I swallowed. 'Let's hear it then.'

Lucas gagged dramatically. I was barely holding onto the conversation. My focus was shot. So I slapped him gently across the back of the head. I was too tired, too impatient, and too miserable for dramatics.

'Alright, geez,' he said as he rubbed the crown of his head and frowned. 'He said to say that he knows the kiss wasn't really your fault and that he still loves you regardless.'

'He really said that?'

He shook his head, all seriousness. 'Actually, it was, "Bloody hell, Elena smells like shit and needs to have a shower before I barf".'

I grinned at him and laughed in spite of myself. 'Now you're projecting. William would never say "shit" or "barf".'

'Are you sure about that? You really do stink.'

'I had a shower,' I said, recalling the brief hose down in the small bathroom with Greg and Adam, and shuddering.

'When? Before or *after* they threw you in a vat of shit?'

I laughed once, covering my mouth with my hand to stem the flow of emotion. It felt wrong to smile or laugh after everything that had happened. Elizabeth would never smile again. Neither would Kate, if that was even her name. I couldn't be mad at Lucas for trying though. Healing had to start somewhere, and I was going to have to heal fast. The Protectors were going to want explanations for my behaviour with John and validation of my claims of a permanent end to the Vânători.

I just had to figure out how to tell them, and how to move past my own fear.

Lucas and I sat quietly for several minutes. He knew well enough not to push me into talking. His comforting arm wrapped around my shoulders was enough to calm me and remind me that I was home and safe.

Susan and George managed to leave us alone for a whole fifteen minutes before the pounding started on my bedroom door. Lucas and I had exchanged a wry look and then let them in, but only because the pounding wouldn't cease until they knew all the gory details.

They didn't get any.

Lucas stepped up to the plate and told them to give me some space for a few hours. He also left, leaving me alone with my thoughts. For the first ten minutes I'd just sat there, staring at the wall, thinking of everything and nothing all at once. After that, I'd finally broken down, pressing my dirty face into my pillows and crying until my throat hurt and the pillows were wet with tears. Afterwards, I felt no better.

A couple of hours later, I managed to drag myself into the bathroom, taking the longest shower in the history of mankind. I was fairly certain that I'd single-handedly drained Copperlode dam, our local reservoir, of its seemingly infinite resources. But justly so, as I wanted to wash off every single trace of the abduction from my skin and the remnants of those I could still clearly smell on me. I didn't want to feel or scent John on me any longer than I had to, even though there was a very small part of me that had relished his touch and craved more. That was over now. Never again would I let myself be put in that position again.

John had made no secret of his desire to use my blood, to take my abilities from me and use them so his kind could destroy the world. And I had no doubt that he had ensured that his alpha companions were aware of me, his latest discovery, and if they weren't they soon would be.

The saddest part of events was that I was probably no longer safe in Cairns. If the other alphas were now aware of my unique blood, then it would only be a matter of time before they sent others to look for me. If I was going to truly do the right thing by my family and myself then I would be better off either on my own or transferring to headquarters in Bucharest, keeping trouble away from everyone I loved.

Even William, with his competent training and endless knowledge of hunting vânătors, could not be expected to hang around in Cairns to protect me from the coming onslaught. That was too much for any one person to expect of another. Deep down I knew that meant I was about to become a science experiment of the IMI, but there weren't too many other options available. Lucas would disagree with me emphatically and hate me for my choice, but if I had to choose between being poked and prodded with needles and living in a soulless laboratory while The Protectors sought answers in my blood, then I would willingly volunteer if it meant that he was safe.

I sighed, running a hand through my now clean hair and watching my smiling family excitedly discuss the downfall of the Vânătors. We were gathered around the dining room table, the site of many household discussions—today was no exception. They were animated, excited by the prospect of finally having solutions to the answers they'd long sought. I wanted to celebrate with them, revel in the wonder of what I had learnt, but I felt drained and oddly detached from it all.

'You did well, Elena.'

'Huh?' I said, snapping back to the present and looking at George in confusion.

'I had my doubts that our training would be enough to get you through the last few days,' he patiently repeated. 'I thought your smart mouth would get you killed.'

'I don't think they were interested in my mouth,' I explained, my hands curling into fists in my lap. 'I'm alive because John had a further purpose for me, nothing more.'

George looked surprised by my answer. 'I expected you to take all the credit for today's victory.'

I bowed my head, not wanting him to see the tears that stung my eyes. 'What victory could there be when two innocent people are dead?'

Because of me …

'You're alive. You killed a few vânǎtors yourself, and you unselfishly tried to save the girl. You can take pride in that, Elena.'

I almost laughed. Pride? Was he kidding? 'Yes, and I'm still alive, at the expense of others. All I can take from that is guilt, not pride. I don't deserve any praise for surviving, especially when I know Elizabeth and Kate's parents don't know their daughters are dead.'

'Elena …'

I zoned out again after that. No excuse would make me feel better. Plus, I could feel them watching me, judging me as I kept my head bowed.

I shook my head, trying to dispel the bitterness I felt. Despite suffering under the hand of such cruelty, there were positives to observe. With the Vânǎtor's secret now uncovered I could at least say Elizabeth and Kate had not died in vain.

I guess some of the change I was feeling also evolved

from the unavoidable reality that this experience had forced me to start growing up. Just like life, death, and love, growing and maturing from the product of our experiences is simply inevitable, and I could no longer pretend that was passing me by. The sooner I accepted that I was no longer a child and that I was responsible for the consequences of my actions, the sooner I could accept my part in Elizabeth and Kate's deaths. If I could free myself of the guilt I harboured and move forward, then perhaps I could also start to let people in—people like William.

My head flicked up as Susan squealed in delight, her face etched with excitement as she performed a happy dance around the table. I looked on, confused, as she danced up to me, patting my cheek, before dashing into the kitchen to assess the contents of the pantry.

'What's going on now?' I said, leaning over to Lucas.

'Mum's just real happy about you discovering a way to destroy the Vânǎtors.'

'Still?'

'It's a big deal, E. Dad's already contacted Bucharest so they can start spreading the news globally.'

'Then why is Susan in the kitchen?' I asked, leaning backwards on my chair and watching her pulling jelly crystals and Tabasco sauce out of the cupboard.

'Haven't you been listening?' Lucas asked.

I shook my head, grimacing as I saw Susan lifting out a jar of peanut butter.

'She's decided takeout is all wrong for the occasion. She wants to put her culinary skills to the test and cook us all something extra-special for dinner.'

'That sounds like a really bad idea.'

'Quiet, you two,' George muttered, getting up to give her hand. It wasn't going to help.

I cringed as I watched her rummaging through packets of out-of-date food, declaring that, 'she could really do something with this'. I didn't have the heart to tell her I'd been tortured enough in the last two days. So I left well alone, and prayed for all the electrical appliances in the kitchen to suddenly break down instead.

The look on Lucas and George's faces said it all, as she lowered a plate of God–only-knew what onto the centre of the table forty minutes later. There weren't enough expletives in the English language to depict just exactly what it was that we were all looking at. But the smell was definitely something—a cross between a jammed-up Port-a-Loo and spearmint-flavoured bubble gum.

It was crap-o-licious.

We talked for a good few hours, discussing every detail of my capture—including both my unwanted attraction to John and the effect that the alpha scent appeared to have on me. I was reluctant at first, mostly because talking about the experience dredged up painful memories, but I found the more I shared, the better I started to feel. We all agreed that avoidance was the best cure for circumventing such entrapment again, and avoidance meant evacuating me from the area.

Much to Lucas's disgust, they both agreed that sending me back to headquarters for a little while was not the worst idea I'd ever had. The IMI had their faults, George had said, and they had their ulterior motives, but they were still my best chance of avoiding recapture. Ten Protectors, three vampires, and one half-breed were not enough to fend off an army of determined vânători should they discover I was still residing here.

The agreed upon plan at this stage was to seek advice from headquarters first and wait for instruction.

In the meantime, Susan and George were going to see how quickly both Vampires and Protectors could mobilise to track down the last remaining alphas. I would be staying put, at least until the IMI had reached a decision.

Lucas still did not look thrilled about my plans to leave.

After dinner, I nervously made my way upstairs, saying goodnight to Susan and George as they headed off to their own areas of the house. Lucas followed at my heels, no doubt hoping I would include him in my reunion with William. I made my feelings clear by shutting the bathroom door in his face, telling him, through the door, to go to bed and that I'd update him in the morning.

I brushed my teeth slowly and thoroughly, and then headed to my bedroom, wondering if my Vampire would be waiting. My heart sank when I opened the door and found that I was alone.

I switched on the light just to be sure and almost groaned in disappointment when the fluorescents illuminated my empty room. Disappointed, I grabbed a pillow off my bed, headed over to the window and threw it up onto the roof above. Without a second thought, I draped a blanket around my neck, climbed up onto my sill, and heaved myself up onto the roof.

Tonight, I wanted to feel the freedom of the breeze blowing across my face as I slept. I wanted to lie in the spot where so many of my teenage fantasies, arguments, and procrastinations had played out in my head. I didn't want to sleep in a bed, confined to my room. I needed open space—no walls, no doors, no vânători. And as my future at the IMI brimmed with the possibilities of enclosed walls, uncertainty, and repressed freedom, I wanted to make the most of my liberty before it was taken away.

On the roof's corrugated surface, I doubled the blanket

over and spread it out to cushion the uneven texture of the metal under my back. I pulled the softness of my pillow underneath my head. I glanced up at the stars for the longest time, watching them with quiet contemplation and trying to avoid heavy thoughts wrought with emotion.

Cold fingers brushed through the silken strands of hair that enveloped my face, and my eyes flicked to the side in an instant to stare up at the emerald green pools looking back at me.

'Hi,' William said as he grazed his fingers down to my cheek and then brushed them across my lips.

He settled down comfortably beside me, propping himself up on one arm.

I turned my head and just stared. 'I thought you weren't coming.'

'Why would you think that?' William breathed, as he took my hand in his. He traced small circles on the back and looked intently into my eyes. The disgust and indifference I had expected was missing from their depths. Even though Lucas had reassured me with William's words of love and understanding, I still couldn't believe that he would want to know me after what he'd seen.

'I thought after all that happened with John that you wouldn't—'

He silenced me, pressing his fingers to my lips. 'Nothing that you ever do or say is going to change how I feel about you. Make sure that you remember that.'

'But what I did ... how I felt when he touched me ... I just don't understand why you—'

'Why I still want to be with you?' he answered, interrupting my mumbling.

I nodded.

He intertwined his fingers in mine and tilted my face up to look at him. 'I love you. What more explanation did you need than that?'

I cringed. 'How can you love me? You don't even really know me and I know even less about you.'

'I just do. I don't know how else to explain. It's definitely not something that I'd planned, but I knew from the very first moment that I laid eyes on you that I'd never be able to walk away from you. I've lived for over four hundred years, roaming from place to place, searching for something and never knowing what it was. I always feel empty and alone, no matter how many people I surround myself with. It wasn't until I met you that I realised that you were the missing piece in my life.'

I turned away and stared back up at the stars. I didn't want to look into those eyes and see truth in his words. Letting myself love him could only lead to pain. In fact, loving anyone at all was far too dangerous right now. I needed to take things very slow—that was the only way I could ever let him get close to me.

'Elena?' he said, pulling my face back to look at his. 'Tell me what you are thinking.'

'Honestly?'

'Yes, always.'

'Honestly, I'm thinking that I can't give you what you want right now. I like you William, I do, but I'm not ready to feel weak and defenceless again. And I can see that if I truly let myself be close to you then you would have the power to do that to me, power that you could use to inadvertently hurt me.'

He brushed a thumb across my lips. I shivered. 'You can't stop your heart from wanting me, Elena.'

I closed my eyes, opened them again, taking a deep

breath in. 'You'll be surprised what I'm capable of if I put my mind to it, William.'

'Oh, I have no doubt about that,' he said smiling, as he leaned forward and brushed his lips across mine.

My heart did a crazy little backflip as his scent washed over me. Sandalwood and spice—oh, how I had missed that smell. 'Things have changed now, William,' I said, placing a hand between our lips before things got too out of hand. 'I may be leaving soon.'

'I know.'

'You do?' I said, surprised.

He smiled and moved my hand away from his lips. 'I hear everything, remember?'

'Then us, this … it's all pointless.'

He kissed me again, lightly, before leaning forward and resting his forehead against mine so our noses were touching. 'Nothing is ever pointless,' he breathed against my lips, his sweet scent pouring into my mouth and filling me with heat. 'A lesson can always be learned from any experience. And my experience is telling me that I will follow you wherever you decide to go.'

'Like a stalker?'

He smiled. 'Yes, like a crazy, jealous stalker.'

'I'm not sure a restraining order would make much difference to you, would it?'

He laughed lightly and wound his fingers through my hair. 'Hmm, no.'

'So, regardless of what I say or do, you're going to persist on harbouring pointless feelings for me and follow me all around the world until I agree to love you back?'

'That is correct.'

'That is insane.'

'But that's also why you love me back.'

I smiled in spite of myself. His perseverance was strangely endearing. 'You're all kinds of crazy, you know that right?'

He laughed and pulled me closer to him. 'I'm going to kiss you now … my love.'

My tongue lolled to the side and I screwed my face up. 'Ugh, enough with that already. I accept that you're going to be my stalker, I'm not agreeing to pet names as well. Not unless you like being called … Willy.'

He cringed, and giving me a steady, almost stony glare, he said, 'You will not call me,' and here he swallowed and shuddered, 'Willy.'

I giggled. 'Then lay off the *love* stuff. It's far too much for an emotional cripple like me.'

'As you wish.' He didn't wait for an answer before he pulled me against him and crushed his lips against mine.

My head swirled with desire, and my hands couldn't help but reach up and entwine themselves in the thicket of short dark hair at his neck, pulling him closer and inhaling every part of him. His lips moved with expertise and purpose, and it was all I could do not to surrender myself to him completely.

When he kissed me that way, it was very difficult to even remember my name, let alone the reasons why I had decided this was a bad idea. Yet through the heat of our embrace and the fire dancing across our lips, I couldn't shake the overwhelming feeling that I was forgetting something very vital.

Hang on a second …

As if reading my thoughts, he pulled away slowly and smiled at me with self-satisfaction, leaving me slightly breathless and very, very frustrated. 'I thought you were holding out on me?' he whispered against my lips before nuzzling the side of my neck with his cold nose.

Crap, there goes my leverage.

My eyes narrowed as I pulled his face back up and looked into his slightly muddied eyes. I frowned as his grin widened. 'Do you really want to pursue this?'

He chuckled lightly and shook his head, running his hand down my back and pulling me hard against him. 'I want to pursue you very much,' he murmured seductively against my lips as he pressed his mouth against mine again, taking possession of me, hungry. I could taste the sense of victory on his tongue.

I couldn't resist. Not when he was loving me like that.

Smug bastard. He knew it too.

So he could have tonight. He could taste my mouth and dream about a world of love and all things la-dee-dah, but tomorrow was a different story. Tomorrow I would make sure that my head was clear of his essence, of any lingering desire I may have felt when his hands had stroked my body. I would let him have a few hours to convince me that he had possession over my heart and soul.

Tonight, they were both unknowingly his.

But tomorrow ... well, that was an entirely different story.

EPILOGUE: ONE MONTH LATER

oshan stepped closer to the glass, his own, borrowed reflection staring back at him as his eyes probed the darkness beyond. He watched the girl as she made a song and dance of saying goodbye to her family.

She wrapped her arms around the youngest male and squeezed him tight, before briefly embracing the two adults who he assumed were her parents. It was hard to say one way or the other given that none of them looked anything like her. They were average, but she was beautiful. Underneath that tightly knit sweater and skin-tight pants, he saw her long, slim legs, dark chocolate coloured hair and skin that was as smooth as silk itself. Roshan could not see her eyes from this distance, yet he had a feeling they'd be as beautiful as the rest of her. No wonder John had taken a fancy to her. She was sublime.

Elena.

John had told him much about this strange girl who was human, yet born to be a Vampire. Even more inexplicably still, she had also been blessed with the blood of his own kind. According to his alpha brother, she could possess a cure that would remove their genetic disadvantages as immortals. Her blood held the possibility of changing their vulnerabilities into strengths, and thus she was vitally important to *his* future.

Roshan watched her carefully as she pulled back from the three, her eyes darting towards the darkness for the briefest of moments before settling back on the youngest male. She gave him a half-hearted smile.

Roshan glanced into the darkness too, mimicking her movements. What could have possibly piqued her interest across the darkened tarmac?

Awareness prickled Roshan's skin and his teeth lengthened involuntarily. He wasn't the only immortal here tonight. He could smell the other's scent. It was slight, but enough for Roshan to pinpoint its source. He wondered if his enemy could smell him too. It was more than likely.

He could see the Vampire clearly now, his glittering green eyes watching her carefully from the cover of darkness, arms crossed in front of his chest.

How touching.

John had been right. The Vampire was quite clearly enamoured with her. His watchful gaze and the cautious readiness of his stance suggested that he would stop at nothing to protect this girl. His past actions had proven that fact. This one persistent vampire had hunted down and decimated the London pack with relative ease. He would not be easy to defeat.

Roshan straightened his coat and tried to keep his temper in check. He wanted to break through this plate glass window and rip out that vampire's throat. The pleasure he would derive from that experience alone was limitless. It had killed one of his closest brothers, and he wanted his revenge.

Not now.

He calmed himself, stretching his neck and cracking his human knuckles to ease some of the tension in his borrowed body. There were much bigger matters to contend with and revenge was a dish best served cold. The fate of the Vânătors was now resting in his hands and he couldn't let his temper get in the way of his plans.

There was too much at stake.

Roshan stepped forward again and looked down at Elena embracing the younger blonde human. Surprisingly, he felt a stab of jealousy that this one, lone human was touching her. Ridiculous considering he'd only just laid eyes on the girl two days ago, but still, she was more than he had expected. Roshan's entire wolf soul yearned to lose itself in her and, at the very same time, sample some of that delicious tasting blood that John had spoken so ardently about. He could almost picture how pure her scent would taste on his tongue and how her soft creamy flesh would feel underneath his lips and fangs.

It was a pity he wasn't going to get a chance to revel in his desires any longer than the next ten minutes. He had checked the flight plan for her imminent departure. The plane belonged to the Institute of Magical Intervention. She had a one-way ticket to Bucharest, and once she was in the safety of the Protector's headquarters there would be no way he could get to her unless every vânător still alive banded together and stormed the facility. He still hadn't decided if that was an option or not yet. He hated The Protectors so much he'd seriously considered sacrificing himself just to spill some of their blood, but common sense had warred within him. The influence of the IMI extended far.

Romania was the Vânător's birth place, but they had been pushed out of the cities and forced into the Carpathian Mountains where many still hid today. Others had spread out to other continents and countries. The only one not inhabitable was Italy—it was crawling with vampires. The leader of their people, the one they called Lucius, made sure his cities were locked up tighter than Fort Knox. It was suicide for a vânător to stray willingly into either region, and though he wanted Elena badly, he wasn't sure if he was willing to risk the safety of all the packs just to feel her against his skin, and taste her in his mouth.

Roshan cursed. He should have taken her earlier. He dared not risk it now given that she was surrounded by the magical ones as well as the Vampire. He did not doubt that he could defeat it himself, but did not like his chances with the others there. He needed to be patient. Bigger things were in the works, things that could guarantee him exactly what he wanted.

He looked down as Elena picked up her backpack and slung it over one of her slender shoulders. She took one more moment to stare off into the darkness before she waved goodbye to her family and headed for the plane.

A man in a tidy uniform with decorated lapels stepped closer to the stairs and helped her into the plane, taking her back pack from her. His hands inadvertently brushed hers.

Roshan growled.

She turned and waved goodbye a final time before the uniformed man ushered her up the stairs, and securing the door behind her.

Roshan swallowed the lump of rage in his throat, fighting the urge to pound his fists into the concrete pillar next to him until they were bloodied, bruised, and broken. The man sitting only a few feet away from him looked like an excellent target. Better yet—he could drag him outside, take his fill and then rip the guy to pieces.

He sighed wistfully as the man stood up a second later, along with a multitude of other people that also looked good enough to eat, before heading over to the nearest gate to wait for boarding to begin.

Pity.

Roshan glanced back out the window again and watched as the aeroplane finished reversing up and then steered out onto the tarmac.

He glanced across at the Vampire again and stepped back in surprise. It was looking directly at him, an angry and vicious-looking snarl spreading across its entire face. Roshan could practically feel the hostility, even from this distance, and his own hackles rose up in response.

It was time to go.

He glanced back one more time as Elena's plane began to taxi down the runway, and then cursed himself silently again for leaving the matter until too late. He should have come over a week ago when he realised that something had happened to John. It was too late now.

He would have to head home again, gather his alpha brothers and figure out a way to capture the girl that would not involve such a costly showdown.

When he glanced out the window again the three Protectors were looking straight up at him, blank expressions spread across their faces. They must have known that he was there. But the part that troubled him most was that the Vampire was now gone.

Definitely time to get going.

He abruptly spun around and disappeared into the massive crowds of unsuspecting people that were oblivious to the wolf stalking amongst them. Roshan could almost taste all of their warm, searing flesh and blood in his mouth. Their mingled scents filled his nose with longing, with hunger, their veins pulsing with excitement and energy.

He licked his lips but repressed his urges for now, distancing himself as quickly as possible from the scent that was now familiar above all others—that Vampire's. He needed to get back to Paris before he did something that he might regret.

One thing was for certain though. The time for the rule of the Vânǎtors was drawing close. And more than anything, he was looking forward to the day when his brothers would finally be on equal footing with the Vampires, the day that they no longer had to hide in the shadows to defend what should be rightfully theirs. The day when they were no longer ... the hunted.

www.ingramcontent.com/pod-product-compliance
Lightning Source LLC
Chambersburg PA
CBHW071332020726
47502CB00001B/65